Brian R Hill

Love, Lies and Treachery

First published by Brian R Hill in 2016.

Copyright © Brian R Hill 2016.

The moral right of Brian R Hill to be identified as the author of this work has been asserted.

This novel is a work of fiction. Names, characters, places, and incidents are the product of the author's imagination or are used fictitiously. Any resemblance to actual events, locales, or persons, living or dead, other than those clearly in the public domain, is coincidental.

All rights reserved. No part of this publication may be reproduced, stored, or transmitted in any form or by any means, electronic, mechanical, photocopying, recording, scanning, or otherwise without written permission from the publisher. It is illegal to copy this book, post it to a website, or distribute it by any other means without permission.

First Edition.

ISBN-13: 978-1537719313

ISBN-10: 1537719319

This book was professionally typeset on Reedsy. Find out more at reedsy.com

*Novels by Brian R Hill*

**Genre - Fantasy**

*The Shintae*
*Shadows from a Time Long Past*
*The Mastig*

**Genre - Thriller**

*Love, Lies and Treachery*

# 1

A filthy mist rolls down the grimy street, the yellowing vapour reminiscent of the smogs of my grandparents' childhood days. Along greasy footpaths, I hasten towards the ageing terraced-house I call home. A lethal combination of fog and the onset of darkness have reduced visibility to a few bare paces. Bus-services stopped running a while before I left work. What a day for it to happen; I have a date with Julie later this evening. At the thought of her, I increase my pace. The day has brought a marked drop in temperature. I shiver in the dank mid-November air.

Through the murk comes the muffled tooting of horns. Streams of foolhardy motorists clog the roads, persistent in their efforts to find a way home. Inside their heated tin cans they sit, their speed a crawl, no faster than my own. Bloody idiots! The worst fog in forty years - or so banal presenters on local radio have been announcing all day. Their voices, filled with false sincerity, promote an inconvenience up to that of a crisis. I imagine it enlivens their day; a change from broadcasting an endless stream of stories about pets, pigeons and the local football team. I swear, each time a player breaks wind, the channel has a three-hour in-depth debate on the subject.

On the third attempt, I find the right house and make it home. In these conditions, how easy it is for the senses to become confused. The Jones and Ashley families will be chuckling still about my unexpected arrival into their homes. My face burns with embarrassment, as I push open my own front door.

"Mum, Dad, I'm back," I splutter as I suffer a coughing-fit, brought on by the change of air.

Away from the swirling fumes, the foul atmosphere has irritated a chest-cold I thought I had conquered. A hot shower and dinner revive me. Dressed in much warmer clothes, I am fit enough again for anything. A last flick of the razor over the day's growth and it is time to go to meet Julie. In the background, the familiar closing-theme of an early evening TV soap fades. Ma rushes into the kitchen to switch on the kettle, and uncover the packet of chocolate biscuits she believes she has hidden from me. A vain hope, but I have left them some. Dad, of course, decides on the rest of the evening's viewing.

"Where do you think you're going?" a scandalised cry comes from the kitchen. "You know you've had that cold for a fortnight. You'll be up all night coughing if you go out again in this weather. Dad, you tell him!"

Silence from the front room. Dad ignores the altercation. His interest lies in the TV section of the evening paper. Sensible chap. Where possible, he avoids becoming embroiled in one of Ma's rants. I shuffle into my coat.

"All right, Nathan, but don't you come running to me for sympathy when you're poorly again!"

"Okay Ma, I won't. Promised I'd see Julie, must fly, seez you later."

In haste, I close the door, cutting-off further comments. With my scarf wrapped over my nose and mouth, I vanish into the swirling darkness. By the dim light coming from the window of a nearby off-licence, I snatch a look at my watch; damn it, late again. It is already a quarter to eight. I promised Julie I would be at her house by half-past seven. Damn the weather! Damn the buses! The meeting we are to attend starts at eight-thirty. Rush-hour traffic has dissipated. Along silent, empty roads I race. The dismal light from street lamps struggles to penetrate the mist. Vague shapes loom out of the darkness. People, walls, hedges, house-sides, all are unrecognisable until close to. From their shapes they could be monsters lying in wait! The clang of the gate, outside Julie's house, alerts her to my arrival. The cheesy sound of door chimes strengthens as the door swings open.

# CHAPTER 1

"Damn you, Nathan Philip Andrews, you're late again," she snaps, her back straight and stiff.

When Julie uses my full name, I know I am in trouble. Her eyes are ablaze and her lips pursed, confirmation, if needed, of her state of mind.

"Sorry, love, the buses stopped running at lunch time. I had to walk home from work. It took me hours. Come on, hurry up, put your coat on, if we rush we can still make it on time to the meeting."

After a quick kiss and struggle in the doorway, Julie, somewhat mollified, grabs her coat from a peg in the hallway. At speed, we set off down side-roads and through claustrophobic, crumbling brick-lined ginnels towards our destination. We burst into the wood-panelled and white-plastered hall. The meeting is due to commence. Breathless, we slide into a pair of seats at the rear of the room.

The inclement weather has kept away many of the potential audience. Row after row of plastic chairs are empty. The speaker-to-be appears unconcerned by this insult to his magnetic personality. On stage, after a brief glare of disapproval towards us at our late arrival, he launches into his well-crafted speech.

"The Party for National Unity…" he booms.

We sit and listen. On and on his voice drones. My eyes droop. There is no lack of motivation in his words, but I have heard them many times. A question and answer session will follow the speech. Later, after the non-party members have left, for the chosen few the evening's important agenda commences. Three years ago, Julie became a party member. Because I was, still am, very much in love with her, I joined soon afterwards to be closer to her. In those days, when we were both eighteen, it was a fledgling organisation. If I am honest, Julie is the fanatical one; but her passions extend beyond politics, which means I reap the rewards of party-membership in other ways.

While the speaker answers questions, Julie and I sneak-out through the stained-glass, wood-framed doors at the back of the room. Down the corridor, in a draughty kitchen at the side of the hall, we prepare tea and biscuits. Well-practised, we work with an economy of effort. We have time to spare before the wearisome session next-door ends. The same issues, which arise time after time, meeting after meeting, the speaker deals with as if they are original and thought-provoking.

Will the Party's policies work in practice? Why does the PNU, which claims to be a party for national unity, seem determined to split the country? Why does the party's name appear, whenever, since Brexit, a strike or demonstration takes place; in fact, when anything happens to challenge the established order of the country?

No matter how trivial, every question receives an erudite answer. Each response, statesmanlike though it may be, bears little, if any, relevance to the original request. In this respect, we differ little from any other political party. Almost without fail, the questioner goes away pacified, if not satisfied. This charismatic speechmaker, whose words overflow with charm and assurance, delivers his replies with confidence, as indeed he should. He is the great Joseph J Emerson, esteemed leader of the PNU.

An exaggerated 'Ahem' comes from the doorway leading into the corridor. Julie and I break apart. She wipes a smear of her lipstick from my face. We look round, trying to appear unconcerned. Old Alf, the caretaker, leers at us. A knowing sly wink he aims in my direction.

"They're about done in there. I thought I'd better warn you two - to put the kettle on, of course," again the knowing wink.

"I suppose that means you'll want the first cup and the pick of the biscuits," Julie says.

Alf's habits are familiar to us. Soon, a majority of the audience, twenty in total, amble into the room at the other side of the serving hatch. They invade our privacy in search of their compensation for sitting through the evening's proceedings. Joseph J circulates. He speaks in broad terms or in confidence, if requested, to those who hang on to his words. After a while, once the plates of biscuits are empty, the non-members drift away to pastures new (home or, in all likelihood, the nearest pub).

# CHAPTER 1

Those invited to remain behind retire to a former function room upstairs, which we rent as the local party office. Julie and I wash up. Ten minutes later, we join the others. Downstairs, Alf keeps a watchful eye for anyone who might try to gain entry or eavesdrop. He takes no interest in what goes on behind the locked door above. The generous payment he receives for his duties is enough to satisfy his curiosity.

☙ ❧

JJ rises to his feet. The idle chatter of the gathering comes to a halt. We wait, eleven of us, for the great man's words.

"Right," he commences. "Is anyone missing? Apologies? No. Good. Let's start, shall we?"

A subtle change has taken place in his tone and accent. It has become down-to-earth, conspiratorial and encompassing toward us, his selected audience. He waits until the usual coughing and fidgeting subside. Once we are comfortable, he clears his throat, then continues.

"As you are aware, our agents meet with great success as they incite unrest throughout the country. The economy is in a mess, although that is nothing new. Strikes have spread nation-wide. Demonstrations against the government take place daily. Our participation in these events we keep secret. Of course, rumours of our involvement abound, which we deny and dismiss as fabrications.

"So the polls tell us, the PNU has the majority backing of the country's electorate. Whenever an opportunity arises, in public or in private, we condemn the government. Everyone knows that, in our opinion, the malpractices of our leaders have led to this widespread disorder. Yet, at the same time, we offer sympathy to the populace, to those citizens in extremis, driven to attempt to bring about a better Britain. By demonising the elderly, the jobless, those on low-incomes or benefits, while squandering billions on unhelpful reforms across institutions countrywide, the government plays into our hands. They make it easy for us to ferment nationwide unrest.

"We know our actions are necessary. A succession of weak and half-brained administrations, in or out of coalition, has dragged our once great island through the mire. Do the ruling parties ever put aside petty jealousies to do the job the people elect them to do? Did they learn the lessons of the Brexit referendum? No! Do we have a remedy? Yes! We are the answer. You, me and our colleagues spread throughout the land. We are the Party for National Unity."

JJ pauses a moment. Enthusiastic applause rings out. His beaming countenance lights up the room. He waits until his audience falls silent before he continues.

"Never before have we fielded parliamentary candidates. Although requested on numerous occasions to do so, we have declined. Now, at last, the time is right. Clamour for our involvement is at fever pitch. Stage-two of our campaign is set for implementation. In twelve months, a general election will be upon us. We shall contest it, compelled, we shall say, to do so by the ineptitude of the country's current political parties. We shall field a candidate for each seat and, my friends, we shall achieve an overwhelming majority. We have the backing of many major figures in business, the police and the military. Once in government, we will put Britain back where it belongs, as a leading international power."

We sit back and listen. The rhetoric continues. Each member of the audience is in awe at the presence of such an incredible visionary. We will dominate the election, achieve an historic victory and, in doing so, secure the futures of those activists involved.

For most people in the room, their involvement with the party has been since its inauguration. We will become leaders of an invigorated nation. Whether our role be a political one, or one of a multitude of other positions, we will take control of the country. Life is amazing. To be twenty-one and to have a bright and assured future is exhilarating. Some of our compatriots might distrust us, even fear us, but we have the backing of the majority - for as long as it matters. Rare it is for my zeal to approach that of Julie's, but tonight is one of those occasions.

# CHAPTER 1

The clock approaches eleven. The meeting ends. After much handshaking and backslapping, we make our ways back to our respective homes. JJ's enthusiasm has inspired each one of us. We are secure in the knowledge of our roles in the momentous events to come. Hand in hand with Julie, I walk her home. The all-pervading mist is thicker than ever. We part at her doorstep. A passionate goodnight kiss, a slapped hand, then away I go, to dream of glory to come. Soon, we will put the country to rights.

ᛒ ᛒ

The months that follow the meeting pass by at an astonishing rate. The owner of the factory, where I work in production-planning, is a party-sympathiser. He allows me extensive time-off, on full pay, to canvass door-to-door, district-by-district. On evenings and at weekends, Julie and I attend political gatherings, far and wide. There, among thousands of other jubilant followers, we listen to, and applaud, our various candidates.

Groups of troublemakers ensure meetings, held by other parties, face frequent disruption. In contrast, our gatherings have tight security, policed by either the appropriate authorities or our own well-disciplined groups. Friends in the right places ensure we receive the maximum amount of positive publicity. As a result, the election in October, as forecast by JJ, is a landslide. The PNU take all but seventy-five seats in the Houses of Parliament. A token resistance now sits on the opposition benches, bereft of influence and effective voice.

Throughout this period, Julie and I become much closer. Two weeks after the announcement of the results, we hold a double celebration, victory and our engagement. Julie's parents have misgivings about the latter, but that is a common failing among parents when faced with their offspring's choice of partners. My parents are the opposite. I am to marry someone who lives in a semi; a huge step up from our well cared-for back-to-back terraced house.

Within weeks, the new government shows its iron fist to the country. Strikes become illegal. Firms must provide monthly productivity figures to the Department for Business, Energy & Industrial Strategy, which then demands improvements. A public outcry from some owners, and near riots by workers, follows these repressive measures, a response we had anticipated.

Twelve months after taking office, JJ's government instigates a state of emergency. The government create a National Security Force, using loyal party elements from both police and armed-forces. Unlike the police, NSF units bear arms and are a law unto themselves. This, of course, was a part of the Party's hidden agenda. Loyal members welcome it with open arms. Now we can begin in earnest to put the country back on its feet. For me, the vicious methods employed by the new force tempers my enthusiasm for them. Their brutality is gratuitous. Julie, as usual, maintains her belief in her beloved party.

With the exception of PNU rallies, a ban on all public meetings comes into effect. Days later, with their leaders arrested or on the run, the disbandment of trade-union organisations takes place. Imprisonment, without trial, for troublemakers becomes the standard method of dealing with opposition. Instead of to prison cells, the authorities put the detainees to work on the many improvement schemes the government has initiated.

These measures stir-up further unrest among the populace; protest groups receive similar treatment. In a calculated escalation, instead of the police, NSF troops become the ones to handle dissent on the streets. On the first occasion in which they see action, several protesters are shot and killed while 'resisting' arrest. Under such harsh treatment, support for open opposition collapses. A massive propaganda campaign comes into being.

In time, people begin to appreciate the advances that appear in everyday life. Public services and transport become more efficient. Industrial productivity soars. The rich become richer, while the less well-off see some improvement in their lives. The populace finds it convenient to forget the plight of thousands of political detainees. These are the people who, by their sweated labour in and out of the political reform-centres and forced-labour camps, bring about many of these changes. Providing no-one voices their thoughts in the hearing of the many informants, the majority of the population find their standard of living rises.

For myself, I reap the rewards for my diligent work within the movement. I become the party representative at a large factory complex in the centre of Sheffield, Dawson's Springs and Metal Forgings. With powers greater than those of the directors, lord, how everyone fawns over me. The board, in particular, are careful to watch their words and temper their actions. One word from me and they could be sweeping the floors. Under my tenure, productivity increases. My reputation within party-circles also rises.

Power! That, I suppose, is the meaning of the game. In many ways, a game it has become to me. I soak up the attention gained through my position. At first, I hesitate to exercise my authority to the full. With the gradual realisation of my true position in society, I try-out my strength and wield my influence with greater confidence.

I learn to quieten my conscience. With practice, it becomes easier to hide my guilt or remorse when, because of some infringement, I condemn someone to several months of re-education in a political-reform centre. Power is a mantle to wear; I wear mine as if moulded to me, or give the appearance of it being so. My sense of right and wrong, instilled into me by my parents from childhood, although suppressed, refuses to abandon me.

# 2

Julie and I wed, in blazing June weather. Four months later, I have my first strike to confront. Production has halted. A picket stretches across Dawson's factory gate. At the age of twenty-four, I have the eyes of the party elite focused on me. This is my first major test. How will I handle the situation? Any indecision, or attempt to negotiate, the watchers will interpret as a sign of weakness. This could be disastrous to my career. Without hesitation, I call in the NSF. They force their way through the barricades. Seconds later, the mindless mob of strikers launches an attack. The platoon falls back, their batons at the ready. The captain in command looks to me. It seems, as party representative, I am the one to give the order to charge. I nod my head before I turn my attention back to the strikers.

From behind, a volley of rifle-fire strikes panic among the rebellious crowd. What the hell! At no point did I intend this. Bodies of the dead and wounded litter the ground. Screams rend the air. Behind my back, instead of a baton charge, the captain has ordered his men to fire into the seething mass. The enormity of what has happened hits me. How could he have misinterpreted my intentions in this way? Now, men with batons move into the crowd. Blows rain down on the panicked mass.

I am too dazed to speak. The captain guides me through the bloody scene. The survivors, cowed with shock, attempt to give aid to their fallen comrades. Back-up teams from the NSF arrive. They drag away those uninjured and the walking wounded, to place them in chains. I excuse myself as soon as I can. In the nearest quiet corner, I empty the contents of my stomach, until nothing remains. I, me, myself, caused this to happen. Because of my inexperience and failure to give a clear signal, twenty human beings have died. Others have injuries from which they may never recover. Many of these people I know – knew – people I have joked with and shared the time of day. Now they have gone. The look of revulsion in the eyes of those who survive burns deep into my mind. They all saw me nod.

For days, weeks, visions of the dead and dying haunt me. I lie awake for hours or toss and turn, crying out from some related nightmare. Julie, dear Julie, whispers words of hope into my bedevilled mind. She is my anchor at this time, attached to the end of my thin chain of sanity.

In time, her words of comfort and logic penetrate my troubled mind. I find life easier if I listen to, and believe her. After all, these strikers were rebellious scum. In the circumstances, I had no other option, had I? Why should I blame myself when it was the fault of the Captain? He was the one who had failed to make his intentions clear, or mistaken the meaning of my command. The daily horror of facing people at work fades. With Julie's strength, I regain much of my self-confidence. Well-concealed though they are, the looks of loathing from the workforce I try to ignore. Its members are afraid of me.

As the weeks pass, my grasp on power returns. The workers' fear intensifies my Julie-fuelled ego. Production shows a rapid increase; no one dares to dissent. The great JJ himself writes to congratulate me on the improved output, and on the way in which I had handled the troubles. My qualms, I bury deeper at the back of my mind. It is in the dead of night when they come back to haunt me in my dreams.

I suppose, after the first time, the taking of a life could become easier. This theory I have no desire to put to the test. I cannot permit anyone to misconstrue my commands, or me misread a situation so disastrously again. There are times when it becomes necessary for me to make hard, tough and brutal decisions. When these occur, I do what is needed to resolve the situation. Afterwards, Julie talks me through these dark episodes. Killing is one weapon I refuse to use. It might be the ultimate power over one's fellow man, but, for me, it is a step too far.

On our first wedding anniversary, Julie and I move into a large detached house on the outskirts of Sheffield. Prior to this time we have been content to live with her parents. Ten months later, on the 15th April, our son, Ian, is born. Julie soon drops out of mainstream party-life to devote her time to our child, something to which we both have a strong commitment. In its early years, a child should have as much love, care and attention as it is possible to give. A policy promoted by our government. Now the country is achieving financial stability, the state can afford to pay higher grants to mothers. With these, they can stay at home longer, to nurture their children. Those who languish in government work camps are plentiful. At minimal cost, they fill the gaps in the labour force. I do sometimes wonder what happens to their children.

Two years later, on the 1st of July, we celebrate the birth of our daughter, Caroline. Our family is complete. This new addition, which spends most of its life sleeping, eating or screaming, fails to impress Ian. He wants her sent back to the hospital. In time, although with some jealousy, he does accept his sister as part of the family.

Over this period, Julie begins to change. The differences in her attitude are gradual and subtle. For twelve months or so, I cannot say I pay them much attention. The odd comment she makes, I thrust to the back of my mind, after all, Julie is the most loyal of party members.

I suppose being at home for most of the day, with less involvement in the political scene, triggers this apparent change in her mindset. With pram, or pushchair, most days she walks into town. There, with time to spare, she observes life and overhears points of view that, in my closed little world, are alien. She talks to strangers in the library, shops, cafés and on the streets.

Sixteen months after she commenced these excursions, one late January evening, we relax in the comfort of our armchairs. In front of us, a log fire blazes. We bathe in the warmth while, outside, frost crackles over deep drifts of snow. Without warning, Julie poses a question that disturbs me, more out of concern for her than her words.

## CHAPTER 2

"Nathan!"

"Yes, love?" I tear myself away from a copy of JJ's latest book of political essays.

"Why does everybody hate us? I mean the ordinary people in the street. I speak to them. They are friendly, at first, but when someone whispers to them who I am, they slink away, fear and hatred in their eyes. What's the matter with them?"

"What the devil are you talking about?" I ask in amazement. "You're imagining it. Why should they hate you? Look what we've done for them. Their standard of living is higher now than in living memory. They eat well, can afford good clothes and holidays; educational standards are higher than ever. They can afford luxury goods, the roads they travel are in excellent order. In fact, they've never had it so good," I exclaim, with a subconscious echo of a famous catch-phrase from the past.

"But we don't allow them the freedom to say what they think," Julie interjects, her voice low, her face serious.

"Now look here," I bristle, angered by this implied treason. "Of course they can say whatever they want, unless it's anti-government. What's wrong with that? If someone out there has threatened you, tell me; I'll put the NSF onto them. The security people can do their job and arrest them. Whatever you do, don't voice such thoughts again about lack of freedom of speech. If someone hears you, you'll find yourself in a correctional facility. I don't understand how you can have such ideas."

"No-one's been bothering me, it's nothing like that, nothing at all. I'll go and put the kettle on." With that, she leaves me.

By the time she comes back, Julie has a smile on her face. She changes the subject and, happy to drop the matter, I drive it from my mind. We have an early night, but our lovemaking is perfunctory. With a sense of mutual dissatisfaction, we drift off into sleep.

We avoid mention of that evening, although, at odd moments, I recall her words. Of course we are right, damn it. My work and lifestyle rest upon the foundation of our beliefs. The means, JJ says, cannot be anything but justified by the quality of its results. If I accept that as true, why do I find myself questioning his methods? Could this be the reason I was angry with Julie? She aired some of the thoughts I prefer to keep buried. When you reap huge rewards from the state, it is easy to gloss over its faults. What I fail to realise is, my family should be a higher priority in my life than my career. It is our misfortune the future reveals itself to us as it happens. For some it comes too late to amend the error of their ways.

At times, I catch Julie observing me, almost as if I am a stranger. If I do say anything, she laughs it off, smiles and acts as though nothing is wrong.

☙ ❧

The months pass by; summer draws near. Ian and Caroline are growing fast and developing their personalities. By the time I reach my thirty-first birthday in June, the weather is hot. We bask in a heat-wave. With the high temperatures comes the annual crop of trouble throughout the country. Groups of militant activists attempt to stir-up unrest. By the middle of the month, duty takes me away to the south to put down an uprising, 'a strike' as they used to call them.

I am away for a week, by which time several hundred insurgents are under arrest. Their leaders face the threat of execution. I am glad to say I have no input in that matter, the courts will decide their fate. To my surprise, I receive another commendation from JJ. Julie, as usual, keeps up-to-date with the details in the papers. She welcomes me home, listens to my fears and talks a strong party line, but the strange looks are back. There are times, when she thinks I cannot see her looking at me, the expression on Julie's face troubles me. Is it sympathy, pity or contempt I glimpse?

We are no longer close, as man and wife. Could there be someone-else? I have no evidence for that. I am certain she still loves me, or so

I convince myself, but some part of Julie, some inner depth I cannot grasp, has left me behind. Something that I am sure is in my power to catch hold of, if only I knew how.

# 3

"Mr Andrews? Mr NP Andrews?" the NSF officer asks as, with ease, he side-steps my secretary.

The poor woman, flustered by her failure to bar his way into my office, closes the door with more force than necessary.

"Yes," I snap, irritated by this sudden interruption. "What can I do for you?"

"The Captain has asked me to call round to see you. Captain Thomas, I mean."

"Ah! Charles, and how is he?" I force myself to relax. "I haven't seen him for a while."

"It's a matter of national security, sir. The Captain sends his compliments and requests you meet with him this afternoon."

"Damn it! Is it that important it can't wait until tonight? I'm rather tied up at the moment."

I am positive it will turn out to be something minor and of no consequence. I have the production figures to go through.

"Captain Thomas did impress on me the matter is of the utmost urgency, something to do with a raid on a group of dissenters."

The man's face is expressionless; in this light, his eyes appear dead.

"Oh! If I must, I must," I concede with ill grace.

With my day's schedule ruined, I grab my jacket then follow the officer. He hastens down the stairs. By the time we pass through the main entrance, I have to sprint to catch him. Having missed lunch, I was looking forward to the pot of coffee, and plate of biscuits, brought into me a few minutes ago. It is the middle of the afternoon. I have eaten nothing since breakfast.

## CHAPTER 3

Traffic is light through Sheffield, allowing the unmarked security-car to travel at high speed through town, and on into the country. Where the devil is the fool taking me? I thought he said we were to go to the local headquarters. In the rush to leave, I have forgotten to pick up my mobile. Damn. I have missed the opportunity to leave a message for Julie, to let her know I might be late tonight. She has been away for a few days, at a retreat somewhere on the North York Moors, but is due home tonight. The children have been staying with her parents.

To speak to her would be better, but to find her mobile switched on during the day is rare. Where she goes, most times I have no knowledge. 'Out walking, for some peace and quiet', is all she will admit to when asked. She has dropped out of most local party events. I attend most functions by myself. Since that time, two and a half years ago, when she asked that question about people hating us, her other self has abandoned me. This last year, her comments about life under JJ's rule have re-surfaced. I warn her about them, but to no lasting effect.

The children, and a thousand-and-one other strands connect us, but the mutual attraction, the caring for one another, and our love, have become somewhat one-sided. On some other level, I lost Julie a long time ago. It is a subject I avoid dwelling on, or questioning in depth. To be honest, I am too afraid to want to discover the real answer. I have a 'bury my head in the sand' attitude to my personal relationships. Damn stupid, I know, but I cannot help it.

ଓ ଃ

It is August. The sun's rays are powerful. Despite the front-windows being open, the heat inside the rear of the vehicle has risen several degrees.

"How much further have we to go?" I complain, as the miles speed by.

We have been travelling for well over an hour. Now, after circling Manchester, we are on the motorway heading north.

"You might have warned me we were going across country. I could have rung my wife."

"Sorry, Sir. Captain Thomas's orders."

Blast Thomas and his orders. I could wring his damned neck for him.

"We're here now," the driver says, twenty minutes later as, in rural countryside, we drive through the entrance gates of a large country mansion.

"Where the devil are we?" I ask.

"Captain Thomas will explain everything when you meet, sir," is the answer I receive.

It has been like this for the whole journey. Everything I say, or ask, receives the same reply. Captain Thomas will explain everything. He had better. I have failed to elicit anything useful from the driver, including his name.

"This way, Sir." His voice remains as respectful as ever.

He directs me through the imposing doorway into the deep-piled carpeted corridor that lies beyond. He knocks on the first door to the left. A voice calls 'Come in.'

"Ah! Mr Andrews," greets the Captain. We are being formal today. "Thank you Johnson, that will be all for now."

"Yes, Sir," Johnson salutes.

He leaves, but now I know his name.

"What's this about, Charles? Your man drags me from my office, drives for hours into the back of beyond and refuses to answer the most basic of questions."

"I'm sorry about that. It is rather important. Please, sit down. Whisky?"

We discuss the weather while we drink. Charles waits until the last drops of our drinks has gone, before he responds to the question of why I am here.

"It's a matter of national security," he states. His face takes on a look of concern.

## CHAPTER 3

"From Johnson, I gathered that but little else. Why does it concern me, and why have I had to travel all this way? Whatever the problem is, I'm sure I could have dealt with it at my office."

"Yesterday morning, at nine-thirty, we raided a private house. We arrested several known troublemakers we've had under observation for some time. We also netted another activist, a woman whose association with the dissidents was unknown to us. Our prisoners, apart from this one, did not survive their interrogation. This woman has confessed to being a member of the group. She's a recent recruit but has no useful knowledge of their inner circle. Because she comes from your area, we thought it polite to ask you first before we process her. You are the top man there."

Have they brought me all this way for this? A simple telephone call would have sufficed. My work is much too important for such trivial matters to delay it. He should be able to deal with someone in this woman's position, without asking me. I make my thoughts clear.

"If it was that straightforward, we would have had no reason to contact you," Charles says, "but she's the wife of an important party member. We thought it better to hear your views on the matter, in confidence, before we instigated proceedings."

"My views?" I utter with some force. "You know my opinions on matters such as this. There can be no exceptions. She is subject to the rule of law, as is everyone else."

As the wife of a senior party member, three months in a re-education centre is the usual tariff for such a privileged offender. Ordinary citizens could expect a two-year sentence of hard labour for a minor offence, life or execution for one more serious.

"I know, but we had to be sure."

Charles's smile, after he acknowledges my judgemental stance, has a strange edge to it. Recent overwork has put me under great pressure. The stress of that and my home life has pushed me towards breaking point. I am hot, tired and hungry. These factors might explain my failure to pick-up on the undercurrent of the conversation. Explain, yes – excuse, no! The large whisky has dulled my senses. I have allowed my concentration to slip; an unforgivable mistake on my part. Once more, I have misread a situation. I have in mind a brief trial and a short term of imprisonment. Charles, I soon discover, has other ideas. He presses a buzzer on the intercom set on his desk. In an undertone, he speaks into it.

"There, that's that. Here, have another drink. Sorry again, Andrews old chap, for dragging you out here, but we have to be sure in a case like this. It wouldn't do to for us to proceed without your authority."

"I don't understand why you need it. You haven't before. Who is she anyway? I suppose I must know her, or of her, if she comes from my area. The wife of a party member, how could she?"

From outside, before Charles can answer, or, before he intends to answer, there comes a volley of rifle-fire. From the look of triumph on his face, I know the answer to my question. There will be no trial nor prison term. I have given my blessing to a much bloodier solution. Too late, I discover Charles is no friend of mine.

I stagger to the window. Waves of nausea threaten to overwhelm me. At the grimy panes, I see a young officer. He walks towards the limp pathetic bundle, tied to a pole skewered into the manicured lawn. He removes the blindfold and cuts loose the body. For an instant, as the soldier lowers the victim to the ground, a gust of wind lifts the long brown hair. Revealed are the features of the one I love more than life itself. Julie, oh Julie, what have I done? How could I have allowed Charles to use my arrogance to deceive me this way?

I turn and empty what little is left of my breakfast over the Captain's nice clean uniform. Within seconds, my hands are round his neck. His eyes glaze over. My grip tightens further round his throat. His desperate struggles and futile clawing weaken. Without warning, my head explodes. I feel myself falling but have no recollection of hitting the floor.

The smell of new Axminster carpet is strong. I am in a heap, my head face down on top of the thick woollen pile. I doubt I have been

## CHAPTER 3

unconscious for more than a few minutes. My head rings with the after-effects of the blow that felled me. Watering eyes make it difficult to focus. My skull seems swollen to twice its normal size. Rough hands drag me to my feet and toss me into a waiting chair. The room appears to revolve and, for a second time, I feel faint. Apart from my head, which throbs with a rare intensity, everything returns to normal. The blurred shapes in front of me come into sharp relief as my eyes regain focus.

Johnson is to the front and right of me, an automatic pointed at my heart. A little curl of skin and hair hangs from the barrel. I watch the scrap fall to the floor, unaware at the time it is from my scalp. I raise my head. The movement causes the beating anvil inside my skull to increase its work rate. Across the desk, Captain Thomas sits, his composure recovered, his clean, neat uniform, now soiled from my outpouring.

"Well!" he says. His voice is husky, but he remains calm and calculated. "Attempted murder of a member of the NSF! Now, this is an unusual reaction from a dedicated Party Member. I understand the penalty for that is death, isn't that correct, Johnson?"

"Yes Sir," he answers, keeping his eyes on me. "A serious offence indeed, shall I see to it now?"

"Mmmh! No, we can save that pleasure for later. I have some questions to ask first. Oh! Sorry, Nathan, did I forget to mention, because trials of traitors take too long and stir unrest among the people, we have new guidelines? They came into effect at the start of the month. The penalty for those who engage in acts of terrorism, or join an anti-government organisation, is execution. Once a senior party official has agreed the severity of the offence – in this case, yourself – there is no right of appeal. Our duty is to carry out the sentence with immediate effect," he turns to Johnson. "Take Mr Andrews to a 'guest-room', and see he has every consideration."

"Come this way please, Sir," Johnson requests with exaggerated politeness.

The effect is somewhat spoilt by his grabbing hold of my hair and dragging me to my feet. The door opens, as if by some hidden signal. I hurtle through the opening, into the corridor. Two men in security uniforms seize hold of me. They manhandle me down the passageway.

My mind is in a whirl. Everything has happened too fast for my poor benumbed brain to take it in. One thing alone keeps running through my mind, Julie is dead… Julie is dead… Julie is dead…

At a run, the guards take me to the end of the corridor. A waiting man in uniform opens a panelled door. For a moment, I have the impression of bright lights and whitewashed walls. The guards rush me down a steep flight of stairs to the depths below. Thrown into an empty chamber, I land with a heavy thud on the cold, damp concrete floor. Behind me, a heavy metal door slams into position. The clang echoes around my pitch-black room. All that breaks the silence that follows are distant moans and an occasional scream.

Brought here to face questioning, Julie must have been tortured until she confessed to something, anything, to stop the pain and humiliation. Although, deep in my heart, I know the charges are true. I doubt she was a mainstream activist, but she was on the outskirts of the dirty business. For the first time, I have my eyes opened to the ugly hidden depths of what I have helped to create. It hurts. Julie, oh Julie, what did they do to you? What did I do to you? I retch again and again until I am empty of all but grief. That is not so easy to expel. My straining eases. I pass out on the hard floor, my eyes wet with tears of shame and sorrow.

The next forty-eight hours are something that, for the rest of my life, I shall have difficulty in remembering without breaking out in a cold sweat. The continual rounds of questioning, pain, degradation, bright lights, mental and physical battering shatter my mind. Combined with lack of sleep, and the utter humiliation this treatment induces, I reach a point where I am ready to confess to anything my inquisitors want.

It is the fact that this can happen to me, myself, a person, a living being, as much as the physical pain and degradation. I suppose we all have an image of ourselves, the complete person, durable and unyielding, no matter how erroneous this may be. We want to believe we are in charge of our destiny. Despite continued doubts about the methods I, and others in similar positions use, my ego has become tremendous. I was the one who gave the orders that sealed people's fate. Now, everything has turned around. I am nothing more than a defenceless lump of beaten flesh, a screaming gibbering frightened animal that needs a corner to crawl into so that it can die. My delusions of grandeur drip, drip, drip towards the floor, into a pool of red sticky liquid.

It has been an efficient short, sharp treatment to soften me up before my interrogators inject me with various drugs. Under the alternating sweating and freezing effects of these substances, I tell them everything in my mind. Of this part of my treatment, some memories are hazy. Without doubt, they learn everything about my subconscious suspicions of Julie. Apart from those, I am unable to betray myself further. I have done nothing treasonable.

After this period, their attempts become somewhat half-hearted. After a while, they take me from the interrogation room, back to my cold, damp cell. Whimpering like some wounded creature in the wilds, I gather the few remaining tatters of my clothing around the bleeding shell I had once been proud to call my body. Despite the agonising pain, I faint into oblivion. Almost three days without sleep gives me that merciful release.

For the next three days, my interrogators leave me on my own. At random times, a light comes on. A grill slides open at the base of the door. Through the gap, a hand pushes a tray, bearing some nameless anaemic broth and a glass of water. No words accompany the delivery, although I try to initiate some response. My captors leave me to lick my wounds in silence. The first couple of times the tray remains untouched. I lie where I landed when they threw me into the cell, afraid to move, my body on fire and my mind numb.

Had I been a traitor, I may have been able to endure what has happened to me for longer, without screaming out everything I could, to ease the pain and horror. The mental scars may have been less deep. I imagine a real traitor would have anticipated what was to come. To live with the fear of capture and questioning must be an occupational hazard. Unprepared as I was, I cracked without any real resistance. My betrayal, my own personal fundamental betrayal of the one I loved, I doubt will ever rest easy in my mind.

I told them everything I could about Julie, towards the end, everything and anything, real or imagined that might stop the pain. At times, I had hated her for bringing me into this situation. I was almost glad she had died under my orders. These are memories that will haunt me forever. Beside the betrayal of our love, I have betrayed everything our life together has meant. She is, was my first and only love. Despite our problems over the last few years, Julie was my world.

Yet, I fear, had she been alive during the darkest hours of my interrogation, I might have condemned her to take my place, by any truth or lie I could have conjured out of my tortured brain. Had we both survived, it is doubtful I could have brought myself to look into those beautiful eyes and caress her body, without curling-up and dying inside.

# 4

"Ah! Good morning, Mr Andrews." Charles's voice is relaxed, with neither a hint of malice nor sarcasm.

He has a smile on his face, but his eyes are expressionless. These are the first words spoken to me in days. After the three in the cold, dark and damp cell, my captors took me to a secure medical room. Here someone in a white coat treated my injuries. I took advantage of a shower and a change of clothes that were on offer. After my treatment, the suit I had arrived in was little better than rags. Once dressed, my guards escorted me to a windowless room, where they locked the door behind me. A bed, a chair and a tiny bathroom became my home for several days. I soon lost track of time. There I remained, in solitude, until twenty minutes ago. Now I am back inside Charles's office. Drapes, pulled across the window, block the view of the lawn and firing post.

"It would appear," Charles continues, "your story bears out. You're a lucky man. You have friends in high places who have spoken to my superiors. They have agreed to drop the charge of attempted murder. Apart from that, all other matters will remain on file. You are free to go. Johnson, will drive you home."

Stunned, and before I can speak, my guards take a firm hold of me. They frog-march me from the room. The last thing I notice is the look of utter contempt on the face of my ex-friend, Captain Charles Thomas. For the first time in days, I have something on which to focus. At that moment, the numbness in my mind fades and hatred flickers. At some time in the future, I shall kill him. How? I have no thought to the detail, but I shall find a way.

I sign innumerable release papers. The journey home that follows is a blur, although I do commit to memory the winding route from the headquarters to the main road. I shall be able to locate it again. The hour is late when we park outside my home. Apart from a light in the hallway, it is in darkness. A sense of dread grows inside me, a confirmation of my deepest fears. I calm myself. Of course, the children would not be here, alone. They must be with my parents, or still at Julie's. Outside, an unmarked security car pulls up to park over the road. It seems I am to remain under observation.

In a daze, I wander through the house. From its appearance, a dozen burglars could have ransacked the place. Each cupboard and drawer is open, the contents strewn across the floors. Once pristine seat-covers now gape where sharp blades have slashed the fabric. The internal padding hangs loose. Ripped floorboards, their nails exposed to careless footsteps, lie in haphazard fashion across the exposed gaps left behind.

The children's rooms are bare; their clothes, toys and furniture removed. I turn to Johnson, who has followed me on my tour.

"Where are my children? I want to see them, now!" I demand.

"You can forget them, Mr Andrews," Johnson advises with relish. He is enjoying this. "For their own safety, they have been removed. What did you expect? With a self-confessed traitor for a mother, and a father who keeps his suspicions to himself, the court has no alternative but to place the children in care. The state's decision is final. In its opinion, it would be injurious to their future welfare for them to remain in your custody. They've become the responsibility of a couple of loyal party members. Earlier today, they finalised the adoption papers."

Johnson's hand reaches for the butt of his automatic as he takes a step back, his expression wary. The look on my face has telegraphed my intentions toward him.

"Be careful Mr Andrews," he warns. "Your friends gained freedom for you once, it won't happen again. If you lay one finger on me, I promise you, your execution will be over before dawn."

## CHAPTER 4

I remain still and silent. He relaxes, but his hand remains on his weapon. Careful, so that he cannot misconstrue my intentions, I walk round him. Downstairs, I open the front door wide and indicate he leaves.

"Well, goodbye, Mr Andrews. From now on, I would be careful with whom I make friends or start a relationship. We'll be keeping a close watch on you for some time. Oh! I forgot to mention, your position at the factory is no longer open to you. We have appointed someone else to do your work, a person whose loyalty is without question. The local party committee is deciding where to place you. They'll be in contact in due course.

"If I were you, I would make good use of my time. It's a pity you've let your house fall into such a mess. In its present state, I doubt you'll be able to cover the outstanding mortgage when it goes on the market. Believe me, sell it you'll have to. On what you'll be earning soon, you'll struggle to afford the price of a tent."

My attempts to keep my face expressionless fail. In haste, Johnson steps outside, then, at speed, moves down the path. He looks back, to see whether I have followed him. I remain at the door and watch as he walks round his car towards the one with the surveillance-team inside. After a brief conversation, of which I hear nothing, he returns to his own vehicle. With a sardonic salute in my direction, he opens his door and, moments later, drives away.

I slam the door on the world. With my back against the hallway wall, I slide to the floor, drained of all emotion and energy. They have taken everything from me. I have nothing but memories and a few broken possessions. After an hour, cold and shivering in reaction to the confrontation and the situation in which I find myself, I move. In the kitchen, food lies strewn over the floor and smeared across the walls and ceiling. The doors of the fridge and freezer gape open, their contents either rotting inside or trodden into the floor. The smell is atrocious. I open the windows, then go in search of the kettle. It is in a corner, its metal body dented and lid twisted. While I wait for the water to boil, I discover an undamaged jar of instant coffee. I sip the hot strong drink. There is no fresh milk, the old cartons long since emptied over the floor. The congealed mess, with its spreading fur coat, adds further to the overall stench.

Coffee improves my ability to think. In need of a friendly voice, I pick up the 'phone and dial some of my contacts. Each time I pick up the receiver, a click follows. The authorities have tapped my line. I should have known; such procedure is standard. Apart from numbers, I provide them with little to record. My contacts, people I have known for years, dined with, partied with, some even holidayed with, disconnect once they hear my voice. Two have the courtesy to speak, but to say nothing other than for me to lose their numbers. It would appear I am persona non grata in my own town. Who the friends in high places might be who saved my life, I cannot guess. If they are among the people I have rung, no-one will admit to it, nor help in any overt way.

Johnson was right about some things. The house does need cleaning, repairing and most of the rooms re-decorating. The salary I earn, too, for the foreseeable future, will be insufficient for me to keep up my mortgage re-payments. As I wander the wreckage, I realise my house is only a shell. It is no longer a home. I have no desire to stay. There are too many memories. Over the days I widen my attempts to contact old 'friends' and colleagues. No-one will speak, nor return my calls. I consult a solicitor. The authorities provide paperwork. It confirms what Johnson told me. My children are no longer mine. Under current laws, there are no legal options open to me that would allow me to re-claim them.

As for Julie's remains, the authorities deny me the closure of a funeral. They have cremated her body and refuse to tell me where they scattered her ashes. Treatment, officials tell me, which befits a traitor to the country.

A month passes. Much to my surprise, my final salary arrives in my account, along with a much larger than expected severance payment.

## CHAPTER 4

With this, and the money Julie and I had saved, I do the work on the house. When complete, I put it up for sale. Along with everyone else, it seems, the estate agents know my circumstances. They indicate to potential buyers that I need a quick sale. The offers I receive are derisory. Because I have enough to live on, I stand firm. Weeks pass, until the third estate agent with whom I place the house, a man more sympathetic than the previous two, sells it at near the asking price. With the money from my severance and the amount left over from the sale, I have enough for a hefty deposit on a much smaller property. For the moment, until settled in a job, I rent a bedsit.

Much to my relief, the offer of employment I receive is for a position in Leeds ("Take it or end up on the streets", was the way the party official phrased it). My new job and home are an hour's drive away from Sheffield - a world away from my solitary existence. I wonder whether my anonymous friends have pulled strings again. By the following March, my low-level office job has benefited from an increase in salary. With money in the bank for a deposit, I can afford to cover the mortgage on a two bed, brick-built inner-terraced house not far from the Kirkstall area of Leeds. I now half-own a house, with twenty-five years to pay off the remainder.

Apart from the trouble at Dawson's, my intervention in industrial disputes took place in the south of the country. In those places, where my involvement was pivotal, I kept in the background. I was happy to leave my media-trained colleagues to take the glory in newspapers and on televised news-reports. With my face unknown, I am able to conceal my past life from both neighbours and work-colleagues. I look different, too, I am around two stones lighter and I've let my hair grow a little longer. At work, no-one but senior management and the party representative are aware of my past. The latter pays particular attention to my work and progress.

I still harbour thoughts of revenge. They burn away, deep inside, but I am in no hurry. I am wise enough keep them to myself. I have no knowledge of who my watchers are. Overt surveillance ended when

I left Sheffield. For a while, at least, it would be foolish to consider regular observation of me consigned to history. I will bet any amount of money that someone among my neighbours is an informant, along with one or more of my work-mates. Those whose duty it is to keep an eye on people of interest, the state pays well.

I continue to mourn for Julie, but whether this is for the girl I first fell in love with, and for a way of life that had already escaped me, I cannot be sure. I yearn for my children; their adoption I cannot forgive.

In my new life, I keep myself to myself and avoid socialising. Whenever possible, I decline nights out with the lads. An unguarded word, spoken in an alcoholic haze, could return me to the clutches of my old friend, Charles. Until *I* am ready, I want to avoid all contact. When we meet again, I want to be the one with his finger on the trigger. The lure of the drink is another consideration. It would be too easy for me to drown my sorrows, to deaden the pain. This ache, my constant companion, keeps me focused.

Word reaches me that my parents have died. In an accident, the party representative tells me. I saw them once or twice before I left Sheffield, but the meetings were fraught. They were afraid. I could understand that. Over the brief period of my incarceration, the NSF paid them several visits. Each time I called to see them, an unmarked car would pull up outside their home. After I left, it would stay for several hours. Although neither of them said so, it was a relief to my parents when I moved away from the area.

Compassionate leave, to attend their funerals, the company denies me. The Sheffield police have contacted the party-rep. They told him my attendance could bring unnecessary attention. It would be better, they said, if I stay away. A few weeks later, I visit the cemetery, to lay flowers on the grave and to see the headstone I have bought.

After Julie's arrest, I heard her parents suffered much worse attention than did mine. As she was their daughter, the authorities suspected the couple must have been aware of her state of mind. Their interrogation had been harsh and, afterwards, they had endured months of separation

## CHAPTER 4

and corrective training. Although re-united, they were shadows of their former selves, broken people. Afraid of becoming pariahs in their local community, as had I, they re-located to another part of the country. These details are hearsay. Since my arrest, they have disappeared from my life.

By now, I am certain I have identified my main watchers. One is Karl, my supervisor in the office where I slave each day. A talent for production-planning has proved a lifesaver for me. After nine months, a few weeks before Christmas, Karl moves to a new position. I gain a promotion, albeit offered with some reluctance. The rise in salary is larger than expected. Do I detect the movement of hidden hands directing my destiny?

My assistant Amanda, brought in to fill my former role, I soon realise is my new watcher. Her work rate is variable and at times slip-shod. My complaints to senior staff meet with no success. They refuse to issue an official reprimand. At times, when I have stayed late in the office, I have caught her deep in discussion with the party representative. Unaware of my presence, I see them through the side window of his office. Between them, on the leather-topped surface of his desk, is a file bearing my name and photo on the front.

At home, my watcher proves to be more elusive. The street where I live houses a diverse cross-section of people. It could be any one of them. Over time, I narrow it down. Of those, a youngish man comes to the fore. He above any of the others has tried to strike up a friendship. Although unemployed, he seems to have plenty of money. At first, I thought him up to no good, a petty crook or conman. Over a period of several months, I realise, wherever I go on an evening or weekend, I catch sight of him, in the background. I keep an eye on his house, which lies across the street, offset to mine. Unlike the row I occupy, the houses opposite are back-to-back.

From my bedroom window, hidden behind net curtains, at an angle I can look down into his front room. Once a week, on a Monday, no-matter what time of year, he draws the curtains for a while, about seven o'clock. As an indicator of clandestine behaviour at best it is flimsy, but twice now, before his drapes come together, I have caught sight of a stranger entering the room. Although out of uniform, this man carries himself with the assurance of a member of the NSF, his close-cropped hair typical of such officers. How he gains access to the house, I cannot tell. I have yet to see him enter or leave by the street entrance.

With my promotion, I can afford to upgrade my old car to a newer model. At the end of January, after a couple of weeks into my ownership, it requires some minor work. On the Monday, I leave it at the garage and pick up a courtesy car. That evening, out of curiosity and in possession of a strange vehicle, I park down the next street. The house behind my neighbour's is empty and boarded up. It is a cold January night. A hundred metres away, huddled inside my car, I wait with lights out.

At five minutes to seven, a van pulls-up outside the empty premises. By the light of a nearby street lamp, I can see emblazoned on its side 'Landlord Services', an old NSF disguise I know from my past life. Laptop-case in hand, the man, whom I have seen before, leaves the vehicle. With a key, he opens the door to the empty house. It is half an hour before he leaves, confirmation enough for my suspicions. There must be a back way through into my neighbour's home. He is my watcher, this man his handler.

# 5

A few weeks after confirming which of my neighbours is keeping watch on me at home, I see him approaching my front door. Wary, I step back from the window, but he has seen me. He waves.

'Oh! What the hell', I mutter, as the doorbell rings.

It is time I convinced the authorities that the past is behind me. If I want to prove to them that I am over the loss of my wife and family, I cannot remain in seclusion forever. I mould my expression into one of mild curiosity, then open the door to greet my unsuspecting enemy.

"I'm sorry," I explain, "I don't buy from people at the door. Oh! Wait a minute. Sorry about that, don't you live over the road?"

"Yes, I'm Tim," he answers. "I know what you mean. Bloody door-to-door salespeople are a right menace. I don't know why the government doesn't do something about them, I think they..."

"I'm sure those in power know best," I interrupt.

Does he consider me a fool, to fall for such an amateur attempt to trick me into say something against the authorities?

"All street salesmen have to be licensed," I add.

"And so they should be," Tim agrees.

"How can I help you?" I ask, changing the subject.

"Ah! Well! You've lived here for a while now. I've noticed you don't seem to have many friends, or go out much. It's Wednesday and quiz night at the pub. My old competition partner has moved out of the area. I wondered if you'd like to come for a drink and join in."

"Er! Yes! Sure, that would be nice." I make my acceptance of his invitation sound as genuine as I can. "It'll be a change from watching the repeats on TV, although JJ's speeches are worth a second hearing."

I make it sound as though I do little else but watch them. Once that would have been true, but, in those days, I had a wife, a family and a belief that our leader's way of running the world was right. That conviction died with Julie.

"Brill!" Tim says. "I'll call for you around seven-thirty."

I nod as, with a quick wave, he leaves. Hidden behind the lace curtains in my bedroom, I gaze towards Tim's downstairs window. He has his mobile in his hand. Several times, he glances towards my house as he speaks to, I assume, his superior. I glance at the clock. It has already turned six-thirty. A ready meal from the freezer is all I have time for now.

Despite earlier concerns that my lack of enthusiasm might be transparent, the evening goes well. We fall two answers short of winning the gallon of beer on offer. Unlike in my younger days, when questions covered a variety of subjects, quizzes these days seem to have a greater nationalistic and governmental bias - one with which I am no longer as familiar. Tim is delighted. Our result, he declares, is better than any he achieved with his old partner.

Despite much persuasion, I keep to soft drinks. I must be on my guard. Tim slips an occasional anti-government comment into the conversation. He assumes I am unaware of his careful observation of my reaction. I either ignore, or respond in the negative to his provocative words. Twice, I have to warn him such talk is treasonous.

Without doubt, he has set me up. I have no alternative, and he knows it. I shall have to report him to my representative at work, otherwise I risk serious attention from the NSF. The thought of another visit to see Charles and his gang of inquisitors turns my blood cold. The following morning, I reach work an hour earlier than usual. When Harry, the party rep, arrives at his office, he finds me outside his door.

"Good grief, Nathan," he says. "What are you doing here at this time? You don't start for another half hour."

"Same as you, catching up on work, but it's another matter I want to discuss with you. It might be of little importance, but I was with someone last night. No, nothing like that," I add at his raised eyebrow. "A neighbour asked me to partner him in a pub quiz."

"Very nice for you, but I don't see what it has to do with me." Harry pretends ignorance.

"The quiz, nothing, but my neighbour, Tim Caldwell, was different from what I expected."

"In what way?"

"He passed several subversive and other, dubious comments"

"Oh! I see. What did he say?"

I spend the next ten minutes going over everything Tim had voiced last night. In the sombre surroundings of Harry's office, many of the snippets sound much less offensive than when first heard. It is possible I am being hypersensitive, but I do know I would have been in trouble had I failed to notify Harry. He feigns interest, and ignorance.

"Mmmh!" He strokes his chin in concentration.

He walks over to the percolator in the corner, then empties the stale contents from the filter into a bag-lined bin. I bet his office cleaner loves him. For a few moments, I wait while he considers his reply. When I spoke, I detected a look of satisfaction on his face. I am in no doubt this is a test. It could be he considers I am ready to have my security-risk rating lowered. If so, I am sure my visit has gone some way to confirm this. What he says next does surprise me.

"We should keep an eye on this chap. I want you to develop this friendship. Would it be a problem for you, to report back on everything you do and what he says, seditious or otherwise?"

"Er! No! Sure," I stutter. "Of course I will."

"Excellent," Harry acknowledges. "Now, I've detained you long enough from your work, I know you're busy. Oh! One last thing, party officials have mentioned how pleased they are with your efforts. Since your arrival here, production and profits have increased by a significant margin. Keep it up."

I step out of Harry's office, flustered but pleased by his unexpected praise. The fact that, had I failed to report Tim, Harry might have had me arrested tempers my delight. Duplicitous rat. Although, is there a vast difference between him and the person I used to be?

Later, when I reflect on my meeting, it occurs to me how cunning Harry has been. The watcher watches me and I watch the watcher. Harry can compare notes and know whether Tim's reports are accurate and, at the same time, prove my loyalty. Clever! This situation has its advantages for me, too. The sooner I convince the authorities I am trustworthy again, the better.

Over the next few months, Tim and I continue with our Wednesday quiz nights. To my surprise, I come to look forward to them. I have been alone too long with my grief. It does me good to integrate with humanity again. I have changed. Now I can have sympathy for people, and empathise with their fear when they realise something they have said, in innocence, might appear subversive to others. No-one knows who among them might be an informer. Anyone, anywhere, anytime could be the one to notify the authorities.

We win the prize of a gallon of ale several times. I take my share in fruit juices and Tim, his in pints of real ale. While waiting my turn at the bar for re-fills, his name crops up in occasional conversations with other regulars. It does appear Tim has told the truth about his regular visits with a previous companion, and their lack of success. His old quiz partner, they tell me, left to take up a new position in the south of the country. I suspect he was a fellow-informer, sent here long enough to establish Tim's credentials, before transferring to another surveillance job. What, I wonder, does Tim do with his time while I am at work? I doubt I can be of sufficient importance to merit him sitting at home all day doing nothing. It could be that others in the neighbourhood, besides me, are of importance to the authorities.

03 80

After six months, I widen my horizons. I start to visit local attractions, enjoy occasional trips to the coast or go for walks in the countryside.

## CHAPTER 5

Tim has joined me on some of the less strenuous outings, others I have been 'unaccompanied'. By unaccompanied, I mean without Tim. It is rare for me not to spot someone in the background. Sometimes it is a man, sometimes a woman. They keep their distance. Whoever it is, they blend in well with the crowds, but, because I expect someone to be there, I soon identify them. I make sure I do nothing to make their job difficult. To lose them would be self-defeating. I want them to believe I am unaware and conscience-free.

One Sunday, twelve months after my first quiz night, I find myself out in the countryside, alone. For once, I can see no distant figure, attempting to blend in with the background and keep up with me. For the first time since that dreadful day when Julie died, a taste of freedom has come my way.

For the end of March, the weather is mild. My fleece jacket and waterproofs remain inside my rucksack, unused. With a rock for a seat, on the valley side overlooking Langstrothdale, I eat my sandwiches. Across my face blows a gentle breeze, the air fresh and clear. I take a deep breath. I wish it were possible to freeze time, so that I could remain here forever, to bask in the sunshine, miles away from my miserable existence. A pipe dream, I want my revenge, and my children back!

A woman comes through a gap in the dry stone-wall, a hundred metres or so back in the direction from which I have come. Dark haired and attractive, she possesses a figure that, unlike mine, shows signs of much regular exercise. She approaches along the dusty path, near to where I sit. Late twenties, early thirties I guess. Her hips swing with an easy stride.

On the path, near to me, she pauses to take a bottle of mineral water from the trouser-pocket of her khaki walking-trousers. She takes a deep swallow from the container's half-filled contents. Between the petite mounds of her breasts, perspiration darkens her bright green T-shirt. She turns towards me. The upper part of her outdoor tanned face remains shaded by a floppy sun hat. She smiles.

"Beautiful day for a walk," she says.

Her voice is melodious and pleasant, her accent Yorkshire, closer to Leeds than the Dales. The fact she speaks confirms her as a regular walker, unlike some of the miseries on the moor, who pass you by with scowls on their faces and never a word.

"It's perfect," I agree. "It's a shame we can't guarantee more days like this."

"Too true. Enjoy the rest of your day."

"You too," I call as she turns and carries on walking.

Within moments, she is through the gap in the next wall and out of sight. I remain where I am, lost in thought. The woman has made an impression on me. I have been alone too long. However, with revenge on my mind, is it fair to involve someone else? No! To become close to another would put their life at risk.

I cram my rubbish into my rucksack, sling it over my shoulders then return to the path. Before long, I descend to Yockenthwaite, a place name of Scandinavian origins. I turn left, to drop down to join a well-trodden path, which will lead me beside the river Wharfe to Hubberholme. From there, it is an easy walk back to the car park at Buckden. The heat builds along the valley bottom. My damp T-shirt flaps in the occasional breeze.

I go through a gate to follow a narrow path between a wire-fence and the remains of a moss-covered wall above the riverbank. On the other side of the fence, a field barn throws its shadow over the pathway. My mind is in a faraway place. A soft voice calls out to me. Taken by surprise, I stop and look round. Standing in the shadow of the barn, is the woman I saw earlier.

"Keep walking, Nathan," she instructs. "Stop when you reach the opposite end of the barn. Make it look as if you have paused to catch your breath. Don't speak," she adds with some urgency, "and don't look my way. You might be seen by your watcher."

My mind races with questions. How does she know my name and what watcher? Since reaching Buckden Rake, at the start of my walk, I have seen no-one except this woman. There, a trio of hikers ahead of me had turned off on the route towards the Pike.

"You do have a follower, but he's a long-way back. Keep your head turned the other way," she warns, when I sneak a glance towards her.

I lift my binoculars and pretend to look for wildlife among the trees beside the river.

"Good," she says, "that's better. Your work's party rep believes it's time for mandatory surveillance of you to end, but, unlike others, he suspects you have become aware of a tail when you go out. He wants to satisfy himself that your actions are no different when you think you're without one. Neither he, nor his masters, realise you know your 'friend' Tim is one of them."

How the hell does she know this? I wonder if this unasked for meeting is an elaborate attempt to trick me into saying or doing something incriminating.

"At the moment," she continues, "I doubt the man tailing you can see you from his current position, although I cannot be sure. If he finds himself in the right place, he might have line of sight down the hillside. He's much further behind than he would prefer to be, still high on the path above. Some of my friends engineered a slight accident for him, which has cost him some time. He turned his ankle over, which is a bonus. That has slowed his pace."

A ring-tone sounds. She pauses for a moment and I sneak a glance. I notice she wears a wireless earpiece. With her head cocked to one side, she listens for a moment or two before she whispers something, the words too faint for me to hear. She disconnects the call.

"I'm told he's half an hour behind. Head back to Buckden; go to the Rake Tearooms. It'll be full inside, as will the garden tables, apart from the one nearest to the roadside wall. There'll be an empty seat for you there. Once you've ordered, return to the garden and take that place. Someone there wants to talk to you. Now, go. Don't look back."

The woman steps away. Troubled, I walk on. Am I about to enter into a trap, if so, whose? One set by the NSF or that of some underground opposition group? I know they are real, although those in authority would prefer to deny their existence. I would have thought such a faction might rather see me dead for my past deeds.

My mind is in a spin as I cross the last field before Buckden Bridge. On the road, a motorbike roars past. The bright green top of the pillion-passenger looks familiar. Occupied by my thoughts, I cannot remember passing Hubberholme Church nor the George Inn, although I must have done. What am I to do? My first instinct is to return to my car then flee. Still undecided, I push myself up the incline from the bridge towards the village green. Left or right, which way should I turn? I decide to risk the meeting.

With a combination of dread and anticipation, I walk towards the tearoom. If these people wanted me dead, they had plenty of opportunity to kill me on the walk. To do it in the village would leave too many witnesses. I shall listen to what they have to say. If I sense this is a set-up by the authorities, I shall ring Harry once I am away from here. Otherwise, it might be of interest to find out what it is these people want to discuss.

# 6

Up a small flight of stone steps at the entrance to the Rake Tearoom garden I go. As foretold by the woman at the barn, groups of people occupy each of the outside tables. One bench seat does remain free, at the table nearest to the roadside wall. Inside, the white table-clothed, dark-oak tables have no empty places around them. Paintings of the local area hang from white painted walls. The murmur of voices fills the room. Apart from an occasional curious glance, no-one pays me any attention. My sandwiches are a distant memory. For now, I ignore the cakes and other sweet temptations on offer in the glass fronted display cabinet. Instead, I look to where the specials are listed on a chalk board. Yorkshire pudding with local sausage and gravy tempts me. It will save me from having to cook when I reach home, which is a plus.

Outside, with severe doubts about the wisdom of my actions, I cross the trimmed lawn to the last remaining seat.

"Do you mind if I sit here?" I ask.

Even though I know I am expected, and everyone in the garden is a 'friend', I prefer to keep up the appearance of a weary walker seeking somewhere to rest.

"Help yourself," a middle-aged man responds.

His short black hair has streaks of grey, as does his trimmed moustache and beard. A nose, tending to bulbous, lies below a pair of the most penetrating blue eyes I have ever seen. Seated, his height is hard to judge, but his long legs stretch out from the side of the table. He has a slight paunch, but I gain the impression he is fit and active. He exudes a sense of power.

The woman I met on the walk sits beside him, confirming my thoughts on the motorbike passenger. Beside me, is a younger man, mid thirties, broad-shouldered and tough-looking. His blond hair is short, but avoids the close-cut style favoured by the security services. A nondescript face, with few distinguishing features, is one he must find useful as a member of the anti-government brigade. I doubt I would be able to describe him well enough to build a decent photo-fit image. His neck is bull-like. Under his black T-shirt, muscles ripple. His protruding arms are muscular. It is possible the expensive camera-bag at his side carries a weapon rather than a DSLR. This is the bodyguard. Ex-military by his look - Special Forces at a guess. He is someone, I suspect, it would be better to avoid having as an enemy.

The woman smiles at me. The blue eyes opposite give me a brief but thorough examination. My three companions continue with an innocuous conversation about the weather, the strength of the wind on top of Buckden Pike, the views, and the pints they will share later. Ignored, I divide my time between gazing into the distance and admiring the flower display along the borders. Cottage gardens have always been my favourite.

A young women, dressed in black, brings me my order and the offer of various sauces. Once she returns inside, the man opposite takes out a mobile. After a few nods and grunts to a one sided conversation, he returns the 'phone to his pocket. He fixes his gaze on me.

"The man tailing you is in a great deal of discomfort," he discloses. His voice, like the woman's earlier, has a Leeds sound to it. "The poor chap's hobbled as far as Hubberholme, which should give us a good twenty minutes at least to talk without interruption. We know who you are, Nathan, so I ought to introduce everyone else. For the moment, we'll stick to first names. I'm Joe."

His hand, which he offers, is soft, used to pushing a pen rather than performing manual work, but his handshake is firm.

"The gentleman at your side is John," Joe continues with his introductions.

## CHAPTER 6

John, if that is his real name, puts out a hand the size of a small dinner plate and takes hold of mine. I brace myself for a bone-splintering grip, but find another firm, non-aggressive response. His skin is hard and calloused.

"Pleased to meet you," he says in a voice that is deep, pleasant and cultured, but without any discernible county accent.

"And the young lady beside me, whom you met earlier, is Fia," Joe concludes the introductions.

Fia's hand is soft and warm, her shake firm like the others. Unlike those, at first touch, what feels like a spark of electricity passes between us. Her smile falters. As with me, there is a moment of surprise and confusion at this sudden attraction. Fia mumbles something. Her face reddens; she withdraws her hand. The moment passes unnoticed by the other two. Joe's attention remains on me.

"For some time now, Nathan, we've been keeping an eye on you," he begins.

"Why?" I ask, unable to hold back my curiosity. "If you know who I am, and you're the people whom I suspect you to be, what's your interest in me? Are you out for revenge, to kill me in reprisal for what I did in the past? Believe me, I wouldn't blame you."

"No," denies Joe, "although I admire your honesty. I admit the thought has crossed the minds of several of my colleagues. They argue we should make an example of people like you. I, on the contrary, consider there are better ways for them to serve us and our country than by becoming martyrs for good old JJ," he spits out the initials. "He duped many with his promises. Young and impressionable, you were an easy target. Although much older than you, I, too, fell under his spell."

"Go on," I urge, "I'm listening, but I can't believe you've had me under surveillance. I've never spotted anyone, other than my official watchers."

"It's possible they want you to know you're under observation, or they are inept. I must say, you've done a good job acting as if you're unaware. I bet you failed to notice the other NSF professionals who kept an intermittent watch over you. Yes. I thought so," says Joe, as I nod my head. "Neither did they, nor you, observe our people who kept eyes on all of you. My people are the best."

"Fine! Your comrades are good. So, what do you want from me?" I ask, my voice sharper than I intended.

If Joe's statement about his men is true, they must be good, but I cannot think why I merit such attention.

"We know a great deal about you, Nathan - your history, your involvement with party affairs and the role you played in breaking strikes. We are aware, too, of your doubts over the years. Since your, shall we call it 'fall from grace', we have monitored your 'rehabilitation' and with interest observed your behaviour."

I raise an eyebrow, but remain silent. I am aware of Fia's gaze, a look of slight confusion remains on her face. She blushes again and looks down when she realises I have noticed. Joe continues, oblivious of his companion's attentiveness.

"You've worked hard to re-establish your reputation as a loyal citizen. On the surface, you've settled down, accepted the loss of your wife and the removal of your children. 'Onwards and upwards' seems to be your attitude, why allow the past to ruin your present or future? Your masters seem pleased with your re-integration, but not enough, yet, to allow you to re-join the party. The reports about you, which Harry, your work's party rep, sends to his superiors, praise your ability and general demeanour.

"Your swift reporting of Tim, your local watcher, met with their approval, as did your subsequent updates on his behaviour. You will be glad to know he is to be re-assigned. Your colleague, Amanda, submits positive reports about your conduct. The authorities are to move her elsewhere, soon, to oversee a new suspect. Constant surveillance of you, at home and at work, is to cease. Harry will remain as party rep, but he will no longer treat you as a special case."

How does Joe know this? His revelations have taken me by surprise. I sit back for a moment and sip from my teacup.

"If all that's true," I say, "how come you know about it? No-one but senior party members, and certain NSF officers, have access to my file. This sounds like another Tim-inspired trap."

"Don't be a fool. You're not the only one with a grudge against the authorities," is Joe's response. He taps his fingers on the tabletop. "There are many others who, daily, risk their lives to provide us with intelligence. You impressed us in the way you used your knowledge of Tim to further your cause. We've watched you in the pub. You want to be careful. When you think no-one's looking, you let your guard slip, which allows your distaste for your companion to show.

"We know about the box, which you've hidden from the authorities - the one with the photos of your children, and a rather self-condemning letter. A note we burnt, by the way. On their own, the photos are innocuous, but that letter would be a death sentence if found. Provided you continue to work hard and stay away from trouble, you're in line for another promotion."

"How the hell do you know about the box?" I am both annoyed and alarmed.

Under an assumed name, I had it locked away in a safe place, or so I thought.

Joe looks at me and grins. "I told you, my men were good."

Arguing about it would be counterproductive. Joe is right. The letter, if found by the NSF, would place me in grave danger. It states, in full, my intention to find my children and seek revenge against those who destroyed my family. At the time, it was cathartic to write down my thoughts, although, in retrospect, an unwise act. If Joe's people have read and incinerated it, they cannot be on the government's side.

"All right!" I speak after a lengthy silence. "Let's say I accept everything you have said. I still have no idea what you want from me."

"Nothing," Joe admits, "nothing at all, for the moment. Once your minders have been re-deployed, we shall be in touch with you."

Joe catches my wary expression.

"Don't worry, we've no intention of involving you in any acts of sabotage. All we want is information. We shall set you up with a new, reliable friend, one who is security-vetted. When Tim leaves, this person will become your quiz-night partner, walking companion or somethin..."

"I'll do it," Fia speaks-out, taking Joe by surprise.

It stops him mid-sentence. Again, there is a quick glance my way and a faint blush in her cheeks.

"I'm not sure about that." Joe is dismissive of the idea. He sounds irritated by her interruption.

"Well I am." Fia is undeterred and determined. She looks straight at Joe. "Nathan's had no female company for a long time. We want to convince the authorities he has moved on. If he finds a new 'girlfriend', those keeping an eye on him will relax even more. I'm clean. There are no detrimental records on file concerning me. You know better than I do about that, because you deleted them before they became centralised. I'm a trusted citizen, and I live little more than a couple of miles from Nathan."

Fia falls silent. Joe glares at her. For some reason the idea makes him unhappy. I wonder why. Is she his lover? I doubt it. The age gap between them is considerable, although that in itself means nothing. There does seem to be a bond between them, but, from my brief observations, it falls short of intimacy. Looking at Fia for a moment, I notice a slight similarity between her and Joe - father and daughter, or uncle and niece.

For a moment, I consider agreeing with Joe. Am I ready for a girlfriend, real or pretend? My gaze returns to Fia. Something inside seems to flip. What the hell, it's time I dipped my toes into the water of relationships again. I keep quiet. If I say anything positive about the idea, I gain the impression Joe will veto it on principle. Should I appear neutral on the matter, it may allow Fia to work on him in private.

"We'll discuss it later," Joe says. "Whoever we choose, they'll contact Nathan in good time."

## CHAPTER 6

"How will I know the person is genuine?" I ask.

"He - or she," Joe adds after seeing the glare from Fia, "will bring into the conversation the phrase *'crafted in Wensleydale'*."

At that moment, Joe's 'phone rings.

"Yes…right…we're off," he says. He disconnects. His attention focuses on me. "We must go. Your watcher's close to the bridge. We'll be in touch."

I have noticed that, while we talk, a slow progression of people has taken leave of the tearoom. Now, others move away from the tables outside. Soon, apart from one other, all are empty. There a young couple sit, hand in hand, engrossed in conversation. A few hundred yards away, out of sight on the main road, cars are on the move.

John and Fia gather theirs, and Joe's, plates and cups. They carry them into the tearoom where they pay their bill. Joe is standing nearby. None of the other tables shows signs of recent occupation. To a newcomer, it would appear I have enjoyed a solitary meal. The young waitress walks towards me.

"Order an apple-pie or something," Joe whispers. "Wait until the man following you reaches here, before you leave."

Without a backward glance, he walks towards the path where Fia and John wait for him. They disappear down the steps then out onto the road. Minutes later, from nearby, comes the sound a motorbike starting. The engine roars. Seconds later, the machine takes off down the road. Farewell, John and Fia. Soon afterwards, a car follows along the same route. I suspect Joe has retrieved his vehicle from the car park.

I am half-way through my apple-and-blackberry pie when a moist gentleman, with a bad limp, struggles up the steps into the garden. I flash a quick look in his direction as, with a dirty handkerchief, he mops his brow. The look of relief on his face, at finding me, is evidence enough that this is my tail. With my peripheral vision, I watch while he takes in everything - my solitary position, the lack of extra plates on my table, the young couple canoodling at the other end of an otherwise empty area. There is nothing here of significance to report to his masters.

I finish my meal, swallow the last of my tea, then follow the man inside the now empty tearoom. Here, someone has cleared the tables already. It gives no indication as to how busy the place has been.

"Was everything all right for you?" the owner asks as, with her usual warm smile, she takes my money.

I am glad there is no comment on how many people they have served over the last hour. We talk about my walk and the weather for a few moments. The man with the limp peruses the menu. He listens-in to the conversation. I pay my bill, leave a generous tip, then depart. As I go, I hear the man swear, and the sound of his chair moving. Before the door closes, I hear him apologise and mention something about the time. With a grin, I walk down the steps. From behind, I hear the creak of a door opening, followed by uneven footsteps. At a brisk pace, I return along the lane, back towards the car park. I keep my gaze ahead. As I drive away, my hungry and thirsty follower staggers up the steep slope, towards a line of empty vehicles.

Within minutes, I am on the road towards Kettlewell, my mind in a quandary about what to do next. Should I report my encounter or keep quiet? If my meeting had been with NSF agents, knowing as they did what was in my letter, would I be free and driving home? No. I would be cuffed and on the way to meet my 'old friend' Charles, and his team of happy torturers.

# 7

Quiz night. Sitting in the pub with Tim, I have my usual bottle of apple and mango. Tim nurses a pint of Guinness, real ale is off tonight. Each of us is part way into his third drink of the evening. Over three weeks have gone by since my stroll round Buckden. I have neither seen, nor heard from Joe, nor any of his contacts. Sometimes, I wonder if I imagined our meeting. Tim has mentioned nothing about leaving. At work, neither has Amanda. Rare for a quiz night, the pub has few customers. There are a dozen or more people huddled round beer-splashed tables. The questions are over, the answer sheets collected. In groups of two or three, the drinkers chatter among themselves while we await the results.

With a loud crash, the double doors into the pub fly open. A group of women lurches inside. Each one is in fancy dress - by the looks and sounds of it, a hen-party making merry. Laughing and giggling, they advance towards the bar. Tim rolls his eyes in horror. Sacrilege! How dare they ruin *his* Wednesday night? I give the party the once over. I do a double take. Impossible! I look again. One of the new arrivals, dressed as a fairy princess, looks familiar. It cannot be, or can it? Under the woman's blond wig and tinsel-band, a line of dark hair is visible. In haste, I down my drink.

"You're slow tonight, Tim," I admonish my companion. "My round; you ready for another?"

"Er! Yes, sure," he says, as he turns his attention back to me.

Transfixed by the group at the bar, he has missed the rapid end to my drink. Tim takes a huge swig from his pint-glass, to leave a thimbleful at the bottom. He belches. I make my way to the bar, where I face a long delay. Members of the hen party take an inordinate amount of time to decide on what drinks they want. The barman finishes their order. In a meandering group, they head-off to a corner of the pub. Raucous laughter breaks out from their direction. The 'fairy princess' who, I am certain, is Fia, has disappeared down the passageway to the loos. She walked past me, without any sign of recognition.

"Same again," I call to the lad behind the bar.

Dan, the barman, slams some ice into a clean glass then passes it, and a bottle of apple and mango, to me. I do the honours while he takes his time with the Guinness. Like an artist, he pulls the pint to leave a perfect head. I pay for the drinks then pocket the change. Hands filled with brimming glasses, I step away from the bar.

Fia must have been watching from the shadows at the corridor entrance. She times to perfection her return. On my first step, she stumbles into me, sending the best part of a pint of Guinness and a glass of fruit juice down the front of my trousers. I am soaked.

"Oh! Shod! I'm shorry." Fits of giggles intersperse her words.

She grabs a couple of beer towels from the bar counter, then tries to sponge me down with them.

"Shush!" she whispers into my ear. "Make out everything is okay and, for now, send me back to my friends."

"It's no problem, it was an accident, as much my fault as yours," I say aloud as, with real embarrassment, I remove her hands and towels from around my groin. "It's fine, I can dry myself. Please, go, join your friends."

"No, pleash, let me buy you shum more drinks, it'sh my fault." As well as slurring her words, she is starting to sway.

"I'm serious, it's ok. I'll dry-off with the hot-air machine in the Gents. Go back to your friends before you fall down."

"You shure?"

"Yes, I'll be fine."

She totters off to join her crowd, who stare my way, laughing aloud at the incident. I bow. The group cheers and gives me a round of applause.

## CHAPTER 7

The barman looks towards the group, his eyes turn heavenwards. The hen-party return to their drinks.

"Two more of the same?" Dan asks.

I hand him the glasses.

"They only need topping up," I point out to him.

"On the house, then. Sorry about that, but they've spent as much in five minutes as have the rest of the pub the whole evening. I'd rather not ask 'em to leave. They may buy another round."

I nod in gratitude. After ten minutes under the hand-dryer, damp, but no longer dripping, I return for the drinks. Tim has already collected them. He laughs when I reach the table - no sympathy here.

"Looks like you've wet yourself," he observes dryly.

"Drunken hen groups," I complain. "It's all we want."

The landlady puts in an appearance to read out the quiz results. We fall short of winning by one incorrect answer. A cheer from a nearby table announces the gallon of beer has found a worthy recipient. The barman appears at my side, with a couple of drinks for Tim and me.

"Courtesy of the fairy princess," the barman explains. "She said she would carry them over, but I thought it might be safer if I did. I didn't think you'd want a second soaking."

"No, I don't," I laugh.

My trousers steam in the warmth of the room. They are black. With luck, any stains will blend in.

"Ayup, watch yourself," Tim warns.

Moments later, a hand falls on my shoulder. A chair moves into place beside mine. Fia sits down, close to me, her breath heavy with some scented alcoholic drink.

"I'm terribly shorry," she slurs. "I must apologishe. I don't drink much, ushually. I shink I've had too mush."

She leans forward and almost falls off her chair. She rights herself in time and giggles.

"Please, I musht pay to have your clothes cleaned, it's the leasht I can do."

"It doesn't matter, it wasn't intentional," I lie, a little light-headed by her presence.

She stirs emotions in me that have remained dormant for a long time. Fia brushes her hand against mine and again a spark seems to pass between us.

"I sherious", she insists. "Oh! I'm Fia," she adds.

"I'm Nathan, this is Tim," I reply by way of introduction. "But, I mean it, there's no need to pay, it was an accident."

"Hi Tim." She acknowledges him with a little wave.

She ignores my protest and picks up the one dry beer-mat left on the table. With a pen, taken from her handbag, Fia proceeds to write her name, address and telephone number on the back of the beer-mat. She places it near to my drink.

"Pleashe, contact me when you have the bill. I inshist," she says, when I shake my head. "Pleashe, do give me a ring."

She winks as, with the help of the table to steady herself, she stands, waves goodbye then weaves her way back to her friends. Tim gives me an old-fashioned look.

"Bloody hell, you've pulled." There is more than a trace of envy in his voice. "She couldn't keep her eyes off you; never gave me a second glance."

He picks up the beer-mat and peers at the writing for a few moments. I assume he has committed to memory her name, address and telephone number, before he hands the piece of card back to me. Fia has been clever. She has established contact between us without the use of any silly code phrases. Tim believes we have met by accident. Because she has allowed him to see her name and contact details, he can have her checked for security. If Fia's record is as clear as she said it was, she should pass scrutiny without difficulty.

"Fia McFadden," Tim rolls the name around his tongue. "It's a nice name for a nice looking woman. She lives in a good area, too. She made it bloody obvious she wants you to contact her. Besides," he adds, "you're going to need a new quiz partner soon."

## CHAPTER 7

"Why's that?" I ask, taken by surprise at the sudden announcement, although I knew it would happen soon.

"I've found a job, at last. It's down in Nottingham," Tim explains. "It's good money, and way too far to travel for a weekly quiz. This weekend, I'm going down to look for a place to rent."

"That's a shame," I'm proud at the amount of sincerity I force into my voice. "I look forward to Wednesday nights. It makes a change from sitting at home on my own."

"Give this Fia woman a ring. Tell her you can't accept payment for the dry-clean, but you'd be happy to meet her for a drink instead."

"Now that is a good idea, I might do that."

The noise levels from the hen-party increase as they prepare to leave. The bride to be, or who I assume her to be by the L-Plates hanging round her neck, is a pretty, blond-haired girl with red cheeks and unfocused eyes. Two of her friends help her to her feet and half carry, half walk her to the door. Fia is last to go. As she reaches the door, she turns and smiles at me. With a little wave of her hand, she steps outside.

"There you are," Tim states, "I told you so, you've cracked it. She fancies you."

Whether that is true or clever acting on her behalf, time alone will prove. The attraction is strong for me. Whether it is the same for Fia I cannot know, but I suspect the feeling is reciprocal. How matters progress depends on many circumstances - the fact she is my go-between, or handler for Joe, will be a major factor. Employers, such as mine, frown on romance at work. I wonder how they stand on romance outside, mixed with a large dose of treachery! Let us hope I avoid giving them the chance to pass judgement. I fear the consequences could be severe.

# 8

On my arrival at work next day, true to my role as a watcher's watcher, I mention Tim's announcement about moving to Nottingham.

"That's good to know," Harry says, playing his part, too. "I'll advise HQ. They can keep an eye on him down there. Oh! I have some good news for you. I'm sure you'll be happy to learn, Amanda has handed in her notice."

I smile with delight. Harry knows my opinion of her work. It would seem odd it I reacted in any other way.

"I thought you'd be pleased," he adds with a laugh. "I agree with you about her work, but her uncle is high up in the party. It would have been a risky career-move, for both of us, if we'd sacked her."

I nod as if I believe his story. The reason she was here was to report on me, although I cannot discount she might have good family connections.

"Any thoughts on who might replace her?" I ask, curious to know if Harry has someone in mind.

"I've been looking at the personnel files for the general office. There is a couple of possible candidates there you may want to interview. Apart from that, for many of our prospective employees we use The Sandiman Agency. Give them a ring. Tell them what skills, personality type and anything else you can think of, for your ideal applicant. You know what you need far better than I do. They'll select several candidates from the people on their books, then set up interviews for you. It'll save you a great deal of time and effort."

To my surprise, it seems I have moved several rungs up the trust-ladder, to a place far beyond any expectations. It's Harry's way of saying

## CHAPTER 8

'over to you'. The party wants to see how you handle the process. We shall observe from a distance, take note of what you do, and what type of person you select. From his drawer, Harry passes me a business card, one of several bearing the same design.

**The Sandiman Agency**, it states in a bold, elegant, gold-foiled font, *We Select the Best for Your Approval*. Beneath, in smaller print, is an address and contact details for a prestigious office in central Leeds. *Joe McFadden, Chief Executive* is the name under the logo at the top of the card. It cannot be! It has to be a coincidence - Joe McFadden, Fia McFadden. If this is the same Joe from the meeting at Buckden, would he want to place Fia in the same working environment as me? I doubt it. We have to be able to talk, away from prying eyes and monitored conversations, which would be impractical here.

If the man is Fia's father or uncle, he has achieved an enviable position, one that he can exploit for the underground. It will allow him to garner much knowledge about the operations of a wide variety of businesses, and about the people who run them. To be in such a role means the authorities must trust him. His security clearance must be at the highest level. For the first time, since my meeting at the café in the dales, my insecurities ease. The agency, I am certain, will select me an ideal candidate, someone who is not an agent for the party nor for the resistance.

I take my leave of Harry and go on to my office. Amanda looks up from her computer. She makes use of her blank screen as a mirror while she applies make-up. For some reason, she has a large old-fashioned monitor with a glass-screen, a rarity these days, almost vintage.

"Oh! Morning," Amanda greets me. Without any preamble she continues, "I've handed in my notice. My parents saw a job advertised nearer to them in Lincoln. I had an interview last weekend. I start the tenth of May." At my raised eyebrow she continues, "That is, if I'm allowed to leave without working my full-notice."

As if my opposition would make a difference to her leaving date, but, I suppose, she must continue to act the part of being a genuine colleague. I have given her no reason to suspect I know her true reason for being here.

"Harry said you'd found another job. It would be silly to miss such a good opportunity, I am sure you'll be happy there." I cannot bring myself to add the lie as to how much I shall miss her. "Have you produced those reports I asked you for last night?"

She presses a button at the side of her monitor. Her screen hums. It comes back to life. It reveals a program page with a large square printer-box at the centre. For once, she impresses me. Whenever she has beaten me to the office, she has failed to switch on her computer before my arrival.

"Another twenty pages ought to finish the last one," Amanda calculates. "In a couple minutes I'll nip down to the printer room to collect them all. Do you want a drink?" she adds, pressing the button again, before returning to the important task of adding lipstick.

"A cup of tea, oh, and a biscuit would be good."

Once Amanda is out of the office, I dial the number on the card. Two rings later, a bright and cheerful female voice answers.

"Good morning, The Sandiman Agency, how may I direct your call?"

I explain who I am then ask to speak to Joe McFadden.

"I am sorry, but Mr McFadden is away on business this week. I'll put you through to Andrew Faulds. He deals with admin staff for the Aitkins Precision Moulding's account. Mr McFadden looks after the executive recruitment-side of the business," she adds, putting me in my place.

I mumble my agreement. The music of Vivaldi fills my ears. It proceeds to loop every few bars, interspersed, every third loop, with *'Sorry to keep you waiting. Your call is important to us. Someone will be with you shortly'.*

"If it were important, you'd bloody-well answer," I snap into the receiver, after the umpteenth hearing.

According to the digital display, I have been on hold for ten minutes. Another five pass, but still no answer. Neither have my tea nor reports put in an appearance. I imagine Amanda is with Harry, comparing notes on how I took the news of her imminent departure. A loud click, followed by sudden silence, comes from the 'phone. For a moment, I think someone at the other end has disconnected the call. I am about to say something rude, but stop myself in time, when I hear another click.

"Hi there, Nathan," a pleasant, but out of breath, male voice comes on the line. "I was with another client. I must apologise for keeping you waiting. I'm Andrew Faulds. I look after general recruitment for Aitkins. How may I be of assistance?"

I explain to him about the vacancy and the type of person I want to fill the role.

"Sounds fine to me," Andrew confirms. "Because of Aitkins's preferred government contractor status, I understand the need for applicants to be party members, have security clearance and be able to keep their work confidential."

After the exchange of a few pleasantries, he rings off, with the promise of half a dozen candidates for me to interview over the next few days. I wonder whether Harry will contact him to see what criteria I have dictated. Nothing I have done should give cause for alarm. It is possible, the fact I have asked for party members who take no active part within the organisation, might raise an eyebrow or two. My explanation, that the department's work is too important for someone to keep taking time out for rallies or meetings, is true. I want someone who can focus on their work, something Harry is certain to understand and accept without dissent.

By Friday evening, I have a list of potential employees. Monday morning I shall spend at Sandiman's offices, in Leeds, where I have three men and three women to see. Back at work, in the afternoon, I have the two possible candidates from here to interview. It should be a good day.

That evening, at home, I study the beer mat with Fia's contact details. Several times, I pick up the 'phone. After a few moments hesitation,

I put it down again. Ridiculous, I know. Fia must be expecting my call. Have I become such a recluse I am afraid to step away from my isolation? With Tim, there was never any danger of our relationship becoming close and personal, but Fia is different. She is someone with whom I have a serious attraction. Could this be the start of a relationship? Am I ready for such a life-changing event?

I remain on the fence. I have avoided going out, or anything else, with a woman, since Julie. I could be misreading the whole situation. Fia may regard our future relationship as nothing other than a business one. The off-putting knowledge that someone records everything I say over the 'phone, does not help. Each time I pick up the receiver, the faint click and hollow sound tell me that.

Whoever is listening-in should be expecting my call. Tim will have told them about my meeting in the pub with Fia, and its probable outcome. By now, they must have checked her credentials. No-one has warned me off. Her record must be clean. If the relationship between her and the Joe McFadden at Sandiman's is what I believe it to be, I would be surprised if her clearance was anything other than the highest.

What am I, man or coward? I pluck up courage to lift the receiver one last time. With care, I press the digits of Fia's number. After a few clicks, and the hollow sound, the ring-tone is loud in my ear. One, two, three times and more it rings - twelve in all; it connects. A mechanical voice says *"Sorry, there is no-one here to take your call at the moment, please leave your name, your number and any message after the tone, and we will get back to you as soon as possible."*

My heart sinks. Damn. After all my deliberations, Fia is out. In frustration, I am about to put down the 'phone when, after another click, the sound of someone's fingers scrambling on the receiver at the other end comes down the line. A voice, which I remember all too well, speaks over the noise.

"Hello, sorry for the delay, I was upstairs."

"Hi, it's Nathan. We met at the pub the other night."

## CHAPTER 8

"Oh! God! It's you." Fia sounds pleased to hear from me. "I hoped you'd call. Look, I'm really, really sorry about spilling your drinks and soaking you. How much do I owe you for the cleaning?"

"Nothing. No, I mean it," I add as she protests. "Instead, how would you like to meet for a drink?"

"Yes, I'd like that." There is no hesitation in her voice. "Be warned, I'm not a great drinker. Wednesday was the exception. It was a hen party for one of my colleagues, I had a few too many. Next morning my headache was dreadful," she groans to emphasise her suffering.

I laugh. She joins in.

"OK. Something different! What if I was to meet you outside Hennies' restaurant, tomorrow-night at eight?" I suggest. "We can have a meal, rather than a drink."

"Oooh! Yes. Now that I would like. My treat," she adds.

"We'll discuss that later," I say.

"Must go," she laughs, "I'm dripping water everywhere; I was in the bath. Bye, see you tomorrow," she has played her part well for the listeners.

She disconnects, leaving an image in my mind on which I find it hard not to dwell. Instead, in haste, I search the net for Hennies' telephone number. I curse myself for failing to check first before selecting the meeting place. In a mild panic, I ring them, seeking to book a table.

"Just one moment, let me look for you, sir. Ah! Yes, you're in luck," a calm voice at the other end of the line informs. His accent has faint European undertones, "we've had a cancellation. We have a table free at eight o'clock, is that convenient? Excellent, eight o'clock it is, sir. Table for two, tomorrow-night, in the name of Andrews," he confirms.

I relax. It would give a less than favourable impression for me to have to ring Fia with a change of plans. The smell from the oven signals a cremation has taken place. Undeterred, I whistle as my burnt-offering hits the bottom of the bin. The local takeaway seems a reasonable alternative.

# 9

Nervous about being late, I arrive half an hour too soon for my date. Inside the multi-story car park, near to the restaurant, I pass the time listening to the radio in my car. The choice on offer, of rousing music or political rhetoric, reminds me of what I once read about Russia under Stalin. Life is too short for constant misery. I switch off, preferring silence to the persistent barrage of political garbage. After a few minutes I check the time, and again at regular intervals.

After twenty minutes, I can wait no longer. I step out of the car then walk away. With a double-flash of the hazard lights, the car locks behind me. Overhead, sodium lamps light up the doorway and litter-strewn floor ahead. On this Saturday night, the car park is busy. I take the stairs down from the third level. Hennies' is on the opposite side of the road to the one that leads to the car park.

No matter how much I slow my steps, I still arrive ahead of time. I am as tense as a teen on a first date. Why? The reasons behind this evening are far from those of a romantic tryst. We are here to set up an indirect communications-link between Joe and me. I must concentrate on this aspect of the evening. Any thoughts of a personal nature, with Fia, are a separate issue. If I take this attitude, I cannot be disappointed. Can I?

Positioned to one side of the entrance, I make a half-hearted attempt to distract my attention from my watch. My wait is short. Within minutes of my arrival, Fia comes into sight. She hurries up the high street. As soon as she catches sight of me, she slows to a steadier pace. A beaming smile appears. She waves. Within moments, she is at my side. Fia stands on tiptoe and gives me a quick kiss on the cheek.

## CHAPTER 9

"Am I late?" she asks, an anxious expression on her face, her breathing heavy from the walk.

"No, I was early."

Fia links her arm in mine. We walk towards the restaurant door, where she leans towards me, to whisper in my ear.

"When we're inside, avoid any mention of Joe or the real reason for our meal. On the way here, we've both been under surveillance. With this being our first time out together, Joe's certain the NSF will bug our table. We have to convince them everything between us is aboveboard. Our behaviour must be natural. If we give them no cause to suspect anything, he doubts they'll go to this much trouble again."

I smile, as if Fia has said something amusing. I assume Joe's man, John, is on the case. That must be how she knows about the surveillance. I force myself to look ahead instead of back. By now, I should be familiar with this type of behaviour from the authorities.

Inside, the door-attendant takes our coats. He escorts us into a cosy bar area filled with easy chairs. We each order a glass of Perrier water. Her hair looks as if she has spent half her day at the hairdressers. It is shorter than I remember, trimmed to rest on her shoulders. The stylish black dress looks new; cut to emphasise her figure in a subtle and alluring way. A thin silver chain, from which hangs a single pearl in a plain silver setting, hangs round her neck. She has a silver bracelet on her right wrist.

"You look beautiful," I blurt out without thinking.

"Why thank you, kind sir." She blushes, but looks pleased by my involuntary compliment.

The nibbles, supplied while we peruse the menu, are delicious, but we eat in moderation. We ignore the starters. Two courses are enough for each of us. We prefer to finish with a dessert. I order *breast of chicken, stuffed with pesto butter, wrapped in Parma ham with a tomato salsa*. Fia chooses *cajun salmon with miso broth, pak choi and rice noodles*.

Twenty minutes later, the maître d' shows us into the dining room. He seats us at a table, to one side of a large room decorated with taste and lit with skill. Low ornamental-screens separate diners from others nearby. These partitions allow for intimacy without isolation. A luxuriant pile carpet covers the floor. Heavy drapes screen the walls. The fabric deadens the sounds from around the room, muting conversations, allowing diners to talk in comfort without their neighbours overhearing. We are careful to say nothing untoward - Fia's warning about possible listening-devices has made sure of that.

The evening passes at much too rapid a pace. To my relief, my fears about being ill-at-ease prove baseless. We talk about everything and nothing. Between us, conversation is easy. Curious to the origins of her name, she tells me she shares it with an Aberdonian grandmother. Our interests, many of which we have in common, are diverse. We both love walking in the Dales and have a love of music; Chopin, Mozart and Beethoven in particular. Both of us play-up to the microphone, concerning the official 'stirring' government anthems streamed in the background. I doubt many of those will be popular a few hundred years from now.

Dessert consumed and coffee drunk, we sit back, replete and content. I call for the bill. Despite my protests, Fia insists on paying. I back down, after the promise of a second date. Arm in arm, we walk into the cooler April night-air. Fia accepts my offer of a lift home. As Tim had said, she lives in an upmarket area of Horsforth.

I bring my car to a halt outside a modern brick-built detached house with a garden and a low dividing-wall. We talk for a while, both reluctant to bring the evening to a close. Before we had reached my car, Fia had warned there might be a bug installed there, too. We steer our conversation away from anything work, or Joe-related.

Fia's head rests for a moment on my shoulder. She looks up at me, her eyes close and our lips meet. Her arms reach up, around my neck and pull me closer. I hold her close, her breasts firm against my body. For several minutes we stay, locked together. Fia releases her grip. We move apart. Again, there is a look of surprise on her face, but none of the uncertainty this time. She smiles with a warmth that radiates

## CHAPTER 9

throughout her whole face. I cannot believe everything is an act, put on for the benefit of any watchers. Fia looks me in the eyes, her gaze penetrating. Whatever it is she seeks to find in my expression, she seems satisfied with her scrutiny.

"Ring me, soon," she whispers as she untangles herself.

The car-door swings shut behind her. She walks up her driveway. I wait until, after turning the key in the lock and one last wave, she closes the door. Whistling, I turn on the engine, put the car into gear and drive off. For the first time in years, life is good. In my rear view mirror, in the distance, I see the lights of a car come on. Even the sight of a vehicle pulling out after me fails to dampen my spirits.

My week at work passes in a flash, I am a different man. I have to stop myself from whistling at my desk. The tunes I have in my head are throwbacks to my youth, such items no longer considered suitable for loyal citizens.

☙ ❧

Monday morning I head to Sandiman's. Andrew Faulds is good at his job. All six candidates he selected for me are suitable, although one woman, Sara, stands out. She has wider experience in production-planning than have the others, and, of greater relevance, has experience in route-planning. This was part of my job-description some years ago. Harry has warned me, it will be something that will soon come under my auspices. This snippet of information might be of significance to Joe.

At lunchtime, I leave Sandiman's, after having informed Andrew that Sara is my preferred candidate. I warn him about the couple I have to see at the office before I can reach a decision. I reach my office invigorated. I had forgotten how good it is to have some control over one's own life. Micro-management is hell for the recipient. I allow myself the luxury of a sandwich and coffee before I take over a nearby empty office to begin my interviews with the internal candidates. One is unsuitable, but the other does show promise, although he lacks experience.

I thank them both for their time, but advise them the vacancy, this time, will go to an external candidate. To the one with promise, James, I mention that, if work continues to grow, I may have room for him in the future, but promise nothing. The lad seems pleased by this faint hope. He is quick and bright. If route-planning does come my way, I am sure Harry will see the wisdom of an assistant to help with the workload. One word from Harry and senior management will approve the expansion of my department.

I discuss my final choice with Harry. He listens and nods in approval. I anticipate he has already spoken to Andrew Faulds, and is aware of the results of my morning's labours. As anticipated, Harry has no objections to my preference for non-active party members. Production-planning is key to the company's success; distractions are detrimental to the smooth running of the business. I mention about the young lad, James, being a potential trainee if my workload becomes any heavier. Harry confirms the board have agreed to route-planning coming under my control. Once Amanda has gone and Sara's training period is over, James will come to work for me.

That night, from behind the curtains in my bedroom, I check on Tim. To my surprise, he has no seven o'clock meeting with his handler. Instead, he appears to be in the process of packing his belongings. My house is different, too. I have the strangest of feelings someone has been inside it during the day. The last time that happened, the day after I moved in, the monitoring of my 'phone calls began. I do have a mobile, but my use of it is rare. I am certain some faceless bureaucrat records the numbers I dial and the calls I receive.

As I am late home from work, a takeaway curry seems a good option. It saves me having to cook, and allows me to test the phone-line. When I pick up the receiver, the dial tone connects without the usual telltale delay. There are neither clicks nor buzzes. The tap on my line has either gone, or been replaced with one less evident.

## CHAPTER 9

Later that evening, I ring Fia. She seems delighted to hear from me. We talk for an hour or more, as if we have known each other forever. Unless she is a brilliant actor, she feels the same way about me as I do her. After everything I have said about becoming involved with someone, I am in danger of doing that same thing, although, this is different from what I had envisaged. Fia already engages in subversive activities, to a greater extent than I might ever do.

The next evening, Fia 'phones me. Again, we talk for a good hour. Wednesday is quiz night. I continue my habit, so go with Tim to the pub. Tim says, this is our last night out. From what I have seen through his window, his packing is complete. I must admit I have been better company. Fia occupies my mind the whole of the evening. Thursday I ring her. We arrange to meet for a meal on Saturday night. This time, I have done my homework and have already made a provisional booking, an Italian restaurant on this occasion. Saturday night cannot come soon enough for me.

What Joe might think about this budding relationship between his protégé and me, I am in ignorance. If Fia has mentioned it to him, I suspect the news will have displeased him. I have some sympathy for him; but one thing even our all-invasive government cannot control, is with whom someone falls in love, or in lust.

At the office, Sara has accepted the appointment. Her last employment, a fixed-term contract, ended a few weeks ago. She agrees an immediate start. Friday, she arrives for her induction talk with Harry. After lunch, he brings her through to the office then leaves her with me. After a quick introduction to Amanda, Sara pulls up a chair and begins to shadow her. Earlier in the day, I had spoken to my new starter, to warn her of Amanda's bad habits. Several times, I catch sight of Sara's expression as she asks questions or passes comment. She appears less than impressed with Amanda's standard of work. My choice seems to have been a wise one.

After Amanda has left for the day, I have the chance for a quiet word with Sara. Already she has ideas and suggestions regarding the work. Some I have already thought of, others are new and innovative. Impressed, I tell her so, but advise any new methods of working must have my agreement, and any implementation take place after Amanda's departure. Sara nods. She is aware that even slight changes to certain processes can be detrimental to others. This is a concept alien to Amanda. Several times, her failure to stick to correct procedures has seen production come to a halt. Sara gives the appearance of having greater business-awareness.

I can look forward to diminished stress-levels. With my private-life set to improve, Sara's input here should mean work impinges less on it. Evenings spent poring over a laptop, correcting a colleague's sloppy work, I am happy to forgo. Sara leaves and, after a quick chat with Harry, I do too. His praise at my choice of assistant is voluble. The noose that, figuratively, the state has looped round my neck these past view years, I feel begin to loosen.

Once the passing of information to Joe is under way, I will be in a better position to make demands of him. I want something in return, quid pro quo. It is the main reason I have agreed to work with him. I want Joe to use his contacts to find out the whereabouts of my children. Whether Caroline will remember me, is another matter. She was four when taken away, but Ian was six. His memories should be deeper. I pray, whoever cares for them now has not turned them against me.

# 10

The following Saturday night's meal is another success. On this occasion, the authorities leave us to enjoy our meal without anyone on our tail. For Fia to be able to confirm this, I acknowledge shadowy figures from her organisation must have kept a distant eye on each of our journeys instead of the state. She is less confident about whether the NSF has bugged our table.

In many ways, this uncertainty is to the benefit of our personal enjoyment. We can concentrate on each other without the distraction of dissident-related business. Talking is an art that seems lost among our fellow diners. They spend most of their evening with their eyes on their government approved smart phones, rather than each other. I am sure a couple sitting nearby communicate by texting each other.

Our plates are empty, coffees drunk; almost in an instant, it seems. Fia's mood is bubbly. We have talked and talked and, in between, laughed long over the silliest of matters. Outside, a southerly breeze warms the air. The restaurant is close to the river. The night is still young. Arm-in-arm, we stroll past shop windows with their seductive lighting, over-spilling bars and packed restaurants towards the waterfront. At ease, we wander along the riverside path.

After a while, in the semi-darkness half way between lampposts, we stop. Our lips find each other's. It seems the most natural thing in the world to do. With our arms around each other, we lean against the ornate wrought iron fencing above the river. The cloud breaks for a moment. The moon's reflection joins those from the multitude of lights on the opposite bank, to wriggle and dance on the flowing current. With her head resting against mine, Fia whispers into my ear.

"Joe sends his regards," she tells me.

"Is there anything specific he wants to know?" I ask, brought back to reality. This is, I have to admit, the supposed reason behind our evening out.

"No, nothing for now. He wants our meetings to become a normal part of life before that happens. He asked me to pass on the news that the NSF classifies you as low-risk now. Surveillance on you has stopped, as has the tap on your 'phone. Incoming and outgoing numbers on your landline and mobile will be subject to routine checks. They might merit a little extra attention than do most people's 'phones, but nothing as intrusive as you've experienced. The NSF will have my number on record. It should cause you no problems. I've been vetted and, according to Joe, passed as a person for whom it is fitting for you to associate."

She laughs at this. We kiss again and for a few minutes forget about the world.

"I have something you can pass on to Joe," I mention as our lips part. "I have a new assistant, Sara. Joe knows Amanda is to leave the company, but what might be news to him is, that route-planning will come under my wing, once she's gone."

"Now, that will be of interest." Fia's brow furrows in concentration. "To know what goods are in production at any one time, and for whom, is valuable. To have access to the routes taken by the finished goods, and their final destination, is gold dust. That snippet will make his day for him."

"What is Joe to you?" I ask. "Is he the Joe McFadden of Sandiman's?"

"Joe's my Uncle. My father's younger brother and, yes, he is CEO of The Sandiman Agency. He and dad joined JJ's party at its inception. As they grew up, dad and Joe were close. Later, when adult and with sufficient capital between them, they went into business. Joe's rise through the party's ranks was rapid. Dad's less so. Business concerned him the more. With Joe's contacts, along with dad's, the agency they founded flourished, after JJ came to power.

## CHAPTER 10

"When Sandiman's owners decided to retire, they contacted dad and uncle Joe. They reached an agreement to buy out the company. A few months later, they re-branded their own business to the Sandiman name. It was well known, respected and had a much broader clientele. For Dad and Joe, it was a step-up to the top rank."

"What happened to change everything?" I ask.

For a moment, Fia gazes into the distance, her mind far-away as if on a distant world. She blinks, then wipes-away a tear that rolls down her cheek.

"Sean happened, he was my baby brother," she continues after a moment's hesitation. "An accident, my mum once told me. His birth was premature. I was eighteen at the time. When mum's contractions began, I drove her to hospital. There was an emergency on the ward. Staff rushed to attend. We were on our own for some time. With a shortage of staff on the unit, no-one realised mum's baby was in distress until it was too late," Fia's tears flow. "They performed an emergency caesarean, but Sean had suffered oxygen starvation. He was born with brain-damage."

Fia sobs at my side. I put my arms round her and pull her close. She has stored this hurt inside for years. Now the dam-walls have burst. I could understand her grief at the loss of a brother, but how it caused such a change of political heart, for both her uncle and father, is beyond me. After all this time, the strength of her feelings, too, seems strange. Fia looks up at me. Through her tears, she continues with her story. Now I come to understand everything.

"Sean survived. He was a sweet baby, but, as he grew, he had mobility troubles. He spent months in hospital. His mental development was slow, but we loved Sean. In his own way, he was happy, with a permanent smile on his face. Once everyone recovered from the shock, we arranged our lives around him. I spent hours looking after him. I suppose I felt guilty, still do. Why? I was there, in the room, when the damage happened. It's absurd, I know, to blame myself, there was nothing I could have done to prevent it.

"Dad reduced some of his workload. Uncle Joe understood. He was fond of his little nephew. He did what he could to help. We fell into a routine for Sean's care. None of us minded. We learned much about ourselves. It's at times such as these, we realise how selfish we have become.

"A few weeks after Sean's fourth birthday, our lives changed forever. We had bought him an incredible electronic toy. With numerous combinations of lights and noises, it had dozens of buttons he could press. He loved it, although, at times, it drove the rest of us to distraction. I had been out at work and, to give Mum and Dad a break, I offered to do the evening shift with Sean. As soon as I entered the house, I knew there was something wrong. It was silent. Sean's toy, I could see, lay broken on the front room carpet. Mum was on the couch sobbing, curled in a foetal position, hugging Sean's favourite blanket. Dad was pacing backwards and forwards, the expression on his face was beyond anger. I cannot remember seeing him like that.

"Uncle Joe arrived. Compared to Dad, he remained calm. All he could say was 'There's nothing we can do, there's nothing we can do'."

Again, Fia lapses into sobs. I hold her close, a sick feeling inside. Over the years, I have heard rumours. I have a dreadful premonition I am to have them confirmed. I remain silent. For now, my role is that of listener, a shoulder on which to cry. I offer her a tissue. She wipes her eyes, blows her nose then continues.

"Child Welfare, (what a misnomer that title is) had visited earlier in the day. They took Sean away. There was no suggestion of maltreatment on our part. Our *wonderful* government had decreed that children with severe disabilities were now the state's responsibility. Housed in specialist institutions, they would receive round-the-clock care. This would release valuable resources back into the workforce for the good of the state. Because Dad had been with a client, mum and Sean were alone when the welfare people arrived. They told mum, parents should be grateful to have such a caring government. Now she was free to do something useful and productive with her time.

## CHAPTER 10

"Mum never recovered from that. Her health deteriorated. That winter, she caught the flu-virus. It was a virulent strain that year. Within days, it turned to pneumonia. The doctors tried several antibiotics, but she had lost the will to live. She died before the week was out. Since Sean went, for mum's sake, dad had kept up a brave front. After her death, he became bitter and withdrawn. I made it my duty to try to find Sean. That was when I fell foul of the authorities. It was my records concerning that period that Uncle Joe was able to destroy."

"Did you find Sean?" I ask.

"No, but the following spring, after Dad died, Uncle Joe disappeared for several weeks. When he returned he had changed. On the surface, he was the same. He serviced the key accounts and socialised with top party officials, as he always had done. Underneath, he was no longer my happy, caring Uncle Joe. He stopped coming to visit me. I inherited my parent's home and, for a while, I lived there. It was as if he wanted to cut himself off from his memories. At work, on the rare occasions he returned my calls, he was cold and offhand. Outside, he turned off his mobile. I cannot tell you how much this hurt me. I had lost my brother, my parents and now my only living relative, Uncle Joe, had distanced himself from me.

"One night, in desperation, I went to his house to confront him. I burst in, to find him chairing a meeting with strangers. I had little chance to see their faces. Instead of them, for the first time, I met John, Uncle Joe's minder. He grabbed me. Within seconds, he dragged me out of the room into the kitchen. Before I could speak or do anything to resist, he had searched me for weapons. He used plastic ties to bind me to a chair and was about to gag me, when Uncle Joe hurried in. He made John cut me free, but told him to keep me there until later. I had to wait until after the meeting had broken up, and Uncle Joe's visitors had departed, before I could join him.

"We had a long talk. To begin with, I was furious at my treatment. Poor Uncle Joe, he sat there and endured a tongue-lashing, the like of which I doubt he had received in years. Once I'd calmed down, he told me he had become involved in matters that were dangerous. They were not my concern. He wanted it to remain that way. I wore him down, over several weeks, until I found out what his secret was. It took some time, but I did discover where he had gone during some of those missing weeks. He had travelled to Scotland. How he obtained the information, he wouldn't say, but he had discovered the location of where Sean should be."

A strange bleak look settles on Fia's tear-streaked face, which contrasts with her eyes. They blaze with an intensity that frightens.

"While in the Highlands, he paid Sean's new home a visit. It was an old country estate. Expecting to find it alive with activity, to his surprise, he found it abandoned. The estate's one remaining occupant was an old man, who acted as caretaker. It took Uncle Joe some time, but, with the offer of a bottle or two of fine malt whisky, and most of the contents of another one, he loosened the old man's tongue.

"He led Uncle Joe out into the nearby woods, to a clearing with a large mound at its centre. Somewhere beneath the earth, the old man told Uncle Joe, lay the bodies of the disabled brought to the house. As promised, the state had taken permanent care of them. It had euthanised each one. Back at the house, the caretaker led Uncle Joe to a room in the basement. There, he found the records of the children who had passed through the house. After his removal, Sean survived less than a week."

"What did Joe do after that?" I asked, horrified, but no longer surprised at the confirmation of stories, which, in my naivety, I had refused to believe.

"By now, the old man had begun to sober. He realised he had revealed too much. He pulled a gun on Uncle Joe. They struggled. During the fracas, the old man fell and struck his head. The blow killed him. Uncle Joe spent several hours, photographing the records and the mound outside. He discovered several other, similar, sites in the wood. Before he left, he set a fire in the cellar and left it burning. With an empty

## CHAPTER 10

bottle of Malt on the lawn outside, the glass covered in the old man's fingerprints, the authorities drew their own conclusions. They decided the caretaker, while in a drunken stupor, had caused the blaze in which he perished.

"Once I learned what had happened, Uncle Joe realised there was no way he could keep me out of his affairs. He had joined the underground opposition and, that night, I, too, pledged my allegiance to them."

"What does he think about you meeting with me?" I ask.

"He's unhappy, but knows too well I'm my own person. He trusts me, and my judgement, so he will go along with me. It will take time for him to have full confidence in you, Nathan, but he's the same with everyone. Please, don't take it as something personal against you."

"And you, do you trust me?" I ask.

Again, the long piercing look into my eyes. She nods, satisfied with what she discerns.

"Yes," she answers, her voice soft. "I do. You're different to most men I've met."

We stay a while longer, until Fia recovers her composure. She dries her face and, when we move into the light, she repairs, as best she can, the ravages to her make-up. Fia is quiet as we walk past the bright lights, back towards the car park. She keeps a firm grip round my waist but her face is stress free, her inner demons released. Sharing her sorrows seems to have lifted a great weight from her soul.

Tonight, Fia invites me in for coffee. Wrapped in each other's arms, we stretch out on a comfortable sofa. Chopin nocturnes, from an old classical CD, play in the background. Fia is aware of some of my history, the basic outline without much detail. My time with Charles at NSF headquarters, and my life with Julie and the children, in particular, is unknown territory to her. In the privacy of her home, I spill out everything. It is my turn to shed a tear. I expect her to recoil at some of the deeds I have done and, under torture, my betrayal of Julie. Instead, she holds my hands and looks at me with compassion and understanding. This woman, I would be a fool to lose.

It is close to two in the morning before I leave. This night, when we have revealed our innermost secrets, fears and hopes, it seems inappropriate to take our relationship to the next level.

"I'll be seeing Joe tomorrow," Fia says, as I leave. "I'll ask him to make discreet enquiries about your children. If anyone can find them, he can. Please don't build your hopes. It could take months before he discovers anything, if at all. The state is secretive about such matters. It would be ill-advised to alert them."

Exhausted I may be on the drive home, but I cannot blame the lateness of the hour for all of that. The evening has drained me of emotion. Although, it has left me with a calmness of spirit, I have never experienced. No longer am I a prisoner of my memories and fears. If Joe can find my children, I shall follow him to the ends of the earth, provided Fia is at my side.

# 11

The passage of time is rapid. By Wednesday, Amanda has dropped any pretence of work. She spends her days chatting with Harry, drinking endless cups of coffee in the cafeteria or, in between, popping out to make arrangements for her move. It is a relief when she's away from the office. There are seven working days until she goes, unless - I know Amanda has five day's holiday still unused. I have a quiet word with Harry. With his approval, I suggest to her it might be easier if she leaves this Friday. She will have more time to prepare for her move south. Without hesitation, Amanda agrees.

The planning-software is straightforward. Sara soon develops a working level of proficiency in its operation. Her thought processes are rapid and analytical. By the end of the week, with minimum supervision, she controls production rotas for several of the minor production lines. Before implementation, unlike Amanda, Sara has no objection to verification of her figures. Going forward, this will make my life much easier. The process is simple for me. As I have my eye on most company production lines, I can adjust manufacturing schedules elsewhere in the system, if necessary, to avoid component shortages. Amanda had a tendency to allocate stock items without checking requirements elsewhere first, which led to many problems.

Fia and I talk on the 'phone most evenings. I mention to Harry about my new relationship. Of course, he is aware of the situation, but pretends surprise. To be fair, his congratulations do seem genuine.

"Well done, Nathan. It'll do you good to have some female companionship. I expect she'll be much better company than a pub quiz pal," Harry smiles at me. "I wish you both the best of luck."

On Friday night Harry, Sara and I, join Amanda, along with half-dozen of her friends from other departments, at the Bishop's Arms near the factory. We did have a collection for her. As anticipated, the amount raised was derisory, a reflection of Amanda's popularity. Harry and I top up the fund to a reasonable amount. We buy her a bottle of her favourite perfume. Amanda seems pleased with the gift. I had warned Fia I would be out. We made our arrangements for the weekend earlier in the week. What I have to do tonight is watch my fruit juices, to make sure nothing alcoholic finds its way into them.

To most attendee's surprise, the evening goes well. Outside of work and no longer on watch-duty, Amanda feels able to let her hair down. She has a great time. Half-way through the evening, a rugged young man enters through the pub doorway. Amanda waves at him, then rushes over to bring him to our table.

"Meet my baby brother, Vince," she gushes with pride, gazing up at her companion. "He's come up from Lincoln to help me pack. He'll be driving the van I'm hiring."

We introduce ourselves. The merriment continues. By ten o'clock, I am on my fifth bottled of juice. No matter how pleasant its initial taste, there is a limit to its desirability. Harry is awash with G&T's. After several large measures of white wine, Sara, her face flushed, is a little unsteady on her feet. It is time for us to leave. We say our goodbyes to Amanda. Because neither Harry nor Sara brought their cars to work, I offer them a lift.

Sara is nearest. I take her to Moortown. Harry lives further out, in a new development built on former green-belt land, near Shadwell. I discover it to be a high-security neighbourhood, designed for members of the local party hierarchy. Razor-wire topped walls surround the area. Uniformed men, with carbines and large Alsatian dogs patrol the outer defences. We approach an ornate, but solid pair of security gates, set into the walls at the entrance to the complex. I pull up in front of them. Two security guards step into view, their weapons aimed through the centre of the windscreen, at my head.

## CHAPTER 11

"Don't worry," Harry says, a slight alcoholic slur to his words, "They don't recognise your car, I'll speak to them."

He presses the button to open his window. At the sound, one of the guards moves to his side of the vehicle. He keeps his weapon at the ready, until a third guard appears. This one shines a torch into the car.

"Oh! Sorry, Mr Wardman, we didn't realise it was you," the guard admits. "Is everything okay?" he asks.

Harry's late arrival, with a stranger, in a small, unknown economy-class vehicle is a cause for concern.

"It's all right Wayne. Mr Andrews, here, has given me a lift from a work's leaving celebration" Harry explains. "Once he's dropped me off, he'll be away."

"Very good, sir. George will follow on, to make sure your companion finds his way back all right."

Harry waves in acknowledgement. Security is tight. The guards take no chance of anything untoward happening. The electronically-controlled gates swing open. Moments later, a small battery-powered buggy approaches. With it behind us, we move off. For several minutes, we drive down a well-lit sweeping avenue lined with beautiful mature trees. Harry's home, when we reach it, is a substantial stone-built detached house, with double-garage and extensive gardens - the plot's privacy assured by the high walls that surround it.

All the houses we have passed have been similar in outlook, if diverse in design. I turn onto a crescent drive. Gravel crunches. I pull up beside a short flight of stone steps. They lead to polished wooden twin-doors. Concealed lighting, triggered by our arrival, illuminates the entrance. Harry thanks me as he steps out. Back on the roadway, the guards' vehicle slips into position behind me. This time, without further delay, those on duty wave me through the gates.

By eleven, I am home. My terraced-house seems smaller than ever tonight. I decide on cosy, rather than tiny. Yawning, I am soon in bed. Fia is expecting me at eight in the morning. We are to head for the Dales. A walk up to Simon's Seat the main part of tomorrow's itinerary.

The day dawns bright and sunny. Ten o'clock finds us on the rocks in front of Posforth Gill waterfall. There has been rain during the week, water enough to enhance the fall's natural beauty. It makes the slight detour, along the muddy path to their base, worth the effort. Leaving the Valley of Desolation, we pass through woodland above to reach open moorland. Once across the stream, we start the long gradient towards Truckle Crags. Long before the ascent eases, I realise Fia is much fitter than am I. Unlike hers, my breathing labours on the steeper sections. We make several stops, to allow me, so she says, to 'admire the view'. Her tact is admirable.

The wide expanse of Barden Fell spreads out on either side. Hand in hand, we walk towards the two rock formations that make up Simon's Seat. This is my first visit. We scramble up the rocks towards the Trig point. The Wharfe Valley opens up in front of us. This time it is the view that takes away my breath. We sit, at the edge of the rocks. Beneath us, the drop is sheer, before the land curves away towards the valley bottom. From there it sweeps up towards Skyreholme's stone cottages. Fia points out Trollers Gill and, in the distance, Buckden Pike. Other names fall from her tongue. Her face, flushed from the walk, glows in the sunlight. With my arm around her, she snuggles closer.

Fia has brought sandwiches, I bottles of spring water. We dine at one of the finest tables in Yorkshire. Several times, other walkers, singletons or pairs, each eager for their natural high from this wonder of nature, join us. Light, cotton-wool clouds float towards us from the Pennines. In slow motion, they drift across the undulating landscape, little higher than are we. Their shadows follow them across the spring green countryside. The contrasts of light and shade bring an ever-changing patchwork across the land.

The sound of someone clambering the rocks reaches our ears. Engaged deep in conversation, a loud cough makes us break apart with a start. Turning round, we see John resting against the Trig column.

"Sorry to make you jump," he apologises, although the smile on his face tells the opposite story.

## CHAPTER 11

"Hi, John," we say, in unison, flustered by his unexpected arrival.

Neither of us anticipated seeing him, nor anyone else we knew, today.

"What's wrong?" Fia asks, a worried frown puckers her brow. "Nothing's happened to Uncle Joe, has it?"

"No, Joe's fine. He said to tell you he'll be in the village tearooms, around three-thirty. If possible, he would like a word."

"Are tearooms his venue of preference?" I ask.

"No," John laughs at the idea. "He does try, whenever possible, to keep his actions out in the open. People who gather in secret invite suspicion from the authorities. He's visiting friends in West Burton. The village tearooms are a convenient place for him to break his journey. What could be more natural, on finding his niece entering such a place, than to invite her and her companion to join him?"

At the word companion, John gives me a hard stare. I return it, unflinching. In a fair fight, I would be no match for him, and much less of one in an unfair contest, but I refuse to be intimidated. I doubt John has any designs on Fia, but he has watched over for her for a number of years. As with Joe, he has yet to be convinced of my suitability. For some reason, John finds my reaction reassuring. He gives a faint nod in acknowledgement. He bids us goodbye. Back on the moor, at a mile-eating pace, he strides away in the direction of Bolton Abbey. I suppose he reached us the hard way, straight up the hillside from Howgill, rather than the somewhat less strenuous route on which we embarked.

"Come on," Fia urges, after checking the time on her mobile. "It's time to make a move, if we want to take in Lord's Seat as well."

Within minutes, with our rucksacks back in place, I help Fia down onto the springy peat-surface below the rocks. Moments later, a paved footpath leads us across the boggy moor top, towards another mound of rocks. After a brief pause, to admire the view from the summit, we follow the line of a wall and second paved section. Lower down, on a service track, we cross the moor alongside where, in August, shotguns decimate the local grouse population.

We re-join our outbound route and return through the Valley of Desolation. Bypassing the turn-off to the waterfall, we take the more direct route towards the road and the eventual riverbank, opposite to the Cavendish Pavilion. Ignoring the crossing there, we follow the riverside footpath for the last mile to the wooden footbridge over the Wharfe. Few of the stepping-stones, parallel to our crossing, break the surface of the flowing waters. As we climb the steps that lead us to the hole in the wall, behind us the Priory glows in the late afternoon sun.

# 12

Inside Priory View tearooms, a sign commands customers to *'Please wait to be seated'*. Within moments, a young man arrives to attend to us. Before he can speak, a voice calls out from a corner table.

"Fia, Nathan, is that you? Over here."

We turn to see Joe. He beckons us to join him. The young man hands us a menu each, our seating arrangements decided without any assistance.

"Why, Uncle Joe, what a pleasant surprise," Fia says, leading me towards him. She gives him a quick hug and a kiss on the cheek.

"I could say the same thing about you two," Joe replies.

He shakes my hand. We take our seats.

"The last people I expected to bump into on my way back from Jack and Mary's, were you two," he continues. After a quick glance at our rucksacks and muddy boots, he states the obvious, "I guess you've been walking."

Other customers, at nearby tables, lose interest as our conversation turns to the usual pleasantries, details of our walk and Joe's day out. The young man returns to hover, while we select scones with jam and cream. Joe orders a fresh pot of tea for the three of us. Coffee is good, but, after a long walk, I find nothing refreshes more than a cup of Earl Grey. The party at the table nearest to us pay their bill. They leave. Within a few minutes, with their table cleared and empty, we are able to talk with some degree of privacy. Joe lowers his voice, but keeps it above a conspiratorial level. To all appearances, our amiable conversation continues.

"Nathan, I hear you're in charge of route-planning."

"Soon, in a few weeks time. First, I have to settle my new assistant, Sara, into the job and make sure she's comfortable with the production-side. Once the work does come over, a trainee will join the team. That should free-up more of my time and allow me to concentrate on oversight and, I hope, take a more active role in company operations."

"Do you know if that will include shipments from the top security, Experimental and Special Mouldings division?" Joe asks.

"Until the work comes over to me, I cannot be sure. To begin with, I doubt it. In many ways, I'm on probation. I'd be surprised if Harry transfers that side over to me before I've proved myself. It's rumoured Experimental's route-planners have made some unfortunate errors. I have worked in that field with some success, which, I assume, is why general routing is to come my way."

"That ties in with what I hear," Joe agrees. "There's no need to look worried. In no way shall I risk your position, nor life, by compromising any shipments you've directed. That apart, many government activities remain a closed-book, even to me. If I can correlate who manufactures what and ships it to where, it could help some of my much cleverer colleagues to work-out to what use your mouldings can be put. I must admit, the experimental work is of greater importance than the standard product."

"You'll want to know more than I can provide. A moulding can be put to a variety of uses."

"We are aware that," Joe stresses each word with exaggerated patience, "but once we have a destination, we can attempt to learn what else goes there. From that information, we can build up a picture of what the end-product might be."

"Wouldn't it make greater sense to infiltrate their technical departments?"

"Those facilities are high security. They want people with specific skills sets. Goods-in and despatch department operatives are subject to less scrutiny. Those areas are easier to penetrate."

Fia looks out of the window.

## CHAPTER 12

"Damn it," she complains. "There's a queue for the loos. I'll nip out to take my turn."

She goes outside, beating, by seconds, a group of women walkers to the end of the line."

"Good, I'm glad Fia's left us for a moment," Joe's voice takes on a serious tone. "I wanted a word with you in private."

"Oh! Anything in particular?" I ask, on my guard in an instant.

"Is it true, there's something going on between my niece and you? John believes you've formed an attachment. This is not what I intended. Your relationship is supposed to be casual, one you can exploit to exchange information, without arousing suspicion - membership of the same gym, or something along those lines."

"You'll have to ask Fia how she views our liaison," I state. "Provided we carry-out our duties without a problem, our private lives are none of your business."

Honesty I consider best, although under my breath, I curse John. He should keep his nose out of other peoples' affairs.

"I did ask Fia," Joe admits with a grimace. "She told me to mind my own damned business, too. It would be a lie to say I don't have concerns, but I've given the matter some thought. In some ways, a genuine connection might be safer for the pair of you. You're both young and single. It's quite natural for you two to develop a relationship. That way, there is less chance your meetings can be construed as suspicious."

I am about to speak, but Joe puts up his hand.

"Hear me out, please. I want to say this out of Fia's hearing. I promised my brother, if anything happened to him, I would look out for Fia. This I tried to do, by keeping her out of the underground movement; but she backed me into a corner. I had to bring her into the organisation, albeit in a minor role."

"I know, Fia told me all about her family, and her brother Sean."

"Bloody hell," Joe looks shocked, "she must trust you if she's told you that. It's rare for her judgement to err. Listen. In the past, I have used Fia, both to gather information and act as a courier, in low-risk operations. Meeting you, at Buckden, was the first time I involved her in anything approaching a pro-active situation. John and I thought you would respond to her charms, rather than his. We didn't expect it to be reciprocal."

"I want her kept safe. Understood?" His gaze is penetrating. I nod. He continues. "Trust me, if anything happens to her because of you, I will hunt you down, then kill you."

I nod but keep silent. The threat is of no concern. If I do cause anything to happen to Fia, I deserve everything that comes my way.

"Something about your situation worries me," Joe continues, changing the subject. "Your being where you are, the position you are in, everything about it is somewhat puzzling. It's too convenient. As you are aware, the state, when it uncovers an underground opposition cell, celebrates its infrequent victories. What the NSF keeps to itself is their lack of success in tracing the leadership. I suppose, if the authorities had anything suspicious about me to go on, no matter how trivial, by now, they either would have interviewed, or arrested me. I have no reason to think I am other than trusted, but others warn me to be careful - and of you in particular."

"If you have suspicions, why permit Fia to meet me?" I ask.

"Gut instinct," Joe answers. "My background investigation of you has been rigorous. I accept you are who you say you are, and, of greater importance, *what* you say you are. That said, it is possible the authorities have you dangling, like a worm at the end of a giant fishing-line. Who knows whom they hope to hook? It could be someone specific, such as me, or a speculative cast, in the hope someone, anyone nibbles. If they arrest me, Fia, as my niece, will fall under suspicion. In that case, her main chance of survival could lie with you."

"Me?" I ask in surprise. "How can you believe that? When I was a man with influence and connections in high places, I was unable to save my wife."

"That was a strange affair. Your wife, I mean. On numerous occasions, she attempted to make contact with the underground, but, because of you and your position, no-one trusted her. The one time she gained access to a meeting, the police raided it. You know what followed that. At first, we were certain your wife was working under instructions and had betrayed us. Her death and your arrest convinced us too late, she had been speaking the truth."

Joe looks out of the window. Fia is out of sight, near the beginning of the queue.

"Whatever the authorities have in mind," he continues, "You're in a good position to hear about it, or see something, first. Be careful, your party-rep is more than he seems. Last night, John kept an eye on you. When you took Harry home, he followed. For someone on a party-rep's salary, the secure area where he lives is way above his pay grade. You should know, you were one, once. This morning, I called in a couple of favours. It seems Harry Wardman is a major, in the NSF.

"I want you to promise me, if at any point you have any reason to think Fia, or I, am about to be exposed, you will take her and flee the country."

None of this is what I want, nor expected to hear, although, certain parts do make some sense, in a crazy way. The suspected guiding-hand, from above, comes to mind. I mentioned it to Joe. He raises an eyebrow as he considers it.

"If true, it confirms what I suspect. It also means this operation has been in progress for much longer than I thought. I shall endeavour to find out more. This will be difficult. I shall have to choose the contacts I use with care."

"That apart, how do you expect me to spirit Fia out of the country?" I ask. "I have no connections who could arrange anything on that scale."

"I would be very surprised if *you* did, but *I* do. I have sources, independent and unknown to the underground. Once I am able to confirm arrangements with them, I shall pass contact details to you. They have done work for me and, if necessary, they will look after you. I have saved their lives a couple of times. They will be happy to return the favour.

## LOVE, LIES AND TREACHERY

"For now, I want you to pass on what information you can. It will help to expand my knowledge, but, for now, to act on it would be too risky. If we did, the NSF may trace it back to you. If that happens, you and all your contacts will come under intense scrutiny."

"Is anyone watching you?" I ask.

"No, not that I'm aware." Joe appears startled by the suggestion. "The NSF would be wary of alerting me, but there are other ways. It's difficult to travel anywhere without being in range of a CCTV camera. Since JJ took control of the country, camera proliferation has been exponential. Having said that, even with facial-recognition software, to track someone this way is difficult, expensive and labour intensive. I'll have John do some long-range tailing of me. If he spots anything, I will have to re-think Fia's safety, as well as my own."

Fia returns. Joe moves the conversation onto something less serious. He glances at his watch; it is time for him to leave. We wait a while longer, before we settle the bill.

On the road, outside the village, Fia asks me to pull into a lay-by. She wants a tissue from her pack in the boot, which is odd; she knows there are some in the glove compartment. Before I can speak, she puts a finger to her lips to indicate I keep quiet. Back in the car, and after some theatrical nose blowing, Fia produces a mobile sized electronic device from her pocket. With practised thoroughness, she scans the whole car before dropping the object into her handbag.

"Good," she declares, "there are no listening devices in your car. Now, tell me, what was it Uncle Joe said while I was away? I could see you through the window. You were deep in conversation. Each of you looked serious. It must be something he wants to protect me against."

I am torn. I know Joe wants to keep Fia from harm, but she is an adult, old enough to make her own decisions. In my mind her safety is paramount, too - but lying to her? Can this be the best way? Secrets had led to Julie's death. This relationship, I refuse to start with a web of deceit. It would be insidious and create a barrier between us. Besides, if Joe is correct in his thinking, I believe it safer for Fia if she has full

## CHAPTER 12

disclosure. This way she can take precautions. Taking a deep breath, I look Fia in the eyes and give her a full summary of everything said to me by Joe.

"Thank God for that. I thought he might be trying to split us," are her first thoughts. "If he believes keeping me in the dark will protect me, if everything goes sour, he's mistaken," she adds. "I shall have it out with him, next time we meet."

"No, you can't do that," I object, taking hold of her hand. "He mustn't know I told you. Be grateful, he cares for your well-being as much as he does. You're the last surviving member of his family. It's right for him to have concerns. If we are correct, and someone is playing me, it is up to *me* to find out why. I must do whatever I can to stop their plans from coming to fruition. I know first-hand what it is to be a guest of the NSF. Trust me, Fia, you don't ever want to find out."

"I'll do whatever I have to." Her tone indicates her stubbornness.

"Think about it. What if it's Uncle Joe, or me, they torture in front of you? I've no idea how long I could last if they made me watch you undergo such treatment. These people have no moral scruples. Once Uncle Joe passes on the details of his escape-route to me, I shall give the contact details to you. If I suspect at any time the authorities are about to pounce, we will use it."

"I refuse to abandon Uncle Joe."

"What, and let his sacrifice be in vain? Once dead, we can do nothing. Abroad, we can work to bring down the tyrants who rule over this country. Few governments tolerate them now. If the international press learns the full extent of what takes place over here, they will mount huge pressure on world-leaders to take action. International sanctions already bite deep. The good old days of JJ's rule have long gone."

There is sense in what I have said. Frustrated, Fia sits back, her thoughts angry with Joe. Because I am with her, I suffer the backlash. She snatches her hand from mine. I put my arm around her. For a moment, she tries to pull away.

"You're right," she admits, after a moment, her body relaxing.

"Don't worry," I tell her. "We'll have to make sure we're careful. If anything does happen, I shall do my best to warn Joe. Promise me one thing. If I cannot reach you, you must go alone."

"No, that is too much," she says, pulling me closer.

"You must," I insist. "If they arrest you, they will use you against me. If, as we think, someone does pull my strings, somewhere in the puppet-master's scheme there may be an escape-clause for me."

Fia looks as though she is about to disagree, but, after a few moments, she nods in acceptance of my words.

"Come on. Let us go home. Until we learn more, we can do nothing. I've left something in the oven on a low light. It should be ready by the time we arrive. Would you care to join me?" she invites demurely.

"It will be a pleasure," I accept.

# 13

"Dinner will be about an hour," Fia says as she adds vegetables to the bubbling dish of meat she left slow-cooking this morning.

It is soon after our return from Bolton Abbey. Rays from the low evening sun shine with bright intensity through her kitchen window. The warm tones highlight her face, already aglow from our day spent in the fresh air.

"I think I'll have a shower," she decides. "I'll be quick. Make yourself at home. Put the kettle on if you want. Tea and coffee are on the shelf next to the kettle. Cups are in the top cupboard, to the right."

As she runs up the stairs, I look around. Fia's kitchen is modern, well lit, with marble work-surfaces and solid wood cupboards. It is clean and tidy, but not in an obsessive way. It differs much from the tiny space I have in my home. A tantalising aroma rises from the direction of the oven. I locate the kettle, throw a tea bag into a cup then wait for the water to boil. My jacket, its lining damp from the day's exertion, I hang up on a hook in the hallway. My T-shirt feels clammy, too.

In a short time, the sound of water, running through the pipes, stops. Footsteps sound overhead. I am about to put the kettle on for Fia, when I hear her call.

"Do you want a shower?" she asks as I reach the stairs. "I've put some towels out for you."

At the top of the stairs, I find Fia, a large towel wrapped round her to preserve her modesty. As we pass, she slips into my arms. Her towel falls to the floor, as our hands, searching and caressing, discover each other. Fumbling fingers strip away my clothes. We stagger towards her bedroom. With fervour and desire that suggests each of us has abstained too long, exploring hands delight and inflame our senses. We join with a passion as intense as is our release. Afterwards, we lie, locked in an embrace, our bodies tight against each other.

Fia, whose head has been resting on my chest, looks up. She wrinkles her nose.

"You need a shower," she says, "and I want another. Come on, I'll scrub your back."

We make love again, in the shower. Long afterwards, dressed in robes, we sit across her dining room table and eat our meal. It is late in the evening; the food is long since overcooked. Wrapped up in our own little world, neither of us cares. That night I stay with Fia. We make love again. This time, our intimacy is slower, gentler, our pleasure greater and more satisfying. In the small hours of the morning, we float happy, relaxed and content, into slumber, our arms around each other.

༺ ༻

Since our first night together, the speed at which time passes takes us both by surprise. Memories of Julie remain. She was a part of my life for a long time, but that part is over. My new-found happiness with Fia is different, somehow, less stressful and much more satisfying. The first few months are hectic. Making time to grow our relationship, against the backdrop of pressure from work, is difficult.

Sara soon proves her ability at work. From the start, she integrates with ease. Her work-rate is phenomenal. Between us, we overhaul the entire system. In the process, we generate marked operational efficiencies, which result in significant financial savings. Two months after Sara's start, the transfer of route-planning to us commences. At the same time, James's transfer to the team receives board approval. He, too, proves to be a quick learner. Hands-on experience improves his self-confidence. Within weeks, he takes a pro-active role in the department.

## CHAPTER 13

The rate at which distribution work transfers to our desks is rapid. Four months after James joined the department, Harry calls me into his office. By this time, we control logistics for the whole of the company, except Experimental. That work remained classified, but, as I have heard from several sources, problems within this department have continued to mount. Much of the task is software-based. They operate the same programs, as do we. Where they fail is in forward-thinking and an inability to take a holistic view. Simple checks on road-traffic reports, for instance, or the weather, can make a huge difference. Adverse conditions can turn an ideal route into a nightmare, for time-sensitive deliveries or receipts.

With the expectation of a brief update meeting, I knock and enter Harry's office. He has company. Beside him is an impeccable blue suit, white shirt, sombre tie, and a pair of shoes polished to an almost impossible shine. Wearing these objects is a lean faced man, in his mid-thirties. What hair remains on his balding head, he has shaved to a fine bristle.

My heart rate rises. This is a member of the NSF. The arrogance and contempt in his stare tells me that. Over the years, it is a look I have seen too many times. At one time, I may have worn the same expression. Whether this is an indicator that something is wrong is unclear; I am sure such people are born with a supercilious look of pre-eminence. This thought is of little comfort. I struggle to contain a rising sense of panic. Is he here to arrest me? What do they know about Fia, Uncle Joe or my involvement, albeit on the periphery, of the underground? I shake the proffered hand, while, at the same time, I attempt to prevent mine from shaking.

"Hi, Nathan, shut the door and pull-up a chair," Harry instructs. "Robert's here to sit in on our meeting."

As I select a chair from the wall-side, a casual brush of my hand against my shirt-pocket confirms I have brought my mobile. Comforted by its feel, I try to relax. Since I obtained her number, Fia has been on speed-dial. If at any time I feel under threat, I can attempt to reach her. We have a secret code word, one that means *run, warn whom you can, but do not wait for me*. The contact details for Joe's escape-group, we have committed to memory.

"You look worried," Harry observes, his tone genial. "You've no need. There's nothing wrong, in fact, the opposite. Robert's heard good reports. He's here to discuss something with you."

"That's right," Robert agrees, moving forward in his chair.

His accent contains faint echoes of the West Midlands, but, by its lack of broadness, I guess it is some time since he last lived there. Harry sits back. By the look of it, this is Robert's show.

"The work you do here has attracted the attention of several of my colleagues at the Department for Business, Energy & Industrial Strategy, in London," Robert starts. "The savings and increased productivity you achieve have set the standard for many other businesses. There was a suggestion you join us in London, to act as a roving advisor, or trouble-shooter, to failing companies. For now, due to the unfortunate circumstances that surround your relationship of a few years ago, the appropriateness of such an offer is in question. The minister, presiding at the head of my department, wants more time for you to prove your reliability, and loyalty to the party."

Somehow, I contain my annoyance at this disclosure. I have worked hard to prove my worth, sweated blood to redeem myself. The truth, that my efforts are a lie, is irrelevant. For me to be in such a position would be a godsend for Joe, and the underground, but, would a move to London be welcomed by Fia? I doubt that. There is something else to consider too - how would those in power react if I declined such an offer, or asked if Fia could accompany me? Questions, again, to which, I fear, I have no answer. Robert, unaware of my thoughts, goes on to offer me something else, something that could be of equal value to the underground.

"In my role at the department," Robert explains, "I have special responsibility for the experimental division here, and similar ones at several other locations throughout the country. As such, I would like

## CHAPTER 13

to make you a proposition. Something that, if you accept it and prove yourself, could lead to the offer of a role similar to the one mentioned earlier."

"Please, do go on," I encourage him to continue.

I adjust my tone to reflect the level of curiosity he will expect from me. Satisfied with my reaction, Robert explains further.

"As with my colleagues, I have taken great interest in your methods, and the resultant improvement in workflow. By their nature, experimental divisions here and elsewhere are expensive to operate, but, when you factor in gross inefficiencies in their operations, their costs become prohibitive. To begin with, we want someone to take control of Experimental's supply and distribution functions here. That person must have the knowledge and experience to provide insightful input into the department's processes. I believe you are that man. Unlike other areas of the company, Experimental have no production lines. They specialise in one-off samples and short runs. Procurement of supplies and delivery of their prototypes can be a nightmare. Too many become damaged, or lost in transit."

"Do you want me to move over there?" I ask. "Sara is good, but lacks the experience, yet, to take full control of my department."

"No, we cannot afford for you to abandon your present work. We want you to remain in overall control. You will have full access to the experimental processing database, and software. This will come via your laptop. Passwords, etc, are for you alone. Under no circumstances should hard copies be made of these, nor anyone else made aware of them. If you agree, we shall issue identity cards and credentials. They will permit you to enter the main experimental areas. For reasons of security, access to the design and CAD facility has its limits, but everything else will be open to you. Now, tell me Nathan," Robert asks, "is this something of interest to you?"

"Of course it is. I shall not let you down"

"Excellent, I shall set everything in motion. Harry will continue in his current role. He'll be your main contact with my department."

Robert stands, his hand outstretched. Dismissed, I leave the office, the deal cemented with a handshake. The following afternoon, Harry brings my credentials. Later, he introduces me to the experimental division. To begin with, I spend two to three days a week with them. Later, as I learn their processes, I am able to reduce my absences from my main area of operation.

The resultant increase in salary is a shock. Overnight, my income doubles. Fia is happy with the promotion, but less enthusiastic about the long hours it involves. Once the work becomes manageable, it allows me to spend more time, again, with her. Sara and James step up to the challenge. Much of my original workload, they split between them. For this, they each receive a generous increment to their salary.

# 14

The need, over this period, for Fia to act as a go-between for Joe is, to some extent, made superfluous by value of my blossoming relationship with her. Most weekends, either Joe dines with us one night, or we call on him. It is the natural thing to do. It would appear strange if we did otherwise. The Sunday after my meeting with Harry and Robert, Joe joins Fia and me for an evening-meal at her house. After dinner we retreat to the lounge with a pot of fresh coffee.

Before Joe's arrival, as usual, Fia had scanned the house with her electronic device. Reclining in easy chairs, with Elgar's Enigma Variations in the background, we are free to speak without restriction. Joe is enthusiastic about my promotion, but, when I voice some misgivings, his brow furrows.

"What's the problem?"

"It's too easy. I sense these mysterious hidden hands at work again, moving me into position. To have Experimental's supply and distribution network come to me is a logical step for the company, but, from a Department of Business's viewpoint, to give me unlimited access to a top-secret area is one leap of faith too far. The government chap, Robert, warned me of the minister's doubts."

"I have to agree," Fia joins in. "No offence to Nathan, but he has been in both the political and employment wildernesses close to four years. Imprisoned, tortured, his family killed or taken from him, then transferred to a dead-end job in a strange town. Now what? He's a phoenix risen from the ashes. One thing we can agree, he has worked hard to prove himself, but, in today's world, career resurrections such as this are as rare as donkey wings. This government, we know, has no moral scruples. It makes use of people who have fallen out of favour, providing they have outstanding talents. Do such individuals live free from constant supervision, allowed an unrestricted life outside a secure hostel? No, Nathan is the exception."

Joe nods in agreement. "What Fia says is true. What we have to work out is why Nathan has this freedom, and why he's achieved such an elevated position."

"I could be in deep cover," I propose, playing devil's advocate.

It is something Joe, for one, must have considered before he first made contact with me. It must remain a possibility in his mind.

"I cannot believe that." Fia is indignant.

"To be fair," Joe admits, "neither do I. Many of my colleagues, as well as I, have thought much about Nathan's position. Over the years, we have dealt with a number of covert agents. Their cover-stories vary, but it is usual for them to have much greater relevance than yours. Although, if you were a spy, you have penetrated our organisation far deeper than anyone has."

"So, what now, a double bluff?" I ask, both gratified and curious. I have my own ideas, but do want to hear Joe's thoughts on the situation.

"For years, the surveillance on you was constant," Joe says, "and, in the main, with little effort made to disguise it. If you worked in secret for the NSF, such activity would have been short-term, sufficient to give substance to your cover-story but nothing more. After that, we would have expected you to make contact with us. None of that happened. We were the ones who initiated the contact.

"That said, I do consider your re-location here to Leeds to be a set-up. The authorities have tried to exploit your experiences with them. They felt sure you would seek out the opposition, in an attempt to use them to help you take revenge – which, in reality, is what you do intend. Because your story is true and verifiable, your words have veracity. With skill, and much luck, you have avoided their trap. Your actions have been the opposite to those they expected. Everything you have done indicates you seek redemption.

## CHAPTER 14

"Had you allowed your bitterness to show, or exhibited any inclination towards subversion, overt surveillance would have faded. Their best teams would have taken over, then compiled a list of your connections. In time, they would hope you would lead them to the top. The reason they kept you in a menial position for as long as they did, was, I think, an attempt to provoke you. What we have now is a conundrum. Have they given up, have they succeeded or, are they trying something new?

"If they have any suspicions about me," Joe continues, after a pause to sip from his drink, "they must believe their operation has shown results. You have insinuated yourself into my immediate family-circle. The current lack of surveillance on you, a promotion that allows you access to sensitive material, all fall in with such a scenario. They control what material you see and are able to pass on, which could lead to me revealing my contacts. Without any conscious co-operation by you, they control the run of play.

"If we take an alternative view, that they accept I am a loyal party-member, your general attitude and current relationship with Fia, may have persuaded them to abandon the whole operation. Your friend, Tim was a deep-cover operative. They used him to worm his way into your confidence. You soon became aware of his motives, then turned the situation to your advantage. He witnessed your first meeting with Fia, which I know from my intelligence, his master's believe to be accidental. They know you have talent in your vocation. Because of that, I suspect they have cut their losses and decided to make proper use of your abilities."

"But, if we suppose I am bait," I say, "even if you were above suspicion before, you may be suspect now. Because we are in regular contact, you will have become a person of interest."

"Has John discovered anything?" Fia interrupts. "You said he would perform some long-range shadowing of you."

"No, nothing at all! He mounted an operation that lasted several weeks, then did a similar detail on Nathan. Apart from random drones overhead, of which we know the government make use, he could find nothing to suggest either Nathan or I are of any concern to the authorities. John scanned my house, office, 'phones and car. He found no listening, nor tracking devices, nor any hidden cameras."

"I scan here, every day," Fia confirms. "I've found nothing."

"There's always me," I speak-out, as a forgotten memory resurfaces. "Could they have planted a tracking device inside me, when I was their prisoner?"

"I suppose it's possible, why?" Joe asks. He looks thoughtful.

"When my interrogation ended, they left me alone for several days. During that time, I developed an infection on my back. A nurse came to look at it. She said it was a problem with a deep cut. She cleansed the wound, gave me antibiotics, afterwards it soon cleared up. A few days later, she removed a couple of stitches. To be honest, I was such a relief to be out of their clutches, I forgot about it until now."

"You told me you received several beatings. What's so special about this cut?" Fia asks

"During the interrogation process, they strapped me to either a high backed chair or a table." The horror of my memories makes me flinch. "Other than grazes, received when they threw me into my cell, I had no puncture wounds to my back. Neither do I have any recollection of receiving stitches."

Fia, her eyebrows raised, explores the depths of her handbag until she finds what she seeks, her trusty electronic device. With it switched on, she runs the machine over a tiny scar she finds at the back of my neck.

"You might be onto something. The needle shows a slight reading, although too faint for whatever it is to be effective."

"After four years, any power-source will have become exhausted," Joe states. "The detector registers the presence of something under the skin, but no signal. To begin with, they must have feared Nathan might run. Once it became clear he had no such intention, nor was he going to enter into any subversive activity, its value would be degraded. Fia, you must scan on a regular basis to see if the tracker becomes active again."

"How can that happen without my knowledge?" I ask Joe.

"Let us hope it's not the same way you received it, while being tortured. To slip you a sedative and replace it would be too invasive for them to perform unnoticed."

"With modern technology, there might be no need for a replacement, Fia advises. "Dependent on what it is, there are ways to re-charge some power-sources remotely."

"That's true," Joe says. "For now, unless it's re-activated, we can ignore it."

"I could have it removed," I suggest. "Once gone, no longer will it be of concern."

"That would be too risky. If the authorities find it missing, you would be in serious trouble. Anyone acquainted with you would fall under suspicion. It's better left where it is. What do you think?" Fia asks Joe.

"For the moment, let us be extra vigilant," he advises. "I shall inform the underground intelligence committee that it's inadvisable to act on any information supplied by Nathan, unless it can be cross-referenced from other sources. If the authorities find anything they can trace back solely to you, it would confirm any suspicions and place each of us in danger. For now, we must build up our intelligence and learn what we can about our government's secrets."

For the next few months, this is what happens. As I learn more about new moulding designs, and the special compounds and materials used to create the prototypes, I give the information to Joe along with details of their destinations. He passes on no details other than what we deem necessary, without compromising my position, to agents in those districts.

It is slow work, piecing together what might be the final designs, and their eventual utilisation. Most of the products are benign, but a few are of concern and fewer still have the potential to pose a real threat to the population. Among these are weapons for public order control, or components for newer, more sophisticated, methods of spying and surveillance.

Fia continues with her courier work. As an executive recruitment specialist, heading a sub-division of Sandiman's, she has permits that allow her to travel throughout much of the north of England. These enable her to deliver packages and messages without suspicion. Fia's face is familiar to many whose job it is to check traveller's papers. Many times, the guards wave her through their mobile checkpoints. I suspect Joe, unless he has no alternative, gives Fia few incriminating documents to carry on her person. He is too fond of her for that.

# 15

Twelve months after our first night together, I put my house on the market. Over this period, the amount of time I have spent at my home has dwindled to zero. We have decided it is time I moved in with Fia on a permanent basis. Outside of work, my life, now centres around her. Her house is larger and no less convenient for work than is mine. Once the sale of my property goes through, we shall have some spare money.

To celebrate this, and the first anniversary of our meeting, we plan a holiday. Work has settled into an efficient routine. Between them, Sara and James are capable of running the department for a few days. I apply for a week's leave, which, to my relief, the company authorises without any objections. Prior to my relationship with Fia, it was rare for me to use half of my annual vacation days. After we met, the increase in workload has compelled me to take little more than an extra day or two around bank-holidays. On a weekend, whenever possible, we do spend a day walking or touring the Dales, or similar activities around the North York moors.

With Harry's assistance, Experimental provide me with longer than usual notice of their projected supply and distribution requirements. This allows me to plan in advance for my week's absence. Working long hours, I complete the details necessary to keep the department operational until my return. Harry takes charge of the schedule. He has my mobile-number on file. He asks for Fia's number too. This, he explains, is a last resort in case of an emergency at work and he cannot contact me on my own 'phone. However plausible this explanation, I doubt it is the main one. With both our numbers, he can arrange to keep track of our whereabouts. For now, the device implanted in my back remains inactive.

The week we have chosen falls in term-time, during the middle of May. As a result, many B&B's have vacancies. We have plenty from which to choose. The week before our break, changing climate-patterns bring about a settled spell of warm weather, which forecasters expect to last until our return. The jet-stream is on our side.

Saturday arrives. Between us, we load Fia's car with luggage. She has a company car, one that is larger than mine. It offers greater comfort over longer distances. With a lightness of spirit that neither of us has felt in years, we forget about work, the underground and the stresses involved in our everyday life. I start the engine and, without a care, away we go, next stop Suffolk. This is a place to which, in my past life, my work for the party never took me.

By nine, we have joined the A1 south of Leeds. According to the sat nav, we have one hundred and twelve miles to go before we make a turn. Fia switches on the radio and adjusts the volume. She settles back with her sun hat pulled over her eyes. I have drawn the short straw to drive first. We had been early to bed last night, but late to rest. At the memory, I smile. Fia drifts off to sleep.

Two and a half hours later, after several stops to show our papers, I turn onto the A14. A short while past the junction, I pull into a lay-by. The silence, when I switch off the engine, wakes Fia. After a quick drink of water and a sandwich, we switch seats. It is my turn to slumber. We have another two hours, at least, to drive before we reach our destination, a four-bedroom guest house a few miles inland from Thorpeness. The online blurb describes it as a medieval, timber-framed house, converted to the highest standards of en-suite comfort. Both its oak beam ceilings and four-poster bed are something to which we look forward.

We find everything as advertised. Our welcome is warm. The building has the scent of age – a faint musty air mixed with the aroma of beeswax. For us, it is ideal. Our room is large; the en-suite modern

## CHAPTER 15

and luxurious. The beams are genuine. Set into the white plastered, timber-frame walls, a wide leaded-glass window looks out over fields of green, where cattle graze. Fia stretches out on the bed.

"Wow," she says, "this is comfortable."

I join her for a moment before she leaps up.

"Come on, lazy. let's go have a look at the sea." Fia's energy levels have recovered. "According to the listing on the web, we can be in Thorpeness in twenty minutes. Let's have a look round there, then go on to Aldeburgh for a meal. The Beacon Restaurant there has an excellent write-up in the local Tourist Guide. I'll go freshen up first."

"You go ahead, the place is listed here in the Guest's Information Pack. I'll give them a ring."

Fia throws off her clothes and runs into the bathroom. Any self-consciousness she might once have felt has long since disappeared. A quick 'phone-call secures us a reservation. The sound of the shower comes from next door. I decide against joining Fia. Let us save ourselves until tonight, when we can take our time and enjoy the novelty of the splendid four-poster. I freshen-up. Fia steps out of the shower. Wrapped in a towel, she gives me quick kiss and my resolve falters. She sees the intent in my eyes. With a laugh, she ducks out of my reach to go dry-off and dress.

The shingle beach at Thorpeness is heavy-going, so we curtail our walk there to head for the mere instead. For half an hour I row, if you could associate that term with my strange action. Twice, with the tips of the oars, I miss the water altogether and end up on the bottom of the boat. Exhausted, we return from our trip, me from rowing, Fia from laughing. After refreshments nearby, we explore further. A short walk takes us to the former water tower, now holiday home, the House in the Clouds folly. The mock-Tudor styled construction on top, with its weather-boarded appearance, from a distance, seems to float in the sky. After taking a few photographs of an old, white-painted windmill nearby, that used to pump water up to the storage tank, we work our way back to the little sandy car park.

The late afternoon sun beats down as, along the narrow coast road, we drive the short distance to Aldeburgh. We find a parking space near to the sixteenth century Moot Hall. It is much too early for our meal, so, arm-in-arm, we set-off to stroll south along the front. Several fishing boats are pulled up onto the beach, their shadows lengthening over the shingle. Nets and lobster pots are piled on the ground beside some of the vessels. One of the iconic old lookout coastguard towers, with its wrought-iron, exterior spiral-staircase, attracts our attention. Strange sounds emanate from inside of the single-story structure attached to the tower. A hand-written poster invites visitors to a recital of experimental music. Fia raises an eyebrow. We continue with our walk, shingle to the left, houses painted in bright or pastel shades, to our right.

Beyond the houses, we follow an unmade road. Ahead of us, a Martello tower looms large in our sight, one of a number of similar, circular defensive forts built during the nineteenth century. Too small to be of current use by the military, or the NSF, this, as with many others, is under private ownership. A cool breeze has sprung up from the North Sea. We turn back. The time for our meal approaches.

Eastwards, waves break in a gentle soothing rhythm. On our left, a low, orange sun reflects on the wide expanse of the river Alde. The light bounces off sailing boats and cruisers, tied-up on the waters beyond the yacht club. We return to civilisation. The smell of fish and chips, wafting on the wind, makes us realise how hungry we are. With little trouble, we find the Beacon, further along the high street. Still too soon for our meal, we peer through the gaps left by dozens of stickers on the multi-paned window. A large party of diners populates the downstairs room. We collect our car, to drive the few hundred metres back into town, to park closer to our evening location.

As we push open the restaurant doors, the sun is close to setting. The room echoes to the clamour of a golden-wedding celebration, so banners proclaim. The maître d' confirms our reservations. Up a narrow wooden staircase, we follow him to a first-floor room, where

## CHAPTER 15

he ushers us to a window table. The noise from downstairs fades to a low murmur. On our first day at the seaside, it has to be a fish dish. The local cod fillet on parmesan and chive mash, with olive, sun-dried tomato and caper salad on the menu, takes our fancy. We order the same. I keep to fruit juice. Fia selects a large glass of dry white French wine. The drink soon takes effect. Fia's fits of giggles and laughter are contagious. After pudding, we pay the bill then leave.

Outside, the sky is black. Half an hour later, after our sat nav has taken us down a series of winding, single-track unlit back-ways, we arrive outside our home for the coming week. Inside, voices from the visitor's lounge sound over the top of a television programme. After a long day, we decide to be anti-social and retire for the night. Fia attempts to stifle a giggling fit as, in stocking feet, we sneak up the creaking wooden staircase to our room. That night we discover the delights of lovemaking in a four-poster live up to expectations.

Breakfast is a communal affair. Two couples, of advanced years, and a single man sit at a large, polished oak-table that fills the centre of the panelled dining room. Two chairs and place-settings remain unoccupied. We take our seats, then introduce ourselves. The couples, Frank and Alice, John and Geraldine, are on holiday. The single man, Roger, works in the area. His look is familiar, a member of the NSF, without any doubt. For a moment, I wonder if he is here to spy on us, but he says he has been here for several months and expects to remain until the year-end. Steven, the guest house owner, confirms this later as we finish breakfast. The other guests have long-since departed about their business.

"Was everything all right for you?" Steven asks, as we eat our toast.

After that, on top of cereal and a full English breakfast, I doubt we shall want much else before evening.

"It was delicious," Fia says, eyeing the last slice of toast but deciding against it.

"Sorry we were late coming down," I apologise. "I am afraid we overslept. Long drive down and too much fresh air on arrival."

"Don't worry. We serve breakfast between eight and nine," Steven advises, "although it would help if I had some idea what time you would like to eat. Did you have a good night's sleep?"

"Yes, we slept like logs. Asleep as soon as our heads hit the pillow," I add, keeping a straight face. Fia struggles to do the same with hers. "Eight-thirty for breakfast, is that all right for you?"

"Oh! Yes, that fits in with everybody. The seniors have theirs then. Roger does, too, on a weekend. During the week, he works in Framlingham; he's away by eight for a nine o'clock start. He's on secondment at the castle. Since the security-forces took it over, two years ago, it's become a high-level processing centre for dissidents. I understand Roger is one of their senior officers."

Steven's manner is relaxed, but the implied warning in his words is clear. So he knows I understand, I smile and nod; Fia does the same. Our host's words are of no surprise, we have already recognised the calibre of our fellow-guest. His duty done, Steven begins to clear the table.

"Where are you two going today?" he asks.

"We're still deciding," I reply. "We thought we might start with a wander round Snape, then have a look at the What's On listing at the Maltings. There could be a performance this week we want to see. After that, we might take in the Tide Mill at Woodbridge and, if there's time, end the day at Sutton Hoo."

"The forecast is excellent, it should be a good day to visit those places," Steven says.

"We might wander down to Felixstowe, tomorrow."

"Old Felixstowe is quaint, but the Bawdsey ferry is under NSF control," Steven cautions. "It's no longer open to the public. The security-forces have taken over the old manor, with much of the surrounding land. It's become their East Anglian Coastal Area HQ. The NSF has commandeered Languard Fort near to the port, too. It would be better to stay well away from both areas. Orford Ness, too, has no public access, though what happens there, no-one knows."

## CHAPTER 15

Again, the warning is unambiguous. We both nod. Much of the information we know already, but think it wise to keep that to ourselves. Joe gave us a list of places to avoid on our travels. Most are military or NSF locations, while others are sensitive industrial areas, near to which it might be unwise for our presence to go on record. The former prison, known to locals as the Hollesley Bay Colony is one such place to avoid. It is now an internment camp and re-education centre. Almost as many leave in wooden boxes as return to society.

After a lengthy wander round the converted Maltings, its shops and antiques centre, we have tea and scones. Neither of us can face a meal yet, instead, we have a desire to step out for a walk. We relegate all thoughts of the Tide Mill and Sutton Hoo to another day. I have a pocket-book of Suffolk walks. We decide to leave the car where it is and stay in the local area. From behind the concert hall, we head out across the fields. Before long, wooden duckboards guide our feet over salt marshes towards a pathway alongside the river Alde. Our destination, Iken.

For much of the way, above the surrounding trees, the tower of the half-thatched, half red-tiled roof of St Botolph's church is visible across the tidal river flow. The sun is warm, the breeze light, the walking easy compared to that back home, although the flat terrain does catch different muscles.

After exploring the medieval church's interior and its grounds, we take our leave. Relaxed, content and at peace with the world, we saunter the couple of miles back to Snape. We are in no hurry. Along the way, for a while, we sit on a grassy bank overlooking the rippling surface of the flowing waters. Why cannot life forever be this wonderful? We talk about everything and nothing.

The week passes much too fast. Days and events blend into one. A walk along the sandy beaches of Southwold, then out to the end of its re-built pier; trips to Long Melford, the medieval village of Kersey and the ancient centre of Lavenham are of equal delight. The sweeping arch of the Orwell Bridge is magnificent. We stop to admire its span of the estuary, on our return from a visit to Flatford Mill and Dedham in Constable country. We sample the local ice creams, fish and chips and, as it is the start of the season, asparagus pie. I even enjoy a pint of the local beer.

On Friday evening, we decide against a restaurant meal. This is our last night. The long drive home beckons in the morning. A picnic by the sea is in order. At a little sandwich bar in Woodbridge, we buy some Suffolk ham baguettes, made to order, some expensive imported strawberries, and fresh cream, to be followed by something sticky from a nearby cake shop. We head out to Aldeburgh with our haul of goodies. It is the middle of the afternoon, so, with some bottles of spring water, we pack our picnic into a rucksack. From the Moot Hall we head north. We walk along the coastal path towards Thorpeness. After a pot of tea and a short break, we head back.

Out on the shingle, on the seaward side of the large metal Scallop (dedicated to the memory of composer Benjamin Britten) we spread a blanket. Alert to any thieving gull that might take a fancy to our food, we spread out our feast. For hours we remain, long after the last strawberry has gone. We are unwilling to tear ourselves away. This week has been the happiest of my life. With my arm round Fia and her head resting on my chest, a spare blanket wrapped around our shoulders, we watch the shadows lengthen. Waves sweep in on the incoming tide, to lap at the shingles below.

To the accompaniment of breaking waters, the ground turns red as the setting sun sinks low in the sky behind. The occasional sound of a car, on the coast-road, does little to disturb our peace. It is time to go. We gather the remains of our picnic. Away from the darkening sea, the sun is below the horizon. The western sky glows deep-amber and yellow. The Scallop, silhouetted against this backdrop, is a remarkable sight. With a tinge of sadness, we retrace our footsteps across the shingle, to leave behind this haven of peace.

A shiver runs down my spine. I have an uncomfortable feeling, a foreboding. This brief interlude may be the last we shall enjoy for some

## CHAPTER 15

time to come. I push the dark thoughts to the back of my mind. I pull Fia closer to me. She hugs me in response and looks into my eyes in the fading light.

"You sense it, too, don't you Nathan," she says, her tone wistful. "Something is in the air."

"Yes, but what?"

"I wish I knew, but at least we've had this week - and there's tonight," she adds, a twinkle returning to her eyes.

"Why waste it?" I laugh. "Race you to the car."

# 16

Monday morning, my first day back at Aitkins after our return from Suffolk, proves hectic. I have no complaints about Sara nor James. During my absence, they have done great work, but, from the looks of relief on their faces, I can see how glad they are to have me back. There have been no major problems, but the line-managers, from two minor assembly units, have taken advantage of my absence to be somewhat difficult with Sara over her schedules.

Once I've listened to her tale of woe, I check and agree her calculations. Soon afterwards, the offending pair arrives at my office. Ten minutes later, chastened, they leave. I doubt they will cause trouble again. Harry drops in for a chat. He is full of praise for Sara's and James's work in my absence. He brings me up-to-date on Experimental. After a quick coffee, he leaves me to catch up on my paperwork.

In the days that follow, both within the company and on the streets, I become aware of an edgy atmosphere. Back from a stress-free holiday, I suppose the change is more noticeable. I doubt the public mood has deteriorated this much in my absence. This past year, I have been too absorbed with my own life to notice much outside my relationship with Fia, and work. How else could this undercurrent of resentment have failed to impinge on my consciousness?

This ill-will directs itself more towards people such as Harry. On a personal level, it bypasses me. PNU members are its main recipients - those who occupy key-roles within companies, or, in particular, are active in local politics. At work, although perceived as a company man, I have no links to state activities. Because the party withdrew my membership, it is impossible for me to become involved, even if

## CHAPTER 16

I wanted. Unlike many of my officious work colleagues, I tend to a more even-handed approach to my fellow-workers. In their eyes, this leaves me in a neutral position.

Now, with my mind attuned to the general mood around me, I take closer notice of my fellows. People seem more afraid than usual to voice their thoughts, to all but their most trusted of friends. As I have no close friendships, no-one confides in me, but I do overhear odd snippets of conversation. Had I a mind to report these, many of the speakers would be lucky to escape spells in re-education centres.

The halcyon days of JJ's dream have receded. No longer do we live in affluent times, those that pertained during the early years of the party's reign of power. Recession has affected economies worldwide. Britain, with its numerous forced-labour camps, can manufacture at cutback prices, but the global market for such products has shrunk. Elsewhere in the world, housing, food and energy bills cripple family budgets. UK wages no longer keep up with inflation.

Luxury goods are beyond the range of the average person. Of course, if you are a loyal party-member, you have access to an almost limitless supply of quality goods at marked-down prices. The gap between those who have and those who have nothing widens at a frightening pace. Rising unrest is the consequence - that and the increasing savagery in which the NSF is putting-down disturbances. It is reports of the latter that have led to international sanctions against Britain, which, in turn, exacerbate our economic woes.

The sense of foreboding Fia and I felt in Suffolk, we realise, was real. The country is on the turn against its masters. For now, the movement is in its infancy, but its spread will accelerate. Bloodier times are ahead. I wonder what part, if any, Joe plays in this rising antipathy. I would suspect he has mixed emotions. His people want unrest to spread, but a massive clampdown could prove counterproductive to their network. They are against anything that provokes the NSF too far, too soon. Only at a time of their choosing will the underground want the population to take to the streets.

Since our return, we have been too busy to visit Joe. This evening, Fia chats with him over the 'phone. She arranges for us to meet at the weekend. All day, at work, my shoulder has tingled. After a quick check with her electronic-device, Fia breaks the bad news. The implanted tracker is emitting a strong signal. The device is now charged and re-activated. What has happened to alter my status? From this moment on, we need to re-double our vigilance.

A thorough scan of the house, from top to bottom, proves negative. The needle of Fia's little machine remains static. The phone-line is next. The dial-tone is clear, no suspicious delays or clicks emanate from the receiver. We look at each other. For the moment, in our home, it seems we are secure, but for how much longer? Until we know more, we must continue as if nothing has changed. To do otherwise would draw suspicion our way.

☙ ❧

On Saturday, before dawn, we set off, rucksacks packed and boots freshly-waxed. In the dark we drive into the Dales, turn off at Buckden towards Hubberholme and the delightful Langstrothdale. We pass by the tiny hamlet of Yockenthwaite, with its stone cottages and single-arched bridge. Across the nearby riverbed, a stone circle, the kerbstones of a ring cairn, remain hidden as the greying pre-dawn light fails to penetrate the darkness.

Our headlights pick out the bridge at Deepdale where we cross the infant river Wharfe. After Oughtershaw, a steep ascent takes us to the summit of Fleet Moss, Yorkshire's highest pass. The sun rises. Shadows race across the fells. We make the long descent to Hawes and Wensleydale's mist-coated valley bottom, then we motor up Buttertubs Pass. The moors are alight in the rays of the morning sun. High on top the air is clear, our spirits high. We drop down to spectacular views of Swaledale and our walk to come. At the valley bottom, we head the last mile or two towards the car park at Muker.

## CHAPTER 16

With the village behind us, we walk through wildflower and buttercup filled meadows complete with their distinctive stone-walled field barns. Ahead of us flow the waters of the River Swale, our destination Keld. The early morning mist that swirls around the riverbed burns-off in the warmth of the rising sun. The vast range of greens and yellows in the landscape, are fresh and bright with spring's re-birth. Kisdon Hill stands proud to our left. We follow the course of the river towards Kisdon Gorge. In the fresh air, birds abound, their songs carrying on the breeze. In time we pass the ruins of Hartlakes (alleged to be the most haunted house in the dale), with the gap of Swinner Gill rising into the hills on the opposite side of the river. We enter woodland before a diversion takes us down to the falls, which lie within the gorge.

On our return, along the steep and narrow path, we rejoin our original route and continue towards Keld. Again, we divert down to the river, this time to view East Gill Force. Stretched out in the warming air, on a rocky outcrop near to the tumbling waters, we sample a sandwich. The breeze here is slight. Apart from a few sheep, chewing on grass and hoping for a dropped sandwich, we are alone. We have passed other walkers en-route, some with a nod and a smile, most with a cheery hello. No-one seems other than genuine. Outside of work, my shoulder no longer tingles. The wretched tracker inside remains live, transmitting my location. Fia confirmed this before we left home this morning. We have seen nothing to make us suspect we might have a tail.

On leaving Keld, for a brief period we follow the Thwaite road. At a footpath sign, we direct our boots onto the corpse road and Kisdon Hill. Over this route, as with similar ones throughout the country, people would carry their dead from areas without a church for burial in consecrated ground. To begin with, the ascent is steep. As the slope eases, we pass a farmhouse, to reach in time a green track that ascends between the crumbling remains of dry-stone walls. Fia grabs my hand.

"Don't look up," she warns, "but we appear to have a drone keeping track of us."

"I know," I acknowledge. "It's been flying around since we left Keld. I didn't want to worry you. How long before that, I don't know. There could have been one in the area for most of the morning."

Hand in hand, we clear the top of Kisdon. Swaledale opens out before us as we start our descent towards Muker. To the southwest, Lovely Seat and Great Shunner Fell straddle Buttertubs. Eastwards, behind and across the valley where we walked this morning, the expanse of Rogan's Seat, with the gaping cut of Swinner Gill, fills in the view. We descend to Muker, where refreshments are in order.

Outside a tearoom, at a table near to the road, we bask in the afternoon sun. Our accompanying drone has flown away. It disappeared when we were part way down Kisdon, at a sign marking the route of the Pennine Way. Whether the drone's absence is a good indicator remains open to interpretation. Without further information, speculation as to the reasons behind its presence earlier is fruitless. It could be paranoia on our part to think we were its target.

Mid-afternoon approaches; we have the best part of a three hour journey ahead of us. We are due to dine with Joe at seven, time enough to reach home and have a quick shower first. Our footsteps turn the corner onto the arched bridge, beyond which is the turn-off to the car park. A large, dark-coloured four-by-four accelerates down the road from the direction of Gunnerside. Without indicating, it ignores the sharp right-turn onto the bridge and continues into the car park. The vehicle's windows are tinted and, although we cannot see its registration, we know it will contain NSF personnel.

Fia grips my hand. Is it us they seek? With relief, I remember Fia's electronic device is at home. It would mean instant arrest if found with that in our possession. The occupants of the black car must have seen us. If they have come for us, we have little chance of escape. Should their interest lie elsewhere, it will arouse unnecessary suspicion if we turn back towards the village. We take a deep breath. All we can do is try to brazen it out. Our car is in a bay close to the entrance. As if we have no concerns in the world, we enter the car park.

## CHAPTER 16

The black SUV has pulled up further-on, obstructing the middle of the car park. Four tall, broad-shouldered men, dressed in black, walk in our direction. The plastic peaks on their dark service-caps glisten in the sun. For now, their guns remain holstered. We continue towards the back of our car. The indicators flash as I press the remote. The doors unlock. I give Fia's hand a re-assuring squeeze.

Engrossed in a discussion of the day's walk, we seem oblivious to our surroundings. Appearing to notice the approaching quartet for the first time, I nod towards them. Fia opens the hatchback. We take off our rucksacks and lay them in the boot. Three of the men stop behind an old white van, parked four vehicles away from us.

"Nice day," I observe.

"Seen worse," the fourth man admits as he approaches us. "Been walking?"

"Yes." Fia's glowing face is testament to her reply. "We went up as far as Keld, then came back over the top of Kisdon," she adds, pointing in the direction of the hill across the river.

"Was this van parked here when you arrived?" He indicates the vehicle beside his colleagues.

"No," I answer. "We pulled in soon after sunrise. Apart from a couple of cars over in the far corner, we were the first ones here. Is there a problem?"

"Nothing to worry you. The van is of interest to us. You didn't come across anyone acting strangely, during your walk?"

"No, a few fellow-walkers along the way, nothing out of the ordinary." Fia's brow furrows as if in concentration.

"That's fine. Don't let me detain you any longer. How far do you have to travel?"

"Back to Leeds," I tell him.

"Drive safely."

The man has already turned away, his attention waning at our lack of knowledge. One of his fellows has returned to their vehicle. He walks back with something metallic in his hand. The man, who had spoken to us moments ago, now holds a conversation on his mobile. He nods at the man with the metal bar. The sound of breaking glass comes from the van. Without delay, we swap our boots for trainers. I start the engine. With a final glance in the rear view mirror, I turn left at the exit to drive over the bridge. Within minutes, we are through Muker, and away. The security men ignored our departure. They were too busy wreaking havoc inside the van.

My legs feel weak and, at the side of me, Fia trembles.

"It looks as if the drone wasn't keeping an eye on us, after all," Fia concludes, as we climb towards the summit of Buttertubs. "Its operators must have been trying to spot the people from the van."

"Perhaps, although it was with us for a long time," I caution. "We'll see what Joe thinks about it. Don't forget, we promised to call at the creamery, to buy him some cheese."

"Oops! I'd forgotten about that. I prefer the fruited ones, but Joe likes the standard waxed cheese. We do have time, don't we, to sample the tasters?"

The change of conversation lightens our sombre mood. Soon the walk and the countryside become our main topics of conversation. I keep a watch in the rear view mirror, but no-one is on our tail. High above the valley, at a viewing point looking down towards Hawes, I pull into the side of the road. We stretch our legs. Instead of the views, we focus our attention on the heavens. No drones are visible, although from the direction of Swaledale comes the steady beat of a helicopter's rotors. I lean towards Fia's theory, the authorities were on the lookout for someone-else, this time.

That evening, over a roast dinner, we talk long to Joe about our week in Suffolk. I am sure the sheer weight of photos, transferred to my Laptop, bore him close to tears. While we eat, from the bushes set back from maturing borders, the setting sun casts lengthening shadows over close-clipped lawns. Joe's large, detached house is set in half an acre of well-stocked and cared for gardens. Well-stocked and cared for, that is, by the local gardener, whom Joe employs to do the work for him. I

## CHAPTER 16

am happy to say, his culinary skills are much superior to his gardening abilities. Later, after pudding, in the comfort of Joe's lounge, we steer the conversation onto matters more serious. Outside it is dark.

Neither Fia nor I mention our presentiments. In the relaxed ambience of Joe's house, such ideas would have sounded ridiculous. Instead, we tell him about the re-activation of the tracker in my back and the events of the day in Swaledale. We apprise him of the drone and the security forces in the car park. I mention the strange atmosphere I have experienced at work and elsewhere.

Joe nurses a large malt whisky. He is lost in thought. Fia and I, each with soft drinks, lie-back on a deep cushioned sofa. We struggle to keep awake. The meal, together with the walk and fresh air, has had a soporific effect.

"The people's anger you sense is real," Joe responds at last, his half empty glass of whisky cradled in his hand. "The authorities are under pressure. No hint of trouble makes it into the papers, but civil unrest is on the rise. Even in the southeast, the base of JJ's greatest support, acts of disobedience have risen. Whenever possible, our agents try to calm such incidents, but most are spontaneous, beyond anyone's control. Increased attention from the authorities is the last thing we want.

"As to the tracker, anyone who has a record with the NSF, and an implant, is to have their devices re-activated soon. I heard the news last week. It doesn't mean you've come under suspicion, yet. If unrest reaches a critical level, the authorities will clamp down hard. Those with implants will be among the first to come under stricter controls. While you were away, I imagine Harry's been instructed to have the equipment installed somewhere in your office.

"I doubt the drone was there to keep watch on you. Because you were in the vicinity, your implant would have shown on their satellite-tracking equipment. They would have observed, to see if you met up with anyone of importance to them. As far as you're aware, the occupants of the white van are unknown to you. The drone's cameras would have shown you to be at the locations where their observations said you should be. You did nothing to arouse their suspicions. I doubt they will check further. In many ways, this implant could be advantageous for you. If there is trouble, the authorities will be able to discount your involvement."

"They could be using me to find out about you, or to lead them to others in the underground," I suggest.

"Nothing has changed," Joe replies. "We keep our heads and continue as if nothing is wrong. For now, it might be better, Fia, if you stop your courier work. There are reports of drivers having their cars and belongings searched, even when their papers are in order. It's best, too, you leave your bug-detector here. If they catch you with that, they could arrest, interrogate and shoot you, before anyone could intercede on your behalf."

"The authorities must be twitchy," Fia says. She passes to Joe the device, which she collected on our return home. "I presume we work on the principle our homes, cars and workplaces have bugs installed. We say nothing incriminating, unless we're out in open country."

"Watch what you say, even out there," Joe says. "If there's a drone nearby, or you are anywhere where you can be observed, don't forget many members of the security-forces are taught to lip-read."

"Damn it! This way of life has become intolerable," I snap. "We cannot go on living like this for much longer."

Although he had assured us he had scanned the house earlier for listening devices and cameras, Joe proceeds to sweep the room again with his device. Fia and I glance at each other. Now what is the problem? He draws heavy curtains across the windows.

"It's all right, we're clear," he states with confidence. "Sorry, about that, I needed to be sure no-one can listen in. John is prowling outside. He will warn us if anyone approaches."

"What's this about, Uncle Joe?" A nervous tone has crept into Fia's voice. "Are we in danger?"

"No more than usual," he answers, "but there's something I think you should know."

## CHAPTER 16

The muscles in my neck tense. I doubt what it is we are about to hear will be good news. Fia moves closer. I put my arm round her.

"Go on," we urge.

# 17

Fia and I wait for Joe's disclosure, our minds no longer sluggish. Instead of an immediate start, he sips from his glass of whisky. He seems in no hurry to expand on his earlier statement. What is it we should know? Joe seems unaware of our impatience. He makes some alterations on his MP3 player, before he slots it back into its docking-station. Deep orchestral sounds, from a new playlist, blast from the speakers. With some haste, he adjusts the volume down to background levels. He clears his throat. After another sip, he starts to speak.

"Do you remember, six months ago, you told me about a special batch of mouldings going to a research establishment in Kent?" Joe asks me.

"Yes," I recall after a moment's thought, "samples for a company called Bio Research. You looked into the company. Nothing to worry about, you said. Don't they specialise in bovine-disease research?"

"Correct, that's the company. They have a purpose-built facility to the south of Rochester, near a town called Coxheath. The place is in the middle of a wood, surrounded by mines and an electrified perimeter-fence."

"That sounds nasty," Fia says. "Why do they need that amount of security for cattle-disease research?"

"The short answer is they don't," Joe answers. "The closest they come to a cow is to choose between skimmed and semi-skimmed milk in their coffee."

"What do they do?" I ask.

"Genetics and stem-cell work, combined with advanced research into miniature electronic devices."

"Where do the electronics fit in?" Fia wants to know.

## CHAPTER 17

"That's what puzzled us," Joe says, "until last week."

"What happened to change everything?" I ask.

"Let's go back to the beginning," Joe says. "When you first notified me about the delivery of parts and of what they consisted, I didn't consider the particulars of any importance. After a quick call to friends in the ministry, the information I gained I passed on to you. The mouldings were to form part of a laboratory-process involved in the manufacture of a new bovine TB vaccine. Laudable, I must admit.

"A couple of months after that, you sent some samples of fine, sterile, plastic moulded tubes to Zavrol Pharmaceutical in Bristol. Unlike their virus research-centres, this unit specialises in medical-delivery systems. Syringes, needles, drips and countless other ways of injecting medicines, plasma and anything else you can think of, into living tissue."

"I know the ones," I remember. "They've approved the samples and placed orders for delivery, starting next spring. I received instructions this week to prepare for the manufacture of twenty-million of the items, all for delivery before autumn next year. Something to do with a new influenza-vaccine the company is to test. It's a denser fluid. For an effective delivery, they require a special hypodermic. Our mouldings form part of that."

"Again," Joe continues, "everything sounds commendable. Now, what would you say if I told you these special hypodermics, when assembled with their other component parts, are to go to Bio Research instead of the vaccine manufacturing plant? To confuse matters further, the 'flu vaccine ampoules are also destined for Bio Research."

"But why?" we ask.

"Because, when people receive their 'flu vaccinations, those whom the great and good consider to be anti-government, or have the potential to be so, will receive something extra in their jab."

Alarmed, Fia interrupts. Her look of concern towards me, gives rise to anger in her voice.

"What are these people going to be injected with?" she asks. "Is Nathan going to be one of those who receive this special treatment?"

"As to Nathan, I cannot say, although it is possible. The sparse details we have about the product, we struggled to uncover. We did succeed in placing a low-level agent at Zavrol in their distribution department. Smokers who work in the vaccine department congregate outside the loading bay doors for cigarette breaks. They tend to gossip among themselves. Our man found a spot, where he could overhear their conversations without them realising.

"That's how he discovered the destination of the vaccine. Because Bio Research is a new name and destination for such preparations, he passed on the snippet to his underground handler, which made its way to me.

"This news provoked sufficient concern for us to send an agent to Coxheath. He was lucky. A deer stepped on a mine and blew itself up before he reached the danger area. The woods have cameras, and infrared sensors located in a grid pattern. Wearing reflective gear, he penetrated to within few hundred yards of the perimeter fence."

"So, what did he find out?" Fia asks.

"Nothing much beyond the high security levels which surround the place. He watched the area for a while. Live-wire warnings were visible along the perimeter fence, which has razor-wire along its top. Dog-patrols make regular passes along the inside. Once he'd seen everything he could, he slipped away to make his report."

"How were you able to find out what was going on inside the complex?" I am curious to know.

"It took some time, because we wanted to avoid drawing attention to our investigation, but we did have a breakthrough. One of our contacts, a lab technician in Birmingham, saw a vacancy advertised for a similar post at Bio Research. He applied and, after several interviews, they offered him the job.

"For several weeks we heard nothing. Their security, as we know, is tight. Most of the research-workers live in an adjacent compound. Visits outside are rare. After he'd feigned problems with toothache, their medical officer sent our man to visit a dentist in Coxheath. A

## CHAPTER 17

security officer shadowed him the entire time, but the dentist is one of our allies. It cost our man a tooth, but he was able leave a message at the surgery. The dentist passed on the details, which I received last week."

"Go on, please, tell us the bad news," Fia says.

She is on the edge of her seat.

"Bio Research has invented a revolutionary implant, one that is part-electronic and part-organic. It takes the one inside Nathan to a new level. As a tracking device, it performs much the same function as earlier ones, but that is where the similarity ends. Once injected via the special hypos, the stem-cells grow and become part of the body. They form tentacles that wrap themselves around the spinal-cord. Within thirty days, the process is complete and irreversible. Genetically enhanced, these cells are benign. The body shows no sign of rejection."

"How horrible," Fia gasps. "What's the purpose behind this thing?"

"Public-order control," Joe answers. "Each chip has a unique signature, which includes a doomsday-code."

"What happens if someone triggers the device?" I want to know.

"Imagine a riot taking place. There are hundreds, or even thousands of dissidents creating mayhem in the centre of Manchester, for instance," Joe says. "At present, the NSF would attend. Bloody street-fighting takes place. Damage to person and property is immense. Now, let's say, you arrive on the scene with your colleagues in the riot squad. You take out a cigarette-packet sized radio-device. Once you've selected a power level and radius strength, a simple press of a button does the rest. Within the designated area, anyone fitted with an implant falls to the ground, unable to co-ordinate their movements. For several hours, they judder like stranded fish. You call in a clean-up squad. They take the victims away for processing. It's unfortunate for those who have no involvement in the trouble, but, if they're lucky, they'll be able to prove their innocence."

"Yuk, that's awful! How does the device work, I mean what does it do to the people?" Fia asks.

"There are several settings in the chip. On its lowest, it transmits sufficient power, through the connections it has made round the spinal cord, to scramble signals to and from the brain. For a period, people lose control of their bodies. For mass control, this process works on the global doomsday coding. On higher settings, it can leave recipients, at best, paralysed for life. At the top of the range it kills.

"For large crowds, it's ideal. The lowest setting, once demonstrated, would put an immediate end to any resistance. Once those inclined to rebellion have witnessed the effects of the implant, few will risk the same happening to them. Unless they go against the authorities, there is no way of knowing whether someone has received a chip.

"With each chip registered against an individual, its unique number can be used to give the same results on a one-to-one basis. Follow the party line or face the consequences. There can be no hiding. At the press of a button, the government has the ability to stop, or kill, anyone in the country injected with the device."

Fia and I are silent. The ramifications of Joe's disclosure have shaken us. I feel certain, with my history, the authorities will include me in the programme. Fia, as my partner, will join me. Another thought occurs. Britain may lack international status now, but other countries would take a keen interest in such a device. Apart from nations such as North Korea, there are others, considered more enlightened, to which such a method of control might appeal. Initial use might be limited to known dissidents and lawbreakers, but, once its effectiveness became apparent, its application would spread wider and be less specific.

"Why are the authorities delaying the project until late next year?" I ask. "We have the capacity to manufacture the equipment by the end of this."

"It takes time to grow the cultures used in the implant," Joe explains. "The process is slow. Incorporation with the electronics to create what is, in effect, a living-chip is complex. There is need for a new satellite. It won't be ready for launch until next summer. Its design, specific to this operation, will give it nationwide coverage. Without it, the effectiveness of control is dependent on the range of local devices. With the satellite, a central command centre will be able to track anyone, anywhere, dispense immediate punishment to the individuals concerned or, if required, the masses, and in total secrecy. Using the cover of the 'flu vaccine, administered at the same time, the authorities hope to have everyone on their priority lists injected before the population becomes aware of anything untoward."

"Bloody hell, what a mess!" I say. "What can we do to stop it?"

"For the moment, nothing," Joe answers. "As far as we can ascertain, the original research, designs and cultures remain on site at Coxheath. Digital copies are on a server located on the other side of the Pennines, at a place you know, Nathan."

"The place they took me for questioning?"

"Yes. Since your visit, additional building work, complete and ongoing, will quadruple its size. It has become the main HQ for the NSF outside London, and *the* place selected to run the implant operation. Over the next year, installation of new computer and communications-systems will take place. Because of the sensitivity of the operation, its planning is on a need-to-know basis. Your old friend, Charles, has received a promotion. He is in control of the whole affair."

At the mention of Charles, I clench my hands. The anger of my betrayal by him has never faded.

"Ouch! Nathan, that hurts," Fia cries out.

"Sorry," I mumble as I realise I am crushing her hand, "Charles has that effect on me." I ease my grip and rub her fingers.

"This is serious. If the government sells-on the technology, it could affect the rest of the world," Fia says, echoing my thoughts. "Is it enough to stop it happening? No! Each part of the process, and the research behind it, must be eliminated."

"That'll be difficult," Joe says. For once, even he looks dispirited by the enormity of the task. "There's a new military base near Coxheath, built to provide back-up to the research centre in case of trouble. The NSF HQ is a fortress."

"Can't we pass the information out of the country? Isn't it our duty to warn Europe and the USA?" I ask. "There must be someone out there who can do something to put pressure on the government."

"Such as?" Joe shrugs. "Europe? They struggle to agree on anything. Would you trust the CIA with information like this? They'd want the technology for their own use and attempt to make a deal with the government. We have considered numerous options, but what could anyone do, even if they wanted to? Invade? We still have a nuclear deterrent. Our air and sea forces, would put up a determined defence.

"If we resorted to the nuclear option, our island would be destroyed in retaliation. If we didn't, an attacking force would concentrate on the destruction of our air defences. With those overwhelmed, we'd lose most of our infrastructure in bombing and missile attacks - all before a foreign boot landed on our soil. I have to agree with Fia's earlier comments. This project has to remain secret, no matter what the cost."

"Is it possible the Americans might have heard something?" I ask.

"Who knows? We expelled their people three years ago, when we caught them using their resources at Menwith Hill to spy on our government. The same applies to GCHQ. There is no American involvement there at all. It's probable they have agents established over here, but no longer do they have the ease of access they once had. This project is top-secret. We discovered it by luck, and through your information. I doubt foreign-agents have learned anything of value, yet, but anything is possible.

"Those involved in component-manufacture in what remains of Scotland's silicone glen," Joe continues, "have no idea into what products their chips go. As to your colleagues in the experimental unit at Aitkins, all they know is that the tubes they design are for a pharmaceutical company, well-known for its life-saving medical products. Other companies involved in the supply of components, are in the dark, too. Some companies' goods go to Zavrol, others to Bio Research, one or two to ghost companies, who ship them on.

## CHAPTER 17

"Apart from your old friend, Charles, I doubt if more than a couple of dozen people know the whole story. Those down the line, involved in any of the processes, hear the 'flu, or bovine vaccine story, dependent on what part of the project concerns them. The electronics company believe their order is for a standard communications satellite, while the components for the handsets that trigger the living cells, go to secret government factories for assembly."

For another half an hour or so, we mull over the possibilities. If Joe has any plans regarding the destruction of the project, he keeps them close to himself. The fewer the people who know, the safer it is for everyone. We both know the ways of the NSF - how they extract information from suspects.

The exertions of the day have caught-up with Fia. She stifles a yawn. We say our goodbyes. There is no sign of John. I have the impression that, unless he wants anyone to see him, he will remain hidden from all but the most skilful of watchers.

At home, exhausted, we head straight to bed and attempt to sleep. Despite my tiredness, it takes some time before my brain shuts down. Joe's words have unsettled me; they refuse to go away.

# 18

With a year to go before the government's 'immunisation programme' comes into being, any scraps of information I uncover are of potential significance to Joe. From a source in the capital, he learns that, towards the middle of next year, reports of an impending pandemic will make the headlines. This disinformation, although under embargo, will go to the heads of various media groups a few months beforehand. In secret, they will prepare for the official release-date. They will have no reason to doubt the available facts. For once, it will seem the Department of Health is on top of its job.

Publicity about this *new* virus, as intended, will create high-levels of anxiety among the population. There will be sensational comparisons made to the Spanish 'flu pandemic that afflicted the country after the First World War. Soon afterwards, the Department of Health will announce they have been aware of the problem for some time, and have produced a vaccine to combat the disease. Because of the severity of its predicted symptoms, the government will dictate that, unlike previous years, take-up of the vaccine will be compulsory. Neither will it be limited to those over sixty-five, those under five years of age or anyone with a relevant health problem. On this occasion, with the ability to produce the vaccine in large quantities, the immunisation programme will encompass the whole population.

Experimental create several new prototypes, intended for either Bio Research or Zavrol. Each one is of interest. Within the constraints of my security clearance, I do what I can to obtain details of the new designs. I add several other names to my watch-list - ghost companies that I think may have links to our main targets. This increases my

## CHAPTER 18

risk of discovery. If I ask too many questions, or someone sees me studying any of the open files I come across in Experimental, it will raise suspicion. A quiet word from them to Harry could prove fatal for my well-being.

Over the past few months, he has become much more relaxed and sociable towards me. A regular visitor to my office, he drops in for coffee and a chat. We talk about life in general, but, unless there is a problem, seldom is business a topic of conversation. He prefers to discuss my walks in the Dales with Fia. In his younger days, before work overwhelmed his free time, he used to indulge in much the same activity. He talks of walking holidays, in his youth, in France, Spain and Germany.

Whether this familiarity is genuine, I have no way of knowing. It may be a ruse to gain my trust, to find out in what, if any, nefarious activities I might be involved. My experience with Charles was a lesson well-learned. No matter how affable Harry may be, he remains a ranking officer in the NSF. Were he the party representative whom he purports to be then, too, it would be advisable to temper my words. His loyalties are to the government first, but, unlike Charles, I am not sure Harry would arrest his own family without the slightest qualm.

☙ ❧

After a mild and wet autumn, a period of cold and wintry weather arrives during the latter-half of December. I finish for the holidays at lunchtime on Christmas Eve. While others make for the pub, I head into town to meet Fia. Our main gifts for each other, long-since wrapped in shiny coloured-paper, are secure at home, but we have several last-minute purchases to make. We both pretend nonchalance about our own presents, but each has caught the other, squeezing and shaking their parcels in an attempt to discover the contents.

Inside a café, situated on the first floor of one of the major department stores, we sit over the dregs of our latte, and the crumbs of some indifferent cake. It is late afternoon, we have bags laden with food, Christmas crackers, and Joe's present, a new government-approved smart phone.

"Nathan, what's up?" Fia snaps her fingers in front of my face. "I've been talking to you for five minutes. Have you heard a word I've said?" she asks, as much in concern at my blank expression and watery eyes than in irritation.

With a start, I come back to the present. I blow my nose, in an attempt to hide a trickle of water from my cheek. "Sorry, I was miles away. What were you saying?"

Fia turns her head, to look out of the café towards where I have been staring. Her expression shows sudden understanding. She takes hold of my hands and holds them in hers.

"I'm sorry, Nathan," she says, "I shouldn't have brought you here."

"It's all right. There's no escape at this time of the year."

"That's no excuse. I try to imagine how this must affect you, but I doubt if I can come close to it," she says, indicating the shopping-floor outside the café entrance.

Rows of shelves stretch into the distance, many half-empty. These bear the last of the store's selection of children's toys and electronic games. The storerooms are empty; everything unsold is now on display. Among the streamers and tinsel, fairy-lights flash and flicker, lighting up the expectant faces of excited children.

"I'm all right," I say, although it is apparent the opposite holds true.

"How old are they now?" Fia asks, keeping a tight hold on my hands.

"Ian will be ten, Caroline eight," I sigh. "Stupid, isn't it. After all these years, I don't even know if I would recognise them, or they me. I keep hoping they're happy and cared for, wherever they may be."

We finish our drinks. It is too public here to discuss this matter further. Who knows who might be watching or listening? An hour later, we return home.

The temperature has been below zero for most of the day, but has risen over the last hour. A fine snow is settling. We take advantage of

## CHAPTER 18

the conditions to stroll through the local park, to admire the beauty of the white-coated landscape. Under the light of the street lamps, children race around, throw snowballs or make snowmen. Anxious parents keep an eye on the younger ones. The temperature rises a little, the flakes become larger. Away from home and the ever-present concerns of potential listening devices, we are able to talk without constraint. No-one pays any attention to us. It is too dark for our conversation to be lip-read from any distance.

"I know Joe hasn't given up on your children," Fia says to me. "He's under a great deal of pressure with work and this immunisation problem, but he does keep putting out feelers for information."

"I know, but it's bloody frustrating. Where the hell are they?"

"We don't know," Fia says, holding onto me, to give me encouragement and to stop her from sliding on the slippery footpath. "Joe has told us everything he's discovered. We know, after your arrest, Ian and Caroline arrived the same night at a children's home near Northallerton. They were there for three nights, before a man and a woman from the NSF arrived. Each wore a long coat, with its collar turned-up. Neither of the couple removed their peaked caps, which left their faces in shadow for the whole length of their visit. None of the staff at the home can give an adequate description. The transfer papers were in order; the pair took custody of Ian and Caroline. That was the last time anyone can confirm their whereabouts."

"That couple could have taken them to their deaths," I say, my mood dark. I find it difficult to remain positive.

"Don't say that," Fia's reprimand is sharp. "Don't even go there. There's no record of that. We know the NSF, for some reason, has put a restriction on information relating to your children's removal. The one fact, of which we can be sure, is that no entry for them exists on any adoption lists. Joe searched them for us and found nothing."

"I know; that's what worries me. My solicitor showed me copies of the adoption papers. Why is there no record? I appreciate your efforts to cheer me up, but I fear something must have happened to them."

"I don't believe that. We *will* find them and we *will* fetch them back."

Fia's face is fierce, her eyes blaze. She faces me now, and shakes me by the lapels. I nod. She relaxes.

"We will find them," she whispers as she puts her arms round me and gives me a hug, "we will."

Splat! A snowball hits me on the back of the head. I release Fia, to scoop up a handful of snow. Within moments, we are at the centre of a snowball-fight with a group of youngsters. Later, with honours even, we head for home. This brief interlude has lifted my spirits and made me laugh. I cannot forget my son and daughter, I think of them each day, but for now, I have my fears back under control.

Christmas-day starts earlier for me than has been usual these past few years. Fia, in a return to childhood, is awake long before dawn. After much pushing, shoving and elbowing in the ribs, I give up and admit I am awake. I leave our warm bed and go downstairs to make a pot of tea. Sitting cross-legged on the sheets, with several unopened presents beside her, Fia awaits my return. To be fair, half of those she has brought from the spare room are mine. Her eyes sparkle. She runs her fingers through her tousled hair. I have never been more in love with her. After a quick sip from her cup, she places it on the bedside cabinet. She passes me a parcel.

"Go on," she says, "open it. Don't hang around."

She is already stripping paper from the one she has selected, the largest of them - a present from me. I open mine. It is a new DSLR camera. I hug her in delight. Fia soon pulls away, to tear away the last of the paper from her present. Revealed is the heavy woollen, dark-blue coat she wants. She throws her arms round my neck and kisses me. Seconds later, she models it in front of the full-length mirror on her wardrobe door. With a puzzled look on her face, she pulls out a small package from one of the pockets.

Curious, she looks towards me, but I keep my face expressionless. Uncertain to what she may find, she opens the package to reveal a leather box.

## CHAPTER 18

"Please don't open it yet," I say, "bring it here."

She hands it to me. I drop to one knee. With the lid opened, I turn the box round so that she can see its contents. Her mouth drops open. She looks stunned.

"Fia McFadden," I say. "Please, will you do me the honour of being my wife?"

Silence. Fia's face registers shock. For a moment, I fear I have made a huge error of judgement. She takes hold of the ring case and looks long at its contents. Tears form in her eyes, she smiles, her face lights up and she throws herself at me. Sometime later, lying among the pile of presents and the empty wrapping paper on the bed, we break apart. I realise Fia has yet to give me an answer to my proposal, but I am sure I can take it as accepted. She is at my side, wearing nothing but a huge smile and a diamond ring on the third finger of her left hand.

"Yes," she says, belatedly. "Yes, yes, yes."

We soon open the rest of our presents, which, apart from to each other, are sparse. I have a couple of small gifts from work. A bottle of some reasonable aftershave from Sara; from James, a book I had mentioned a while back at work. Fia has fared better than have I. She has a bundle of shop-wrapped gifts. Most appear to be glass bottles, filled with either whisky or brandy, which we put to one side for Joe. We keep a couple of bottles of quality wine for ourselves. It is Christmas; work is ten days away. If I suffer a wine-induced migraine, I can sleep it off next day.

Earlier, when I made the drinks, I had turned on the oven. The smell of roasting turkey wafts upstairs. It is time to dress and go downstairs. The vegetables need preparing and the table setting. Joe will join us at noon, for dinner at one o'clock. He is to stay over tonight. Without the hassle of having to drive, I am sure some of Fia's Christmas bottles will soon have their contents sampled.

Joe arrives on time and, true to expectations, within minutes he has a glass of Oban, fourteen-year-old, single malt whisky in his hand. It may be a new one to him, but, from the look of contentment on his face, I expect the level in the bottle to have dropped much lower by evening. Much to Fia's frustration, although she flashes her ring whenever an opportunity arises, Joe seems oblivious to her attempts to attract his attention. Without warning, he dashes outside to his car. Moments later, he returns wearing a pair of sunglasses. Fia stares at him in amazement.

"Come here," he says to her, laughing, "let me have a closer look at this giant rock on your hand, now I can see it without going blind."

Fia sticks her tongue out at him, but is at his side in seconds, wafting the ring in front of his face. Joe takes hold of her hand, to steady it. He takes a good look. With a broad smile, he turns to me.

"Congratulations! Congratulations to you both." He hugs Fia, then offers his hand to me."

Joe disappears into the kitchen. After a loud popping sound, he returns. With him, he carries glasses of Bollinger champagne, poured from a bottle he brought with him.

"I intended saving this for later in the day," he says, "but, what better time than now to crack open the bottle? Good health and happiness to you both."

We clink glasses. Fia and I stand arm in arm. Joe takes several photos of us with his phone's camera, including a selfie with us all pulling silly faces. A similar series of photos, Joe repeats later, when he has worked-out how to use the camera on his new mobile. Fia has received a beautiful silver pendant, I a pair of 10x42 binoculars, something I will use when Fia and I go walking.

Soon afterwards, Joe checks the house with his electronic-device. We have remained free from bugs. We have no need to watch our words. JJ gives his annual Christmas message on the television. The main members of the Royal Family withdrew co-operation with the government, once they realised the severity of the treatment suffered by their subjects. Those in power responded by re-locating them to Balmoral Castle, in effect, placing them under house-arrest. International pressure caused the regime to release them. Within

## CHAPTER 18

weeks, the Royals voluntarily went into exile in Canada. Since then, JJ has taken-over the monarch's afternoon spot on Christmas day TV.

Most of the nation watches the speech. It is compulsory, more than compulsive, viewing. With the aid of digital television and add-on boxes, details of programmes watched nationwide, and by whom, register on a central database. Any family who misses JJ's speech receives a visit from a compliance officer, and a fine. To think, this man I once worshipped. How could I have fallen under the spell of his words? It is patent to me now how false they are. Lies flow without effort from his tongue. The man has turned from a charismatic champion of the people into a creepy charlatan. Knowing we are free from surveillance, we delight in dissecting the 'great' man's speech and ridiculing its content.

After a short afternoon nap, Fia and I leave Joe with his whisky and go for a walk in the park again. The air is raw, the wind light but bitter. Yesterday's snow is a memory. Overnight, the temperature rose. By this afternoon, the ground, apart from lumps of white, where snowmen had once stood, is clear. Rosy-cheeked and refreshed by the exercise, we return. We eat cold turkey sandwiches and delve into packets of mixed-fruit and nuts. We finish with a large slice of Christmas cake each, and wedges of Wensleydale cheese. The bottle of champagne lies empty. We play childish games and, by nine o'clock, we are asleep in front of the television.

Joe stays with us until the day after Boxing Day. Now, we study the weather forecast. The following morning has a better-than-expected prospect of sunny periods, with a front moving in for late afternoon.

After a good night's sleep, we rise at dawn. By lunchtime, in the beautiful Washburn valley, we have walked round the edges of Fewston and Swinsty reservoirs. On the way home, we divert to a local village where we find the inn's doors are open. Lunches are on the menu. After the amount of rich food we have eaten these past couple of days, we crave something simpler. Hungry, we ignore the Christmas menu and order beer-battered haddock, with hand-cut chips and garden peas. I look round at a room filled with happy, smiling faces, the words, *peace on earth, goodwill toward men,* comes to mind – I wish that could be true. I should send JJ a memo to remind him!

# 19

If we become active participants, or find ourselves implicated, in any way, with Joe's plans to sabotage the immunisation program, our chances of surviving the summer are low. Because of this long-term uncertainty, Fia and I decide against any delay in our wedding plans. We arrange a quiet spring ceremony.

On the first Friday in April, at 12.00 noon, we assemble at the side of Leeds Town Hall. Our wedding party, apart from Fia and I, consists of Joe, with Harry, Sara and James from Aitkins, and a couple of girls from Fia's office, Adele and Rosaline. I cannot say Harry was someone who came first to mind as a guest, but he has been generous in authorising time away from work for me to make arrangements. He had expressed a desire to attend. Because our guest-list was short, and we had no wish to antagonise, we included him.

Fia spends the night before the ceremony at Joe's house. I have yet to see her in her wedding dress. Joe, determined we enjoy the day, has hired a chauffeur-driven car for the event, and afterwards. Bedecked with white ribbons, a sleek black Mercedes pulls up at the side of the Town Hall. A man, in a freshly-pressed uniform and peaked-cap, steps from the vehicle. Joe walks round the car. The chauffeur opens the kerbside door. Fia, her face alight, accepts Joes offered hand.

I am lost for words. To my eyes, Fia is perfection. She wears a knee-length ivory coloured wedding-dress. There are gasps from the women in our party. Comments about A-lines and princess-scoops are a mystery to me. I can appreciate it is simple, satin and lacy, but the finer technical details are beyond my knowledge to appreciate fully. Her hair is half-up with braids and twists. Again, I have the women standing behind me to thank for the details. All I care about is that she is Fia, the love of my life, soon to be my bride; to me, the most beautiful woman in the world.

With Fia on Joe's arm, we enter the registry office. We have booked the Fredrick Suite. The ceremony is brief. We say our vows. I kiss the bride. Joe and Harry act as witnesses. We are man and wife. I walk on air; Fia is radiant. Outside, the Mercedes has moved to park in front of the building. While we pose for innumerable photographs on the Town Hall steps, a parking-enforcement officer walks towards the vehicle. The driver remains unmoved by the approaching threat. The officer takes out her book. She is about to write a ticket when she spots a notice on the windscreen. With a look of disappointment, she puts away the tools of her trade, salutes then walks on.

"Before I followed you into the Town Hall, I slipped a priority parking-permit to the driver," Harry whispers in my ear. "Nobody will challenge one of those."

Nearby, in the private-room of an Italian restaurant, off the Headrow, we hold our reception. Garuda, Sara's fiancé, joins us. Sara has dressed for the occasion in traditional Indian dress, instead of the business-suit she wears for work. Her gold, satin Sari sparkles in the restaurant lights. James's girlfriend, Leila, arrives soon afterwards. He introduces her to everyone. As is he, she is of Caribbean descent; her accent that of Leeds. Nervous in the company of strangers, she stays close to James's side. Their relationship is in its early stages, but they seem enamoured with each other. Fia's friends from work, Adele and Rosaline, are a couple. Our party is complete.

Champagne flows; waiters open wine bottles. The food is delightful. The room resounds with talk and laughter. After a little wine, Leila loses some of her shyness and joins in with the merriment. Joe makes a speech, I make a speech, even Fia insists on saying a few words. There are a few tears at the mention of Fia's parents and her brother Sean, and sadness on my part at similar references to my parents. The mood soon passes; nothing can spoil our day.

## CHAPTER 19

By seven o'clock, the party breaks up. Our guests, including Joe and Harry, are to head into town, first to a bar before they end the evening at a nightclub. How they can cope with the amount of alcohol they have consumed, and yet want more, is beyond me. I cannot drink those quantities. Fia and I have had sufficient for us to be happy, but remain steady on our feet. As is usual, after a drink, Fia is prone to fits of giggles. Our guests escort us out through the main restaurant. Diners turn, stare and smile.

The Mercedes awaits us, parked on double yellow lines with impunity. The driver, with grateful thanks, hands back the permit to Harry. Both he and Joe have ordered taxis for later in the evening, so, in style, Fia and I return to our marital home. In the fading light, our immediate neighbours spot our arrival. They rush out to cover us in confetti. They applaud my success in carrying Fia over the threshold, without dropping her or tripping. I take Fia in my arms as the door closes on our audience.

It is the middle of the following morning before we rise. We were late to sleep last night. With our bags ready to be loaded into Fia's car, we are in no hurry. Our honeymoon hotel does not expect us until three o'clock at the earliest. We have chosen a location in Borrowdale, Cumbria, a little over two-and-a-half hour's drive from home. At our leisure, we take the A65 past Settle and Kirkby Lonsdale to cross the Pennines. The sky is overcast, the countryside drab in the dull light. Occasional patches of drizzle smear the windscreen. We by-pass Kendal and follow the A591 into the Lake District. At Windermere, we break our journey, to walk for a short while beside the waters. At a café, with a gloomy view over the lake, we drink coffee.

Staying on the same road, we drive through Ambleside, on to Rydal Water and the edge of Grasmere. Dark skies remain with us; we run into a band of rain. Low grey cloud shrouds the sharply-etched mountaintops. Mist rolls down into the valleys. When a sudden deluge hits us, the wipers struggle to cope. With dipped headlamps, we drive on. No matter how heavy the rain, it fails to dampen our spirits. The mist thickens. Through the billowing miasma, we catch occasional glimpses of Thirlmere as we drive past.

The narrow streets of Keswick are awash. We head through the town to take the Borrowdale Road. Across Derwent Water, the undulating ridge of Cat Bells is invisible in the cloud, as is, beyond Keswick, all but the lower reaches of Skiddaw. Taking the narrow route beside the lake, we head for our hotel at the southern end of the waters. The winding road is, in parts, cut from the hard volcanic rock that built this spectacular valley. We pull into the hotel car park. The clock on the dashboard registers four-thirty. What a relief it is to switch-off the wipers. The downpour has faded to an annoying drizzle, but the sky remains heavy. More showers look imminent.

Our hotel is everything for which we could wish. The honeymoon suite is lavish, the en-suite opulent, its whirlpool spa-bath and double walk-in shower are things to which we could become accustomed. A bottle of champagne awaits us in our room. The realisation that, after the hectic planning and arranging of the past couple of months, we are now man and wife hits us. For the moment, we leave our luggage and open the champagne. Fia sits on my knee and snuggles close. From the comfort of one of the easy chairs, we look out onto the misty landscape. We are content.

That evening, after a candle-lit dinner, we take a torch and step outside for some fresh air. The rain has passed, the clouds have lifted and, away from the hotel lights, darkness is complete. We switch-off our beam and look up. Living in an urban area, light-pollution draws a veil over the glory of the heavens. Out here, the sky glows with a myriad of stars; even the line of the Milky Way becomes visible, as our eyes become accustomed to the dark.

Morning brings with it skies of blue. We have arranged an early breakfast. This sets the pattern for our week. The weather is kind to us, although, this being the Lake District, it comes with the occasional shower. I have yet to visit without at least one day of rain to break-up the stay. Although we are keen Dale's walkers, neither of us knows

## CHAPTER 19

well the Lakeland fells. We leave the higher, more strenuous routes to those who do. We are here to relax in a gentler fashion.

Traffic at this time of year is much lighter than it will be within a couple of months. We take advantage and tour the narrow winding roads in comfort, drive over mountain passes, walk beside lakes, and take a trip down a slate mine. Life is good. Fresh air, excellent food and a daily dose of some of the finest views in England (outside of Yorkshire that is), refresh our spirits. From the waterfront jetty at Keswick, near the oft-photographed rowing-boats that line the beach, we take a boat trip round Derwent Water. The air is still, with little more than the boat's wake to ruffle the water's mirrored surface. The reflections of Cat Bells and Skiddaw are near perfect.

Friday, our final full day, dawns much too soon. We wake to bright sunshine and a light frost. After a hearty breakfast, we drive towards the village car park at Rosthwaite. We pull on our boots. With rucksacks on our backs, we stride-out along the flat valley bottom, towards the steep-sided lower Stonethwaite Valley. Across the beck, smoke rises from the chimney of a white-painted cottage.

Once inside the valley, all is silent. Ahead, rugged Eagle Crag dominates the view. High to our right above Base Brown, the fells of Green Gable lead on to Lingmell. The sun rises higher. The frost burns off in the warming air. We are in no hurry. Wherever the terrain allows, we walk hand-in-hand. For much of the time we walk in silence, the scenery speaks for us.

The numerous sparkling falls of Galleny Force are behind us as we take the footbridge over Greenup Gill, above its confluence with Langstrath Beck. From here, our path leads us away from Stonethwaite and, beneath the large cliffs of Heron Crags, we stroll into Langstrathdale. There are neither houses nor roads here in this deserted area. Apart from the sound of the breeze, running-water and the occasional bleat from one of the groups of white-faced Herdwick sheep, nothing but our footsteps disturb the silence. We follow the footpath deep into the valley.

The stream widens. For a while, we rest beside the shallow waters. We watch as they flow among the scattered pale-coloured stones and boulders. Downstream, steep valley sides, with their ragged crags, draw the eye back through the gap toward the serrated top of Stonethwaite valley. The green of the grass surrounding our route blends with the browner valley-sides and areas of bracken. We rejoin the path to follow it until we approach the end of the valley, the halfway mark of our walk. Below the union of Snake and Langstrath becks, we cross a footbridge, to find a rock on which to sit and eat our lunch.

For an hour we stay. At peace, we feed each other cherry tomatoes and grapes, provided by the hotel as part of our packed lunch. With the increasing lack of foreign imports, how they obtained either at this time of year is a mystery. It is time to move on. I pack our scraps. Fia starts to fidget.

"Nathan, do you remember when we visited Keswick?" she asks.

Her voice is hesitant. She takes hold of my hand.

"Yes," I say.

"I stopped at a chemist, to buy some paracetamol, while you went-on to look in the Outdoor Clothing store."

I nod, puzzled by the direction of her words.

"I bought something else," she confesses.

"Why, what did you want?"

"I bought something for a test."

"A test? What type of test... Oh! That test!"

"Yes. I used it this morning. Erm! You're going to be a father again."

Fia, although overjoyed, is unsure what my reaction might be. We have discussed the subject of starting a family, but, with the vaccination programme and its associated dangers looming, we had decided to wait until the crisis was over, before trying. For a second or two I am unable to articulate an answer. Fia's face takes on a worried look. A sudden, up-swell of joy unties my tongue. I stand, grab hold of Fia, lift her high, and swing her round. Laughing, I put her back onto the ground.

## CHAPTER 19

"I don't believe it, how, when?" I ask, my delight impossible to conceal.

"I planned our wedding so that it wouldn't fall at the wrong time of the month," she explains. "When I missed last month, I thought it was stress. When nothing happened again this month, I kept thinking, it would be like me to be late and it fall on our honeymoon, but it didn't. For a few days now, too, I have felt sick at times. I thought I ought to check. It must have happened when we went away for that long weekend in February. You're not upset, are you?" her eyes are large, her anxiety high.

"A little shell-shocked," I say, grinning like a fool, "but nothing could make me happier. Come here." I add, taking her in my arms.

With thoughts bouncing round my head, we start our return journey. A foot caught in a dip brings me down to earth with a thud. Uninjured, apart from pride, the fall concentrates my mind on negotiating the pathway. The ground is uneven, while isolated boulders rise up from the grassy surface. The terrain deserves my full attention.

The distance travelled has been moderate, but we have made frequent stops, to sit, admire the view and talk. It is the middle of the afternoon. On this side of the valley, parts of our route are in shade. Our fleeces, which earlier we stored in our rucksacks, we bring back into use. Near the lower end of the valley, we return to full sunlight. On the opposite side of the beck, Heron and Eagle Crags bathe in a warm yellow glow. There is a chill feel to the air. We increase our pace. Without a cloud in the sky, we need no forecaster to tell us a frost is due again tonight.

With bracken bordering the edge of the stream, we turn left into the confines of Stonethwaite Valley. The path takes us down the valley, with Galleny Force visible through the trees. The valley broadens out as we approach Stonethwaite. Once through the village, we turn right, before crossing its bridge to re-join our outward path and return to Rosthwaite. We are weary, more from the time spent in the fresh-air than from the miles under our boots. It has been an idyllic ending to our honeymoon, with the knowledge of parenthood to come, the icing on the wedding-cake.

By ten o'clock next morning, we are on the road. Soon after daybreak, dark clouds have swept in. The earlier frost has gone, almost as soon as it appeared. The cloud-base lowers, the peaks disappear. A fine drizzle turns to heavy rain. Now, there are three of us to consider. With headlights and wipers on, I slow our pace. I am still a little in shock. Fia is radiant.

As on the journey north, we stop for a drink in Windermere. Trade must be slow. The waitress remembers us. She asks if we want the same again. Amused, we say "Yes." At a window table, we sip our coffees. In comfort, warm and dry, we watch the pounding rain as it bounces off tarmac and splashes into the surface of the lake. A ferry emerges from the wreathing mist to dock at the jetty; the opposite side of the mere is lost to view.

In the downpour that precedes us, the Pennine hills are bleaker than ever until, a few miles after Settle, the clouds lift and lighten. By the time we reach the Addingham bypass, we drive under the edge of the cold-front, with blue skies and bright sunshine ahead.

The economic downturn has left Ilkley with a greater number of 'To Let' signs in the shops than I remember. With the Cow and Calf rocks behind us, across the valley Otley Chevin is resplendent in the afternoon sunlight. Further away, the pimple of the Wharfe valley, Almscliffe Crags stands proud. We drop down through Menston, re-join the main-road and head for home.

Fia opens the front door. She heads inside to put the kettle on, while I pile our luggage in the hallway. We can empty our bags later.

"Fia, are you in the kitchen?" I call, as I shut the front door.

Silence! The whole house is still. I wander into the kitchen. The kettle stands cold and empty. There is a draught from the back door, which is open. I step outside.

"Fia," I shout.

There is no sign of her in the garden. Puzzled I return inside. I suppose she could have gone to the bathroom. In the hallway, I call out her name, still no response. I run upstairs. The rooms are empty.

## CHAPTER 19

"Come on Fia, this isn't funny," I grumble in frustration.

Where the hell is she? I descend the stairs, two at a time and, almost at a run, I enter the lounge. As I open the door, I hear the sound of an engine revving. From the window, I see Fia, struggling with two men in peaked-caps. They drag her from the side of the house, towards a dark-coloured car. Its back door is wide open. Panicked, I run into the hallway and turn towards the door. Tyres squeal as the car outside races away.

Bang. In the confined space, the noise is deafening. A picture beside my head explodes in a shower of splinters and broken glass. With blood pouring down my face from several embedded shards, I turn round.

"Good afternoon Mr Andrews, I cannot tell you how much of a pleasure it is to meet you again," says a voice.

Despite the ringing in my ears, the rich tones I remember all too well from down the years. The uniformed owner of the voice stands at the kitchen door. Hazy smoke spirals from his service-automatic. He moves his arm and aims the gun at a point between my eyes.

"What's this about, Johnson?" I say - my heart pounds.

A tightness round my chest grows by the second.

"Where the hell are you taking my wife?"

# 20

Johnson laughs. The sound, which matches his personality, is far from pleasant. I take a step towards him. His finger tightens on the trigger. I stop. He eases some of the pressure.

"Please, do be careful, Mr Andrews, we wouldn't want any accidents, now, would we? My instructions are to bring you and your wife in, unharmed, unless..." He raises his eyebrows and leaves the sentence open.

I shake my head. At this moment, I can think of several accidents I would love to see happen to Johnson. Getting me killed will be of no help to Fia. What has happened to bring this upon us? On honeymoon, apart from a text to tell Joe we had arrived in Cumbria, we have been out of touch with the world - no television, no newspapers, no radio.

Joe! He must be the source of the problem. What has he done? It must be something serious to bring the NSF back into my life. Why didn't he warn us, so that we could escape? Fia's relationship to Joe has to be the reason for her arrest. I pray there is still room for me to manoeuvre, to initiate her release. Somehow, I have to make our captors believe Fia and I are ignorant of any wrongdoing by Joe. I must be careful that no-one misconstrues anything I say.

"Don't have much luck with your women, do you?" Johnson sneers. "Your first wife is shot for treason. Now your second is helping us with our enquiries. To have problems with one spouse is unfortunate, for the same to happen with another gives rise to certain questions. Either your judgement of women is poor, or there is something more sinister going on with your motives. Such a delightful house you have, too. It would be a pity if you were to lose this, as you did the one in Sheffield."

## CHAPTER 20

Steeling myself, I succeed in bringing my anger under control, and calm a rising sense of panic. Under the circumstances, I make my expression as least threatening as I am able. When he realises his provocation has failed to provoke any reaction, a look of disappointment crosses Johnson's face. This time, there will be no charge of assaulting a member of the security force.

"Why have you arrested my wife?" I ask, keeping my voice firm and steady. "We returned from honeymoon less than half an hour ago. We've done nothing wrong. I demand to know where you've taken her. There has to be some mistake, an error somewhere. She's been in the Lake District with me for the whole of last week."

"Sorry, I'm not at liberty to disclose anything." Johnson's smirk shows the depth of his remorse. "If it were my choice, both of you would be under arrest, but that decision is for others to make. Your old friend, Charles, has expressed a desire to renew your acquaintance. So, if you would be good enough to step outside, now, please."

I have no survivable alternative. Johnson's gun remains steady. My position is hopeless. Either I go as a willing guest, or Johnson's people drag me outside, wounded and bloody. I doubt he intends to put a bullet through my head, but, I have equal confidence, he could place a non-fatal shot elsewhere about my body before I could reach him. As if to leave home at gunpoint is the most natural thing in the world, with a half-smile, I step round the pile of abandoned luggage.

"There will be no need to lock the door." Johnson snatches my keys before I can stop him. "My men will be making a search of the property. I'll take care of these for you."

"Tell the bastards to tidy-up afterwards," I snarl. "As I recall, they have no respect for private property."

I take a deep breath and change tack. I ask, "How is Charles?"

"Charles is well. We shall have to see if the same applies to you, once you two have had a chat."

Outside, an officer stands guard, the gun in her hand angled towards the ground. Any attempt to make a run for it - she could shoot me before I reached the road. Another dark-coloured car pulls up at the end of my driveway. It kills any vague hope of escape I might have. The back door of the vehicle swings open. An NSF officer steps out.

"After you, Mr Andrews," Johnson speaks in my ear.

He hands my keys to the officer at the door.

"Keep going, straight ahead into the back seat. It would upset the neighbours if we had to shoot you during an attempted escape."

I look around. None of my neighbours is in sight. No-one with sense wants to become involved. To my surprise, my hands are still free. Inside the back of the car, flanked by two officers, I gaze through the tinted windows to take a last look at my home. Will I live to see it again? Of much greater importance, will Fia and our unborn child live to see it? Johnson heaves himself onto the front seat, next to the driver. He slams the door. How can it be possible to go from the pinnacle of happiness to the nadir of despair in twenty-four hours?

Our route takes us into Leeds, towards the football ground. Dozens of regular police are on duty. Crowds pour out of Elland Road. The roundabout nearby has come to a standstill. I wonder who won. The driver blasts his siren several times without result. We come to a halt. Johnson opens his window. One flash of his identity badge and a police escort guides us through the crowds onto the slip road, where we speed, westbound, onto the motorway.

The siren comes on again. Match-day traffic opens up for us. We pick up speed. Once on the M62, we speed past Bradford, take the Halifax turn-off, to head towards Hebden Bridge before we cross over to the other side of the Pennines. After a couple of miles on the M65, we turn onto winding side-roads. In the evening light, I recognise where we are. My body turns cold. I shiver. With some effort of will, I push back a dreadful feeling of nausea, and the black memories from when I last travelled this way.

Dark clouds cover the Lancashire skies. In the gloom we approach a barrier, placed before the entrance gates to a tree-lined drive. Ahead of us stands the NSF HQ. Since my last visit, a grey, two-storey concrete

## CHAPTER 20

and armoured glass-gatehouse has replaced the old brick one. The ugly dark grey construction flanks each side of the entrance, connected by a covered walkway over the gates. A large sign, attached to the walkway, reads *Mangnall Hall, NSF Head Quarters 6th Group*. If nothing more, I learn the name of the place.

Spaced at two-hundred metre intervals or so, along the perimeter of the grounds, watchtowers face outwards. Behind a barrier of barbed wire connecting these is a three-metre high, wire-mesh fence. Lit along its whole length, it carries large yellow signs, warning of electrification. Armed guards patrol the inside. High above them, on top of poles, CCTV cameras swivel in random movements. From inside the gatehouse, through a firing-slit in one of the bleak concrete walls, the barrel of a light-machine gun points in our direction. An armed sentry comes into view. He walks towards us. Johnson opens his window, to show his badge and credentials.

"Myself, three other officers and a guest for Charles Thomas," Johnson says.

He hands a sheaf of papers to the sentry who examines them. With the car doors open, the guard compares the passengers and driver with the photos on their identity documents. For a moment, he studies my civilian ID card before handing it back.

"Everything's in order, Sir." The sentry's tone is deferential to Johnson. "Good to see you back with us. I understand your visit today is unofficial. There will be no record made of your stay." With a salute, he turns towards the building behind him. "Let the major's party through, George," he calls out.

The unseen hand of George presses a button somewhere inside; the entrance barrier lifts, the gates swing open. Through the windscreen, the illuminated, original facade of the four-storey, stone-built country-house grows large as we approach. As I know from my previous incarceration, apart from the shell, nothing remains of the original building. The once grand, elaborate interior, the Philistines from the NSF have gutted and re-built. From here, there is no sign of the extensive building-work underway to accommodate the new implant-control-and-tracking centre. I suspect that takes place at the rear of the old hall.

Our car drops us at the bottom of a flight of balustraded stone steps. While the driver parks the vehicle, Johnson climbs the stairs to the main entrance. With my two security guards flanking me, I follow. Our leader speaks into a panel built into the door-surround. At a command, he lays his ID card on a flat-screen beneath. A beam of green light scans the sealed plastic rectangle. A soft beep sounds, followed by a clicking noise. The double doors swing inwards. Our driver arrives to bring up the rear. I enter the building, which has become the sum of all my fears. I am back where nightmares begin.

The entrance-hall is large, the ceiling high. The furniture is sparse and oversized. Its design's main purpose is to intimidate, to make a suspect feel small and insignificant. Knowing this brings no relief from its effects. Again, I fight back the nausea. My legs are weak and my throat is dry. The recent upturn in my fortunes has reversed. I have no need of a clairvoyant to predict my future! This time, I am better prepared; my resistance will be much greater. Will this be enough to save Fia? In my heart, I fear today will have no positive ending.

"This way, Mr Andrews, if you please," Johnson says.

Our footsteps echo inside the almost empty chamber. I follow him through a doorway into a long corridor lit by harsh, bright lighting. Since my last visit, the building's interior has seen much structural alteration. We continue through a maze of corridors, stairways and ramped walkways. Each office we pass is empty and silent. At this time on a Saturday, most staff will have left.

A few minutes later, we arrive in a comfortable reception room. It has several easy-chairs, arranged in a symmetrical pattern around a low table. Chilled-water and hot-drinks dispensers stand nearby. In front of one wall stands a veneered hardwood-desk, complete with monitor and keyboard. The mesh trays on either side overflow with folders in various colours. A dark-red, high-backed office-chair is empty.

## CHAPTER 20

Reproduction, or so I believe them to be, impressionist paintings hang on the cream-coloured walls. On a mahogany-panelled door, next to the desk, a gilded sign bears the legend *Colonel Charles Thomas*.

Joe was right; my nemesis has risen in the ranks. I wonder how many bodies it takes to achieve a promotion to colonel - ten, fifty, a hundred, maybe even a thousand. Johnson raps on the door twice. He opens it then steps inside. One of my escorts gives me a none too gentle shove. I stumble through the doorway, followed by Johnson. The door closes. My escorts remain on the other side.

The first person I see, strapped to a chair at one side of the room, is Fia. Her face is white and fearful. A tough-looking, grizzle-haired woman in a white coat stands behind her. Fia's tear-stained face shows no marks of violence. For now, to my relief, she seems unharmed. A strip of pale adhesive tape covers her mouth. At the sight of me, the initial look of relief turns to one of warning. She struggles, until the woman behind produces a syringe and threatens to inject her with its contents.

The colonel, Charles, sits at his desk, his face smug. Johnson stays behind, to guard the door. I sense another presence in the room. Whoever that might be, they are lost in the shadows on the periphery of my vision. This must be the one against whom Fia has tried to warn. I force myself to focus ahead. I have no desire to give the impression of a trapped animal, casting furtive looks round for a way out - no matter how true this may be.

"Ah! Good evening, Nathan, do come and sit down." Charles indicates a chair in front of his desk.

I obey. It would be foolish to do otherwise. For Johnson to compel me to sit, at gunpoint, would be demeaning and, psychologically, put me at a greater disadvantage.

"Oh, dear me, Nathan, what have we been up to now? I thought you might have learned your lesson, after your last visit here."

"Nothing," I say, "I've done nothing, and neither has Fia. Release her, now."

The figure in the shadows moves further out of my line of sight. Footsteps sound on the polished parquet floor. They halt behind me.

"Now, now, Nathan, we both know that's a lie."

The voice is so well known to me, it takes me by surprise. Now I understand the warning in Fia's eyes. In shock, I turn my head and look into the face of someone I have come to know, like and trust.

"You, bastard," I say, my voice choked with anger.

# 21

My attempt to rise ends in failure when someone else moves over to stand behind me. Johnson's powerful hands slam me back into the chair. The cold barrel of his gun pushes hard into the back of my head.

"Tut, tut, Nathan, such language, and I thought we were such good friends, too," Joe remonstrates.

He comes to stand to the front and to one side of me. His face wears its usual charming mask. This man has reeled me in, netted and landed me straight at Charles's feet. What of Fia? Could she be involved? I refuse to believe it. Joe might be a duplicitous wretch, but his niece? No! With some effort, I relax my muscles. Johnson lifts his gun. He moves to a position where, without fear of hitting the others, he can keep me within his line-of-fire. Joe smiles, his face one of benevolent concern. I notice he keeps his body out of range of my feet. Charles's look of self-satisfaction has deepened. I am a mouse, trapped between vipers. Which will be the first to strike?

Charles presses a button on his desk, to summon the guards from the reception-area. After a few, swift instructions, the pair carry Fia, still strapped into her chair, and drop her beside me. The guards leave the room. Without thought, I reach across to squeeze her hand in encouragement. I snatch mine away, as Johnson raps my knuckles with the side of his automatic.

"How touching." Charles cannot keep the derision out of his voice. "Our newly-weds, so much in love! You can remove the tape from her mouth now, Johnson," he commands.

Keeping out of my reach, Johnson takes hold of a corner of the adhesive tape. He rips away the fabric. Fia cries out in pain. I make a move towards her. This time, the tap from Johnson's gun strikes the back of my head. I wince.

"If you can't keep still," Joe says to me, "I'll have you tied to your seat."

"You bloody traitor," I spit out. My voice cracks with anger.

"Oh! Don't be a bloody hypocrite, Nathan." Charles is enjoying himself. "You've been up to your eyes in treachery for the last couple of years, at least. We can thank Mr McFadden, here, that your success rate has been zero. I cannot tell you how much I look forward to our sessions in the interrogation room…and those with your sweet wife," he adds, after a slight pause.

Charles's threats are far from subtle. What I do realise is, he has addressed Joe as Mr McFadden! No first name terms here. Neither has Charles used an unadorned 'McFadden', as he would to an inferior. This surprises me. It would seem Joe ranks higher than that of an associate. By the tone of voice and deference paid to him, it seems dear 'Uncle' has risen to the heights in the party, the NSF or both.

"That's enough, Charles. I hope to obtain my answers without resort to such primitive means of encouragement. To begin with, *I* shall do the talking to our young friends," Joe's voice is sharp.

The words are an order, not a request. They confirm my suspicions. He outranks Charles.

Charles's "Yes, Sir," carries no trace of sarcasm. With a smirk, he sits back to watch what happens.

"Charles shows great dedication to his work," Joe continues, "but his methods of extracting information are somewhat limited. He blinkers his mind to other, less barbarous but more effective approaches."

"How can you do this to us?" Fia asks, too upset to understand the significance of Joe's words. "I trusted you," she shouts at him, "I thought of you more a friend than an uncle."

"You're like your bloody father, Fia. He was a daydreamer, too. A weak man, he allowed your wretched brother to distract him from his work and his ambitions. It would have been better if Sean had died at birth. To be fair, I did try to keep you out of trouble, but you would

## CHAPTER 21

interfere. To complicate matters further, you fall in love with Nathan, someone whose loyalty to the state is more than questionable."

"But you worshipped Sean, you joined the underground to seek revenge for him." Her anger is palpable.

"Hah! I'm sorry to have to disappoint you," Joe laughs, "and to dispel any illusions you might have about that. I've never been a member of the underground. The meeting, you interrupted, was with several of my area-handlers, those who run my undercover agents. I concocted the story I gave you, to keep you out of trouble. You caused me enough embarrassment when you attempted to find out what happened to your brother."

By now, Joe is pacing in front of the desk.

"Once Sean was removed, I thought your father would return to Sandiman's to immerse himself in his work again, but no! Whenever he did bother to show up, his mind was elsewhere. After your mother died, (and that I do regret) he was useless. I had to maintain my cover, and everything that involved, while managing my clients and most of your father's. After he died, life became much easier. I was able to take on new staff, loyal to me, and to re-arrange my workload. Once rid of your father's commitments, I could devote myself to my real work. Sandiman's provides an excellent front for me. It allows me to travel anywhere in the country, anytime, without comment. Your father remained unaware of my activities up to his death."

"It was *you*. You arranged for Sean to be taken away and murdered." Choked with emotion, the horror in Fia's voice is evident. Another awful thought occurs to her. "Did you kill my daddy, too?" she asks, hesitation in her voice.

I listen, my mind struggling to accept the revelations.

"No, I didn't kill your father." Joe looks affronted by the question. "He had a heart attack after I told him he was redundant. I'd carried him for long enough; he was no longer a valuable asset to the business. As to Sean, for as long as he lived, he would have been a drain on the state, and of your parent's time."

Joe's face remains expressionless. Everything is matter of fact, without empathy in his words. Deceit comes natural to him. Fia sobs at my side. Throughout her life, Uncle Joe has been her hero. To have her belief shattered in this way goes beyond cruelty. I stir in my chair; Johnson taps me on the head. I cannot comfort her.

"I don't understand," Fia flares, "you were furious when you told me about Sean. Was that a lie, too, and the burning of that place in Scotland?"

"No, that's true, in the main. I was angry when I returned from Scotland, but Sean's connection was incidental. The reason for my visit was to oversee the completion of the Highlands removal-programme. I told you it was a holiday to keep you quiet. Everything went well, until that damned drunk of a caretaker burned down the place, with him inside. He didn't require any assistance. At the same time, he incinerated the collated records of half the removal programme, and a couple of my team who had stayed late to finish some work. That was the reason for my extended absence and anger. It took weeks to bring together again the different area-information, to enable us to re-construct the database.

"Telling you what had happened to Sean was a mistake. I didn't realise the effect it would have on you. I thought, once you knew he'd died, it would be enough to stop you from making further enquiries. Bloody hell, his death was painless. There was no suffering involved," he adds, as if that makes everything all right and absolves him from any blame.

With a cold chill, I realise Joe cannot see a problem. There is no room for compassion in his world. I risk a quick glance at Fia. The look in her eye, I have never seen; it is fortunate for her well-being, her restraints prevent her from moving. Otherwise, I fear, she would have flown at Joe, and received a bullet for her efforts.

"After you burst in on my meeting I had to do something," Joe explains, oblivious to his niece's reaction. "You were a loose rocket, fired up, ready to fly in any direction and do something stupid. So, while John kept you in the kitchen, I invented my role as a senior member of the

## CHAPTER 21

underground. While you thought you played a useful part, I controlled everything you did."

"What were those messages and packages I carried for you?" Fia demands to know.

Joe continues to pace along the front of the desk. Behind it, Charles fidgets. His patience wears thin. Why waste time with chitchat? He wants to set his tormentors loose on Fia and me; but Joe is in command. His ego demands everyone knows the extent of his cleverness.

"Those! They were orders for my people on the ground, and their handlers. I cleared those journeys with the area commanders. You were in no danger. Instead of furthering the resistance, everything you did worked against their cause." Joe laughs at this huge joke against Fia. "The one time I did give you a worthwhile assignment, you screwed-up. The idea was for you to become Nathan's handler, not his flaming mistress, although, in retrospect, it did turn out for the best. It meant I could keep an eye on both of you, simultaneously."

"Where do I fit in?" I ask, trying to divert attention from Fia. She has suffered enough.

"Ah! Yes, you, Nathan. Twice now, sex has brought about your downfall. Although, it wasn't a lapse of moral judgement by you that caused your original trouble, was it Charles?" he snarls at his subordinate behind the desk.

Charles shuffles in his chair. He glares at Joe, who ignores his discomfort.

"On second thoughts, Nathan, you must share some of the blame. It was you who introduced Charles to Julie, at a party conference I believe. From the start, there was a serious attraction between them. Later, while you were away on business, or at work, they spent a great deal of time together. To provide cover for their clandestine meetings, Charles recruited her into the service as an agent. I'm told she tried to infiltrate the local underground, but they were too suspicious."

"I can't believe how stupid you were." Charles, unable to restrain his contempt, indulges in a little provocation. "Did it not occur to you

157

to question the discrepancies between Julie's support for everything you did for the state, and her calculated disloyal comments about the party? She used to practise those on you, before she went on missions to meet with dissidents. We used to laugh about it in bed, your bed."

"Shut up, Charles, you're not helping." Joe glares at him.

"What's he talking about? Julie and Charles weren't lovers." I turn to Joe in disbelief. "That cheapskate excuse for a man tortured her. He shot her as a traitor. I watched her die on the lawn outside this office."

Charles's face carries a wicked smile. He presses another button on his desk. To his left, in a deep alcove, a door swings open. Silhouetted by the bright lights behind her, a female officer walks into the room. With her head down, under the intense light of the LED spotlights her face remains shaded by the peak of her cap. She wears the uniform of a senior officer - grey shirt with epaulettes, dark-green trousers and leather boots. Unlike standard, off-the-peg officer's clothes, these are expensive, tailor-made items; they fit to perfection.

The woman walks up to Charles. Her touch on his shoulder is affectionate. She turns in my direction, then removes her cap. Blond hair bounces onto her shoulders. The colour is new to me, but the face that stares at me is one of which I remember every detail.

"Hello, Nathan," Julie says. "I cannot say it's a huge pleasure to see you again, but your new wife, isn't she pretty? I'm going to enjoy getting to know her."

I attempt to stand, but a blow to the back the head knocks me to the ground. Stunned for a moment, I splutter as water splashes onto my face. Johnson's rough hands drag me up. They sit me back in my chair. Fia struggles against her bindings. At a warning look from me, she calms down.

"That merits a charge of attempted assault against a member of the security forces," Charles says in delight.

"I've already told you, Charles, keep your damned mouth shut," Joe shouts. He bangs a fist on the desk. "When I want your input, I'll tell you. Most of this is your bloody fault. What a pity you lacked the moral

## CHAPTER 21

courage to take Nathan's wife from him without subterfuge, instead of inventing the stupid charade you pulled-back then. To make him believe he was responsible for her death with your staged-execution, then to discredit him afterwards, in the manner you did, to cover your tracks, was a disgrace. Nathan was a valuable asset to the party. His recent work has proved that. At the time, had it become known, a court-martial would have been mandatory."

"It wasn't Charles's idea," Julie admits. "It was mine. I was having no success in my attempts to infiltrate the locals. I'd grown tired of listening to Nathan's tales of woe. He'd no stamina for the harsh treatment needed against industrial saboteurs. *I* was the one who carried him through his dark moods. He cannot cope with the realities of life, unlike Charles. He's a real man."

I am unable to speak. Shock has robbed me of my tongue. With my head ringing, I sit and listen.

"You don't know a real man when you see one," Fia whispers. The level of antagonism in her tone I understand. She senses a rival.

Julie ignores the interruption. "I worked out a long-term plan. I put it to Charles that, if the state took everything from Nathan, when we set him loose his situation would drive him towards the underground. The first part went well. After we implanted a chip in his back, to monitor his movements, we sat-back and waited, and waited. We waited some more, but you," she addresses me directly, "you did nothing, did you, you spineless sod.

"Over time, we tried to provoke you. We kept you in a dead-end job, under constant and evident surveillance, pushed you hard, but did you re-act? Did you hell! You didn't even spot your tails, even though, to avoid any awkward questions about funding, most were recruits on training exercises. You didn't even try to find your children. Since you've settled in Leeds, all you've done is try to ingratiate yourself back into the system.

"We expected you to seek retribution and, in doing so, lead us to some useful members of the underground, but nothing came of that.

In the end, we gave up. We allowed your tracker's power to run down. Under questioning, you were quick enough to betray me, you bastard. It's apparent the same lack of courage prevented you from seeking revenge. It took Mr McFadden, here, to learn about our operation and approach you, before you showed any spirit." She looks at me, as a snake might its prey. "I wonder how long you'll last this time, before you betray your new wife?"

"Never," I find my tongue. "I thought you dead, so nothing I said could hurt you. I had the children to consider."

Julie gazes into my face. Despite being at the other side of the desk, what she sees makes her take a step backwards.

"Your resistance may be higher, now," she admits, "but it'll be fun to see how long you hold-out, once we start work on, erm, Fia isn't it?"

Johnson's hands yank me back into my chair. This woman is a stranger to the one I thought I once knew. Was she ever that person? Only Johnson's powerful arms stop me from breaking her neck.

"That's enough. Stop riling him," exasperation has sharpened Joe's voice. "As for you," he points towards me. "Another attempt to move and I *will* have you bound and gagged."

Julie's face flushes with anger. I doubt many people dismiss her in such a cavalier way, but, like Charles, she lacks the nerve to disobey Joe.

"There's going to be no ill-treatment of anyone, unless I say so," Joe's voice has risen. "I have no preference either way, but I want answers, now, rather than in two days time when you've reduced them to pulp. They'll admit to anything after that, true or false."

"That's nice," I say, my voice heavy with sarcasm. "I suppose, now, you're going to tell me my marriage to Fia is a sham, seeing that *she*," I indicate Julie, "is still alive."

I cannot bring myself to call her by name. What she and Charles have done to me over the years, the true awfulness of it, begins to register with me. Could this be the final twist? I can envisage no remorse on their behalf, nothing but sadistic satisfaction at their handiwork.

## CHAPTER 21

"No, your marriage is legal," Joe confirms, much to my relief. "You can rest happy in the knowledge that, when you die, it will be as man and wife. I did confirm before your wedding. When you were here the first time, you signed dozens of papers to ensure your release. In among them were your divorce papers and others, relinquishing custody of your children. You were in shock. After the first couple of sheets, you stopped reading them. Charles tells me you signed everything and anything they told you to."

"That's right Nathan, the kids are mine, you've no claim to them," Julie cannot resist the jibe.

Joe turns and, in a flash, leans across the desk. The crack, as he slaps Julie hard across the face, resounds around the room. The blow sends her spinning into the wall. She leans against the wooden panels to steady herself, blood trickling from her lips. Charles sits, tight-lipped. He knows better than to intervene. With exaggerated slowness, she returns to his side, but remains silent. Julie licks the blood from her lips. She smiles, as if in enjoyment of the pain.

In the moments of silence that follow, I take the opportunity to study my resurrected ex-wife. For many years, I shared my life with this woman. She bore my children. I had loved her above anything in the world. This person I had thought dead, shot in front of my eyes. Compared to what else is going on around me, I suppose the shock of Julie's re-appearance has been less debilitating than it might have otherwise been.

Her physical appearance differs little, apart from the change of hairstyle and colour. Her face has altered most. It is thinner, meaner; the softness, I remember from our years together, has gone. Julie appears to have embraced the NSF and its ideology, as well as its colonel, with open arms. Fia has nothing to fear in respect to any feelings I might still harbour for Julie. She has killed them, and any fond memories I might have retained.

What worries me most is Joe. I am at a loss to know what he wants. For over a year, in the guise of an underground leader, he has run me as an agent inside Aitkins. He knows everything I have learned in the course of my daily work. I am sure, from his position within the party, this was information of which he was already aware. I have been away for a week. In that time, I have had no contact with work, nor with anyone who may have some connection to it. What has happened to turn Joe from someone, whose intention was to protect his niece and, by association, me, from causing him political embarrassment, into someone who wants our blood?

Johnson eases the pressure on me. He stands back. This allows me to settle in my chair. I master sufficient courage to risk another blow, by asking the question:

"So, *why* are we here?" I ask. "We've been acting under your instructions. All I have done is provide you with information you already knew. Fia has carried messages to your undercover agents. So, why arrest us now? Why risk the shame of having family members named as traitors? Any convictions will reflect ill on you."

"That's the problem," Joe says. "While I thought you were harmless, I was happy to maintain the status quo. To be honest, it amused me. What I now want to know, does that still hold true? At Aitkins, we are aware of an active mole. Harry, although unaware of the immunisation programme, became involved in the hunt for him, her, a couple of years ago. We have studied everyone on the workforce, their records, history and home-life to the nth degree. We have moved people around; dismissed some, interrogated others, but still the leaks kept occurring. After you joined the company, Nathan, from the beginning Harry wanted to promote you; he recognised your talents, but Charles forbade it.

"In frustration, Harry mentioned the matter to me, along with what little he knew about Charles's operation with you. Harry was unaware of the deceit involved. That was the first inkling I had about Charles's unauthorised activity. Until then, I had no reason to doubt the stories I'd heard about you. I wasn't even aware Charles's wife was your ex. I brought him in. It didn't take long to extract the whole story. Instead of putting him before a military tribunal, I determined I could make use of someone such as you. I decided to recruit you, to join Fia in my imaginary *underground* cell."

"Why?"

"Little is known about the underground's hierarchy. We have detained activists and saboteurs, interrogated them, but they have scant knowledge as to who runs them. We have evidence there are several autonomous groups that function in a loose alliance. Each runs its own operations. It is rare for them to allow their work to overlap. Because they pool their results, they avoid the risks competition could bring them. To communicate, they use a network, routed through foreign satellites and servers, over which we have no control. No matter how many transmissions we jam, some go through. When possible, we attempt to trace a link, but they are online for only short periods before operators change areas and computers.

"Nathan has no expertise in spying. He's bright and, without doubt, a genius in his field of work. To a practised eye, however, his attempts to obtain information are something an experienced agent would detect. With the national importance attached to the factory's current output, I thought the real mole would soon realise he had competition. I expected him or her to attempt to warn-off Nathan. The long-term infiltrator would resist any attempts by an amateur who could draw attention to the areas that concern him. A slim chance, I know, but we had tried everything else.

"There was also the possibility the mole might attempt to discredit Nathan, to have him dismissed. Another alternative they had was to kill or incapacitate Nathan. That was an acceptable risk. Either of those actions could have led us to our traitor."

"Oh! Thank you," I say. "That's nice to know, but nobody has said, or done anything on those lines. Nothing you've said so far explains why Fia and I are here."

"Last night," Joe explains, "Bio Research suffered an attack by a group of saboteurs. A series of explosions, and the subsequent fires, destroyed the main building, research Labs, offices and storerooms. Several scientists and senior lab technicians have disappeared. Despite a large manhunt, the culprits have yet to be apprehended."

"So your immunisation programme has been set back," I say with a feeling of hope, "or was that another lie?"

"Don't be naïve, Nathan," Joe snorts in disgust. "The programme does exist, but it was never at Coxheath. Everything you send to Bio Research, unless for their own use, they tranship. All that happened was that someone destroyed an excellent bovine research-facility. Did you think I would tell you the location of the actual establishment employed by the scheme? The problem I have is that no-one, apart from you, Fia and I knew about the fictitious research at Coxheath. Even Charles and Julie were in ignorance of that part of the story.

"So, Nathan, I want the names of anyone to whom you might, by accident, have mentioned Coxheath. Of course, you could be an agent for the underground and, as such, succeeded in blind-siding us for years. I have one other possibility - one that finds my dear, sweet niece proving to be much more devious, than I give her credit."

"Apart from you, and with each other, we've not discussed the programme with anyone," I protest.

A cold chill has descended on me. If true, this creates a serious problem. I have no answers. Nothing comes to mind that could prove my innocence. Charles and Julie could torture me, or Fia, for days without learning anything. In the end, they can force us to confess to anything. This might satisfy the need for a scapegoat, but cannot answer the fundamental question, 'who is the original mole'?

For a moment, neither sound nor movement disturbs the room while everyone assimilates what Joe has said. Charles looks as surprised, as does everyone else. Whatever he expected my crime to be, it was different from this. Not that he cares. He wants to vent his jealousy at Julie's first love. If he can, he will destroy Fia, and, in doing so, me. Into the silence, the sound of Joe's mobile rings out. Angered by the interruption, he snatches the device from his pocket.

## CHAPTER 21

"Yes, McFadden here. What do you want? I'm in a meeting."

Muffled sounds come from the direction of Joe's 'phone. He nods several times, and, apart from a few grunts says nothing until the end of the call.

"WHAT!" he yells into the mobile. "Don't wait. Set off now. I want you here as soon as possible. Bring Harry, but leave Sara in custody for now. You can release her later, once we've decided on her innocence."

"What's wrong?" Charles asks.

"You'll find out soon enough," Joe says. "Johnson, untie my niece, then take these two downstairs. Give them something to eat and drink, but put them in separate rooms. Under no circumstances, allow them to talk to each other."

Charles looks at Julie. He winks and they both smile with satisfaction. Joe catches the exchange out of the corner of his eye.

"If anything happens to them," he says to the pair, "a court-martial will be the least of your problems, do you understand? Johnson, if either of these two approaches the detention area, shoot them."

Johnson pauses a moment from cutting Fia free, to nod. He might be Charles's right-hand man, but Johnson knows who has ultimate authority here. For a few hours, Fia and I appear to be safe. With her bindings removed, I help Fia to her feet. We embrace. Johnson moves to stop me, but Joe waves him away.

"Let him help her, Johnson, but remember, no talking. Do you two understand?" he demands of us.

We nod our agreement. Because of the tightness of Fia's bindings, her legs are stiff and painful. With my arm around her in support, Johnson escorts us through the doorway Julie had used to make her entrance. At the side of the box-room we enter, a lift-door stands open. Behind us, Joe's voice booms out, his dismissal of Charles and Julie peremptory.

"Go on, get out of my sight," he shouts at them. "I have work to do. If anyone's still at their desk make sure they leave now. It's Saturday evening, there shouldn't be many people left in the building. Those on duty in the communications centre won't interfere. Their unit's self-contained; they don't change shift until eight in the morning. The last thing I want is for news of this mess to become common-knowledge. It was bad enough having to cover-up for you two, but our involvement in the loss of a multi-million pound research-facility will take some ingenuity to conceal. We have to find the mole, and now."

What has happened, I have no idea. Neither do I know who was at the other end of the 'phone, nor what Sara's involvement might be. I assume it is Sara from work whom Joe mentioned. For now, the pressure has eased from Fia and me. For that, I am grateful. With one last hug and a quick kiss, I leave Fia in her detention room. I allow Johnson to escort me to mine, his aggression, for once, in abeyance. There are no other guards down here, nor sounds from the other cells. Charles must be running short of victims. Within half an hour, Johnson returns, with an offering of plastic-wrapped sandwiches and large cartons of coffee for his prisoners. He tempers his generosity by turning out the lights. On our own, in the darkness we eat his excuse for a meal.

# 22

To my relief, after a lengthy period, during which my thoughts sway between negative and positive outcomes, my mind switches off. On the narrow cot, I slip into a troubled sleep. I wake with a start. Light blazes into my eyes from the anti-ligature, shatterproof light-fittings in my three-metre-square room. It seems the authorities have a disliking for prisoners escaping execution by hanging themselves, or slitting their wrists on broken glass.

Down here, without external view, I have no knowledge of time, nor of how long I have slept. On the way here my escort confiscated my watch and my mobile. Until my eyes become accustomed to the brightness, I shade them against the glare coming from the stark white-painted walls and ceiling. From my previous time here, I have no problem identifying the various stains on the walls and floors.

My first thoughts are for Fia and our unborn child. I pray, after her rough treatment, they have suffered no permanent harm. Whether from the cool air, shock, or both, I find myself shivering. There are no blankets on the bed to keep me warm. I draw up my knees and wrap my arms round them, in a vain attempt to keep warm.

My suffering is short. In the distance, I hear the sound of high-security electro-magnetic fail-safe bolts sliding into their holding sockets. A couple of minutes later, those on my cell slam back. The door swings open. Johnson is standing outside.

"Come on, out," he orders, his voice neutral in tone.

I step outside. Fia rushes into my arms. To feel her body wrapped against mine I feared might never happen again. I dread for this to be the last time. She, too, is icy cold. In a rare moment of compassion,

Johnson walks towards another, empty cell, to re-emerge with a pair of blankets.

"Here, take these," he says, throwing them towards me.

Through chattering teeth, we thank him as we wrap them round our shoulders.

"Follow me," Johnson says, ignoring our gratitude.

I take Fia's hand. We follow him down a sterile white corridor, towards the lift in which we had descended earlier.

"Are you all right?" I whisper into Fia's ear. "The baby?"

"Yes, everything's okay." She keeps her voice low to prevent Johnson from overhearing.

I take a close look at Fia. Her face is drawn and pale. She looks ill.

"Are you sure?" I murmur.

Fia nods, although it is apparent she is otherwise. At the lift, Johnson turns, impatient at our slow progress. We keep quiet while we shuffle into the tiny box. After a swift ascent of several floors, we come to a rapid halt. On our previous ride, I was in no state to appreciate the depth to which we had descended. I wonder how many more subterranean-levels this building conceals.

Johnson pushes open the door into Charles's office. He ushers us inside. Here, the temperature must be ten degrees warmer than it was in our cells. This time, Joe is the one behind the desk. To his right, perched on two uncomfortable plastic chairs, are Charles and Julie, minus their arrogant expressions. Whatever Joe has said in our absence, it appears to have been a painful experience for them. Our chairs are where we left them. Joe indicates we re-occupy them. Fia keeps a tight hold of my hand. Without warning, she lets go. She reaches for a nearby bin. For a short while, she retches into it.

"What's up with her?" Joe glares at Johnson, his tone accusing. "I told you to leave them alone."

"I've not touched them," Johnson protests, indignant at the accusation. "I kept watch, as you said. No-one else came down. They've had a coffee, sandwiches but nothing else."

## CHAPTER 22

Julie watches me, as I help Fia, still clutching hold of the bin, to her chair. My ex-wife has a strange expression on her face. In sudden understanding, she speaks, a tinge of jealousy in her voice.

"I know what's wrong with the bitch. She's pregnant. Nathan's going to be a daddy again, aren't you? How long, a couple of months?"

Fia nods. For once, Joe is the one to look startled. We had intended telling him over dinner tomorrow, or today as I suspect it might be now. Somehow, no matter what direction our future takes, I doubt we shall share any more cosy meals with Uncle Joe. He shakes his head.

"This whole mess becomes worse by the hour," he groans in despair.

For several minutes, we sit. Joe studies an open file on the desk. Apart from the rustle of his papers, the room is silent. A loud knock sounds, in the direction of reception.

"Come in," Joe yells.

Fia makes use of her bin again. Johnson takes a step further away from her as the door opens. Harry and John walk in. Under his arm, Harry carries what appears to be my work's laptop.

"What's wrong with Fia?" Harry asks on seeing her, head in bin.

He is the only one to have shown any real concern. John's expression, as usual, remains neutral. It is rare for him to show any sign of emotion, good or bad.

"She's pregnant," Johnson explains.

He looks with distaste at his shoe, which carries signs of being too near the bin.

"Congratulations," Harry says, his reaction genuine.

"Oh! What the hell?" Joe is impatient. "That's immaterial. What I need to know is what you and John have discovered."

The newcomers place a couple chairs, near to me, away from Fia. She removes her head from the bin. Although still white-faced, she looks a little better. Joe beckons everyone to move closer. Harry puts the laptop onto the green leather desktop.

"It was John who made the first discovery," Harry starts. "During the search of Nathan and Fia's house, he came across a device, hidden inside the vent for their kitchen extractor-fan. The apparatus had wires connecting to the fan's power supply. The equipment uses technology new to us. What is a worry is it fails to register on our scanners. John called in an electronics expert. He says it's a relay transmitter, designed to boost signals from a short-range bug. He and John searched everywhere, but could find nothing. John 'phoned me. I met the two of them at Aitkins.

"Because the original device didn't register on our detectors, we dismantled Nathan's office. We found similar equipment wired into the lighting-circuit, behind one of the tiles in his suspended ceiling."

"How far do you think these devices can transmit?" Joe asks, as, on the desk, John places two tiny plastic boxes, wires hanging loose.

"Without further testing, our man cannot be sure, but he estimates a range anywhere up to five miles."

"Where did you find the bug?" Joe asks.

"Inside Nathan's laptop. The expert noticed a couple of tiny scratches beside one of the screw holes in its base. He took the machine apart."

"Show me," Joe says.

Harry produces a precision-screwdriver. He turns-over the laptop. Taking care, he removes a couple of the re-fitted screws. With the back off, he points to a tiny box with several loose wires attached, nestling against the battery compartment.

"Two of the wires connect to the battery, the others to the internal circuitry," Harry explains.

"What does the thing do?" Joe asks.

"It's a mini-recorder and transmitter. As with the main relay transmitter, it's untraceable by our detectors. Our expert says, once installed, its drain on the battery would be negligible. The device connects to the machine's built-in microphone. Noise-activated, it records everything within a few metres distance. Nathan's laptop uploads the recordings whenever it comes in range of one of the relays. It sends a signal back, to wipe clean the flash-drive in the laptop."

"How long has it been operational?" Joe wants to know.

## CHAPTER 22

"We know the device in Nathan's laptop, and the relay in his office, have been there for about six weeks. When, and who installed the equipment inside Nathan's house, we don't know, but we assume the object has been there for a similar length of time."

Joe turns to me for a moment. "Nathan, any ideas?"

"We had problems with the line about that time," I recall. "An engineer arranged to come and fix the problem. We left a key with a neighbour. She said he was in the house for no longer than twenty minutes, before he returned the key to her. The 'phone worked all right after that."

"Is that enough time, Harry?" Joe asks.

"It's a bit tight, but, for someone who knows their trade, it's possible."

"Where does Sara fit in to this?" I am curious to know.

For once, I escape a gun barrel across the head for speaking out of turn. It seems I am in reprieve.

"I heard her name mentioned earlier," I add in explanation.

"Sara's the person who wired the bug into your laptop. She fitted the relay into the ceiling at work," Harry says.

"Sara? But she can't be the mole, there's no way she's been at Aitkins for long enough. I understood the mole has been there for years."

"That's right, but someone duped her into doing the task. When we found the bugs, I called both Sara and James into the office," Harry says. "She confessed straight away. She believed she had been working for the NSF the whole time."

"It's unfortunate her efforts have allowed the mole to learn much of what you found out," Joe says, glaring at me. "His bloody masters must believe I'm on their side. They must think they've done me a favour by blowing-up the facility."

"How did they trick her into placing the bug?" Charles asks. It seems Joe has excluded him from any of his 'phone conversations. "Why wasn't she brought in for questioning? We'd soon have the truth from her, wouldn't we Julie?"

"I'm starting to worry about you two," Joe scowls. "You've begun to enjoy your work too much. Your methods should be a means to an end, instead of the entire means. Continue Harry, I'd like to hear this as well."

"It was simple. In the street one night, on the way home from work, a man approached her. He told Sara he was Wayne Hogarth, from the Special Investigation Office. The man was persuasive. His NSF ID card and badge were either stolen or excellent forgeries. He explained, because of the sensitivity of the case, he was unable to contact her during working hours. Hogarth gave her a number to call, which Sara did. The voice on the other end said the right things, *2nd Group Security Headquarters, how may I direct your call*? She spoke to a Major Jones, who confirmed the agent's identity and investigation. We traced the number to a suite of offices in the centre of Leeds, which, at the time, were empty. They're occupied now, with no chance of finding any fingerprints. 2nd Group have no record of a Major Jones, nor an SIO called Wayne Hogarth.

"Why choose Sara?" Julie speaks for the first time.

I struggle to look at her. My thoughts at best are ambivalent. There is no love left in me for her. I have long-since recovered from the dark hole of her loss. Fia is my life now, but I fear for her, should Julie or Charles gain control over her future. They appear hell-bent on destroying me. Now they know Fia is pregnant, to satisfy their malice they would take great delight in causing harm to her and the baby. Harry is speaking. I pull my mind back to what is happening.

"...as you can see," I hear him say. "Sara was the ideal person for the mole to involve. She has extensive knowledge of computers. A course on computer maintenance undertaken for her last employer added to her suitability."

"I wasn't aware of that," I say. "There was no mention of that in her CV, was there Harry?"

"No," Harry agrees. "She told me last night. It's something she dislikes. For that reason, she failed to mention it in the interview for Aitkins."

"How did the mole know?" Joe asks. "He must have done some research on her, it might be possible to back-track him."

## CHAPTER 22

"We can try, but I doubt he'll have left any traceable clues. He's yet to slip up," Harry says before moving on. "Once Sara had confirmed Hogarth's identity, he told her about Nathan's past. The man said Nathan was under suspicion again. To aid their investigation, NSF wanted Sara to bug his laptop and fit the relay. Hogarth and Sara met a couple of times at a local café. We were in luck. After a couple of attempted robberies, earlier in the year, the place had CCTV installed. The café keeps several weeks'-worth of records.

"You've had a busy night," Joe says.

"John called in several favours with the local police, who did much of the footwork. They brought us the hard-drive with the CCTV footage. We studied the recordings of the relevant nights. The video bears out her story. The person she met was cute enough to know where the cameras were. He wore a hat and kept his face out of the line of sight."

"Can Sara describe him?" Joe asks Harry.

"Only in general terms. It could be anyone of medium-height, medium-build, with cropped dark hair and blue eyes. When Sara said she wasn't happy about it, he told her it was in the national interest. It was her duty, as a citizen, to help the security-forces. Hogarth made no direct threats, but did make it clear the NSF knew where to find her family. Sara capitulated. He explained what to do and gave her a diagram of what to connect to where. The following week, when Nathan took a day off, she stayed late, until everyone else had left for the day. She did the modifications then. Sara knows, unlike most weekdays and weekends, it's rare for Nathan to take his laptop home if he's on holiday the next day."

"I agree with Charles, you should have brought her in," Julie interrupts, her eyes alight at the thought.

Again, the thought of Fia in Julie's clutches terrifies me.

"Forget it," Joe says. "Sara was a fool, I doubt she'll be as trusting in the future - plus, she may be needed at Aitkins." Joe directs this last barb at me. "Going forward, we have a conundrum. Do we carry on as if nothing has happened, allow Sara to re-instate the bug into Nathan's computer and try to trace the receiver of the signals? Or, do we move on and try something new?

"From the conversations the listeners will have recorded, we can assume the mole's people are aware that we hold real-time back-ups of the immunisation programme-research on servers here. Despite that, the underground must be confident they have set back our agenda for a year or more. If they had destroyed the genuine facility, it would take at least that amount of time to find people capable of understanding the research, fit out alternative labs and re-create the living chips."

"You can forget about Nathan's computer," John speaks for the first time. "Whoever's monitoring it will know it's been compromised. The moment someone removed the back from the computer, the device would have sent out a warning signal. The relays, apart from transmitting uploads, would be sending regular signals to confirm the unit's integrity. Once we disconnected their power-source, the people monitoring them would have aborted their operation and fled."

"You're right," Joe says. "For now, we must continue to let them think the programme has been set back. In six months it won't matter, it will be too late. By then, the majority of those on the list to receive the doctored vaccination will have had the chip injected."

"So, what do we do about Nathan and Fia?" Charles is determined in his efforts to destroy us. "If Nathan disappears from public view, we can produce a confession where he acknowledges his guilt for acts of industrial sabotage. With that, it shouldn't be difficult to lay the whole blame for Coxheath's destruction on him. When we release news of our intention to hold a trial, in camera, the mole will suppose his actions have been successful in diverting attention away from himself."

"For once, you're thinking straight. Until then, what do you suggest we do with these two?" Joe asks. "I know a place in Scotland where we can hold them."

"Is that wise," Julie jumps in. Unlike Joe, she knows what Charles's has in mind – reports of a fake trial, after our lingering deaths. "They already know too much and are sympathetic towards the resistance."

## CHAPTER 22

"Be fair," Joe says. "You're the ones who made Nathan that way."

"How he reached his political conclusions is immaterial," Julie counters. "He's now a potential risk. If you won't allow Charles and me to deal with the pair, I have another suggestion."

"Hold on," Fia speaks-out for the first time, interrupting this, to me, surreal discussion concerning our fate. "You've played God with Nathan and me long enough. Don't we have a say in this?"

"NO!" is the answer, almost in unison from Joe, Charles and Julie.

"Julie's right, Joe," Charles insists. "We've come too far and done too much to risk the programme now. Apart from a few scientists, those of us here, JJ and several of his closest allies, no-one else is aware of our agenda. If the rest of the leadership knew about it, they might agree to a limited implementation of the chip, but most would shy away from its blanket-use.

"The resistance knows about the programme, but believe they have neutralised the threat, for now. I doubt they'll want to publicise the affair. Mass panic, followed by a crackdown, would be as disruptive to their operations as to us. To find out what else Nathan and Fia know, the resistance might hunt for them. Because these two know the programme remains viable, no matter where we keep them, they will remain a threat."

Joe nods in agreement. He turns to Julie.

"What's your solution?" he asks.

"Either kill them now, or inject them with the chip. We have samples here we can use. We've tried the injection on women in the later stages of pregnancy, without ill-effect. It might be of value to see what consequences the chip and vaccine have on the development of a foetus at such an early stage. We can keep Fia here or, incommunicado, at your place in Scotland. Nathan is irrelevant. You can do what you want with him. If you keep either of them alive, and the underground attempts to liberate them, we can send out a 'kill' signal to the chip."

Joe looks at Fia and me. His mind calculates the odds of which method might be better. Kill one, kill two or turn one or both of us into state-controlled zombies. Johnson has moved to stand behind us, his gun no longer in its holster. If I try anything, he will shoot. Fia squeezes my hand. I look into her eyes. Resignation shows on her face. She glances at the gun in John's holster at my side. I nod my head a fraction. Fia responds likewise. We have reached the end. Charles looks at us. With calculated cruelty, he delivers our death sentence.

"We can't permit them live," he states. "What if they've discovered the actual research centre is at Orford Ness?"

The look of triumph on Charles's face is obscene. Joe cannot allow us to live. I wonder whether Harry and John realise they could be in the same position. This is something neither of them should know. John stands. He moves back and to one side, his weapon beyond my reach. Fia tightens her grip on my hand. If we are to try to escape, this is our last chance. Better to die in the attempt than to accept our deaths, or a robotic existence, without a fight.

I move my eyes in the direction of Johnson. Joe and Charles occupy his attention. Fia tenses her muscles. She kicks down hard with her feet, to throw herself and her chair backwards. With the heavy wooden back rail, she catches Johnson on the shin. I spin round and go for his gun.

As I hit the floor, bullets pepper the air above. The lights go out. Thick dark drapes cover the windows. If there is daylight outside, it fails to penetrate in here. Flashes light up the room. Our captors appear to be targeting each other. Rolling around on the floor with Johnson, I have no time to worry about that. His hands tighten around my throat. A roaring sound is in my ears. I bring up my knee, hard into his groin. For a second, his grip eases. I pull myself clear.

My hand finds the barrel of his gun. His fingers find my throat again. I grab the weapon. With all the force I can muster, I bring the weight of it down on top of Johnson's head. He grunts. His grasp weakens. I hit him again and again. After a final groan, he collapses on top of me.

The lights come back on. I push him away. I have his gun in my hand, still held by the barrel. The bloody handle has a patch of hair

## CHAPTER 22

attached. I look up to find John leaning over me. Blood runs down his arm, but the injury appears superficial. The gun in his right hand is steady. It points at my left eye, so close I can see the rifling, spiralling away inside the barrel.

# 23

For what seems forever, the gun remains pointed at my face. John, the room, everything, apart from the barrel end, has dropped out of focus. My life is over. There is no coming back from this. As if from a great distance, I hear Harry call out.

"All clear," he yells.

To my amazement, John steps back. He drops his gun back into his holster. With his good arm, he reaches down and helps me to my feet. On the wall, behind Joe's last position, a mess of blood and brain matter slither down the expensive wooden panelling. Charles and Julie are no longer in the room. Neither is Fia.

"Where's Fia?" I croak, my throat hoarse from Johnson's attempts to throttle me. "What's happened to her?"

Harry appears from the side room. There are a couple of holes in the front of his shirt, but no sign of blood. He sees my stare.

"Bullet-proof vest, hurts like hell, but I'll survive," he explains.

Despite my fears for Fia, I am wary. Ignoring the blood on the handle of the gun, I turn it round and aim it somewhere between John and Harry.

"It's okay, Nathan," Harry says, "we're on your side. I'm sorry, but Charles and Julie escaped. They've taken Fia with them. Joe's dead."

"Why should I trust you? You're both members of the NSF. John, is, was, Joe's right hand man."

"Haven't you worked it out yet, Nathan?" John asks. He pauses a moment then answers for me. "Harry's the mole; the latest in a long line of them. We've known each other since army days. A while back, Harry sought me out. Once he'd recruited me into the NSF, he persuaded

## CHAPTER 23

me to apply for the role of aide to Joe. He wanted someone with my experience and skills. Joe never found out about my past service with Harry. Some classifications are above even Joe's clearance level. I've been sharing information with Harry since then.

"Until now, we've been missing one vital piece of information, the location of the genuine research centre. Joe, Charles, Julie and their masters kept that nugget to themselves. We'd heard about the programme, but all our information was unofficial. I was never brought into their confidence."

"We doubted it was Coxheath," Harry takes over from John, "but we arranged for the attack in an attempt to force Joe into making a mistake. I'm sorry you and Fia became embroiled in the mess, but the implications of the immunisation programme are much too serious for individual considerations to be taken into account."

"So, you and John are members of the underground?" I ask, keeping the gun where it is. "You expect me to believe this?"

"That's up to you," John answers. "We're against JJ, and the way the government runs the country. At the same time, we serve as members of the NSF. Despite public displays of solidarity among the highest ranks of the party, some disagree with JJ's methods, along with the resultant state of the country. These members of the hierarchy want a return to a freer, multi-party model, but one fairer and more representative. Hell, no matter how bad the old days were, they were a damn sight better than the misery we have now."

"Nationwide, we've brought together a broad coalition of underground groups," Harry explains further, "with members across each arm of the services and civilian life. From the start, despite support for JJ by many high-ranking officers, the military's rank-and-file and junior officers have been wary of his motives.

"Our strategy is well advanced, but we need more time to build our capacity to strike a decisive blow. If the government brings forward the living-cell project, we may struggle to interrupt it. Security at Orford Ness will be intensified. Once deployed, the vaccine injections will render the resistance movement impotent. The state will control the majority of those who follow, or sympathise with, our aims."

I have heard sufficient to convince me, for now. If John's intention was to kill me, he would have done it when I was on the floor. I lower my gun. There are other matters on my mind.

"To hell with this talk, where have Charles and Julie taken Fia?" I demand, my voice less strained. "I must find her. Once her use as a shield is over, they'll kill her."

"They reached the lift before I could stop them. When it reached the fifth level down, they disabled it," Harry explains.

"There must be another way to reach them."

"Oh! There are, several. Stairs and other lifts, but we must wait for back-up to arrive," John says.

"What back-up?" I ask.

"We didn't come alone," John continues. "By now, the gatehouse, nearby patrols and watchtowers should be under our control. We have two hours before the next shift comes on duty. It's six o'clock, Sunday morning. Apart from a few keen souls today, no-one will be working inside the building. It's doubtful they'll arrive much before eleven."

"What do you intend to do?" I am suspicious.

"Demolish the server-level, once we've downloaded the records we want."

"I thought you wanted to destroy the immunisation back-ups?" My misgivings turn to alarm at the prospect.

"We do. It's those concerning the clearance-programme Joe mentioned we're after; also the national records of internment, prisoner interrogation and re-education centres. Once we have these, to cover our traces we shall blow out the whole floor."

"Good luck with that, but it's Fia I want. How do I reach the lower levels?" I plead.

Harry and John look at each other.

"You go with him, John. I have to supervise the work on the servers. Only I know from which ones we need to download the information."

## CHAPTER 23

Behind me, someone groans.

"Bloody hell, I thought you'd killed him," Harry says, as Johnson stirs.

John doesn't hesitate. He fires once. Johnson's body judders as a bullet hits him between the eyes.

"Nasty sod that," John's voice is tinged with bitterness. "Some years ago, a close friend of mine was visiting a relative. The NSF raided the house next door. As she was a stranger to the area, Johnson decided to arrest her on suspicion of anti-government activities. He tortured her to death. I was away when it happened. When I learned what he'd done, I made a promise I would avenge her."

I shiver. My thoughts about John, the first time we met, were close to the truth. He's not someone of whom you want make an enemy. He turns and moves towards the reception door.

"Come on," he calls to me. "There's an underground car park on level five. We have to block the exit before Charles can reach it. When we arrived, to avoid rousing the main compound behind the Hall, we disabled the alarms. Several units have their quarters there. If Charles and Julie make it to the surface, any gunfire could attract unwanted attention to our operation."

I rush after John. No matter how well-deserved, I feel sick after witnessing Johnson's execution. On my way out, I look back. Harry is on his mobile. Nearby, the crumpled body of Joe is on the floor. Light-headed, I run after John. Outside, in the corridor, a party of heavily-armed men, dressed in NSF uniforms, moves towards us. The leading pair brings their weapons to bear. John shouts at them. They lower their guns as they recognise him.

"Our backup," John says to me. To them he yells, "Harry's through there."

We stand to one side. The group dashes past us. On their backs, they carry huge packs filled, I assume, with explosives.

"Come on," John shouts.

He sets off at a run. Down several pristine-white corridors we race. As we enter each new area, sensors switch on lights to guide our path.

On either side, doors lead into offices and meeting-rooms, all silent and empty. We make little noise on the carpeted floor. We burst through swing-doors. A few security ones, disabled with the alarms, we slam open with ease. John has no thoughts of going to a lower level. His intention is to cut-off Charles, from the outside, before his party can exit the building.

We lunge through a side-entrance. Two of Harry's men stand guard. At John's command, they follow. In a ragged group, we sprint across the parkland. In the distance, a brick-built structure angles back towards the ground. Red and white striped pole-barriers lie across the twin lanes at its entrance. From the depths, we can hear the sound of an engine revving as a vehicle climbs towards the surface.

"Quick," John urges, "they're almost there."

We are still two hundred metres short of our target, when a Range Rover screeches round the final curve. The vehicle smashes through the barrier. Both men with us have rifles. Before they can bring them to bear, the vehicle veers off the roadway. It weaves at high-speed over grass, before it swerves through a line of trees to reach the main drive near the entrance. With its gates left open, to allow Harry's men to escape, those on guard have split-seconds to react. Whoever (Charles or Julie) is at the wheel, they aim straight at the men. As the guards dive out of the way, the Range Rover, hurtles through the opening, to fishtail, as it makes a sharp turn onto the road. The driver regains traction. The vehicle speeds away.

Bent double, I gasp for breath. A runner I am not. My chest burns, my lungs strain for oxygen. Fia has gone. She is in the clutches of those who seek nothing better than to harm her. Beside me, John's breathing is close to normal. The man has incredible stamina.

"You two," he orders the sentinels who followed us, "back to your posts. Nathan, you okay?" he asks at my apparent distress.

I nod, bent double, unable to speak.

"Good, head to the gatehouse, I'll find a car and meet you there in five minutes. Go on, hurry."

## CHAPTER 23

While John, mobile to his ear, returns to the Hall, I stagger through the trees. Ahead looms the well-lit drive and gatehouse. Unsure about my reception, I thrust my gun into my pocket. It could be fatal to give Harry's men the wrong impression. On arrival it seems, as the result of John's call, they expect me. Behind the gatehouse, several bodies lie, dumped in a heap. Inside, someone works on the CCTV monitors and equipment. I assume they are in the process of removing the hard-disks that recorded the group's arrival, and the takeover of the perimeter. Another intruder lays explosive charges.

In the direction of the Hall, comes the sound of an engine turning over. It roars into life. In front of the entrance steps, several large military trucks stand. From their open backs, men lift out boxes. More explosives? A black SUV appears at the end of the drive and, within moments, screeches to a halt beside me. The passenger door swings open.

"Jump in," John yells, but I am already on the move.

I slam the door. John floors the accelerator. The wheels spin. As we slide onto the road, I hit the door hard. With smoking tyres, we speed away as I fasten my seat-belt. My mind focuses on Fia's abduction. A sense of panic overwhelms me. I find myself short of breath. I feel dizzy, my heart palpitates and there are pains in my chest. Sweat pours from me, my mouth is dry and hands clammy. John sees my distress and slams on the brakes. We skid to a halt.

"Hyperventilating or having a heart attack won't help Fia," he says, rummaging inside the glove-compartment.

He swears when he finds nothing. From the back seat, he grabs a discarded paper sandwich-bag. He thrusts it into my hands.

"Open it up and breathe into it. It'll calm you down."

Without another second's delay, he revs the engine. We are on the move again. The bag stinks of stale onion and burger, but soon has the desired effect as exhaled carbon dioxide relaxes my breathing.

"We'll find Fia and bring her back safe," John says, when I have removed my head from the bag. "I won't allow anything happen to her. I tried hard to persuade Joe to keep her out of his scheming, but I couldn't dissuade him. She was persistent and, despite what he said, he found it amusing to play her and, later, you. His bonhomie disguised an amoral disposition, but Fia, she's the opposite.

"When Joe first mentioned you, I thought you'd turn out to be another self-centred ass similar to him. When Fia fell in love with you, I thought she was a fool. You've proved me wrong. I cannot remember seeing Fia happier. Revenge might motivate you, but it doesn't rule you. Your main wish is to find your children and change the system. You worked with Joe because you thought he had similar aims.

"I'd come across Charles a number of times, but, until today, I'd never seen Julie. On the way here, I heard the full story from Joe. He rang and brought us up-to-date. How Charles and Julie succeeded in keeping everything concealed for this long amazes me. I do agree with Joe on one thing, Charles should have been court-martialled."

"How's the arm?" I ask.

I had noticed, when he fetched the car, John had found time to wrap a strip of cloth round the wound.

"It's fine, it was a scratch."

Long past dawn, we have good light, but John drives at speeds that would be madness if I were behind the wheel. At the start of our chase we were about ten minutes behind Charles. John seems confident that, if we are not gaining on them, we must be keeping up, and that they are heading for the M65.

"How are you feeling now, any better?" John asks.

I nod.

"Good, there's a tablet PC on the back seat, grab it will you."

I look back. It is on the cushion, sliding about with the movement of the vehicle. After a couple of attempts, I grab hold. John gives me instructions and, soon, I reach a screen that asks for vehicle registration-numbers. John tells me ours, and, after a quick 'phone call, the one that belongs to Charles's vehicle. Once they are input, I touch the screen. A map appears. All military vehicles have trackers fitted.

## CHAPTER 23

Two dots appear on the screen. The map zooms in to cover the area between the highlighted points.

"Where are they now?" John asks. "There's a turn off ahead."

He skids sideways round a bend, missing by a narrow margin the front of a tractor edging out of a gateway.

"Keep going," I say, "they've gone straight on."

"How far in front are they?"

"About six miles."

John presses harder on the pedal. The SUV surges forward. I concentrate on the screen. It is less frightening than watching the road. I warn John our prey has turned left onto the motorway. We have gained a little, but, on the motorway, Charles can accelerate to his engine's capacity.

"Why did they run from the Hall, instead of heading for the compound?" I ask. "He could have sought help from the NSF units there." This has puzzled me since we gave chase. I hope the vehicle we follow is no decoy.

"Charles and Julie are part of a clandestine project set up by JJ, recruited by Joe. Official records will show neither he, Charles nor Julie were at the Hall today. Of greater importance, they have a prisoner, whom they must keep isolated. Given an opportunity, they know Fia will reveal the truth about them and their project. I'm sure they're on their way to a safe-house, to consider their options. To involve too many others, would risk inconvenient questions and alert the wrong people. They have to find a plausible explanation to absolve themselves from blame regarding Joe's death, and the loss of Coxheath."

"Have you any idea where they're heading?"

"It could be anywhere, but they'll ditch the car before too long. They cannot be sure, but must suspect someone is tracking them. Their ultimate destination has to be London. If they succeed in reaching JJ, he'll purge anyone whom he considers a potential threat to him or his programme."

"What of Fia?"

"Until Charles and Julie reach safety, she'll be safe. They may make her life uncomfortable, but no more. They want her in good condition, to use as bargaining-tool should we catch them. After that, I cannot say. It may be her value will remain high, as bait to ensnare you. One way or another, they seem determined to make you suffer, Nathan."

I take some comfort from his words. Julie, I fear, carries the greater threat. It is possible she will take out her anger on Fia, by trying to make her miscarry. I still my returning panic by concentrating on the scrolling map.

"They've turned off," I warn, "onto Accrington Road."

"Keep your eyes on the screen, see if they divert again."

We are about five miles short of the motorway. I watch the dot (representing Fia's location) move forward. The time they had spent on the motorway was negligible. We continue to maintain our distance from them.

"They're still on the 679," I say, "heading towards Burnley, but they've slowed down."

"Damn it," John swears under his breath. "There's housing and a mixture of commercial and industrial units along there. It looks as though they're about to bail."

After a couple of anxious minutes, the dot representing our target stops moving. I did not think we could travel much faster, but John increases speed. With siren blaring, we burst onto the motorway. This time on a Sunday morning, we have the road to ourselves. John powers along the carriageway towards the next Junction. We take the slip-road, screech round roundabouts before we accelerate away. With our siren blaring-out a warning, at a junction, John ignores the red lights. How he misses an ancient van that skids to a halt, part way into the crossroads, I don't know. The dots on the screen are close, but only ours has movement.

With trees to our left and industrial units to our right, we speed away. Commercial units appear on the left. Beyond grass-banking and open land to our right, a residential-area comes into view. Our dot moves

## CHAPTER 23

closer to the stationary one. We pass three car-dealerships on the left. Ahead, beside a recent addition, the dots merge. John slams on the brakes. We judder to a halt as the ABS kicks in. With guns in our hands, we leap from the SUV. The business appears closed, but someone has retracted the entrance bollards. The Range Rover, doors wide-open, engine running, is at the side of a glass-fronted showroom.

John bends low. He runs to the car. I follow him to the other side. The vehicle is empty. Despite my disappointment at Fia's absence, I admit to a sense of relief. Had she been there, I am sure she would be dead. John moves round the selection of vehicles on display. There are numerous gaps between them. Which one have Charles and Julie taken? For its model and registration number, we need a member of staff to tell us.

"They won't go far," I say to John. "No vehicle on a dealership forecourt will have much fuel in its tank."

"There's a garage a hundred metres back down the road."

"Would they risk appearing on their cameras? They must know it's the first thing we'd look at."

"There's CCTV here, too." John indicates a camera fixed to the side of the showroom.

A side door, already ajar, leads to offices. An alarm-box inside is silent. Charles has been here before us.

With an unerring instinct for what he seeks, John opens an internal door. He sits at a desk. In front, a computer screen shows a grey blur. He presses a few buttons. Recordings from fifteen minutes earlier appear on screen. These time-lapse images show the forecourt in detail. The Range Rover appears at the entrance. Over a series of images, Charles can be seen to lean out of the Range Rover window. He points something at a box at the side of the entrance. The bollards show half-way retracted on one image, level with the ground on another.

"Have you one of those gadgets?" I ask.

"Most field agents and NSF officers do."

The Range Rover moves forward, until its bonnet rests against the showroom wall, beneath the camera. I hold my breath. The next shot shows Julie. She escorts Fia at gunpoint from the car. Fia looks unharmed, but frightened. In the next image, the two of them are near the forecourt. The final picture, with everything visible on screen, pictures Charles standing on the front of the Ranger Rover, a rag in his hand.

"He's crafty," John admits. "The sod's smeared thick grease over the CCTV lenses. No wonder there's nothing to see after that," his voice carries a hint of frustration.

"Can you wind it back again," I say, "frame by frame?"

John nods. After a couple of frames I say, "Stop, there, look. That car, the black Mercedes, it's missing from the forecourt."

"You sure?"

"Yes, it's gone. It's a pity the number plate's obscured by that sandwich-board."

"A luxury car, such as that, will have a tracking-device fitted. Without a plate, we cannot trace it. I bet Charles noticed the sign, and camera angle, when he made his choice."

Back on the forecourt, John points to a petrol-pump at the side of a workshop. A glistening rainbow reflects on an evaporating pool of liquid from the nozzle that lies on the ground beside it.

"They didn't need to use the petrol station, they filled up here. We can't have missed them by more than a minute or two. Damn it!"

For the next hour, we tour the area, but none of the Mercedes we see is the right colour nor model. Of the one we seek, we find no trace. In whatever direction they've gone, by the time we find the registration number, they will have changed cars again. John's mobile rings.

"Yes! Oh! Hi, Harry. Big bang was it? Did you download the information we wanted? Good. Everybody escape? Great. No, we've lost Charles. He's abandoned the Rover and taken a Merc. No idea, but I imagine he'll lose that soon enough. Say that again? On the edge of Stanbury, near Haworth. You sure? Keep in touch."

He disconnects the call.

## CHAPTER 23

"Is it safe to discuss details over an open line?" I ask in surprise.

"Encrypted 'phones. Without a matching receiver, a call is almost impossible to intercept, or decipher. Harry's discovered something. He forced open a locked drawer in Charles's desk. Inside was a bundle of correspondence, including several communications from a builder and mortgage lenders. Charles and Julie have a weekend cottage near Haworth. It's probable they have a private vehicle stored there, too. Reading between the lines, Harry's positive the couple kept their hideaway a secret. It's the logical place for them to stay while they decide on how to proceed. Let's go, we can be there in thirty minutes."

# 24

John leans over to press a button on the dashboard. The inbuilt sat nav comes to life. He taps in the cottage's location. Our search has brought us close to the centre of Burnley. The mechanical voice of the sat nav directs us back towards the M65. With engine screaming, we hurtle along the motorway. We flash past a police patrol car, but, with our siren blaring out, they ignore us. Once the speedometer passes a hundred and twenty, I stop looking.

We run out of motorway, then dual carriageway. On the single carriageway, John eases back our speed, but keeps the siren going. Vehicles in our path pull to the side to allow us to pass. Colne, sleepy at this time on a Sunday morning, is a blur of stone-walls and shop windows. With the siren, John bullies his way through traffic and any red lights that threaten to delay our progress.

Clouds, blowing in from the west, thicken. Within minutes, a fine drizzle turns to heavy driving rain. Strong gusts blast the downpour towards us, obscuring all but the nearby landscape. The car shakes in the ferocity of the wind. With headlights on and wipers at high speed, our pace slows. Opposite a pub, at Laneshawbridge village, John slams on the brakes. He takes a sharp right-turn onto School Lane and over the slight hump of the bridge. Within a few hundred metres, we are back out in open country.

The heavy shower blows over. Dry-stone walls and bleak Pennine slopes are our backdrop as the sky lightens, and visibility increases. After a couple of squalls, the sky clears, to leave us in bright sunshine. Isolated hamlets and farms flash by as we travel the winding route. We have the road to ourselves. Spray from the turbulent waters of

## CHAPTER 24

Watersheddles Reservoir falls like rain onto our windscreen.

On the approach to Pondon Reservoir, John switches off the siren. Our pace slows. We are close to our destination. It would be foolish to announce our arrival to Charles and Julie. Any error of judgement on our part could put Fia's life in greater danger than it is already.

Lush green fields slope away to our left, down to the valley bottom. To our right, some cottages comes into sight. John reduces speed. Metres beyond them, is a low, stone-built block, labelled Stanbury. A signpost to Bronte Waterfall and Top Withens points us in the direction we want to go. John makes a sharp right turn, onto a narrow lane, which leads us back past the rear of the cottages. After a couple of hundred metres, we come to a fork in the road. We keep left, where, in a patch of mud, fresh car-tracks are visible. A tone sounds on his mobile. John brings the vehicle to a halt and switches off the engine. He studies the message before he passes the mobile to me.

Harry has forwarded several images. They show the plans for Charles and Julie's cottage, and a map of the area. The structure is a new build on open fields; in such a location, something few but a senior member of the party, or NSF, could push past planning authorities. Hidden from our prey by the brow of the slope ahead, we are at most a couple of hundred metres from their weekend-retreat.

"We'll leave the car here," John says.

He manoeuvres it to one side of the single-track roadway. From now on, my reliance on John is total. He has the expertise for this type of operation. If anyone can extricate Fia unharmed, it is he. We remain inside the vehicle for several minutes. John studies the house plans on the mobile before, on the tablet's screen, the area as photographed by satellite. The house is too recent for images of it to appear, but its location is easy to ascertain.

John slips out of the vehicle. From the floor, behind his seat, he pulls out a rifle. It has a suppressor screwed to the end of the barrel. It will not silence the weapon, but will reduce noise, muzzle flash, and the likelihood of another target finding the shooter's location.

With the passenger door up against a wall, I clamber over to the driver's side to follow John. The chill winds suck the warmth from our bodies. We take advantage of a couple of bulletproof vests stored in the boot. I hope they are more effective against bullets than they are against the gale. At a steady pace, we move up the worn tarmac-track. To our right, a house stands across a field, but without access to our route. From the satellite images, we know, much further along the lane, there are more houses. With luck, their occupants will have either no reason to journey this way for a while, or be able to pass our vehicle without drawing attention to its location.

Grassy banks, topped with dry stone-walls, rise up on either side. Near the head of the slope, the banking lowers. Stooping, to prevent our heads from becoming visible over the top of the wall, we draw near to the cottage. A rusty, tubular metal-frame gate fills a gap in the wall to our left. We drop to our knees, to peer through the open metalwork.

On a diagonal-line down the slight slope, the rear of the cottage comes into view. The place must have cost Charles and Julie a considerable sum. The building is extensive, single-story and stone-built. Its well-stocked terraced garden stretches down the slope. It shows signs of being the work of a professional landscaper - a near instant garden, no landowner hurt in its making. After the earlier rain, the views down valley, and beyond Lower Laithe Reservoir towards Haworth, are radiant in the sunlight. Across the valley to the open moorland beyond, in the direction of Top Withens, is a sight of which I could never weary.

At the rear of the cottage, on the lane side, parked on the driveway in front of a double garage is the missing Mercedes. Someone, Charles I assume, lies on his back, underneath the rear of the car. As we watch, he pulls himself clear. Back on his feet, he drops an object onto the ground. With his heel, he grinds it into the concrete drive.

"There goes the tracker," John whispers.

Its loss is no longer relevant, we know where they are, as does Harry. Charles walks to the garage. He flicks a remote control. The roller-

## CHAPTER 24

shutter door opens to reveal, to one side, a high-powered sports car with tinted windows. He returns to the Mercedes, to park it inside. Moments later, the garage door closes behind him. He must have access to the house from inside the garage. On the positive side, it does not seem that Charles and Julie are ready to leave yet, but we may have little warning when they do. They can load the car without our knowledge. The first we shall know is when the garage doors open.

John wriggles on his stomach, past the opening. I follow. Wearing dark-green walking-trousers, and a similar coloured shirt, I blend in with the background. I find it hard to believe, these clothes are the ones I put on in the Lake District yesterday morning. It seems such a long time ago. No longer do John's dark-coloured work-clothes look neat and pressed.

The air warms in the morning sun, but the winds remains strong and the ground is wet. I shiver as I crawl through a puddle. Keeping low, we make our way towards the driveway that leads down to the cottage. Large, solid, wooden gates block the opening. John ignores them as a means of entry. Under their cover, we stoop past to reach the wall at the other side.

With our heads kept low, we move another twenty metres further along. A wooden, barred-gate gives access to a field adjoining the cottage. Another wall, which follows the slope downhill, separates the land from the grounds of the building. John slides over the top bar. With less grace, I follow. Bent double, we progress down the slope. He peers through a gap in the wall for a few moments, then stands to look over the top. I do the same. We are at the side of the garage, its stonework bare and windowless.

I point to a corner of the roof, where several wires hang loose.

"Looks like there's a camera or sensor missing," I whisper. "I noticed an alarm box fitted to the rear of the cottage, when we were on the slope above. It's possible the full system hasn't been installed yet."

"We can't take a chance," John says, keeping his voice low. I struggle to hear him. "There could be other cameras, elsewhere, that are operational. Charles does not appear lax in anything to do with his personal security."

John hands me the rifle.

"Stay here. Don't use that. If you need a weapon, use the automatic you took from Johnson. It's better for close-range work."

He tests the stonework on the wall, before he clambers over the top, to land, light-footed, on the grass between it and the garage wall. On his knees, he disappears from sight. At most, his absence lasts no more than ten minutes, but it is long enough to allow my imagination to run amok. Dark clouds float overhead. The temperature drops as they cover the sun. I shiver. My clothing is inadequate to cope with a downpour. To my relief, blue sky soon returns.

The label, that said my trainers were waterproof, lied. My feet and the legs of my trousers are sodden. The grass is wet, the ground boggy in places; the muddy soil is cut deep by the tracks of animals and farm vehicles. The smell of damp earth and vegetation is strong in my nostrils. The sound of sheep bleating carries on the wind. Along the main Haworth road a motorcycle roars. A rustling against the other side of the wall brings me to full alertness. I raise my gun and point it towards the top stones.

"Nathan, are you there?" I hear a whisper.

I relax; it is John, his clothes smeared with mud.

"Have you seen Fia?" I ask, frantic with worry. "Is she all right?"

"Yes, for the moment, she seems unharmed. There's a lounge at the other side of the garage. Fia's tied to a chair, up against the back wall. At the rear of the cottage, there are cameras and sensors installed to cover that side of the house and driveway up to the lane. Those at the front, where the cottage overlooks the valley, have their wires hanging loose. The fitters must be part-way through the installation. Let's hope they don't work Sundays."

"Charles, Julie, where are they?"

"I didn't catch sight of them. They could be in the kitchen, or one of the other rooms at the back of the house. I cannot be sure how

## CHAPTER 24

operational the exterior alarm system is. I didn't risk exploring that far."

"How do we rescue Fia?"

"I'll open the patio doors. With people inside, the internal alarm system should be switched-off. You release Fia, while I keep watch. Leave the rifle at your side of the wall," he says when I try to pass it to him, "I'll cover you with my gun."

With my automatic, I would struggle to hit anything I aimed at further away than a couple of metres. I see the logic in his guarding my back, rather than the reverse.

"When we've released Fia, what do we do about Charles and Julie?" I ask.

"Leave them to me," John says, handing the SUV keys to me. "Once Fia's free, you leave. Make your way over the wall and back to the car. Don't wait for me; help is on the way. Drive through Stanbury. On the other side, before you reach the turn-off to the reservoir, there's a chicane. Pull into the space on this side of it. Wait for me there."

"What will you do? It's two against one. I've no idea of what Julie's capable, but Charles is an experienced officer."

John looks me in the eyes.

"If you had to shoot Julie, could you? Unless she posed a direct threat to Fia, you'd hesitate. I doubt Julie would return the favour. Charles is a dangerous man with a sadistic temperament. For a long time she's been his willing partner. In the army, before he transferred to the NSF, Charles had a similar role to mine. Unlike me, he enjoys killing and inflicting pain. Sitting behind a desk may have taken the edge off his fighting skills, but to underestimate him is to risk death. Your role is to escort Fia to safety, mine to contain Charles and Julie until help arrives."

"Contain?"

"Capture or kill," John expounds. "Harry's orders."

At the corner of the garage, we fall silent. Keeping low, John peers round the edge.

"Come on," he says, darting out of sight.

Bent double, I follow him. John is several steps ahead, part-way across a grassy patch leading towards an extensive decked area. He ducks beneath a picture-window to squeeze his large frame between the uprights of a safety-rail. Before he shows himself in front of the patio door, he takes a quick glance, steps back, then puts a finger to his lips. I stop moving.

Several minutes pass. John is keeping his eye on whatever is taking place inside the room. He moves to the middle of the glass-doors. Within seconds, with a device he takes from his pocket, he has the lock open. He smiles and beckons me forward. I reach the decking. He pulls open one of the doors and, gun in hand, steps inside. There, on a carpet with the type of pile in which you could lose yourself, John tiptoes towards a doorway on our right.

Through the opening, I can hear a distant mumble of voices. To my left, Fia, eyes wide, gazes at me in disbelief. Bound and gagged, she looks strained, but otherwise unharmed. John passes me a knife. I drop to my knees beside her.

"Shush!" I whisper, as I remove her gag.

It takes seconds to cut her free. I help her to her feet.

"Go, now," John urges.

With my arm round Fia, we stagger to the patio door. Once we are outside, John closes the door, to remain on the inside. With difficulty, I help Fia under the safety-rail towards the back of the garage. On the opposite side of the decking, a flagged path leads from the other side of the house, past a raised bed, to a large shed at the bottom of the first terrace. Footsteps sound from the side of the cottage.

Charles strides into view. We freeze; any movement might attract his attention. His mind is on other matters, his gaze straight-ahead. At the shed door, he produces a key. Once he's inside, I grab Fia and half carry her to the relative safety of the garage side.

With the briefest of stops, to help her over the wall, we reach the field. I take hold of her hand. We keep our heads down as we move up

## CHAPTER 24

the slippery wet slope, towards the lane above. The stiffness, caused by her bindings, eases. Fia's pace increases. Over the gate, we keep our bodies low to move past the driveway and away from the cottage.

I help Fia into the SUV. She slides over to the passenger side. As I slam the door, a fusillade of shots sounds in the background. At the first turn of the key, the engine starts. I reverse down the lane to swing the back-end onto the other fork of the track. We are away, the main-road and Stanbury ahead of us. As instructed, I pull in at the chicane. Fia is in my arms, her look of disbelief still visible.

"I thought I'd lost you," I say.

"They told me they'd keep me hostage until they reached safety," Fia whispers. "They said they'd kill you if you interfered. They kept repeating what they would do to me, later, at their leisure. Both of them are unstable. The methods they described about the treatment I could expect, I…" her voice is lost as a large sleek, black helicopter speeds overhead.

Could this be John's back-up arriving, or support for Charles and Julie? A 'phone rings. I scrabble around. I find John's mobile stuck under the back of my seat. It must have dropped from his pocket when we left the vehicle. Harry's name flashes. I touch the screen and put the 'phone to my ear.

"Harry, it's Nathan," I say. In reply to Harry's rapid words, I add, "No, Fia's here with me. John stayed behind at the cottage, to take care of Charles and Julie. Your back-up flew overhead a moment ago."

"That must be Charles's people, we're on the road," Harry utters the words I had feared. "We're about half an hour away. Don't interfere, John's a professional, he can take care of himself. You have Fia to consider. Drive towards Haworth. Find a side-road, anything, anywhere where you can hide yourselves and the vehicle. Stay there until you hear from me again."

He disconnects. Fia is close enough to have heard the conversation.

"You take the car and do what Harry says," I tell her as I throw open my door.

# 25

"I'm coming with you," Fia's response is immediate.

There is determination in her voice and her face carries a stubborn look.

"You can't," I object. "Think of the baby."

"I am. Without John's and your intervention, Charles and Julie could have done to me whatever they wanted. There would be no child. If John's in trouble, I'm going to help him. Moreover, you know as well as I, if Charles and Julie escape, we'll be in danger for as long as they live."

There is no time to waste in arguing. The helicopter is hovering, close to the cottage. With the engine running, I spin the wheel. We hurtle back through the village, towards the lane we had left minutes ago. This time I park at the cottage gates.

Gunfire comes from the other side of the building. The helicopter has landed on the slope beyond the cottage. The aircraft's doors are open, but its rotors still spin. Apart from the pilot, who remains at the controls, the cabin is empty. Several armed men, in body-armour, run across the field in the direction of the cottage. A pistol shot sounds. One of the newcomers falls to the ground, shot through the head. It is a hell of a shot, or a lucky break, for John.

Thick black smoke pours from under the garage door and roof. John has destroyed that means of escape. As we watch, smoke spreads to the cottage. One of its windows shatters. Flames shoot through the opening.

I have my automatic. Fia throws open the boot. With one of the keys from the vehicle's key ring, I open a metal panel on the floor. In

## CHAPTER 25

the compartment beneath lie an automatic pistol and several loaded magazines. Fia takes the weapon. We share the ammunition between us. From near the helicopter, a burst of fire smashes the side-windows of the SUV. The shots might be accidental, but I grab Fia. We duck for safety beneath the level of the wall. I give her my vest and help her into it.

"This way," I say.

With Fia at my heels, we move towards the barred-gate at the other side of the cottage entrance. The need for silence is over. Fia lifts the rope holding the gate in place. I push open the creaking barrier. On the slimy surface, we slither downhill. John's rifle remains where I left it. Charles and Julie must have him pinned-down. I aim for the rifle, which will be more effective than my pistol. We have another fifty metres to go, when an explosion sends the garage roof into the air and blows-out most of its walls. The force of the blast hurls us to the ground. I throw myself over Fia as debris falls round us. Fragments pummel into my back. As the fallout eases, I roll off Fia and allow the mud and wet grass to put out a small blaze on the back of my shirt.

The dry-stone-wall has deflected some of the blast, and spared the rifle. Below the weapon's position, a length of stonework has collapsed. I am metres from the gun when, much lower down the slope, a dark shape leaps over the wall where it remains intact. An NSF trooper slides on the muddy surface. As he recovers, he looks in our direction. The trooper raises his gun. He fires. The bullet whines past my head. It ricochets off the top of the wall, towards the remains of the garage.

Behind me, Fia opens fire. Several bullets hit the man's body armour, throwing him off balance. I lift my automatic and fire at his head. My aim is less than accurate, but the bullet does strike him in the chest. The impact of this blow, following those of Fia's, knocks him onto his back. Winded, he loses his grip on his carbine. His helmet flies off. We race past the collapsed section of wall. If anyone sees us, no-one has time to fire. I reach the downed man. He snatches at his pistol. I kick it from his hand. With the butt of the rifle, I had grabbed on the way,

199

I smash it against his exposed head until he becomes still. His eyes remain open, but no longer seeing.

I grab his automatic. Fia picks up his carbine. Thanks to the enemy, we now have a greater selection of weapons than earlier. I feel nauseous at what I have done, but there was no alternative. Kill or be killed, a simple choice. A stray bullet whines overhead. I kneel down to strip the bulletproof vest from my victim. The pounding it has received might have weakened its integrity, but it has to be an improvement on my current lack of protection.

Before we can help John, we must locate him first. If he has remained inside the house, his position must be precarious. After the blast, the whole building is ablaze. Flames shoot from the roof. Thick black smoke rises into the morning sky.

"I hope the bastard's insurance isn't valid," Fia says, looking at the conflagration.

For some reason I find this funny. I struggle to control my laughter. This release of tension frees my mind to think with greater clarity. With Fia at my side, we return up the slope towards the fallen wall.

On my knees, I ease myself into a position where I can peek round the rubble. Fia keeps watch down the slope. She holds the carbine as if she knows what to do with it.

"John once showed me how to use one," she admits.

I assume she must be a better shot than I am. Her earlier shooting, with the automatic, showed prowess. My lovely wife continues to surprise me.

The roar of flames is loud, the heat tremendous. A huge shower of sparks accompanies the collapse of part of the roof. At first, the smoke blows across the lawn. I can see nothing to indicate anyone's whereabouts. The breeze changes direction. I detect movement at the other side of the garden. For a moment, Charles's head is visible behind a raised bed of herbs. Of Julie, I see no sign. The raised area has enough bulk to conceal a couple of people. She could be with him. To my right, I catch sight of John. He is about five metres away from me,

## CHAPTER 25

lying on his front, gun in hand, wedged between two stacks of unused paving stones.

He is in trouble. The helicopter group have entered the confines of the terraced garden. From the shelter provided by the landscaping, they keep up a constant barrage around him. If he attempts to break cover, they will have clear sight of him. Had we stayed away, the man I killed would be where I am now, with a direct shot at John's back. I warn Fia to keep her attention on the slope. The NSF troops will come soon to investigate, once they realise something has happened to their colleague. John cannot advance, nor retreat; neither can Charles. This stalemate could be short lived. I watch as John ejects his magazine. He checks how many rounds remain. From where I am, there appears to be few. He slams the magazine back into place.

From across the garden, Julie shows her head. She ducks back as John fires. Dust and splinters fly from the edge of the supporting frame, behind which she shelters. From my pocket, I take out three full magazines. Manoeuvring myself out the attackers' line of sight, I take aim. The fist clip of ammunition lands beside John's head. Startled, he looks round and sees me. I toss the other two in his direction. He scoops them up. I show him the rifle. He gives me a thumbs up when I indicate I am about to move down the slope, in an attempt to outflank his attackers. The NSF troops have noticed my actions. I duck out of sight as bullets chip slivers of stone from the wall nearby.

"You stay here," I say to Fia, indicating where Charles and Julie have taken cover. "They're unaware of us. Charles is on the left. They keep showing themselves, to tempt John into exhausting his ammunition. I've thrown him some extra clips. He can survive a little longer. If Charles or Julie show themselves, they will be in your line of sight longer than John's. See if you can wing one of them."

"Where are you going?" Fia asks, nervous about our separating.

"I'm going further down, to see if I can draw the troopers' fire long enough to allow John to pull back. Now they know we're here, they'll go on the offensive against us soon. I'll try to discourage them."

"Take care," Fia says, moving to my side.

We touch fingers for a brief moment. I wriggle backwards. When clear, I push myself to my feet. Bent double, I hurry down the slope, towards the body of the fallen trooper. I have his automatic tucked under my waistband, the rifle in my left hand and my handgun in my right.

From the other side of the wall, the sound of gunfire is loud, but from a little higher up the slope than my position. Someone's hand lands on top of the wall. A figure looms into view above me. He or she? With a combat helmet and visor, covering most of the head and face, and the chest encased in body armour, it is impossible to tell which gender. At a disadvantage, with both hands on the wall, the figure releases one to reach for a gun. I stretch up, thrust my gun into the gap between the bottom of the chinstrap and the attacker's throat. I pull the trigger.

The body collapses and slides down the wall beside me. Above, I hear Fia's carbine bark twice. I ease two of the capstones away from the wall. Through the gap, I see three men crouched on a terrace. The nearest is ten metres away, the furthest about twenty-five. They are to my left, on a level with me. I put down the automatic. The rifle is a better weapon. With the barrel resting on the stone-base of the opening, I take aim. Firing on the level should improve my accuracy.

I take a deep breath, release it, then tighten my grip on the trigger. The recoil throws me backwards. With a throbbing shoulder, I move back to the wall. The man nearest to me, the one I aimed at, looks round, trying to locate the source of the shot. In agony, the middle one of the three gunmen rolls on the ground, holding the back of his left leg. Luck! I fire three times more, before the rifle jams. I don't hit anyone, but do come close enough to send the remaining pair back across the terrace. They drag their wounded companion with them. I snatch one of my automatics. As they drop to the level below, I open fire.

From above, rapid fire comes from Fia's position, followed by a cry of pain from Charles and Julie's location. I risk a look up the garden.

## CHAPTER 25

John has taken advantage of my intervention, to leave the protection of his shelter. He races across the garden, towards the raised bed. He throws himself to the ground and slides the last couple of metres to take Charles and Julie by surprise. I cannot see what follows, but I hear a rapid exchange of shots. John re-appears and waves. He ducks as an NSF trooper fires in his direction.

I put a fresh magazine in my gun. I hit no-one as I empty it in the direction of the attackers, but I come close to killing several plants and destroying a nearby urn. The retrieval operation has failed. One of the gunmen half-carries his injured companion to the wall at the bottom of the garden. The remaining man retreats, giving covering fire to his colleagues. I fire a couple of shots to keep the men moving. The rotors on the helicopter spin faster as the pilot prepares for take-off. It lifts a few centimetres as the wounded trooper's companions toss him into the back. They scramble on board as the pilot increases power. The machine rises, turns, then dips its nose before it accelerates down the valley.

Without further delay, I move up the hillside. When I reach her, Fia is pale-faced and shaking. I hold her for a moment. She gasps aloud.

"Look, John!" she says, pointing in his direction.

I stare across to where I had last seen him. He leans against the side of the raised bed, his blood-streaked face white, his dark shirt growing darker around a hole in the fabric. For some reason he appears to have lost his vest. We run across the lawn. Behind John, Charles and Julie's lifeless bodies lie sprawled on the ground. An explosion, from the blazing house, shoots flame across the grass several metres away. The heat is intense.

Between us, Fia and I drag John to a safer location, a couple of terraces further down. We ease him to the ground. I rip off his shirt, fold it several times, then press it against the wound. The bullet appears to have missed his lungs. He has no difficulty breathing. A deep gash, caused by another bullet, crosses the side of his head. It appears to have been a glancing blow, but it could account for his disorientation.

"Blasted vest caught fire before I escaped from the cottage," John says. "I had to take it off."

In the distance, sirens blare. The wailing-noise draws closer. I pull Fia down beside me. She keeps pressure on John's wound. I check our guns. We sink lower, keeping below the level of the terrace. Whoever approaches, before we put down our weapons and show ourselves, I want confirmation of where their loyalties lie.

# 26

A fire engine heralds the first of the emergency services. It races along the lane above the cottage, to come to a halt behind our SUV. Within minutes, water and foam arch onto the flames. Out of sight of the fire fighters, we re-locate several terraces down, to the bottom level of the garden. While Fia tends to John, I keep watch on the activity above. Several police cars follow in quick succession. Within minutes, the officers find the bodies by the cottage, and those of the gunmen in the field. A text-message arrives from Harry. He and his men are ten minutes away. The question is, Will he arrive before the police find us? It is to our good fortune the NSF object to the constabulary bearing arms. It means regular civilian-forces continue to patrol without guns.

In streams, dirty, foul-smelling water pours down pathways at the edges of the terraces. The steps nearest to us create a series of cataracts. Foam and debris speed along the surface, to collect in a pool rising against the bottom wall. Because the builders of this barrier had the foresight to build-in drainage channels, the water level remains below our position. Thick black smoke hangs overhead. For a short while, with the movement of the breeze, the acrid fumes drift across us. Our coughing fits attract the attention of a patrolling constable.

From over the side-wall, to our left, she locates our position. For a moment, she speaks into her radio.

"Who are you and what are you doing here?" she calls out as she hoists herself onto the stonework.

At the top of the wall, she pauses. She has noticed our guns.

"Throw down your weapons and kick them away from you," she commands, producing a taser from her belt.

"Sorry, we can't do that," I decline. "They stay with us until we can be sure of our safety. An NSF task force will be here in a few minutes. They'll take command of the situation. If necessary, we'll surrender our weapons to them."

Despite the pain from his wounds, John has recovered some of his wits.

"I'm an NSF officer," he says. "My superior, Major Wardman, is with the task force. He'll provide all the details you want. Please, wait until they reach us."

"Throw me your ID," the PC orders, unsure as to her next move, but courageous, or foolhardy enough to refuse to back-down in the face of an armed threat.

"I'm working undercover," John says, "I don't carry it with me."

"Here, catch." I throw John's mobile towards her. "Press the last incoming call. Speak to the person who answers."

Far away, sirens sound, too distant for anyone to be of immediate assistance. The PC presses the number. After a short conversation, she nods in our direction. She disconnects. With her taser returned to her belt, she jumps from the wall. After splashing through the running water, she offers the 'phone back to me. Fia keeps her automatic pointed in the officer's direction.

"I've to assist you until your people arrive," she says. "I'll take a look at that wound, shall I?" she asks John. "I've had paramedic training."

John nods.

"Go ahead," I say, moving out of her way, and out of range of her hands and feet.

The PC kneels down beside John. Fia comes to sit beside me. Away from the blaze, reaction to events and the cool wind makes us shiver. We huddle for warmth and comfort. The officer's radio bursts into life.

"Two men, one wounded, and a woman," she speaks into her radio.

The squawking sound of a distressed sparrow comes from the device. She seems able to translate the noise.

## CHAPTER 26

"Negative," she responds. "I'm in no danger," she looks at me. I nod, "but the suspects are armed. They say they're undercover NSF officers and that their colleagues are on the way. I've used one of their mobiles to speak to a Major Harry Wardman. He confirms their story."

More screeches blast from the officer's radio, which she listens to, as she tends to John's wound.

"Yes the man could be someone impersonating an officer, but he did identify himself and give his ID number. We'll find out soon enough when he and his team arrive. Sorry sarge, but I've a wounded man to attend to," the PC ends the conversation.

The PC's sergeant has a probable case of arson, several bodies, and others, alive, armed and loose on the property. Under these circumstances, such a person would be a fool to take at face-value an unsubstantiated claim about our identity, nor their subordinate's affirmation of her personal safety. Soon afterwards, half a dozen police officers appear at the other side of the wall. Their tasers point in our direction. The approaching sirens are closing. They fall silent.

In a tone that demands instant obedience, the sergeant in charge commands us to drop our weapons. I whisper into Fia's ear. In a flash, she raises her gun and aims it at the young PC.

"No," I respond. "We wait for my people to arrive."

The sergeant considers his options. He would like his men to fire, but knows, if they do, the resultant effect on Fia could cause her finger to snag the trigger. The young PC keeps her head. She continues to apply pressure to John's wound.

"I'm okay sarge," she calls out. "Do as the man says. We can wait a little longer."

The sergeant orders his men to stand firm, but, to hold fire unless ordered. Stalemate it is. Several minutes pass before, on the terrace above, another voice barks out an order.

"Stand down your men, sergeant."

To our relief, Harry has arrived. Three of his men, weapons in hand, splash down the steps to stand between the police and us. They flash their IDs at the sergeant. A medic follows them, a large first-aid box in his hand. He sprints over to John.

"It's all right officer, I'll take over now," the medic says.

Fia had dropped her gun at the sound of Harry's voice.

"Thanks for all your help," she says to the PC. "You weren't in any danger. My gun's empty."

"Remind me never to play you at poker," the PC says, smiling.

John seems smitten by the young officer. He whispers something into her ear. She blushes, but nods. Without hesitation, she accepts his card before leaving via the steps. Her colleagues have already stepped away from the wall. The sergeant has issues. He has a major incident on his hands, but all his potential suspects and witnesses are either dead or placed beyond his reach. I have some sympathy for the man, but my relief at being out of his custody is greater.

"Come round here, please, sergeant. I want to talk to you."

The sergeant nods in reply to Harry. He climbs up the hill to where the wall is lower and easier to scale. He stops for a few minutes to talk to one of his men.

"You two are bloody idiots," Harry says without rancour, his attention directed at Fia and me. "I told you to stay out of it. John has the skills to take care of such matters by himself. You could have been killed."

Much to the medic's disgust, John staggers to his feet. Wincing with pain, he turns towards Harry.

"Leave 'em alone. I was all right until the helicopter crowd dropped-in. They had me trapped. When this pair of amateurs arrived, I was down to my last couple of rounds. Without them I'd have been dead long before you arrived. They did all right."

"That might be so," Harry's voice is serious, "but they disobeyed instructions. That's a serious offence," he winks at Fia. "I suppose, John, this means you'll be recommending them for a medal."

Two stretcher-bearers come down the steps. Despite John's protests, they insist on carrying him to a waiting ambulance. Fia goes with him. I climb to the next terrace to talk with Harry. The sergeant arrives,

## CHAPTER 26

red-faced and disgruntled. Before he can give vent to his frustration, Harry's mobile rings. He walks away a few steps. After a couple of minutes, he returns, to hand the 'phone to the sergeant.

"Your chief-super' wants a word with you," Harry says. "I've thanked him for your assistance."

The sergeant listens to what seems to be a long monologue, before he says 'Yes, Sir'. He passes the 'phone back to Harry.

"My people are at your disposal," the sergeant accepts his orders with some bitterness. "What are your instructions?"

"The official record of this fire must show it was an unfortunate accident. Colonel and Mrs Thomas returned home after a night out. They went to bed. Faulty wiring in the garage caused a fire. This released toxic fumes that spread to the cottage. The occupants, overcome by these, died in their bed. After a vehicle's petrol-tank exploded, the ensuing inferno spread throughout the building.

"As a member of the NSF, Colonel Thomas was within his rights to store arms and ammunition at his premises. In the heat of the fire, these armaments exploded, the noise of which might have caused people to think there was a gun battle. After a passing NSF helicopter had seen the blaze, it landed nearby. Its occupants attempted a rescue. Three security-officers from that intervention died in the explosion. Other officers received injuries in the blast. The helicopter flew them to a military hospital. A private ambulance is on its way to collect the charred remains of Colonel and Mrs Thomas and the bodies of the other three. Make sure your people know what to do and say."

"I'm sorry, sir," the sergeant says. "I thought you knew. Colonel Thomas survived. He has several suspected cracked ribs, concussion and severe burns to his arms and legs. His wife died from a head-wound, but his vest protected him from the bullets."

"What!" Harry exclaims. "Where is he?"

"He's on the way to hospital."

"Damn it man! Raise the ambulance on the radio now. Tell them to bring him back here. He's a dangerous man."

Via his radio, the sergeant speaks to the control room with a request for them to connect him through to the ambulance. He paces along the terrace-edge. His radio crackles, the operator comes through.

"They've lost contact with the ambulance, sir," the sergeant confesses, bracing himself as chief recipient of Harry's displeasure.

Harry has too much on his mind to waste time on blame.

"Bloody hell! Who's in the ambulance with him?" he asks. "Is there access to the cab from the back?"

"One of the crew was in with the patient, and a member of my force. The driver was on his own in the front. There's a door to the cab from the back. Didn't you pass it on the way in? They were on the way to Airedale Hospital."

"No, I came through Keighley," Harry says. "If they went Laycock way, or diverted across the embankment towards Haworth, I wouldn't have seen them. Is the ambulance fitted with a tracker?"

"Yes, all our emergency vehicles carry them as standard."

"Good, contact your control-room. I want the tracking-number of that vehicle. I'll leave a couple of my men to assist you, sergeant. Give them the information the moment you have it. They'll contact me. Make sure your people, and those from the brigade, know the story I want made public. The press will be here soon. Keep them away from the immediate area, until my people have removed the fatalities."

"Yes sir." The sergeant is happier now he has direct orders to follow.

"Come on Nathan," Harry says. "Let's collect Fia. We must find Charles."

Fia is down the lane at the end of a line of police-vehicles and two black SUV's. An ambulance, I assume with John inside, reverses towards the main road. Fia's face lights up when she sees me. Harry jumps into the back of the end SUV. 'Hurry up' he yells to us. I explain to Fia what has happened, as I bundle her onto the back-seat, beside Harry. One of his men leaps in behind the wheel. Another pulls himself into the front passenger-seat. I stash our handguns and the rifle inside the boot, before I squeeze onto the back seat beside Fia.

## CHAPTER 26

While the driver starts the engine, the man beside him uses a tablet, similar to the one we left in John's car. Harry's 'phone rings. He takes down some details. The man with the device inputs them. As the vehicle reverses down the track, a map and two familiar dots appear on screen.

"It looks as if the target altered direction at Laycock. He's already through Keighley," says the man with the map. "He'll make for the ring-road round Bradford, on his way to the motorway. If we take the Halifax Road to Keighley, it'll cut the distance for us. We won't be far behind him"

The driver spins the vehicle round. We are away.

# 27

At a minimum, we are half an hour behind Charles. Harry's 'phone rings. After a brief conversation, he disconnects.

"The missing PC's made contact," Harry says. "Both he, and the crewman at the back of the ambulance, have minor injuries. They're lucky. Charles could have killed them; he has the capability. He took the PC's taser, threatened the driver then made him pull over. Once the others were out of the vehicle, Charles drove away. They were lucky. There was a farm near to where he abandoned them."

"Can't you call up assistance and have him pulled-over until we catch up?" Fia asks.

"Matters are not that simple," Harry says. "If he's called for help, we could be the ones on the run. As a colonel, Charles outranks me. Without question, he can request help from anyone in uniform. As a major going against someone of senior rank, it limits the number of people I can call on for assistance. What we have in our favour is the severity of Charles's injuries. According to the paramedic, Charles is in agony from his burns. He's acting more by instinct than rational thought

"The paramedic attempted to administer a morphine injection. No-one's sure how much went in. When Charles felt the prick of the needle, he attacked the others. The medic is certain, what did enter Charles's bloodstream will have some effect. With luck, Charles might fall asleep at the wheel and crash into a bridge. I have a couple of vehicles heading in his direction. They'll observe and keep us informed."

Harry falls silent. Fia leans against me, looks up and smiles. This last twenty-four hours have seen an end to our honeymoon neither

## CHAPTER 27

of us had anticipated. I would give anything to be with her, back in Langstrathdale, without a care in the world.

Within the hour we are on the M1, heading south. All the while, Harry receives updates on his mobile. Somehow, he acquires the use of a helicopter, with the result we divert off the motorway at Junction 41, Wakefield. After a short while, our driver pulls up. In the field to our left, between a row of buildings and the road, Harry's ride awaits him, its rotors spinning.

"You two stay with the car," Harry orders us, as he and the man with tablet leave the vehicle. "The driver will take you home."

"Won't we be at risk there?" I ask.

"I doubt it. The ambulance has been weaving about for a while, switching lanes erratically. Now, it's come to a halt on the hard-shoulder, about thirty miles south of here. Charles is unconscious. My men are with the vehicle. They tell me his condition doesn't look good. Since we've been able to track the ambulance, there's been no signal transmitted from it. It doesn't look as if Charles has attempted to contact anyone. There's room in the chopper for one of my men and me, but no more. For the moment, you two should be safe at home. I've requested a protection detail for you. By the time you reach there, there'll be someone outside."

The pair slams their doors. In the hedgerow, close to where we have pulled up, a rotting wooden-gate hangs loose. Harry pushes it open. Within seconds, they have run across the long damp grass to the waiting aircraft. The doors close. The helicopter lifts off. We head back to the motorway. To our relief, our part in today's adventures has ended, or so we hope.

For several miles we lapse into silence. A combination of shock, exhaustion and the after-effects of the adrenaline-rush at the cottage mean we have run out of energy. On the outskirts of Leeds, Fia begins to cry. Tears stream down her face.

"Uncle Joe," she says, looking at me, her eyes red-rimmed. "How could he betray us like that?"

"I don't know," I start to say.

I stop myself. Of course, I know. In earlier years, had I been much different? I, too, had been all for the party, or had I? At first, my belief in JJ's utopian vision had been absolute, but, in the end, the methods employed to achieve and maintain it had disillusioned me. Now, I would settle for a taste of freedom in a land that promised an absence of slavery and fear. A consensus on what constitutes an ideal model for living I now think impossible to achieve.

"Power," I say aloud. "Joe became a slave to it. JJ sees himself as some godlike deity to the nation. Joe thought himself an elite acolyte. He was the ultimate follower, willing to do anything to bring about his master's dreams. Between them, and others of a like mind, they want to build a nation of people who, without dissent, do the government's bidding. Once injected with the living chip, its recipients will become worker-ants, programmed to follow orders, or commit suicide by rebelling. Whatever feelings Joe might once have had towards family and friends, he was happy to sacrifice them all, for influence."

"So, we were nothing to him, me, mum, dad and Sean. He used us, and dad's business, as cover. When we were no longer of use to him, he discarded us. How could we have been so stupid?"

"You weren't stupid. Joe was a master; he fooled everyone. He duped me, yet I was on my guard. Don't forget Julie. That day, Charles convinced me she had died. I was certain I had condemned her out of my own mouth, yet all the time both were in the background laughing at me."

"What a useless pair we are," Fia acknowledges, with a wan smile.

"At least we have each other. That will do me for now."

"For now?" Fia raises her eyebrow.

I pat her on her middle.

"There's junior to consider, too," I explain with a grin.

I become silent again. An awful thought has entered my mind.

"Fia," I say, alarm in my voice, "at the cottage. There were no children there, were they?"

## CHAPTER 27

If they were, the flames had claimed them.

"No, when we arrived, the place was empty," Fia answers, to my great relief.

"Where the hell are they?" Worry intensifies my tone.

"Harry might be able to help," Fia replies. "Joe must have known, but I'm sure he kept the information to himself."

"That's the type of rotten trick he would play. He used hope and snippets of information to persuade me he could find Ian and Caroline. I wonder whereabouts in Lancashire Charles and Julie lived? It couldn't have been too far away from their HQ."

"I doubt very much the children lived with them on a regular basis. Charles didn't strike me as the fatherly-type. Neither he nor Julie kept regular hours. She gave the impression of deep commitment to her work in the NSF. I suspect the children will be at a private boarding school. I'm sure Harry will contact us soon. If we ask him, his people should be able find-out something."

"I hope so." I remain unconvinced.

For a while we lapse into silence. When Fia does speak again, her voice is wistful.

"Home, I cannot wait to be back."

I have a flashback, to the state in which I found my home when I returned to it after Julie's supposed death. Yesterday, after Johnson took Fia and me away, his men were to search our house. I dread the mess they will have left behind. I break the news to Fia. She sighs, but her relief at our release, and being able to return home, transcends any negative aspects.

"Well, we'll have some tidying up to do," she says, ever practical.

I nod, but fear we may have greater need of a builder than a local cleaning service.

# 28

Mid-afternoon, the driver pulls up outside our house. Fia's car stands where we left it on the driveway. Outside our front door, a lone officer is on duty. A dark blue car has parked on the opposite side of the road.

"Harry's men," states our driver, when he sees the look of concern on my face. "For a few days they'll work shifts, until he's certain you're no longer in danger. The officer outside is one of his people. She's been keeping watch on the property for you."

He puts out his hand. We shake it in turn.

"Thanks," we say to him.

The officer at the door hands me my keys.

"Nobody's been in, since yesterday," she says. "You've some nosy neighbours. I told them there'd been a misunderstanding; you would be home today. They seemed more relieved they weren't going to be involved, rather than from any concern for you."

"That's understandable," I reply with wry smile. "Thanks for making sure everything here is secure."

"My pleasure," she says.

She jumps into the passenger-seat of the car in which we arrived. With quick waves, they are away. I look at Fia. She looks at me. With some trepidation at what we might find, I turn the key.

Much to our relief, we find our luggage stacked in neat piles at the side of the hallway. The bags are open, the contents searched, but not strewn everywhere. The inside of the house is dark and gloomy, the curtains left drawn. In the lounge, with them pulled back, the room's contents are visible. A cushion on the suite is the wrong way round, books and ornaments have been disturbed, furniture moved out of position, but there is no sign of the wanton damage nor destruction I had expected.

The rest of the house is in much the same condition. The search has been thorough, but done with care and regard to property. The one sign of damage is in the kitchen, which we visit last. The cover from the extractor fan, behind which John found the transmitter, is on the floor. A thought occurs to me - he would have had little difficulty in finding the equipment. It is probable he was the one who installed it. It was part of Harry's plan to use me as bait, in his attempts to find the location of the living-cell production unit.

"I don't understand," I say. "I expected to find the place gutted. When the NSF went through my former house, they smashed or tore everything apart. They ripped up floor boards and pulled cupboards from the walls."

"This must be John's doing," Fia says. "He was in charge of the search here. It's he to whom we should be grateful."

I pick up the 'phone extension. It has a clear dialling-tone. There are no clicks, nor buzzes associated with a tap. I switch-on the kettle. The important things come first. We have had nothing to eat nor drink, since those provided by Johnson in the early hours of the morning. Fia finds some powdered milk. After thawing-out several slices of bread from the freezer, we dine on tinned-tuna sandwiches.

"What first?" Fia asks. "A tidy up, trip to the supermarket or shall we split the tasks?"

We toss a coin. Fia hands me the shopping list, then starts to sort clothes from the open cases. As I disappear to the shops, I hear the washing machine start its cycle. A couple of hours later, when I return, everything looks to be back in its rightful place. Fia runs the vacuum round the lounge. She looks weary, but happy to be back in control.

"Leave it," I say. "I'll finish the cleaning. You put your feet up. You don't want to do too much in your condition."

"I'm pregnant, not ill," she says, in some indignation, but she stops. "Okay, I'll make a drink while you empty the bags."

With the house back to normal and everything in its rightful place, we stretch-out on the sofa to watch the late evening news. I can remember when this TV channel was independent and respected, one of hundreds available. Now, with all media under government control, only a handful remains. Censorship is rigid, the resulting news stories believed by few. Foreign TV and radio stations remain jammed. It used to be possible to access some overseas news via the internet, but now computers come pre-programmed to block everything but government-sanctioned sites. Some people modify their machines to by-pass this control, but, if caught, the perpetrators face severe penalties.

Nearby, the remnants of a take-away curry litter the coffee table; a spicy aroma permeates the room. Neither of us had the energy to cook. On the news, speculation abounds concerning an explosion that destroyed an NSF HQ in Lancashire, today. The report quotes unnamed sources, close to the NSF, as saying there could be links to the saboteurs who blew up a research-centre in Coxheath. House-to-house searches are ongoing in the area. I exchange glances with Fia. We pity any poor soul caught-up in the mayhem. A news-flash interrupts the programme. Sombre martial music plays in the background. A solemn-faced presenter appears on screen.

'It is with deep regret, we announce the deaths of two senior members of the NSF, officers who devoted their lives in the service of our glorious country. Colonel Charles Thomas and his wife, Major Julie Thomas, died this morning, when fire broke out at their cottage in the Yorkshire Dales. Three other members of the security-forces, who attempted a rescue, also perished when the fuel tanks in Colonel Thomas's garaged vehicle ignited...'

The broadcast continues for a while longer. To our surprise, Harry appears on screen. He pays glowing tribute to Charles's record in the NSF and his previous service in the army. Harry talks about the couple's devotion to the state. We know he has to maintain his cover, but to us, the effect is stomach churning. Fia grabs the remote from

## CHAPTER 28

my knee. The TV goes off. She selects another controller. Soon, the soothing sounds of Mozart fill the air - something in itself that would find little favour with our militaristic music-minded ministry of entertainment. However, the news flash does pose a conundrum.

"So, do we take it Charles has died?" I ask.

The question is rhetorical. Fia's knowledge is no greater than mine.

"I don't know," she replies. "He could have, or Harry might have placed him somewhere out of the way, before recording the eulogy."

"After that announcement, there's no way Harry can permit him to live. If Charles is alive, I suspect Harry will extract as much information as possible, before a quiet execution takes place."

I can find no sympathy for Charles, nor Julie. Fia has told me some of the things the couple had intended to do to her, and our future child. Joe had been right to be worried about them. What they had planned was the product of twisted minds. The sound of a ring-tone comes from upstairs. It is not one of ours. Those, we assume, were lost in the explosion at the NSF HQ.

"Whose 'phone's that?" Fia asks.

"It must be John's," I say, as Fia removes her head from my chest. "I slipped it into my pocket when we were in Stanbury, after Harry rang."

I hurry upstairs. The mobile should be in the pocket of the trousers I changed out of earlier. The ring-tone stops by the time I reach the landing. With the 'phone in my hand, I tap the 'missed call' message. A dial-tone sounds, as I reach the bottom of the stairs. Moments later, I hear Harry's voice.

"Nathan, is that you? I called at the hospital, earlier, to see John. He thought you might have hung onto his 'phone."

"Yes, I forgot to give it back. How is he?"

The mobile uses secure transmissions, so we can speak freely.

"He was about to have surgery to remove the bullet. I spoke to the surgeon. He said it was nothing; the bullet had missed everything vital. John will be in hospital for a few days. They expect him to make a full recovery. The head wound was of greater concern. He had a scan, but they found no signs of internal bleeding, nor swelling of the brain; he was lucky. When I arrived, that young police constable was with him. John seems enamoured with her. Did you see the news report?" Harry asks.

"Yes. Is it true?" I want to know.

"Charles? Yes, he's dead. He had severe burns to his arms and legs, a deep head wound and had lost a lot of blood from a bullet wound. The morphine he received deadened his pain enough to allow him to drive, but, at the same time, impaired his mental capacity. He died before we reached the ambulance. His hands had welded themselves to the steering wheel. His mobile was in his pocket, but I doubt he would have been able to use it. Much of the flesh was gone from his fingers. According to the medics, he suffered heart failure, brought on by hypovolemic shock. How the hell he managed to drive that far, or subdue the people in the ambulance, I've no idea. Sheer willpower, is my guess."

Because I have the mobile on 'speaker', Fia can hear everything.

"Hi Harry," she calls out.

"Oh! Hello Fia. How are you?" he asks.

"Never better," she says, pulling me down next to her. "Are you sure we're safe at home?"

"Yes, for now. Over the years, Charles and Julie kept to themselves details of their shenanigans over Nathan's treatment. Later, once Joe found out, he did the same. The surveillance of Nathan, they disguised and passed-off the costs as training exercises.

"The living-cell programme is top secret. No-one is supposed to know about it. For that reason, Joe didn't want you talking to other members of the security-forces. To do so could have created problems for him. To prevent that, he had you both classified as informants. Anything that might identify you, Joe restricted or redacted. It meant no-one but he could contact you. Information linking you to Charles and Julie, or identifying you as members of the opposition, was either lost in the HQ explosion or the fire at the cottage. Apart from family

## CHAPTER 28

and marriage connections between you two and Joe, I've found nothing physical that might incriminate you. We've searched Joe's house, but it was clean. He appears to have committed nothing to paper nor his computer."

"Won't the people, who came with Johnson to arrest us, say something?" Fia asks.

"There was no formal arrest," Harry answers. "Those who brought you to the HQ died there. John told the people, who aided in the search of your house, you were assisting authorities, but neither of you was under suspicion. He told them, to gain intelligence on you and Nathan, the Underground planted the device he found. Few people have knowledge of the incident. Loyalist members of the NSF, who are aware of it, consider you as victims rather than perpetrators. Those who know your full history, if they come to hear the story, may harbour suspicions, but I doubt they will voice them."

"Much of what you've said sounds a little thin on credibility to me," I say, unconvinced.

"Charles, Julie and Joe are no longer around to contradict," Harry explains. "Those who worked for them are aware, now, they have participated in operations of doubtful legality. These people are no different to the rest of us; they want to survive. To avoid arrest, or a new posting to some godforsaken island off the coast of Scotland, they'll do and say anything I want. That includes those from the helicopter who survived the gunfight today. I'm in charge now."

"Is work going to be a problem?" I ask.

"It shouldn't be. You will be without Sara. She's been charged with sabotage, and leaking sensitive information. Because she knows too much, there will be no court-appearance. Sara, her fiancé and family, will disappear."

"You cannot kill them," Fia exclaims in horror. "They've done nothing wrong. That makes us as bad as Joe and Charles."

"Of course they won't be killed, nor imprisoned," Harry laughs. "They're at a safe-house. By the time we report their 'execution', for crimes against the state, they'll have new identities, homes and jobs in New Zealand. Arrangements are close to completion. In a week or two, they'll be shipped-out on a cargo vessel."

"Oh! That's all right," Fia says. "Are they happy about it?"

"To be honest, they're glad to be leaving the country. Our contacts out there will set-up bank accounts for them, with a generous amount of compensation. They'll own their homes outright, without a mortgage. At some time in the future, when it's safe for them to do so, they'll have the option to return or stay where they are. It will be up to them to decide."

"That seems fair," I say. "I'd hate Sara to suffer through no fault of her own. She should do well out there."

"What shall I do at work?" Fia asks.

"You have to go back and act as if nothing has happened," Harry says. "Despite Joe's decision to kill you both this morning, I do know when he revised his Will, after your parent's death, he left everything to you, Fia. The business is yours, or it will be once the legal details are complete. That might take some time. For now, news of Joe's death must remain a secret.

"We have to wait for the clean-up operation to go ahead, and forensics to identify the bodies once they are recovered from the rubble. For now, Fia, if anyone asks, as far as you know, Joe is alive and well. After a few days, show concern about his absence. If forensics hasn't come up with anything by then, report him missing.

"Let your deputy take charge of your division, while you take the reins at Sandiman's head office. Contact Joe's solicitor then. He has an affidavit signed by Joe that, if through mental or physical incapacity, or, as now, unexplained absence, he cannot run the business, it gives you power of attorney to do so. He set it up in case of accident, but, until his death is official, it will permit you to operate the company. Because you're an executor of his will, that should allow you to keep the business going, once we uncover and identity his body."

"How do you know all this?" Fia is amazed.

## CHAPTER 28

"Joe told me about it a while ago, after a major incident on the motorway. He said if ever he was involved in something such as that, he had his wishes covered, then he told what he'd done. Are you both in tomorrow evening?" Harry asks, "There are some matters I want to discuss."

"Yes," we say.

"Okay, see you then, must go," Harry disconnects.

Fia and I digest what we have learned. I am lucky, I have no-one but James to face in my department. He might know a little about the weekend's events, but I can bluff my way around that. If the directors question anything, I shall refer them to Harry.

Fia has a larger problem. She has an office to run. Somehow, she has to pretend nothing untoward has happened over the weekend, and her *wonderful* Uncle Joe is still alive. That will be tough. Despite Joe's duplicity, he was central to her life for many years. She has grief mixed with feelings of anger and hatred.

For me, it is different. My betrayal by Joe has left me with little sorrow nor sympathy for the man. As for Julie? That is somewhat more complicated. I have mourned once. I want to believe that contempt for her is all I should have, but the shock of her re-appearance and subsequent death has had some effect. I expect these next few weeks and months to be tough for both Fia and me.

We retire to bed, early. Neither of us finds sleep easy to come by. In each other's arms, we are content with the closeness of our bodies, but our minds are elsewhere. Each time I close my eyes, I see the faces of the men, who died at my hands today. Unlike Johnson, Charles or Joe, I derive no pleasure from the act of killing. Since the first time, when my error was responsible for those deaths at the factory, sudden, violent death has had a detrimental effect on my psyche. I am no different now. Or am I? Although, sickened, I have avoided the dark place into which I would once have descended. These men had tried to kill Fia and our unborn child. I suppose that has made the difference. I drift off to sleep, wondering what Harry wants to discuss tomorrow-night.

# 29

Bleep. Bleep. The alarm sounds. I look at the clock – six thirty in the morning. After a weekend of surprises and horror, our honeymoon seems a distant memory. This is to be our first day back at work. Fia's eyes have dark rings around them. She spends some time trying to disguise the marks.

"Don't worry," I say, giving her a hug. "We've been on honeymoon. Your staff will exchange knowing winks behind your back. Nobody will suspect anything else."

She blushes.

"I suppose so," she agrees. "No, not now." With a laugh, she wriggles out of my grasp. "We both need to have an early start at work. Harry said we should act as if everything was normal."

Morning sickness interrupts our conversation and my desires. We miss breakfast. Fia leaves first. As soon as she is out of the driveway, I open the garage doors. My car has been idle for over a week. After several attempts, I persuade the engine to start. The drive to work is automatic, the rush hour traffic undiminished during my week's absence.

From the outside, nothing much has changed. My name remains on the wall behind my parking place. I am a good hour ahead of my usual start-time; most other reserved-spaces are empty. I cannot shake the guilt I suffer about Sara. She does not deserve the destruction to her reputation that will happen soon. Sad to say, to preserve my position, and that of Fia's, this slander is something I shall have to promote.

Unlike my home, my office has received the full NSF treatment. Ceiling-tiles hang loose, drawers and their contents lie strewn across

## CHAPTER 29

the floor. Two desks are on their ends. In a corner, upended chairs lean against the walls. Groaning, I set about restoring as much as I can to its original order. Our office chairs are swivel ones on castors. From a waiting-room down the corridor, I borrow a four-legged chair to stand on to re-insert the ceiling-tiles into the grid. After returning the borrowed item, I find James in the office. He looks-round in a daze.

"Oh!" he says, on seeing me. "I didn't know whether you'd be coming back, er, in today," he corrects himself. "I hope Sara's in soon. Did you have a good time on your honeymoon?" He blushes when he realises what he has said. "I mean was the weather good, the hotel and stuff?"

His experience with the NSF, on Saturday, must have been traumatic. He has developed a tic round his left eye. He appears nervous.

"Yes, we had a great time, weather was excellent. We did plenty of walking. A pity our return home was a bit rubbish. We spent most of the weekend answering questions and trying to work out what's been going on here. You won't be seeing Sara again."

"Sara! Why?"

"I don't know too many details at the moment," I lie, "but it's something to do with industrial espionage and sabotage. She bugged my laptop. Some of her friends did the same to my home. Take my advice, distance yourself from any connection you might have had with her. It's bound to attract suspicion to you."

James's shock is genuine.

"Bloody hell," he says. "I can't believe it. The NSF took me in for questioning on Saturday, but released me late evening. They asked in detail about you, Sara and your work here. I never suspected either of you of doing anything wrong. I told them so. What's going to happen to Sara?"

"I doubt that's something you want to know, James, but it does mean that Sara's position is now yours. Before you can concentrate on that, we have to recruit someone to take over your current workload. Until we do, are you happy to take on extra work? For a few weeks it will mean longer hours."

"Er...yes...sure!" James stutters.

He will come to see this as a golden opportunity to further his career. I have little doubt he will make an excellent replacement for Sara. Unlike her, I hope we can avoid having to sacrifice him on the altar of deceit.

It takes half the morning to put back everything into its rightful place. I re-instate the computers into the network. James re-connects the 'phones. Between us, we sort jumbled piles of paperwork back into some order. The loss of my laptop, in the blast at the NSF HQ, could be a problem. It holds the software I need to establish a connection to special projects division. Until I receive a replacement, I am unable to access anything on their server. That machine will contain back-ups of my work, but, without the link, those are denied to me.

June, from reception rings.

"There's a special delivery down here for you, Mr Andrews," her voice chirrups in my ear. "It's from Mr Wardman. It has to be signed-for by you."

"I'll be right down."

James is busy on his computer, dealing with new requests from production. I leave him to his work. On my way down, I puzzle as to what Harry has sent me. On arrival, I find the deliveryman is the person who drove Fia and me home yesterday. We exchange pleasantries while I sign for the package. Curious, I take it back to my office. On unravelling the wrapping and thick padding, to my delight, I find my laptop and a note from Harry.

*Hi, Nathan. Before I left yesterday, I picked-up this. One of my techies put it back together, minus the bug, then tested it. I thought you might need it. See you tonight, although it might be late. Harry*

The charger had remained behind, when John removed the machine. I plug-in the laptop. Twenty minutes later, I am into special projects' server. My files soon update with everything that has happened at work, since my wedding day. James and I stay late. In my absence, he and Sara have kept on top of the work. He has nothing outstanding to

## CHAPTER 29

distract him from today's new requests. Harry, too, had followed my instructions. One or two additional items have appeared, but I soon programme them into the schedule.

James takes on more than half of Sara's workload. I absorb the remainder into mine. One of the first matters I deal with is to contact Andrew Faulds, at Sandiman's. By close of work, he promises to email me a selection from which to choose to interview for James's former role. Because news of Joe is still under wraps, Andrew remains unaware of his boss's demise. He is aware of my marriage to Joe's niece, who is a director of the company. As a result, he is more talkative than during our last encounter.

The seven o'clock pips sound on the car-radio as I pull into the drive, behind Fia's car. She had rung earlier to let me know she expected to be home first. I open the door to the aroma of something delicious cooking. I realise how hungry I am. We had missed breakfast and, for me, lunchtime had consisted of half the sandwich James had fetched from the local supermarket. Had I tried it, the plastic wrapping might have been tastier.

Within half an hour, Fia and I are at the table, enjoying our first home-cooked meal in our own home, as man and wife. With a candle on the table, we dine with that and some subdued-lighting in the background. Afterwards, with reluctance, we each take a pile of paperwork from our briefcases. It is time to start work again. Fia has a couple of new contracts to study. I have a dozen CVs I'd printed-off to go through. Out of the prospective hopefuls, I select five to interview. Fia, the expert in such matters, scans my selection. She nods in approval.

"Andrew's excellent at his job," she says. "Within minutes, he has the knack of discerning a candidate's strengths and weaknesses. I'm pleased he has no involvement with Joe's other work. Those party members he set-on after dad died have moved on. Only agency specialists are employed now."

No longer can she bring herself to call Joe, 'uncle'. His betrayal has stripped him of that right, and of any acknowledgement that he was a family-member. When the news of his death breaks, it will be difficult for Fia. To her will fall the task of shedding crocodile tears at his funeral. Shock, at his premature death, I can summon by harnessing my thoughts at his duplicity.

"Today, I've been thinking," Fia continues. "When I move over to head-office and assume control, I already have someone who can run my division. Whenever I've been away from the office, Rosaline has stood in for me. She's done a good job. If I promote her to divisional manager, Adele has the experience to take over Ros's role. There are several juniors capable of added responsibility, but those arrangements, Ros and Adele can handle."

"That should work," I say, after a moment. "I can't remember you having had any problems when you've been away. Have you considered head-office? In a few months, you might struggle to devote your full attention to the business. After the birth, too, you'll be away from the office for a while."

"I know, I've given that plenty of thought too. I have an idea I want to discuss it with you. What do *you* think about Andrew?"

"He comes across as knowledgeable, efficient and pleasant; the staff there seems to respect him. Why?"

"I think he's the best person to take over in my absence. I shall return on a part time basis as soon as I'm able but, while on maternity leave, I intend to hold weekly meetings with him. It had crossed my mind about making him general manager, while I remain as CEO, retaining overall control. Andrew can manage the day-to-day running of the business. He's too good to lose. I'd hate him to go elsewhere, or set up in competition. If this offer keeps him at Sandiman's, it'll give me the freedom to spend time with our baby."

"That sounds sensible, and reasonable."

"One other thing. I'm going to bring you onto the board, too."

"Me! I know nothing about the recruitment business."

"That's true, but I want you there. I want someone I can rely on to back me, whenever necessary."

## CHAPTER 29

Convinced I shall be more a hindrance than a positive influence my agreement is tentative. A seat on the board, in an advisory capacity to Fia should have no effect on my position at Aitkins.

By nine-thirty, we have completed our paperwork. Stretched-out on the sofa, we have the television on in the background, while we await Harry's arrival. There has been no message from him. He could be anywhere. Later, on the news, the presenter gives an update on last-night's story about the NSF HQ explosion. Something has changed; she now refers to it as a terrible accident. There is no mention of Sara. A vehicle pulls-up outside our drive.

"That'll be Harry," Fia says. "You let him in; I'll switch-on the kettle."

"Sorry I'm late," Harry apologises, as he breezes into the house. "I've driven straight from the airport, meetings in London all day," he explains. "JJ summoned me down this morning. Allow me to introduce you to the new head of NSF, North of England Special Operations Task Force, me."

"Congratulations," I say. "How the hell did you manage that? I know from the news you've diverted suspicion about the explosion in Lancashire, and covered-up Charles's death as an accident, but how will you explain Joe's death?"

By now, we are in the lounge. Fia brings in the coffee. Harry declines an offer of something to eat.

"I ate on the plane," he says. "I told JJ the truth, or a version of it. I said Joe had died in the explosion at the NSF HQ. Forensics would provide proof of that. I also informed him I had authorised the deaths, if necessary, of Charles and Julie."

"You did what?" Fia asks in disbelief.

I am speechless.

"There was no other way," Harry says. "No matter how much we tried to keep our involvement hidden, other than those under my control, there are too many people who can tell tales. Mass-murder might preserve my secrets for a while, but I am averse to Charles's methods. I told JJ a version of the truth - that Sara was the mole at Aitkins. I said she worked for Joe, as did Charles and Julie. I explained they had hatched a plan to sabotage a secret government project. It was they who had arranged the destruction of Coxheath."

"Didn't JJ ask how you knew about the project?" I ask.

"He questioned me in detail about what I'd discovered. I said the details were unknown to me. I knew it was top-secret, but nothing more. I told JJ you had become suspicious, at work, about Sara. When you discovered the bugs, you reported the discovery to me. I said I recruited John. Between us, we traced the source of the devices to Joe. Afterwards, I did the rest."

"Didn't JJ query why Joe planted a mole at Aitkins when he already knew what went on there, or why you hadn't reported to him earlier?"

"Oh! Yes. He asked why I'd kept quiet. I explained that, until I'd found the extent of Joe's treachery, there was no-one whom I could trust. As Joe, Charles and Julie, had JJ's confidence, I had to be sure, before I went to him with my findings. I revealed the three had kidnapped you and Fia, on your return from honeymoon.

"Sara was a part of Joe's plan, to divert suspicion from him and to frame you for Coxheath. I explained I'd sent John, with a couple of loyal men, to the NSF Lancs HQ, to rescue you. When they arrived, they found the place under the control of Joe's followers. John's men succeeded in infiltrating the area, where they found Nathan. Joe died in a gunfight, Charles and Julie escaped, taking Fia as a hostage.

"I told him you and John fought your way out, unaware that other members of Joe's team had set explosive charges on the lower floors. When I arrived, later, it was to find the place in ruins. I told JJ you and John had given chase to Charles and Julie. You caught up with them at their cottage, where Julie received fatal wounds in a gun-battle. You and John were able to free Fia. Later, I went in pursuit of Charles. By the time I came up to him, his injuries had proved fatal."

"JJ believed all this?" Fia is sceptical, as am I.

"He made several calls. Everything checkable confirmed what I told him. By the end of the week, he wants a full report on his desk.

## CHAPTER 29

I've several people working on it. By the time it's complete, it'll be watertight. He agreed with the release of the story, about the deaths of Charles and Julie, being an accident. The last thing JJ wants to become public knowledge, is a plot by senior personnel against him.

"As to Sara, he wants her to disappear. No court case, no publicity, nothing at all. Once we've extracted everything we can from her, I've to put a bullet through her head. The official report into the explosion at the HQ will conclude there was no terrorist involvement; it was a tragic accident. JJ is conscious of unrest, which makes him want to deny giving any publicity to the dissenters. We know how he intends to solve his problems - with the immunisation project."

"Sara is going to be all right, you promised?" I know Harry has made assurances, but I have to ask.

"Of course she is. I have someone composing her confession now. It will include everything for which I want Sara, and her 'co-conspirators', to take the blame. Sara and her family, with her fiancé, are in a 'safe-house'. I informed JJ I would keep them away from NSF main centres, in case there were further rogue elements. JJ agreed. He charged me with routing-out any subversive elements."

"I am glad Sara's safe, and her fiancé's with her," Fia says.

"Once we have the confession complete, and Sara signs it, they'll be away," Harry says. "In a matter related to that, there's something I want to put to you," he adds.

"Well, go on, tell us," Fia prompts after a long pause from him.

"JJ believes I know nothing about his plans to subjugate the population, neither does he intend to tell me. Whoever has his confidence, the loss of Joe and his people does not appear to have affected their ability to keep that programme under control. With my promotion to Colonel, and my additional responsibilities, my base of operations has moved to York. In a couple of weeks a new party-representative will arrive at Aitkins. He'll leave you and your department alone, Nathan. That aside, I have something I want you to consider." Harry comes to the point at last.

"I can offer you both, with Sara, safe passage out of the country. You would have new identities, and a home in either Canada or New Zealand. The choice is yours. Here, you risk exposure for the work you do to help the resistance and me. If you accept the offer, it means you would be safe and out of the reach of the authorities," the hesitancy in his words is noticeable.

"That sounds attractive, but I have an idea you want something different. Come on Harry, stop prevaricating," I urge, with more than a suspicion I already know the answer.

"The underground still needs to know when the components for the syringes ship-out from Aitkins. Because I'm no longer involved with the company, I cannot keep up with developments, there, in special projects. JJ is no fool. If I attach an unnatural importance to Aitkins's work, now I've severed my connection with the business, he'll become suspicious. I'm sure, from now on, he intends to keep an eye on what I do, and how I behave. After his supposed betrayal by Joe, he's distrustful of everyone."

"Harry, please, tell us what you want from us." Fia says, exasperated by his long-winded approach.

"I want Nathan to remain at Aitkins, to continue gathering information. It will be more dangerous than before. The new rep might have no specific concerns about Nathan, but he will pay close attention to what goes on in experimental. JJ cannot allow anything to interfere with component production."

"We'll stay," Fia's agreement is instant.

"No, I'll stay," I contradict. "Fia must go to safety. She has our child to think about. Before I can leave, I need to find Ian and Caroline."

"That won't be possible," Fia says. "Either we both go, or we both stay. If I disappear, you will come under suspicion, Nathan. Over the years, too much has happened around you for your wife to disappear without question. I can see two scenarios. One, the NSF will think I've fled or, two, they'll believe you've killed me. Either way, Harry won't be able to keep you out of trouble."

## CHAPTER 29

"That's a little far-fetched," I differ.

"She's right, Nathan," Harry says. "If Fia disappears, either one of those two circumstances is a distinct possibility. In those circumstances, and with my past connections to you, there's little chance I could intervene again. If I did, investigators would suspect me of collusion. There is too much else at stake to risk suspicion falling on me, or my associates."

"In which case, neither of us can go," I say. "If we do, your past links to us would direct suspicion your way."

I take Fia's hands in mine.

"Are you sure about this?" I ask.

She nods.

"There's your answer Harry, we carry on as usual. How do we keep in touch?"

"Through John." Harry sounds relieved at our decision. "For a number of years, he's been a friend to Fia and, over recent times, to you, Nathan. You can continue that relationship without arousing suspicion. Pass on any information to him. Keep his 'phone for emergencies.

"As to the information you acquire, Nathan, you must be more circumspect than in the past. The new rep will be watching everyone, like a hawk. His appointment comes via the party in London; he's a strict loyalist. You cannot take copies of anything you see. Neither can you show any interest in unattended papers, nor computer screens. Over the next few months, all we want from you are shipment dates and destinations for the components ordered by Zavrol Pharmaceutical, normal production runs and experimental samples. Because you handle works and route-planning, these are matters you have every right to know."

"That sounds sensible," Fia says.

"How is John?" She asks, changing the subject.

"He's sore and grumbling about his stay in hospital although, when she's off duty, the lovely constable Linda keeps him entertained. The doctors won't release him until the end of the week. The operation on his shoulder went well, it's his head-wound they want to keep under observation for a while longer. He's in a private room at the Infirmary in Leeds."

"I'll take an extended lunch and pop round to see him tomorrow," Fia offers.

"That'll please him. He hates doing nothing. His lady-friend is on duty during the day tomorrow."

Soon afterwards, he takes his leave. His day has been longer than has ours. The watchers in the car across the road have been withdrawn. For the moment, we are in the clear. I lock the door on the world. Tomorrow is soon enough to return to the realities of life.

# 30

On Wednesday evening, sitting round John's hospital bed, we find him in good spirits. His new friend, Linda, had left minutes before our arrival. When we entered the room, he had a smile, and a lipstick-mark on his face. His headaches, caused by a glancing bullet striking the side of his head in the fight at the cottage, have eased. In the morning, on the provision he has a good night's sleep and shows no signs of relapse, he expects the doctors to discharge him. He declines our offer of a lift. Linda, it seems, is to pick him up from the hospital. Fia gives him an old-fashioned look, to which John blushes. It seems, under the gruff, tough exterior, he has a soft centre after all.

"Oh! Harry popped in to see me this morning," John says, before Fia can ask leading questions. "I mentioned both of you would be visiting tonight. He asked me to pass on some news to you, Nathan."

"What's that?" I ask.

"He has a lead to where your children might be."

I sit back, feeling faint in the overheated room. Fia passes me a glass of water. She puts an arm round me in support. It is rare for me to mention my children, but she knows they are never far from my mind.

"Go on," I croak.

"What Julie said, about the children being hers, was nonsense. You signed no documents giving away your rights. Because it would have been difficult to make an application for custody, without you finding out she was alive, a court-order was not applied for."

"Why did she say that?" Fia asks.

"Pure evil," John says. "She wanted Nathan to suffer as much as possible before they had you both killed. The whole charade, about whether Nathan would lead Charles and her to the underground-hierarchy was ill-thought out and, at best, a long-shot. No matter what they told Joe, it was sadistic pleasure at Nathan's downfall and struggle that motivated them. Once Julie had fallen under Charles's spell, she became a willing participant in all his schemes. They kept you under sufficient pressure to keep you from questioning your treatment. With you banned from PNU membership, and them based in Lancashire, they knew it was doubtful you would ever cross paths."

John stops for a moment as he struggles to sit higher in his bed. Fia adjusts his pillows. He returns to the topic that interests me most.

"Yesterday morning, Harry discovered Charles and Julie had a large detached property on the outskirts of Clitheroe, near to their base at the NSF HQ. Harry sent a team to search the house. There were no signs of the children. That would have been too easy. The housekeeper, once she learned her employers had died, became most informative. She has few fond memories of Charles or Julie. They treated her like dirt, but the job paid well.

"At the time of Julie's supposed execution and Nathan's arrest, the children were at her parents'. Straight away, Julie moved them to a house in Northallerton. The stories about her parents' arrest, subsequent treatment and of being a broken couple were total fabrication. After a couple of months, the children came to live with Julie and Charles, in Lancashire. He was against the idea. The last thing he wanted was to have children under his feet.

"Julie told them to forget about Nathan; Charles was their daddy, now. According to the housekeeper, young Ian said Charles would never be his dad; he already had one. Julie slapped Ian; he kicked Charles between the legs. After that, the relationship between him and the children deteriorated. For a couple of months, they co-existed. Julie had a choice to make. She chose Charles and her career rather than the children. They went to live with her parents again."

"Are Ian and Caroline there now?" I ask, fearful that attempts to brainwash them against me may have taken place.

## CHAPTER 30

"No, Julie's mum died eighteen months ago. Alone, her dad was unable cope with two young children. Charles refused to have them back. Julie arranged for a family to foster them. Harry has someone trying to trace them. The housekeeper believes they are somewhere in the Darlington area, but she doesn't have an address. The house-search yielded nothing useful. The housekeeper said Charles and Julie had transferred most of their private papers to the cottage. We have sent someone to talk with Julie's father, to see whether he has any contact details.

"The housekeeper overheard a number of heated 'phone conversations between Julie and her parents. Julie's parents, it seems, disapproved of Charles and his treatment of their grandchildren. This may come as a surprise, Nathan, but they refused to bring-up the children to believe you were a traitor, who abandoned them to their fate. Julie's mother was not your greatest fan, Nathan, but she knew the children were your life. She hated Charles."

I can say nothing. Fia produces a packet of tissues. John looks the other way while I wipe my eyes. It feels as if the weight of the world has lifted from my shoulders. My children are almost within reach. Fia hugs me. How will the children react to her? They hated the idea of a stepfather. How will they cope with Fia? How will Fia cope with them? She has a baby on the way and, now, the probability of a nine-year-old girl and an eleven-year-old boy to help rear. There are times I think Fia can read my mind.

"We'll work something out, Nathan," she says. "When I married you, I did so in the firm knowledge that this day would come. I've known from the start about your children and your desire to have them back. Your family is my family too."

Soon afterwards, we leave. Fia drives. My mind is too distracted to concentrate on traffic.

"I'm glad we didn't spend all the money from the sale of your house," Fia says. "Once the baby is born, we'll want a larger home, with at least one extra bedroom."

Trust Fia to be practical. These are matters, I realise, I should have considered. It looks as if the next few months will be even more hectic than I had imagined.

"An extension over the garage might be less disruptive," I say, after a moment's thought. "Others in the area have done the same. That way, we can stay where we are, and cut out the stress of a move. I like our house and the neighbourhood."

"Mmmh! That's an idea. I must admit, I love our home, too. No sooner would Ian and Caroline have settled-in with us and into their new schools, then we would be uprooting them again. Let's see if anyone we know can recommend a good architect."

We drive home, talking and planning. I am more buoyant than I have been for years about seeing my children; but Fia cautions me. She is right. We cannot assume anything until the children are in our custody. In the meantime, much could go wrong.

Engrossed in our plans, we are brought back to reality when a car pulls up behind us, at the entrance to our drive. I have the keys ready for the door. We turn round to see two police officers step clear of the vehicle. One looks to be senior, the other a PC. My heart skips a beat, but I keep my anxiety under control. These are civilian police.

"You go in," I whisper to Fia, "I'll see what they want."

The officers march up the drive. I meet them on the doorstep.

"Hello," I say. "Is there a problem?"

"I'm Inspector Zarowsky, this is my colleague, PC Bradley," the senior officer replies. They flash their warrant cards at me. "We would like to speak to a Mrs Fia Andrews, is she at home?"

"I'm her husband, what is it about?" I ask in return.

I guess it has to do with Joe.

"We have some bad news concerning her uncle. We would appreciate your being there when we tell her."

"Come in," I say, a look of concern on my face, as would be expected. I escort them to the lounge and call out, "Fia, have you a minute?"

"Coming," she answers.

## CHAPTER 30

"Oh! Hello," she says, catching sight of our visitors. "I haven't been speeding have I? I try to be careful, but sometimes I do slip over the limit."

"No, you've done nothing wrong. Please, do sit down. There is something we need to tell you."

"Oh!" Fia says, looking alarmed.

She acts the part to perfection. She sits beside me. I take hold of her hand as the inspector starts to talk.

"I am sorry, Mrs Andrews, but I have to advise you of the death of your Uncle, Joseph McFadden."

"Oh! No! You must be wrong. He was at our wedding a few days ago. He can't be dead. How? Why? What's happened?"

"I'm sorry," the inspector says. "He was involved in an accident, an explosion at NSF HQ in Lancashire last weekend. It's taken some time to identify his remains."

"Not the incident we saw on TV?" I ask.

"Yes, I'm afraid so."

Despite already being aware of her uncle's demise, and his true nature, Fia needs to show some reaction to the blunt report of his death. She feigns tears and buries her head in my shoulder. I put my arm around her and comfort her. The inspector turns to his junior colleague and whispers something. She stands up.

"I'll find the kitchen and make everyone a drink," she says as she leaves the room.

Ten minutes later, after a long silence, broken by Fia's sobbing, PC Bradley returns with a tray filled with mugs of tea. Fia's and mine are strong and sweet. It tastes disgusting, but seems to be a staple for those receiving bad news.

I look into Fia's eyes. To my surprise, the news has triggered a genuine response in her. Although, I sense her tears are more the result of everything that has happened to her over the last week. She has bottled up her emotions for days. This release will be good for her.

"I'm sorry," she apologises. "It's such a shock."

"We understand," the inspector says. "PC Bradley will leave you her card. You may contact her at any time. If there's anything you want to know, please ask her. She will help you, to the best of her ability."

"Thank you," I say.

"I'm sorry, but I do have a few questions, if you are up to it?" the inspector asks. We nod. "When was the last time you heard from your uncle?"

PC Bradley has her notebook out.

"We saw him at our wedding, a week last Saturday," Fia says.

Both officers congratulate us on our nuptials.

"Thanks," I say. "The following evening we texted Joe, to say we had arrived at our honeymoon hotel."

"Last Saturday, we had intended to see him, on our return from the Lake District," Fia adds, "but, during our absence, there had been a crisis at Nathan's work. We spent the weekend helping the security-forces resolve the problem."

"What was the nature of this trouble?" The inspector asks.

"I'm sorry," I say. "We cannot tell you more. Much of my work falls under the official secrets act. The matter is one of national security. If you contact Colonel Harry Wardman, head of NSF North, he will be able to confirm everything. It was late Sunday afternoon before we arrived home."

We had agreed, with Harry, it was ludicrous to pretend no incident had taken place at our house. If asked, we would give a brief explanation of the events. Anyone in authority who wanted more, we would refer them to him.

"I tried to 'phone uncle Joe, on Monday," Fia says. "We work out of different offices, but we are directors of the same company, Sandiman's. His secretary said he hadn't come into work, but, over the weekend, had left a message to say he might be away on business for a few days. She was to re-schedule his meetings for next week. This is a regular occurrence with uncle Joe. Major clients sometimes contact him on a weekend. If they have an urgent recruitment-problem, he can be away

## CHAPTER 30

for several days. I had intended phoning him on Friday. We wanted to ask him over for a meal this Sunday. It won't happen now," she bursts into tears again.

Whether Fia has convinced our visitors about her grief, I cannot say, but she has me.

"Do you have any idea why Mr McFadden might have been at NSF HQ?" The inspector asks. "It seems a strange place for a recruitment specialist to be."

"Uncle Joe worked as a consultant for the NSF," Fia explains. She dries her eyes. "He knows, knew, several high-ranking officers socially. They appreciated his talent for selecting the best people for the job. Uncle Joe was an expert. His work there was confidential. I assume they had some positions to fill, so wanted uncle Joe's input into the selection process."

"I see," says the inspector. "That does offer a logical explanation for his presence there. The NSF works unsocial hours, expecting everyone else to fit-in with them."

I detect an acerbic tone to his voice. The civilian force's relationship with the NSF is, at best, one of uneasy co-operation. Their right to bear arms, in particular, is a cause of resentment. For the police to speak of their concerns is rare. Not even they are immune from persecution.

The inspector asks a few more questions before he stands to leave. We turn down the offer of the PC to stay for a while. She promises to contact us when the authorities release Joe's body for burial. At the door, the inspector declines my offer to identify the remains.

"That won't be necessary, Mr Andrews. I thought it better to keep the details from your wife, but I'm afraid Mr McFadden's injuries are so severe, there are no identifiable remains in a physical sense. We used his DNA, on the national database, to confirm his identity."

I nod in understanding. Had it been otherwise, I would have been surprised. The amount of explosives I had seen going into the building, should have precluded any other result. It must have blown-out several floors below the level where Joe's body lay, and brought down much of the building on top of him. If there is any surprise, it is at the speed they have excavated the rubble and identified individual remains.

I shut the door and return to Fia. She has remained on the sofa, tears streaming down her cheeks.

"I don't know why I'm crying," she says between sobs. "I hate Joe for what he's done. I feel as if he's ripped me apart inside. Yet, I keep remembering the happy times we shared."

"Don't forget, he was about to have us executed," I remind her.

"I know, but from a little girl, I worshipped him."

There is no answer to that. I hold her close and wait until, for now, her well of sorrows is empty.

# 31

On Thursday, the sun rises at the start of a difficult day. One of the first things I do is inform Aitkins of a death in the family, and that I shall be away until Monday. The HR director offers his condolences, but sounds relieved when I tell him I shall do some work from home. I speak to James. He can cope with the general workload, while I link-up at regular intervals to process any experimental jobs that arrive on-line. He has my mobile-number, should it become necessary.

A good night's sleep has worked its magic on Fia. She is back to her usual self. Soon after breakfast, we drive into the city, to Sandiman's head office. Fia has to break the news of Joe's death to Andrew Faulds and the staff. I have come along to lend moral support. Fia can handle the situation on her own, but she wants the staff to be aware of me, before I join the board. There is another reason. She wants me to sit in and observe Andrew's response. Will he accept Fia as his new boss and potential owner of the business? How will he react to the offer of promotion?

Surprised at our unexpected arrival, staff hasten to congratulate us on our marriage. Their cheery words turn to stunned silence when Fia delivers the sad news. I can see Joe's charisma has cast its spell over the workforce. Many appear devastated by the revelation. Several are in tears. Fia assesses those least affected. She sets one to operate the switchboard and a couple to make drinks for everyone else. While the personnel huddle together for mutual comfort, Fia calls Andrew into Joe's office. She takes Joe's seat behind his desk, thereby asserting her position of authority. I sit to one side. Andrew pulls up a chair to sit across the desk from Fia.

"I assume you will be taking over the business, now that Joe's gone," Andrew says.

His face is white and strained. The news has shaken him. Unlike his colleagues, his mind continues to function on a business level.

"For the moment, I shall run the company," Fia says. "What I need to find out is what arrangements, if any, Joe made to cover his affairs in the event of his death. That could take months. Joe had a sixty-percent stake in the business. I inherited the other forty-percent from my father. Until we finalise legal details and find out who controls Joe's shares, I shall operate from here."

I had asked Fia about this earlier. If her father and Joe had been equal partners, why had her inheritance amounted to less than a half-share of the company's equity? It seemed a third, silent partner had owned the other twenty-percent. Whoever that had been, they had supported the decision to make Fia's father redundant. Once he was out of the way, they sold their stake to Joe. I wonder if the third party was one of Joe's PNU colleagues? It seems logical.

"Everything goes to you," Andrew says with confidence.

He looks puzzled by Fia's apparent ignorance.

"To me?" It is Fia's turn to show surprise (at Andrew's knowledge of this detail).

"Some time ago, Joe asked me to witness a legal document, which gives power of attorney to you to run the company, in the event of his incapacity. He told me that, in the event of his death, you are both an executor of his will and sole beneficiary. You should make an appointment to see his solicitor as soon as you can."

"Thank you, Andrew, I shall do that," Fia says. "I know Joe had great respect for your talents, and I have been happy in my dealings with you. The coming weeks and months are going to be hectic. On a day-to-day basis, there will be periods when I won't be able to devote as much time as I ought to the business. Until we finalise everything, and complete the legalities, I want you to act-up as general-manager. Your efforts will not go unrewarded.

## CHAPTER 31

"I shall promote Rosaline to run my former division. As of now, you will take over Joe's accounts, while I familiarise myself with the financial side of the business. Once I am confident I have a grasp of that, I shall assume responsibility for some of the major accounts, to allow you time to source new business. When the legalities are complete, we will discuss further your position within the company. I don't think you'll be disappointed."

Andrew is speechless, but a little colour has returned to his cheeks.

"Yes Fia," he stutters. "I won't let you down. I'll start right away."

He stands to leave.

"The staff," he says, turning back, "they're in shock. We should send them home for the day. We can keep back Mary, the girl on the switchboard. Mary's new. She didn't know Joe well."

"That's a good idea. Tell them they won't lose any pay. Let Mary know she will receive a day in lieu. I'll leave it to you to arrange."

Andrew closes the door behind him. Soon afterwards, the employees drift away. The girls, who made the drinks, remain at their desks. As with Mary, they are recent additions. Joe's death has affected them far less than the long-established employees. With Andrew, there are sufficient here to keep up to the 'phones, answer urgent queries and schedule less important ones for tomorrow.

Between us, we go through Joe's desk. We find nothing to suggest a link to the NSF. Apart from notes, blank contract forms and, in one, an empty petty-cash tin, the drawers are empty. Most contract-forms, clients complete online. The paper ones have a fine layer of dust on them. At one side, a filing cabinet stands, its contents old and musty. Ancient CVs fill the concertina-dividers. Again, everything now is digital.

Joe's computer has password-protection. Fia tries several combinations of names and dates, but fails to gain access. She thumbs through his telephone and address book. There is no help on the password, but she does locate a number for Joe's solicitor. He can see us at twelve-thirty. The finance manager is away on a VAT seminar. Fia contacts him, to tell him of Joe's death and to arrange a meeting in the office, tomorrow. She spends the remainder of the morning phoning clients to inform them of Joe's death and to reassure them of Sandiman's continued commitment to their needs. At noon, we set off for our appointment with the solicitor. The day is fine and dry, his office a few streets away. We walk.

We weave our way through throngs of office-workers out on lunchtime strolls, or visits to sandwich-bars and shoppers on the move between stores. Soon, quieter thoroughfares lead us to our destination. We arrive five minutes ahead of our appointment. Jerome, Jerome and Simpson, solicitors have their offices on Park Square that overlook its open green spaces. In the bright sunlight, the air has warmed in this sheltered haven. Wrapped in heavy coats, several book-readers and sandwich eaters, take advantage of the mild April weather, to occupy the wooden park-benches.

We are to see Mark Jerome, the only remaining partner who bears the name of one of the original trio. Once through the door, we find ourselves inside a relic of a bygone-age. Ancient wood-panelling, a carpet that looks as though it might outdate the Titanic, and a woman of some years, greets our eyes. She sits behind an antique wooden desk at the back of the room. There is a faint musty smell, and a hint of spray-polish. On enquiring our names, and whether we have an appointment, she asks us to take a seat. She speaks into an ancient intercom. Fia and I exchange looks.

Accustomed to Joe's predilection for modern surroundings and the latest in electronic gadgets, we had expected something new and shiny. Fia stifles a giggle as we seat ourselves on some dusty padded seats. I take note of the computer, on the secretary's desk. It is one of the latest, most powerful, government-approved models. The woman ignores us; her fingers dance over the keyboard.

To the right of the desk, a door, swings open. To our further surprise, a youngish man in his thirties walks into the room. He has a well-fed, genial look about him. A razor sharp parting cuts through his receding

## CHAPTER 31

mousey hair. His pinstripe-suit looks new and expensive, as do his shirt and silk tie. Despite his air of bonhomie, his eyes are sharp. He studies Fia and me in detail. We appear to be satisfactory. He extends a hand.

"Hello," he says, "I'm Mark Jerome. Please come through to my office. You must be Fia Andrews, Mr McFadden's niece, and this will be Nathan, your husband. I'm sorry to hear of Joe's death. It must be distressing for you. He was a gentleman to deal with."

We nod. Fia dabs an eye with a handkerchief. She has recovered from the extreme distress of last night, but it is more natural for her to appear upset. We decline the offer of a drink. He closes the door behind us. Inside this room, we have moved forward at least a century. White walls, modern desk and filing cabinets give an air of professional competence. Two comfortable, upholstered chairs await us. Mark waves us to them. He sits in a high-backed leather swivel-recliner. On his desk lies a folder with *JOSEPH MCFADDEN, LAST WILL & TESTAMENT*' in bold.

We are with him for almost an hour. The Will is brief. There are a couple of bequests. A small one to his housekeeper, while a second, more substantial, is to a woman unknown to Fia. Beyond saying this woman, at times, acted as a companion to Joe, Mark professes to know nothing about her. Either that or he intends to keep hidden the type of relationship she shared with Fia's uncle. Whatever services this woman provided for Joe, it might be better for us to remain in ignorance. His portfolio of shares, amounting to over a hundred thousand pounds, he liquidated the previous year, a few weeks before the stock exchange dived to an all-time low. Insider knowledge?, I wonder. With the money, Mark says, Joe cleared his mortgage.

Once we have probate granted, we can deal with Joe's estate. His share in the business, his house, its contents and some substantial sums in his bank accounts will come to Fia. It seems hard to imagine that, a few short days ago, he had ordered her death.

"What will you do with Joe's house?" Mark asks. "Sell or move in?"

"I haven't thought about that yet," Fia says. "I don't think I would be comfortable living there. What are your thoughts, Nathan?"

"Sell. We have a home. Joe's may be more desirable than ours, but it would have too many memories for us."

I neglect to say that those memories are tainted and far from pleasant.

"I agree," Fia confirms. "We shall put it on the market."

"You will need a valuation of both it and its contents," Mark says, "to assess what, if any, inheritance-tax is payable. You should obtain three separate valuations to confirm a fair price. Because Sandiman's is a private company, the shares will transfer to you without liability."

"If we arrange the valuations, would you handle the legal details and forms for us?" I ask. "We can come in, to sign anything, as required."

"That won't be a problem. First, you have to obtain copies of the death certificate. We cannot proceed much further without it. Make sure you order several copies. That will speed up matters. It is fortunate, Mrs Andrews, you are one of the three authorised signatories for cheques and financial transactions at Sandiman's, as is your financial manager. He can set-up payments, but they have to be authorised, or cheques countersigned, by a director. This should allow you to run the business, and access its bank accounts, without difficulty. You must advise the bank of Joe's death, but, as you are already a director and shareholder, I doubt there will be any problems. I would advise you add a third signatory as soon as possible, someone you trust, in case one of you is absent."

"We will take care of that when probate is at an end," Fia says. "Once the shares pass to me, I intend to transfer a thirty-percent stake in the business to Nathan. He will take a seat on the board and be the third signatory. I have made Andrew Faulds general manager, but might appoint him to the board later. I did think of offering him a small number of shares."

"If you do, there will be a tax-liability," Mark advises. "Instead, I would consider a profit-share. That would reward him, but keep the business within the family."

## CHAPTER 31

We leave the solicitors with a list of things to do. On top of work, we shall be busy for a while. We find a café on the Headrow where, over coffee and sandwiches, we discuss what we have learned. Between us, we plan how we can progress our part of the process.

"There's something else you must do," I say to Fia.

"What's that?"

"Make an appointment to see the doctor. You have to make sure everything is all right with you and the baby."

"You're right. I'll ring when we're home. With luck, I'll be given an appointment before the baby's born," Fia jokes; it could be a week or two before she can expect to see anyone. Party-members take priority - others have to wait their turn.

Back at Fia's office, I contact Harry. With NSF involvement, I know of no other whom I can contact to find out about the availability of Joe's death-certificate. Fia has an in-depth meeting with Andrew, where they discuss current business, and finalise details of his new role. They agree to promote his deputy, Marion, to take over Andrew's current clients. Somehow, in the middle of this, for the position at Aitkins, the pair arrange for my selection of candidates to come in for interview, tomorrow afternoon.

Mid-afternoon, Harry 'phones to tell me that, because of the circumstances surrounding Joe's death, a report has gone to the coroner's office. As this is an NSF-linked incident, they will fast-track it through the system. The security-forces' forensic pathologist, who performed the autopsy on Joe's remains and confirmed their identity, is to provide a report to the coroner.

Under the cause of death, the report will list 'catastrophic injuries sustained in a building collapse', with a 'gas-leak' and, 'subsequent explosion' noted as major contributory factors. Because falling stonework crushed Joe's body beyond recognition, no physical evidence remains to show the damage caused by the bullet that killed him. After the coroner has checked the report, she will open an inquest, then adjourn it until a later date. Provided she has no further questions, the coroner will issue an interim death-certificate and a cremation-certificate. The process will take a few days. By the end of the following week, Fia should be able to provide paperwork, to allow our solicitor to progress probate and us to arrange a funeral.

I have my laptop with me, so, using a spare desk and an encrypted-link, via the office broadband system, I spend my time arranging deliveries and supplies for special projects. It is late afternoon before Fia finishes with Andrew. We have to visit her old office yet, to break the news there. Fia 'phoned Rosaline earlier in the day, to advise her she would be away for most of the day, but gave no explanation why.

This time, although the workforce receives the news with some shock, Joe's death has less effect on them compared to head office. He was a distant figure, whose visits were rare. This office was Fia's domain. Joe left her to run it. Ros relishes her elevation to branch manager, Adele, likewise, her promotion to assistant. There is less to do here, to hand over the reins to Ros. For several years now, she has run the office in Fia's absence, without problem. We stay for a couple of hours, before we return to our car. It is the height of rush-hour. We reach home, exhausted, but relieved at the way our day has gone. We have set matters in motion.

# 32

Weeks pass. We settle into a new routine. At Sandiman's, the transition from Joe's to Fia's reign seems to be passing without any serious problems. One or two major clients, Fia tells me, are wary of her when she takes over their accounts. Progress is steady. Her choices of candidate are first-class. The greater the use made of her expertise by her new clients, the greater their satisfaction with the results. So far, no-one has removed their business. Andrew proves his worth as he gains in confidence. Although a hard taskmaster, he is fair. He uses encouragement and support, rather than a large stick and sarcasm to move the business forward. The atmosphere, on the occasions I visit Sandiman's, appears to be a happy one.

After preliminary interviews with my selection of candidates, I select a shortlist of two. James joins me for their second interviews. Between us, we choose Rachel, a middle-aged woman whose easygoing first impression is deceptive. She has a sharp mind. Within weeks, she is working with minimal supervision.

In early May, after an ultrasound, our fears, that the stress of the past few months might have affected the baby, appear unfounded. Its development is normal. We have a projected birth date of November 11th, which is a worry. We have heard, via John, the immunisation programme commences in October. Whatever has to happen to halt its inception must take place before then. Whether this intervention means another raid, a targeted attack on shipments, or a coup, is supposition on our behalf.

John's recovery from his wounds is steady. Regular physiotherapy sessions bring their painful, but worthwhile results. His visits, on either a Saturday or Sunday evening, to exchange news between Harry and me, tend to be brief. On occasion, when Linda is on duty, he joins us for a meal. Otherwise, he heads to her home in Oakworth where, we gather, he spends most of his free time.

The main news, of which we wait, that of Ian and Caroline, remains in abeyance. Julie's father is in a care home, suffering from dementia. In his lucid moments, he remembers the children, but to where, or with whom they went, he has no memory. Harry has made inquiries with social services in the Darlington area, but Ian and Caroline are not with any of their foster-parents. The NSF has higher priorities. Harry cannot appear to be too involved. An eventual search of school-records, in the area, yields no clues to the youngsters' whereabouts.

◌ ◌

The last Friday in May is upon us. I arrive home, after a long and tiring day in the office, to find John's Range Rover parked nearby. He and Fia are in the kitchen. With relief, he welcomes my arrival. Fia, it appears, has been relentless in her quest for information about his relationship with Linda.

In our household, it is usual for the first one home to start dinner preparations. On this occasion, there are no signs of activity. The cooker is cold, the hob empty.

"Quick!" Fia says. "Change into something casual, we've somewhere to go."

"Why, what's happening?" I ask.

Whatever it is, it cannot be anything bad, because Fia has a smile on her face.

"We have an appointment in Alnwick, tomorrow morning."

"Is there news of the children?" I ask, hope flaring.

"More than that," John says, in triumph, "Harry's found 'em."

He is grinning too. For a moment, stunned, I am unable to say anything. It is a while before I can take-in what he and Fia have to say.

## CHAPTER 32

"The couple, caring for the children, came from Darlington," John says, after I ask him to repeat everything, "but, several years ago, they moved to Berwick-on-Tweed. Because their application to become foster-parents came after the move north, they don't appear in Darlington's records. At ten, tomorrow morning, we're meeting a social worker in Alnwick. She'll take you to meet the children. Harry has sent various documents, by courier, today. Among them, copies of a court-order that grants custody of the children to you. As a matter of course, you need your IDs with you. Everything should be straightforward."

"I've booked rooms for us in Alnwick," Fia says. "John's coming too. If there are any problems, he should be able to smooth over them. He'll drive us there. I've packed an overnight bag."

In a daze, I head upstairs to change. Can it be possible I am to meet Ian and Caroline again? Excited beyond measure I may be but, at the same time, fearful. Do they remember me? Will they want to come with me? How much of what their mother has told them about me do they believe? I hope what Charles and Julie's housekeeper said is true, that Julie's parents refused to lie about me to the children.

Sometime after six-thirty, with our overnight bag in the boot, I join John at the front of the vehicle. Fia makes herself comfortable at the back. Darkness will be upon us before we arrive. The journey will take close to two and a half-hours, plus the time it takes to eat at one of the motorway services on the way. We drive out of Leeds, bypassing Harrogate and Knaresborough to join the A1M near Flaxby. From here, it is straightforward, apart from numerous checkpoints that add to our journey time.

"JJ's nervous," John mentions, at our second stop. "Rumours of unrest are rife. He has upped the threat-level for the NSF. We are lucky Harry's people issued our travel-permits. We won't be searched, unlike these poor souls," he points to a car at the side of the road.

It has had everything removable stripped out and dumped at the side of the carriageway. Open bags, with their contents piled in a heap, are to one side. Even the spare-wheel and tools stand on the tarmac. The unfortunate couple, whose vehicle it is, retrieve its contents, with the likelihood they may have to repeat the same procedure further along the road.

Soon after Washington Services, where we stop for coffee and sandwiches, we speed past the Angel of the North. As John is in some discomfort from his shoulder, I have taken over the driving. By ten-thirty, after another series of road checks, we reach the outskirts of Alnwick.

I allow the sat nav to direct me to our hotel, situated at the centre of town. The inn is popular, with many bedrooms. It is somewhere where we can remain anonymous. Our fellow guests appear to be a mixture of commercial travellers, business-people and holidaymakers. Among them is a sprinkling of NSF personnel, those whose missions most would prefer to remain in ignorance.

Before he acknowledges we have rooms booked, an officious ass, behind the desk, demands to see our IDs and travel permits. John is weary and in pain. He is in no mood to be civil. From his pocket he produces his credentials. He whispers something to the desk-clerk. John's words are too faint for Fia or me to hear, but the man's face pales and his attitude changes.

"Yes sir, at once sir," he says. "If you would sign the register, please, I'll have someone show you to your rooms," he beckons to another man in a gold-braided uniform, hovering nearby. "Would you like tea, coffee, or anything to eat, compliments of the hotel?"

Fia and I accept the drink, but decline the offer of food. Our nerves are on edge at the thought of tomorrow; the meal we had at the services has settled heavy. John has no such worries. He orders a snack for himself. At our door we say 'goodnight'. He has a room nearby. Within fifteen minutes, our drinks arrive. Exhausted, I pour the tea. Fia samples the chocolate biscuits, which came with the tea tray. Such items are a rare luxury in these austere times. Cocoa, like many other goods, is in short supply.

## CHAPTER 32

Soon after, we fall into bed. Unlike the accommodation, sleep denies me the same luxury. My stomach churns, a mixture of anticipation and apprehension at the thought of seeing Ian and Caroline, in the morning. Fia is little better. She approaches tomorrow with even greater trepidation. In the early hours, after much restless stirring, we drift-off for a few precious hours, to recharge our batteries, and dream of things soon forgotten.

I wake soon after dawn. Before Fia's eyes are open, I have showered and dressed. On a silver tray, a kettle boils. The clock shows six-thirty, two hours before we arranged to have breakfast.

"Don't pour mine yet," Fia says, leaping out of bed. "I'll shower first."

She stands beside me and gives me a hug. Her body is warm from the bed and she is still a little sleepy. We kiss before she breaks away. Moments later, I hear the shower running. Half an hour later, we go for a walk. Neither of us can settle. Both have butterflies in our stomachs.

For an hour or more, we wander the streets of the medieval market-town, our minds occupied by thoughts of the day to come. Afterwards, neither of us can remember much detail of the area. Alnwick Gardens, which we might have explored, remain closed until later in the day. Arm-in-arm, we stroll back to our hotel. John waits for us in the lounge, reading a newspaper.

"Oh! There you are," he says, as we enter. "I knocked on your door, but there was no response. I couldn't decide whether you'd overslept or gone out for some fresh-air."

"Fresh-air," Fia says. "Neither of us slept well."

"I did," John says. "It's a while since I've had such a comfy bed. Come on, I'm starving, let's have breakfast."

"You two go ahead," I say. "I'll take our coats up to the room. Be back in a moment."

An aroma of fried-food greets me, when I enter the dining room. My stomach turns over. Too agitated to feel hungry, I join the others. A waiter comes over and takes our order. John has the full-English, I order toast. Fia helps herself to cereal. Those items, and a pot of tea, are sufficient for us. While John tucks into an overflowing plate, I struggle to eat a slice of toast. Fia abandons her cereal half way through, in favour of my remaining toast.

At ten o'clock sharp, we are in the main lounge, our room vacated, bill settled and overnight bags at our feet. In the comfort of the lounge's easy chairs, we sit round a low table, to await the arrival of the social-worker. We make an effort to read the morning-papers. Concentration is difficult. Each time someone new appears in front of the reception desk, through the open doorway we stare at them. At ten-past-ten, a middle-aged woman arrives at the desk, a large briefcase in her hand. The receptionist points towards us. The woman strides in our direction.

She is stocky, about five-foot-seven, with grey-rooted, brown hair stretched into a bun. She has a thin face and a jutting jaw. Dark-red lipstick cakes the pursed lines of her lips, which fail to smile. The milk of human kindness appears to have dried onto her pale cheeks. In her green tweed two-piece and sensible brown shoes, she bristles up to the table.

"Which one of you is Mr Andrews?" She snaps, her attitude officious.

Her voice is harsh, with a strong north-east accent. There is no preamble. I stand and offer my hand.

"I'm Nathan Andrews, this is my wife Fia. Our companion is John."

The woman ignores the outstretched hand.

"Sit," she commands, leaving everyone half in, half out of their seats.

I wonder if she resents having to give up her Saturday to meet us. Had it been a weekday, I have an idea our reception would have been as frosty. The woman appears to have a dislike of the human-race.

"I'm Ms Fenwick," she says. "I must tell you now, Mr Andrews, I am against this whole charade. As far as I can tell from my records, neither you nor your wife has shown any interest in the children, for years. Now, hallelujah, you decide you want them back. It isn't good enough. Children are a lifetime's commitment, not objects to pick up or put down, whenever the fancy takes you.

## CHAPTER 32

"At great effort, I have found two couples, each wanting to adopt a child of your offspring's age. It's disgraceful that, because you decide you fancy the idea of being parents again, I have to give back-word to them. I can assure you I have taken this to a higher level, and been overruled. How you succeeded in thwarting my efforts, I fail to understand, but I shall do my damnedest to ensure your local social-workers put you under the microscope. Any sign of neglect, or problems, I shall have the children removed from your care, without recourse."

"Well now," John interrupts before I have chance to explode, "I think the introductions went rather well, don't you?" he asks of no-one in particular.

He takes out his ID and shows it to Ms Fenwick. Her face, somehow, turns a shade paler.

"There are some facts you might like to know, Ms Fenwick," John makes her name sound like a disease, "before you start throwing accusations and going off half-cocked. To start with, if any social-worker causes problems, because of you, be assured you can look forward to several months in a government re-education centre."

"For your information," I interrupt, struggling to suppress my anger. "Fia is my second wife. She is not the children's mother; she supports me in my attempts to find them. For legal reasons, I am unable to tell you the full story, but what I can say is, when my first wife and I split up, she obtained custody of Ian and Caroline.

"My ex, who worked for the NSF, was vindictive. She prevented me from seeing the children. My work took me to another town. When I applied to have access granted, the authorities informed me my wife had died, my children adopted. As a result, any chance for me to re-establish contact was over. A few weeks ago, I learned the original reports of her death, and the adoption details presented to me, were a fabrication. It seems my ex died in a house-fire earlier this year. It's taken me until now to trace my children."

"My records say otherwise," Fenwick snorts.

"Of course they do," Fia snaps. "My husband's already explained to you how his ex wife falsified them."

While this exchange goes on, John fiddles with his mobile. He stands, walks away for a moment to hold a brief, whispered conversation with someone. We await his return. Frosty stares and silence have replaced the heated words. Back at the table, John thrusts the 'phone into Fenwick's hand, his voice acidic.

"Colonel Harry Wardman, Head of NSF North of England, would like a word with you. NOW!"

## 33

The 'phone conversation is brief and one-sided. After several attempts to interrupt by Fenwick, Harry loses patience. The irritation in his voice, coming through the earpiece, is audible to us as he tears into the woman. Despite my antipathy towards Fenwick, I do have some sympathy for her. Her face is closer to grey in colour now. The call ends. Shocked by the lambasting, she remains silent. We refrain from making any comment. After a couple of minutes, the mobile rings. Fenwick, it seems, is expecting the call. She answers it before it can ring again.

"Yes, minister, I'm Ms Fenwick," she says.

From her posture, it is apparent she wants to speak, but, after Harry's outburst at her previous interruptions, she holds herself in check.

"Yes, minister, I understand. I shall process the paperwork without delay," Fenwick says.

The conversation ends. With some force, she tosses the mobile back to John. Her face has returned to its white, chalk-like texture, with the addition of pink highlights on her cheekbones. Before she impales Fia and me with her glare, the look Fenwick gives John is one of pure hatred. Heaven help anyone unfortunate enough to come under her tender care. I bet Fenwick is a wow at team-bonding sessions.

She snatches up her briefcase. With a crash, she slams it on the table. If there is a tablet, or similar piece of electronics inside the case, I fear for the device's future viability.

"Watch that," she snarls before stalking off in the direction of the ladies' loo.

Fia raises her eyes. She leaps up to follow Fenwick from the room.

"Minister?" I query, looking at John.

"Yes. Roger Dainton, the minister in charge of education. He's a friend of Harry's. I know they've discussed your case. Just now, when I rang Harry to advise him about Fenwick's attitude, he said he would ask the minister to ring her, straight-away."

Ten minutes pass. I order a pot of coffee. In reception, the same desk-clerk as yesterday is on duty. He observes the arrival of our drinks. He calls-over the waiter and has a quick word with him. Moments later, the man returns to remove the fancy, leather bound bill-holder from the table.

"Compliments of the hotel," the waiter says with a smile.

I glance towards reception and wave in acknowledgement. I look at John.

"I don't know what you said to him yesterday, but he's a changed man."

"Only until we leave," John says, with a wicked grin.

Another five minutes pass before Fia and Fenwick return. Fenwick's eyes are red, as though she has been crying. Fia squeezes the woman's arm in re-assurance as they re-join us. Whatever the pair has discussed during their absence, as with John and the desk-clerk, it appears to have wrought a miracle in the social worker's demeanour.

"Shall we start again," Fenwick says. "I'm Miranda."

She extends her hand. We shake it in turn, as we re-introduce ourselves. This is a vast improvement.

Miranda opens her briefcase. She takes out sheaves of paper. We produce our IDs, and our copy of the court-order. Miranda compares our copy against hers, to confirm they agree. It takes an hour to go through the paperwork, read and sign the appropriate documents and for Miranda to check our IDs online against the government database. Much to my surprise, her tablet did survive the briefcase's impact against the tabletop.

"Everything is in order," Miranda says, "but I would caution you. This whole affair has happened apace. No-one has been able to prepare the

## CHAPTER 33

children for such a major change of circumstance. It may be better, albeit on a temporary basis, for them to remain in the care of their foster-parents. A short period, to allow the youngsters to become acquainted with you, might be beneficial. A few regular visits, until everyone is comfortable. I cannot say this is what the children will want, but, in some circumstances, it can be for the best."

"I understand," I acknowledge, "but, if possible, I would prefer for them to come home with us today."

"I agree," Fia says. "It is time they came home."

Miranda nods. She has given her advice. Our papers are in order. Fia and I are the legal guardians of my children. We have official sanction, at the highest level. I have permission to take them, no matter what; but Miranda's concerns are genuine. She is the expert. The children's welfare is her top priority. Let us see what happens when we reach Berwick-on-Tweed.

"Oh! One other thing," Miranda says. "As a matter of course, you will receive visits from your local social-services. This is usual. They will want to be sure that the children are happy, content and well looked-after. Now we have spoken, I doubt this will be a problem."

We have no objection to this; on the proviso such visitors come with the right attitude. We appear to have made peace with Miranda. There should be no problems. Impatient to be off, we realise, first, we should eat something. Again, sandwiches arrive courtesy of the management. I make a mental note to have John with us whenever we visit a hotel. His presence holds great potential as a money-saver.

On the stroke of noon, we leave the hotel. Miranda will travel ahead of us. John's shoulder feels better. He is back in charge of his Range Rover. Once on the A1, it is straightforward. The road follows the coastal plain. Mile after mile of open countryside flash by on either side of us with, later, occasional glimpses of the sea. Away to our left, beyond our horizon, the land rises to form the Cheviot Hills.

After forty minutes, we follow the A1 round Berwick. Miranda indicates right. We turn off towards the town. Soon afterwards, after another right turn, Miranda brings her car to a halt outside a stone-built detached house. It appears to be of recent construction, a match to the ones on either side. It has a stunning view, overlooking the River Tweed. John pulls up behind Miranda. We step out. Fia takes my hand; we walk towards the gateway where Miranda awaits us.

John remains with the car. Unless we need to call on his help, for now, he believes his inclusion in the proceedings would be an intrusion. He drives-off into Berwick, to explore and, without doubt, find somewhere to eat, drink and ring his beloved Linda. We shall call him when we are ready to leave.

"This way," Miranda says.

She marches up to the door, briefcase in hand. We follow, our hands locked together. Miranda presses the doorbell. From inside, the faint sounds of chimes ring out. At once, the door swings open and a stocky, bearded man, with thinning dark hair, fills the opening. Laughter-lines criss-cross his weather-beaten and leathery face. With a beaming smile, he welcomes us. He shakes Miranda's hand with enthusiasm. He wears grey, casual trousers and an open-necked red and green checked shirt. On closer view, I see grey streaks in his hair. Late forties, early fifties I estimate.

"Good afternoon, Miranda," he greets. "It's a pleasure to see you again. The missus is in the lounge; please go through."

"Hello," he turns his attention to Fia and me. "I'm Bill McAuslan. You must be Mr & Mrs Andrews. Pleased to meet you."

He shakes our hands in turn. His grip is firm, the greeting enthusiastic.

"Come in, come in, this way," he directs, as I close the door.

He ushers us down a narrow hallway into a large room. Of a similar age to Bill, a matronly woman stands at its centre. She, like Miranda, is dressed in a tweed two-piece. Her collar-length wavy hair is a vivid shade of unnatural red. She, too, wears a broad smile as she greets us. Once introductions are complete, we take a seat on one of the leather couches. Sally, Bill's wife, leaves us for a moment, to 'pop the kettle

## CHAPTER 33

on'. Fia and I sit in silence, while Miranda and Bill exchange small talk. They seem well-known to each other.

I take the time to look around. Although the furniture is minimal, the room has a lived-in appearance. The atmosphere about the house is warm and welcoming. A large bookcase stands against one wall, the shelves stacked with volumes ranging from early readers up to the classics, with much variety in between. Of toys, I see little evidence. To one side of the lounge, there are several suitcases, stacked in a tidy heap. On top of one, a pink teddy bear sits. My stomach flips. I bought it for Caroline on the day of her birth. On a separate case is a blue bear, which I purchased for Ian when he came into this world. Both look well-loved. It appears the children are ready to leave, but where are they?

Sally re-appears with a tray carrying a large teapot and several cups, alongside a plate of home-made scones. Bill pulls out a nest of tables and spreads them between us. The tea is scalding hot, of builder's strength. I prefer it a little weaker, but drink it without comment. The scones are delightful.

"Miranda rang to say you were on your way," Sally says. Unlike Bill, whose accent is pure Tyneside, she speaks with a soft Highland inflection. "Freda, Bill's sister, has taken the children for a walk. We thought it best to speak to you first, before you met the youngsters."

Which is, I suppose, I polite way of saying *'We want to see what you are like and make sure we approve of you'*.

"As you can see," Bill interrupts. "Their cases and belongings are ready."

"They're such lovely wee bairns," Sally says. "We've enjoyed having them, but we knew it was temporary. The first thing young Ian told us, the day they arrived, was that his daddy would come for them some day, didn't he Bill?"

"Aye, that's right," Bill replies. "Whenever we suggest anything different, the lad says, no, you'll come for them. No sooner had we told them you'd be here today, they began to pack their bags."

"Why has it taken you this long to find them?" Sally asks.

It is a valid question. Before I can answer, Miranda steps in.

"It's a long story," she says. "Several years ago, after Mr Andrews's first marriage broke-down, he learned his children had been put up for adoption (and shown falsified papers to that effect). As you know, in adoption cases, there are no visiting nor contact rights for natural parents. A few weeks ago, he discovered the truth. Since then, he has been seeking them."

"Oh! You poor man," Sally sympathises with this variation on the truth. "This must be a great day for you."

Unable to speak, I nod. The sight of the bears on the suitcases has released emotions I have tried to keep under control. I wipe my eyes. Sally gives me a long penetrating look, one that belies her soft and gentle appearance. She turns her gaze on Fia. Sally smiles, a look of satisfaction and relief on her face at our reactions. For half an hour, both she and Jim quiz Fia and me. They ask about everything related and, to us, unrelated to the children, our lifestyles, jobs and home. Sally looks at Jim. He nods. She delves into her handbag, extracts a mobile and presses a speed-dial number.

"Hi Freda, it's Sally. Yes, everything's fine. You can bring Ian and Caroline over in, say, half an hour. First, we have some paperwork to clear up."

It is our fierce social-worker's turn to smile. It is evident she values Sally and Jim's insight. Miranda seems relieved that both foster parents are happy to release the children into our care. During the next half-hour, we exchange paperwork. We receive letters to pass onto local schools, doctors and dentists. Pages of notes on the children's likes and dislikes, diets, temperaments, favourite books, TV programmes, games, toys and numerous other concerns we are grateful to accept.

Soon after two, the doorbell chimes. Fia and I stand.

"You two wait here," Sally says.

She leaps to her feet. With Jim and Miranda, she leaves the room. The sound of voices echoes down the hallway.

## CHAPTER 33

"Are they here?" I hear a boy's voice ask.

We hear a murmur of conversation. Moments later, the door opens. Sally ushers in Ian and Caroline. Ian has changed little. Older, wiser, his body has grown, his face matured, but he is still the child I remember. Caroline has changed much more. No longer is she the little girl I remember, but I would know her anywhere. She has taken after Julie in looks. Ian has an old photograph in his hand. He compares it to me, several times. After one last comparison, a look of satisfaction comes over him.

"See, Caroline, I told you daddy would find us."

Seconds later, he is in my arms. Caroline is a little slower, more hesitant, less memory of me than has Ian. Moments later, she runs across. My arms close round them both. Tears stream down my face. Through blurred vision, I can see Fia is wiping her eyes. The door closes on us, leaving us to our own private re-union.

It is some time before we are able to talk. I take the children and sit them down beside me on one of the couches. Fia comes to sit nearby.

"Who are you?" Caroline asks.

"This is Fia," I answer. "You are to live with us."

"You're not my mummy," Ian says. "She's dead."

I cringe. The story about what happened, when Julie tried to impose Charles as a replacement father is large in my mind.

"That's true, I'm not your Mummy. I'm your daddy's new wife. Julie was your Mummy. No-one can ever replace her. Instead, could I be your friend?"

I can almost see Ian's mind working. After a moment, he nods, satisfied with Fia's response.

"That's cool," he says.

Fia has said the right thing.

"Will you be my friend, too?" Caroline asks.

Fia nods. Caroline puts out her hand and Fia takes it solemnly. Within moments, we are in a huddle. How long it is before a knock on the door interrupts us, I have no idea. It opens. Miranda steps inside.

One look is all it takes for her to see how successful the meeting has been.

"John's on his way. It's time for you two to leave," she says, "to take Ian and Caroline to their new home."

## 34

We stop several times along the way, once for a meal, the others for more mundane, but necessary, comfort breaks. The checkpoints are a nuisance, frustrating us with their delays. Despite having top-level clearance and our papers being in order, questions as to why we have children with us on our return journey, require answers at each stage. John and I share the driving. Sitting in the back, Ian and Caroline have slept for the last couple of hours. With one on each side of Fia, she has a child cradled in each arm. It is ten before we arrive, tired, but relieved to be home.

After helping to bring the children's luggage into the house, John waves us goodbye. He is going on to see Linda in Oakworth. Fia and I are alone with two sleepy, somewhat grumpy children. A quick look through their suitcases reveals nightclothes and toothbrushes among the piles of clothes.

Upstairs, we show the Ian and Caroline their rooms. Although impressed by their size, neither furnishings nor decorations are child-orientated. We promise to take them shopping in the morning. The beds are new, but I am sure the bedding will look different by this time tomorrow. Within seconds, Ian and Caroline drift into slumber, Caroline with her teddy bear. Ian was too old to have a stuffed-toy with him, he said. He leaves his on the dressing table. Twenty-minutes later, Fia and I are in bed, fast asleep. For everyone, it has been a long stressful day.

Sometime after midnight, I wake to the sound of crying. For a moment, I cannot understand what it is. Memory returns. With my heart racing, I jump out of bed. On the landing, I switch-on a light. The sounds come from Caroline's room. Huddled in bed, she sobs. I put out my arms. She leaps into them. Waking in the dark, in a strange bed and room has frightened her. It seems there is a night-light somewhere in her luggage. She was too sleepy to think about it when we put her to bed.

After a drink, she calms down. I stay until she falls asleep. It seems we have much to discover. Caroline was four years old when taken from me. Back then, the darkness had been of no concern, but a lot has happened to her since then. The landing light remains on.

When we rise, Ian and Caroline are already awake. The cereal we have is of the wrong variety, but a couple of boiled eggs, and some toast, satisfy their hunger. Fia takes an hour to empty the suitcases and sort out the children's clothes. We soon discover the reason why few toys were on view at the McAuslan household. The couple had packed them ready to take. Ian's main find, among his collection, is a tablet computer, for which he soon finds our broadband wireless key. Caroline's bedroom fills with a collection of soft-toys and adventure-books. As with her brother, a tablet is high on the list of her favourite possessions.

Soon after lunch, we arrive at the shops. Several hours later, with a significant drop in our bank balance, we return home exhausted. New bedding, curtains and clothes we bring with us, along with a selection of foods of a variety new to our cupboards. Modern, child-friendly bedroom furniture, computer desks and bedroom carpets are to follow later in the week. A local charity-shop agrees to collect our redundant furniture, on Wednesday morning, before carpet fitters and new furniture arrive later in the day. There are many people in need, for whom our unwanted items will be of benefit.

On Monday, neither Fia nor I go to work. Apart from occasional brief visits to our respective offices, for the next few days, we shall work from home. We have too many domestic arrangements to make. Harry's people have arranged a meeting with the headmaster at the local junior school. We arrive at ten. By eleven, arrangements are

## CHAPTER 34

in place. The children will start there on Wednesday. Caroline will be a pupil here for a couple of years, Ian until the summer. We have plenty of school reports to hand-over. Most show promise. The head arranges an appointment for me at the nearby comprehensive school, to try to find Ian a place there in September.

That afternoon, we buy a uniform for Caroline. The headmaster has given his permission for Ian to wear his old one for his few weeks there. Because the main difference in uniform is the school tie, we purchase one. To stand out is to become an easy target, both for fellow-pupils and staff.

By the end of the week, education has ceased to be a problem. The headmaster at the senior school agrees to enrol Ian as a pupil, to start in September. I suspect the smoothness of the process involved here, and at the junior school, owes much to the background involvement of Harry's close-circle of followers. I am sure that, for the next academic year, a long time ago, this highly-regarded school will have closed its doors to new applicants.

The new furniture and carpets have arrived, the old removed. With much assistance from the children, we select wallpaper and paint-colours for their rooms. The decorator we chose assures us everything should be complete by the end of June.

To begin with, Fia takes on the school run. On Friday, she meets Andrew at Sandiman's. To allow senior staff to absorb much of Fia's workload, they decide to appoint a new junior, to take on some of the more mundane tasks. The pregnancy is beginning to show. Andrew had anticipated she might work reduced hours, once the baby's due date drew near. The arrival of Ian and Caroline has brought forward that moment.

Maternity-leave notwithstanding, apart from when in hospital, she will hold regular meetings with Andrew. He is content with his rise in salary and stature within the company. His share of the profits is generous. The remainder of the staff will benefit from a profit share, albeit a much smaller one, but sufficient to improve morale.

The long summer holidays approach. We decide to take Ian and Caroline away for one of those weeks. Until the new school-term begins, the remainder we shall split between us, working from home alternate days to mind the children.

During June, probate of Joe's Will progresses. His house, now valued, goes on the market. To our surprise, after dire warnings a sale could take some considerable time, within days, the estate agent receives a firm offer. There are, it seems, a few people with money to spend. A high-ranking party member wishes to purchase it for his son and new daughter-in-law. The price is high. We will incur inheritance tax, but this will come from the proceeds. After several attempts, we find an architect whose work we like. He starts on the designs for our house extension.

Whether it is because of the extra responsibility of having the children in our care, I cannot say, but I do notice increased activity by both NSF and civilian forces. It has become routine for them to stop and search people and perform ID checks.

08 80

The first Sunday in August, with the children in bed, we sit back to watch the late news. The day has been hot, the children bundles of energy. Fia, in the sixth month of her pregnancy, stretches-out on the sofa beside me, exhausted. Her head rests on my shoulder. First item on the headlines is a health warning.

The newscaster reads out a statement from the health minister. Our fears about its content prove warranted. A flu pandemic is on the way. Surprise, surprise, the authorities, we learn, have made preparations to counteract its effects. A vaccine, in production, will be ready by autumn. Inoculations, sufficient to cover the whole population, are to commence in October. Through the post, each citizen will receive an official appointment, to attend his or her local health centre for an injection.

## CHAPTER 34

The ministry anticipates everyone shall have immunity by the middle of November. The statement goes on to say, this shows the wonderful caring nature of our government towards its people. Cue - rousing music, followed by a recorded speech by JJ, extolling his, and the PNU's achievements. The newscast ends with scenes of a large crowd applauding. The whole charade is nauseous.

"So, whatever is to take place, it must be soon," Fia says.

"Yes, but we don't know what, nor when. Harry is aware Aitkins have almost completed their orders for the syringe components. The last batches are due out by the end of the month."

"If we had some idea, we could prepare. This suspense is terrible. In case we have to flee, I've packed some rucksacks with spare clothing and provisions."

"Is that a good idea? If the NSF decide to search the house, we could have difficulty explaining that to them."

"You're right. I hadn't considered that. I keep forgetting Harry, and those loyal to him, are a dissident group working within the NSF. The rest remain the thugs they've been from the start. I shall empty the packs tomorrow, but keep some clothes stacked in each of our wardrobes. That way, the bundles won't be as conspicuous. If necessary, we can throw them into bags without any delay."

"That's a better idea. We can't be too careful. This afternoon, when I took Ian to play football in the park, we saw an old couple arrested. They were out for a stroll, enjoying the sunshine. At random, two members of the NSF stopped them. It seems the husband had left his papers at home. Within minutes, both were inside the back of an armoured van. It would surprised me if either one of the couple was under eighty. What threat did they pose?"

The answer is - none. In reality, no-one is safe; from the media, a visitor to the country would gain a different impression. They pour out streams of pro-government propaganda promoting stories of happy, contented citizens. I suppose some people still believe, or want to believe, this rubbish.

Many do well out of the one-party state, big business in particular. They pay their contributions to the state coffers, or into the pockets of those in power. In return, these wealthy industrialists, bankers and merchants have free rein to maximise their profits – usually at the expense of their workers. It would be a generalisation to say all are corrupt, but an avaricious minority does have a disproportionate effect on those living in the lower stratum of society.

This coming Saturday, we go on holiday, seven nights in a cottage at Robin Hood's Bay. Foreign holidays are the privilege of high-ranking trusted party members. Ian and Caroline's excitement is high. Since the time of my original arrest, this will be their first holiday.

I would like to say, since their arrival, our journey has been smooth. In many ways, I suppose, it has. They have settled into their new life. Their bedrooms are now to their individual tastes. We reached a compromise over food; a mix of what is good for them and that which they would prefer to have as an exclusive diet. Despite the shortness of the period they spent at their new school, they both made friends, with whom the children spend time. Because these are local, it has been a boon to Fia and me. On our days at home, the pair's absence allows us free time to work unhindered, although we reciprocate on a weekend.

On the negative side, both children have pushed the boundaries to see how far they can stretch them. This has proved stressful, for Fia in particular. Using firmness and an even-handed approach, we have set standards for behaviour. When initial tears and tantrums fail to sway us, the youngsters tend to accept the imposed limits.

To my surprise, there have been few squabbles between the pair. Ian is protective of his sister. A result, I believe, of their treatment over the years. For the first couple of weeks, they remained almost a separate unit from us. As they settled and trust developed, they opened up and integrated more. Caroline, in particular, follows Fia like a shadow. A real bond has evolved between them. Ian is more reserved and self-contained, but he has taken to her. Both chatter away with her about school, friends and their earlier lives.

## CHAPTER 34

Fia has risen to the challenge of having an instant family thrust upon her. Her earlier fears, that Ian and Caroline might reject her, have dissipated. In her present condition, she is weary at the end of each day, but, with each passing week, the attachment between the children and her grows stronger.

We have kept in touch with Bill and Sally in Berwick. Ian and Caroline have spoken to them over the 'phone. They assure their old foster-parents, they are happy where they are. We owe the couple a great debt. They looked after the children with kindness and love, and, for that, I shall be grateful forever. They have another child, a three-year-old boy, fostered with them. He keeps them busy. We have the occasional visit from social workers, but, as Miranda promised, they seek to find the children are happy and well cared for, rather than to pick fault.

The holiday is a success. We build sandcastles on the beach, search for crabs in rock pools, or look for fossils in Boggle Hole. The weather is variable, but we do explore the area, even climb the hundred and ninety-nine steps up to Whitby Abbey. One fine day, we take a trip in a motor-boat along the coast. It is with some sadness we reach the end of our break and return to the real world; constant reminders of which have been present throughout our stay.

Checkpoints on the coastal roads are numerous, with foot patrols following cliff-top paths. CCTV cameras are everywhere. To an irregular timetable, Customs and Excise boats patrol along the coastline. A couple of times each day, further out to sea, a frigate sails back and forth. With few luxury items available, smuggling is big business, both of goods in and people out. If caught, penalties are severe, but rewards for success are high. Before sailing, searches take place on fishing-boats; the same when docking. Cats versus mice - who is in the lead is open to question. With such a flourishing black-market, I suspect the mice.

Towards the month's end, preparations are complete for the start of the new school-year. Uniforms hang in wardrobes; books and equipment await the start of term. Now, Fia waddles more than walks. Caroline's excitement, at the prospect of a new addition to the family, grows. Ian, we think, is more concerned as to how it will affect him and his sister. Their mother discarded them when someone new came into her life. He fears, when the baby arrives, the same might happen here. Fia and I reassure him as best we can. We involve both children in our plans. As I explain to Ian, if there was no intention for us all to live together on a permanent basis, the last thing we would do is build an extension.

Probate is complete by the middle of September, the transfer of funds made to our account. After settling our tax-liability, for once, our finances are more than healthy. How long that remains will depend on what happens over the next few months. Harry, we have neither seen, nor heard from, since he acknowledged news of the last shipment of syringe-parts south, a few weeks ago. Since that time, John's visits have been rare. The recovery from his wounds is sufficient to allow a return to full-time work. That, and Linda, occupy most of his time.

Before we went on holiday, builders commenced work on the new extension. They promise it will be complete by the end of November. From the speed at which he and his men work, it appears to be going to plan. We shall have two extra bedrooms and a second bathroom. Before then, we have to cope with noise, dust, dirt and inconvenience.

03 80

The weeks have sped by. It is the third Friday in September. The children are in bed. It is time for Fia and I to sit-back and relax. In among the dirge of propaganda-programmes on television, there are a few quality ones. With the lights low and the thermostat set at a comfortable temperature, we stretch out on the settee, snuggled-up to watch a wildlife series we have been following.

Five minutes into the programme, the screen flickers, the picture disappears. What looks like a snowstorm replaces it.

## CHAPTER 34

"Damn, don't tell me the TV's gone wrong," I groan, pressing the remote control. "It must have. I can't find any channel."

"Never mind," Fia says. "Each programme's repeated at least a dozen times, we'll catch it later."

"I suppose so," I grumble, "shall we have some music instead?"

"Yes, why not? We can listen to the end of 'Friday Night is Music Night.'"

This is one of the few programmes to have survived regime change. It is a pity that martial music and new anthems to the great and good have replaced much of the varied light-offerings of the past. I turn off the television. A variety of hisses and crackles greets my attempts to switch-on the radio. Again, each station appears to be off air.

"That's strange," Fia says, "both Radio and TV! Switch on your laptop. We might find some news on there. I can't believe all our equipment's gone down."

The laptop is at the side of the settee. I retrieve it and open the lid. After a few seconds, it wakes up. I enter my password. After an interminable time, when I click to open my web-browser, instead of my home-page a notice appears, *'Server not found'*. No websites are available. We appear cut-off from everything. I check the router. Its red light confirms we have no internet connection.

"This is odd," I say. "I'm going to pop round next door to see if they're experiencing any problems."

"I'll switch on the kettle."

As I open the front door, Fia is behind me in the hallway.

"What was that?" she says, startled by a loud noise from outside.

"It sounded like an explosion, or fireworks," I say.

No sooner have the words left my lips, than the sound of further explosions reaches us. Over in the direction of Leeds and the nearest barracks, a red glow emerges from the darkness. Flames shoot high. Over the night air, a barrage of gunfire joins the noise. Sirens shrill. All around, flashes light-up the sky. Like thunder, the rumble of heavy explosives floats towards us. Neighbours have come to their doors, or have drawn back their curtains, to stand at their windows with their lights out. Fia comes up beside me, her hand clutching my arm.

"Bloody Hell" I say, transfixed. "Someone's started a war."

# 35

Over the next half hour, the vicious crackle of gunfire and the sound of artillery spread throughout the district. The bulk of the activity seems to come from the direction of various NSF barracks. Landlines are down, the mobile networks also. Our area is residential, so, for the present, we are escaping whatever is taking place elsewhere. The question is, do we flee, or stay?

The noise has wakened Ian and Caroline. White-faced, they huddle on the edge of our bed. They watch wide-eyed as we throw garments into rucksacks.

"Give Harry a call," Fia says, as I squash extra items into a bag. "He might know what's going on."

"That's a thought, his mobile's on a secure network. It's worth a try."

With no thought to worry the children, more than I have to, I hurry downstairs. In haste, I find John's old 'phone, then press speed-dial for Harry's number. After a few moments it connects, but goes straight to ansaphone. Blast. I leave a quick message. I have given no details. Harry knows my voice. If he is still alive, or able, he will know who rang. After a moment's hesitation, I 'phone John. This time, a stranger answers the call. In the background comes the sound of intermittent gunfire.

"John's 'phone," a voice answers. "He's a tad busy right now. Who wants him?"

"A friend," I say.

It could be anyone at the other end. Until I know it is safe to do so, I would prefer to keep my identify secret.

"A friend, who?"

"Nat, from Buckden," I say, after a moment.

The sound of muffled voices follows that of a hand going over the receiver. A scraping noise comes through the earpiece, as the mobile passes from person to person. The sound of gunfire in the background increases.

"Is that you, Nathan?" John's voice is in my ear.

"Yes," I say with great relief. "What's going on?"

"Can't talk for long," John replies. "We received word that the first shipments of vaccine were to leave Orford Ness at the end of the week. We couldn't delay our plans any longer. We've cut communications networks for most of the country, apart from our private one. Many units of the armed forces have joined us, while most others remain in their barracks, refusing to neither go against civilians nor support the security-forces.

"The NSF troops are well-armed, highly-trained, motivated. They're split, about 70/30, between those who are loyal to the government and those who have pledged allegiance to the underground. Because both sides wear the same uniform, the situation is open to confusion. If you come across any, make sure they're wearing green armbands before you make contact. Even then, be careful.

"Earlier tonight, several sorties by the RAF blasted the storage units and research centres at Orford. Troops loyal to us are on the way to take control there. Apart from the top brass, who hold their allegiance to the party, once we convinced the higher military ranks beneath them about JJ's plans, the majority threw-in their lot with us. We showed them some of the information we downloaded from the Lancs base. They weren't impressed to find their names on the list of those to be vaccinated with the doctored-doses."

The sound of shouting in the background becomes louder.

"Sorry," John says. "I have to go. Someone from the civilian police should be with you soon. They've instructions to escort you and your family to a place of safety, until we can bring the situation under control."

## CHAPTER 35

"You think we're in danger?"

"It's possible. There are others in a similar position to you whom we hope to protect. Your association with Harry, though not common knowledge, is far from being a secret. Once his leading role with the dissidents becomes public knowledge, you risk becoming a target for members of the NSF still loyal to the government. In addition, there are ordinary, local people, who may deem your recent help from the authorities a reason to vent their anger against you and your family.

"Even without communications, word has spread. People have taken to the streets. They're attacking small groups of NSF - and anyone against whom they hold a grudge. You could be in danger from all sides. I'm surprised the police aren't with you. Look, I must go. Until they arrive, stay calm and keep a low-profile."

John disconnects. My anxiety levels are higher than ever. The radio, which I had forgotten to switch-off, crackles into life. Whatever channel I had abandoned the radio on, I cannot say, but instead of martial melodies, the long-forgotten sound of a Joan Baez protest-song blares out. Part way through the track a 'News Flash' jingle interrupts the music. Seconds later, an American voice comes over the speakers.

"We interrupt this broadcast with breaking news. Reports are coming-in from our correspondents in northern France, of the sound of heavy explosions from across the English Channel. Aircraft, flying in international airspace, have reported seeing widespread flashes and huge fires, visible over wide-areas of the UK. Britain's jamming of foreign broadcasts has stopped. So, too, have their media transmissions. Stay tuned. We'll bring you further updates as we receive them."

Music from a rock band blasts out. I dash upstairs, two at a time.

"Quick," I say to Ian and Caroline, "put on some outdoor clothes; something warm, it's cold outside."

They sense the urgency in my voice. Within seconds they have gone. In a low voice, I explain to Fia what John has told me. Worry lines crease her face. We are potential targets for everyone, it seems, no matter what side of the political divide they belong.

"I'm sure, once everything settles down, we'll be able to come out of hiding," Fia says.

"Providing Harry's people come out on top."

"That's true. Harry's assistance in our troubles is no secret. Former colleagues of his who remain loyal to JJ, if they defeat the underground, will take their revenge on anyone with links to him."

"I wish we'd left when we had the chance. The other day, I heard Sara and her family have reached safety. They're settling-down well into their new lives."

"I'm pleased for them, but you had a job to do; my place is with you. Had we gone, you would have lost the chance of a reunion with Ian and Caroline."

"I know. I can't think straight," I say, trying to focus my mind.

The children return, dressed and ready for the outside. We leave the rucksacks by the door. It is probable we shall travel in whatever vehicle the police arrive. With the lights out and the front door unlocked, we are ready for a quick exit. To the children, Fia, bless her, has made out the whole affair to be an adventure.

I keep watch through the front-room window. With a squeal of tyres, a NSF jeep races down the road towards us. Behind it, an armoured car gives chase. With shots fired from both vehicles, I pull the children and Fia to the floor. Bullets slam into the wall above the window. I wait until the sound of revving engines fade before I look out again. We have been lucky. The house across the road has several windows, either shattered or scarred with bullet-holes. I hope the Mansels, who live there, had the sense to duck.

The children are frightened now. Ian is at my side, clinging to me. In Fia's arms, Caroline, white-faced, looks ready to cry. Both of us talk to them, our voices calm and reassuring, though neither of us feels any better than do they.

A few minutes later, round the corner at the end of the road, a dark-coloured SUV comes into view. Illuminated by street lamps, headlamps off, it coasts towards the house.

## CHAPTER 35

"Be ready to move," I warn. "There's someone coming. I don't know if it's them, but be prepared."

At the entrance to our driveway, the vehicle stops, its sidelights turned off. The driver keeps the engine running. In the faint glow from a street lamp, I can see two people sitting in the front of the vehicle. At this moment, I wish I had a gun. The passenger-door opens. A darkly-clad figure steps out onto the driveway. There is sufficient light for me to make-out features that seem familiar. After a couple of seconds, I recall where I had seen person. With a sigh of relief, I grab hold of Ian.

"Come on, quick, they're here. One of them is the WPC, who came with the Inspector to see us after Joe's death. Bradley's her name," I say to Fia.

With Ian, I make for the door. Fia puts down Caroline. Hand-in-hand, they follow us out of the house.

"Hurry," Bradley says, as we draw close. "It's not safe. Someone's followed us once already, that's why we're late. It took my driver a while to shake them off."

The car is large, a seven seater. Fia and Caroline jump into the middle row, Ian into the back. I run to the house where, with a struggle, I gather the rucksacks. Back at the car, I throw them into the boot. On my final visit to the house, before I have chance to lock the door, there is a momentary gap in the sound of small-arms fire and explosions. Coming our way is the sound of vehicle engines, pushed to their limit.

With sparks flying, as it strikes the curb at the corner, followed by a Jeep, a military truck, hurtles into view. Bradley, to my surprise, is armed. She fires a couple of rounds towards the vehicles. The response is instant. From the passenger-side window, a machine gun opens fire on the SUV. Bullets ricochet off the bodywork. The SUV driver guns the engine. Bradley leaps inside. I have left it too late. In a cloud of burning rubber, the vehicle shoots off. The open back door swings shut with the momentum of the exit. Through the side window, the last thing I glimpse is Fia's look of shock and horror.

On my own, in the darkness, I doubt anyone in the approaching vehicles has spotted me. At the rear of the house, over the fence, is a field with woodland at the other side. If I can reach that, I might yet escape. I turn to run away. My foot catches against one of the builder's scaffolding supports. I feel myself tumbling. Head first I go, into the low wall at the side of the driveway…

# 36

As consciousness returns, I find myself face-down on the floor. Inside my head, a hammer makes use of my skull as an anvil. Wherever I am, it is away from where I last remember being. By the feel of the material against my cheek, I am on a carpet. Behind my back, plastic ties bind my wrists. I open one eye. It would seem someone has dumped me on my own lounge floor. Nearby, I can see child's red, plastic building brick.

Why cannot I open my right eye? Beneath my throbbing forehead, my eyelids seem glued together. At a pace that is pedestrian, my brain recalls the events that led to my plunge into darkness. An image of Fia's frightened face comes into my mind. Has she escaped, or, is she, with the children, taken prisoner? Worse still, could they be lying somewhere, wounded or dead? With my good eye, I search further afield. Stout military boots, beneath a pair of dark NSF fatigues, attracts my attention. Groaning, I try rolling-over onto my back.

Before I can turn, two strong pairs of hands drag me to my feet. For a moment, the room swims in and out of focus. I feel sick. As I sway, those supporting me keep a firm grip. The blurred shape, of the owner of the fatigues and boots, comes sharper into view. A fresh-faced young man looks me in the face. He wears no green armband round his sleeves. To me, he looks as if he should be still at school. A dark beret covers much of his close-shaved head. Despite the youthfulness of his unlined cheeks, and lack of stubble on his chin, his blue eyes are cold. They look much older than his apparent years.

"Ah! You're awake at last," says the young man, a Captain (from the insignia on his jacket). "I have orders to take you and your family into protective custody. Our commander has some concerns about your loyalty. After what happened here, earlier tonight, I consider those justified, don't you?"

"I don't know what the hell you're talking about," I say.

My throat is dry. My voice cracks.

"Where's my family? What have you done with them?"

"Done with them? I've done nothing." The man is taken by surprise at my anger. "Your people opened fire on us. They're the ones who spirited-away your family. From where I stand, it seems you're in league with these troublemakers on the streets," he accuses. "That's something that bodes ill for you."

He steps forward to stand inches away from me. For a moment, I fear he is about to strike me in the face.

"Who the hell are you, and what are you talking about?" I demand, my sluggish brain moving into a survival response. "What's going on? You're the ones who have them. Someone knocked on the door. I opened it. A couple of men, wearing NSF uniforms like yours, but with green armbands, grabbed hold of me. They yanked me outside. I can't remember anything after that. Tell me, damn it, where the hell are they?"

I struggle to free myself, but my captors are too strong. The captain studies my face for a long while. He seems convinced by the vehemence of my words. His body relaxes. It is fortunate I had thrown my coat into the back of Bradley's car. Still in shirtsleeves, my appearance is far from that of someone fleeing their home.

"The name's Sutcliffe, Captain Sutcliffe. What's going on is that we're in the middle of an uprising." He appraises me again. "Cut him free," he says to my guards. "Sit him down, before he falls."

"Do you have any idea where anybody might take your family?" he asks, while someone uses a knife to release me from my bindings.

"No," I say, as his men guide me to a chair. "Why target me?"

"Because of the work you do at Aitkins," Sutcliffe says. "It's of great importance to the state, so I'm told. I imagine the kidnappers hoped to persuade you to tell them what you know. When we approached your house, we found a car outside. We gave chase, but the vehicle escaped. It wasn't until we returned we found you on the driveway. It's lucky for you we disturbed the kidnappers when we did. Another minute and they would have grabbed you, too."

"If you don't have my wife and children, I must look for them," I say, attempting to stand.

I have no need to put on an act. I am desperate to find my family. The effort proves too much. Dizzy, I sit back. One of my former guards leaves the room for a moment. He returns with a wet cloth. With a shortage of care, he dabs at my forehead. I take the cloth from him and work on my right eye. Dried blood from a head wound has glued my eyelids together. How long have I been unconscious? Now, with the use of both eyes, I am able to make out the clock-face on the mantelpiece. The hands show ten-past eleven, at least half an hour since Fia escaped.

"Are you fit enough to travel?" Sutcliffe asks.

"Yes, but I have to find my family."

"Sorry, sir! My orders are to bring you in. The valuable work undertaken at Aitkins is something we cannot ignore. You are an integral part of that. I have instructions that, under no circumstances, must you fall into the hands of the insurgents."

I cannot fail to understand the inference. As I see it, I can go either as a passenger, or as prisoner. There is no way he will leave me – alive, that is. I am in the worst of situations. My options have shrunk. From his last sentence, I gather his instructions are to kill me rather than let the rebels have me. If the rebels find me with Sutcliffe's people, they will draw their own conclusions about my allegiances, then attempt to do Sutcliffe's work for him. I have to find a way to escape. In my present situation and condition, that is unfeasible. At best, I am fit, a walker, but unskilled in the art of killing, unlike my escort.

I have a moment of panic. What if these people find John's mobile? One look at the people on speed-dial will seal my fate. Where did I leave it last? With relief, I remember Fia putting it into her pocket. I hope she is able to contact John, to apprise him of the situation; though I doubt there is anything he can do about it. For now, I must rely on my own wits to survive long enough to engineer my disappearance.

☙ ❧

"Come on," Sutcliffe says, "we have to be leaving."

Twenty minutes have passed. He has allowed me time to have a hot drink and take some painkillers. My head aches less; I can move without feeling nauseous. I have taken advantage of the delay, to change into waterproof walking-clothes and boots. Who knows when I might see a chance to break-away? I need to be dressed in a manner that enables me to take advantage of such a situation. If I go on the run, I have to be able to survive in the open.

Sutcliffe nods in approval at my choice of attire. If we come under attack, he realises it may be necessary to go on foot. Since Fia's departure, the temperature has dropped. Rain lashes against the windows. As promised by forecasters earlier in the day, squally showers have arrived. With my waterproof hat resting against the top of my pulled-up collar, I step outside. Sutcliffe's men stay with me while I lock the door. They accompany me to the waiting jeep. The truck is no longer with them.

A driver has remained with the vehicle. Sutcliffe jumps into the passenger-seat, while I sit, dripping water, between my watchers at the back.

"Where are you taking me?" I ask.

"We have a base on the outskirts of Ilkley," Sutcliffe says. "Last reports say it's still secure. Major centres in Leeds, Bradford and their central districts are under heavy attack. It's too dangerous to try to reach them. Many outlying areas have escaped attention, for now. My instructions are to take you out of the way, until we can clarify and assess the situation."

## CHAPTER 36

He talks into a satellite 'phone. As do the rebels, he has access to the private communications network.

"Blast," he says, throwing the 'phone to the floor. "I've been cut off. Bloody rebels have taken control of the satellites. They've blocked communications to many parts of the network used by us. They're well organised. This must have been in the planning for years. But why strike now?"

I know, but decide it too risky to say anything. Would Sutcliffe believe me? Even if he did, I would think him a supporter of the living-cell project. He could expect his name to be missing from the list of recipients. Would it occur to him that, as governmental paranoia grew, in time, his name would join those on the programme? Total control means what it says. Why have absolute power over half your citizens, when you can exercise it over them all?

The wipers are at full-speed. The downpour intensifies as we drive along side-roads. When we pass behind the airport at Yeadon, the crackle of gunfire, coming from the direction of the terminal buildings, is loud and constant. We continue. After a left turn, we head towards Harrogate road. Using dipped headlamps, our driver negotiates the winding road. He would have preferred to drive without lights, but conditions are too inclement for that. He ignores the traffic lights to cross the empty main road. On Otley Old Road, a flash of light from beyond woods of Danefield Estate, followed by the sound of an explosion, reaches us.

"Go left," Sutcliffe orders the driver. He spins the wheel. We slide onto the side road of Yorkgate. A few metres past a darkened inn, Sutcliffe directs his driver into the car park by Surprise View on Otley Chevin. At the end of the tarmac, the vehicle skids to a halt.

"Let's try the radio," Sutcliffe says. "With luck, from up here, we should be able to contact Ilkley. There're no hills in the way to block transmission."

As if on cue, the rain eases. It stops. Overhead, the ragged edge of a storm-cloud scurries past. Stars appear. With his driver carrying a heavy box from the rear of the jeep, Sutcliffe makes his way along the ridge, towards the rocks. Within seconds, the pair is lost to sight.

Behind the jeep, district by district, huge swathes of the Aire Valley, between Leeds and Bradford, drop into darkness. It would seem power to the whole area is being cut. Within minutes, all that are visible are sporadic flashes. Most are brief, but, on occasion, spectacular explosions light-up the night sky. In many areas, flames rise high into the air. At the end of the airport's main runway, a large military transport-plane is on fire. While we watch, it explodes in a ball of fire. The distant sound of sirens is all-pervasive.

My two watchers step outside to smoke and watch the pyrotechnic displays. The door to my right is ajar. For the moment, I am alone. The painkillers have worked. My headache has eased. My forehead remains painful, but the gash has stopped weeping. No longer am I light-headed. At the rear of the jeep, my guards' attention remains fixed on the blazing aircraft. Now is my chance.

I manoeuvre towards the open door. With care, I ease down, onto the tarmac. Wind buffets the car. That, combined with sounds of battle and the murmur of the watchers' voices cover any slight noise I make. With care, I ease away from the vehicle. The last thing I want is to splash into a puddle. The soles of my walking boots make little noise.

I climb the couple of steps from the car park onto Surprise View. Without delay, I have to place myself below the skyline. Up here on the ridge, despite my dark clothing, it is possible to pick out my silhouette against the background of stars. Higher to my left, towards the rocks, comes the muffled voice of Sutcliffe, as he struggles to contact someone on the radio. Praying I keep my feet in the darkness, I cross a dirt-path onto grass. Bent low, I make my way over the top to reach the steep descent beyond. It is merciful the distance is no more than a few steps.

The Wharfe valley below lies in darkness. The disruption of power-supplies is evident here, too. With caution, I descend. A huge flash, followed seconds later by a loud rumbling bang, comes from an area across the river beneath. Flames shoot skyward. The sound

## CHAPTER 36

of heavy, tracked vehicles, moving along the valley bottom, carries up the hillside.

Below the ridge-top, the wind eases. I slither downhill over wet grass. Large tufts and brambles are a menace, snatching at my ankles as I pass. If I can reach the trees, partway down the slope, I have a good chance of remaining free. A heavy machine gun opens up in the valley bottom, triggering a cacophony of small arms fire in response. With a dog-chewed branch, I feel my way to the megalithic boundary stones, at the edge of the woodland. From above I hear shouts. Someone has noticed my disappearance.

Sutcliffe's voice is loud and harsh. He tears into the men supposed to keep watch over me. Two pistol shots ring out. I wonder if the pair has paid the ultimate price for their negligence. The sounds of battle from below grow louder. From above I hear nothing more. On the skyline behind, headlight beams sweep overhead, to disappear behind the ridge. Sutcliffe and his driver, I assume, have driven off. To find me in the dark is too great a task. I could have fled in any direction. Now, without accident, I have to make my way down the hillside.

More by good fortune than skill, I reach the tearoom next to the White House ranger station at the base of the woods. Apart from a few bruises, after slipping several times on the stone steps on the way down, I have sustained no serious damage. From here, the way is easier. I follow the lane down to Birdcage Walk. At the side of a darkened building, I keep watch until certain the road is clear.

From the other side of the by-pass, towards the centre of town, the sound of gunfire is persistent. On the opposite side of the road, a dark shape has embedded itself in a low stone-wall. I approach with care. On closer inspection, it appears a shell has exploded beneath the rear of a military truck, sending it careering into the stonework. Nearby, a large crater cuts deep into the middle of the road.

I stumble over something in the gutter, a body. In the darkness, I cannot decide whether the unfortunate person was army or NSF. He does have an automatic strapped to his waist. I relieve him of that, and two fully-loaded spare magazines. With or without a weapon, if caught by either side in the conflict, I am open to instant execution. With a gun, I do have a chance to defend myself. I slip the weapon into my pocket.

Desperate for news of Fia and the children, I push back my fears for their safety. After leaving home, they could have gone anywhere. For now, my main priority has to be my own survival. Alone, out in the open, I am vulnerable, an easy target for anyone with a gun and night-vision goggles. I need to find somewhere safer to rest for the night.

In the dark, I stumble along, feeling my way along the road until I reach its end. Turning right, the main highway is within easy reach. Towards the centre of Otley, flames have spread wider. The sound of gunfire has become sporadic. Lower down, a fire engine hurtles along the main road.

Before the roundabout, leading to the by-pass, a jeep has mounted the pavement. Its doors are wide open, its keys in the ignition. The windscreen shows scarring from bullet-strikes. Of the vehicle's former occupants, there is no sign. I jump into the driver's seat. As, I lean over to close the passenger side, I rest a hand on the seat next to me. It is wet and sticky. Something jams the door, which prevents me from closing it. I scrabble around the sill with my hand, to recoil in horror. The blockage is a leg attached to the body of one of the jeep's previous occupants. Without further investigation, I lift it and drop it over the edge of the sill. With a shudder, I close the door.

The engine starts at the first turn of the key. I switch on the sidelights. The instrument panel lights up. The fuel gauge shows a full tank. With care, I drive towards the roundabout, where I turn right towards Burley-in-Wharfedale. I want to cross the river, into more open countryside where I consider it might be safer. With a battle raging in Otley, any attempt to use the bridge there would be foolhardy.

According to Sutcliffe, the NSF base, he hopes to reach, is on the other side of Ilkley, off the main road towards Addingham. I have to

## CHAPTER 36

reach the iron bridge at Ben Rhydding, which I can use to cross the river. Once on the opposite side, I can make my way along that side of the valley, towards Bolton Abbey, via Ilkley. That way I can avoid any activity around Sutcliffe's base. Clouds have swept over again. Driving rain bounces off the windscreen. It forms rivulets across the road. I have no alternative but to switch on dipped headlamps. It means I can maintain my speed, but at the expense of advertising my approach over a longer distance.

As fast as possible, in a cloud of spray, I speed along the dual carriageway of the Burley by-pass. Off the other carriageway from the entrance to the mills, a flash of light catches my eye. Moments later, the back-end of the jeep lifts into the air as an RPG explodes behind me. The wheels crash onto the carriageway. For several seconds I skew over the wet surface, before I have the vehicle back under control. Forty metres behind, another explosion sends a blast-wave my way. The back-end sways, but the wheels retain traction.

Sparks fly from the bonnet. Two more stars appear on the glass of the windscreen. Ahead, parked sideways across the width of the road, are three dark-coloured vehicles. In front of them, several people are firing at me. I switch on full beam, hoping to blind them for the few moments it will take me to reach their position. The effect is better than anticipated. Powerful spotlights, mounted on the roof of the jeep, light up too. There is a gap between two of the blockade vehicles. I push my foot to the floor, then take aim as the jeep leaps forwards.

The opening is too narrow for me to pass through without impact. As those operating the blockade dive out of my way, I plough into the gap. The armoured front and wings of the jeep smash into lighter, less protected vehicles. The two cars I hit career sideways, one into the remaining vehicle. The impact sends my face into the steering wheel. With bleeding nose, and head throbbing again, I regain control and straighten the jeep. Small-arms fire pings off the rear metalwork. I power the vehicle away.

# 37

With tyres squealing, I speed round corners, heading towards the iron bridge. Safety cameras flash. Good luck to whoever has the task of collecting on those tickets. Frequent glances in my rear-view mirror convince me no-one has taken up the chase. The damage I have caused to the blockade vehicles must be severe. Without further incident, I cross the river. At a more sedate pace, one less likely to attract attention, I head for Ilkley.

At a crossroads, after the town's Lido, I take the narrow winding road that leads to the sleepy village of Beamsley. On dipped headlights, my progress is slow as I splash my way along the pot-holed roadway. Through there, within minutes, the Skipton-Harrogate road looms ahead. Rain has eased again. There is no traffic on the main route as, with lights out, I pull-up a few metres short of it.

On the back seat is a pair of binoculars. Across the main road, on my knees, I focus the glasses down the slope, towards the roundabout on the other side of Bolton Bridge. Arc lamps light-up the area. On this side of the junction, pole-barriers are in place, across the road. Armoured vehicles, carrying heavy machine guns, guard the route.

These could be members of the insurgent forces, but, from this distance, I cannot tell. According to Sutcliffe, while major centres were under attack, most outlying areas remained under government control. Whomsoever these people are, dependent on their perspective, if I am recognised, my welcome could be a handshake or a bullet. Otherwise, being an unknown civilian in possession of a battle-scarred, military registered vehicle, I could languish under arrest for days, or weeks before someone decides my fate.

## CHAPTER 37

Back at the jeep, with the revs down and lights off, I turn right out of the junction, towards Harrogate. In the dark, I almost miss my turn-off onto a narrow road I know from past trips into the Dales. Away from the highway, with headlamps on, I increase speed. Past the stone-built cottages of Storiths, the road descends to the deepening ford at the base of Pickles Gill. I drive on towards Appletreewick.

Sometime later I glance at the dashboard. The digital clock reads three-seventeen. It will be turning light before long. Exhausted, I look for somewhere safe to pull over and sleep. Wharfedale lies behind me. I am on the moors above Nidderdale, heading towards Pateley Bridge. A short drive after Greenhow, a single-track road leads off to the right. A few hundred metres along there, I find a gateway into a field, beyond which a barn stands. I pull in at the entrance. The engine falls silent. I switch-off the lights. High on the slope above, silhouetted against the stars, I can make out the faint outline of the monumental artwork of Coldstones Cut. Minutes later, with doors locked, I am asleep.

Cold and shivering, I waken to grey overcast skies, and a loud banging on the passenger-side door. Startled, and unsure where I am, I turn my head. A ruddy-faced, middle-aged man, wearing a flat cap, glares at me through the window. I switch on the ignition so that I can lower the window. I drop it a fraction.

"Ayup, shift yu car, will you? I want access to that field."

The man, a farmer I assume, gesticulates at something behind me. I look in the rear-view mirror to see, parked on the road, an old battered land rover, with a box-trailer of equal vintage attached.

"I've a dozen sheep to drop off," the farmer explains.

"Sorry," I shout, starting the engine.

Something seems odd. The passenger-side of the bonnet appears higher than it should.

"'old on," the farmer shouts. "You've a flat, nearside back. Bloody hell, that's going to slow things down."

Groaning, I switch off and step outside. The farmer meets me at the back of the jeep.

"Thar's not going far wi' that," he states the obvious.

I notice he has placed himself beyond my reach. In his right arm, he cradles a shotgun. Although the weapon points to my left, the slightest change in his stance would bring the barrels to bear. Something other than the flat tyre occupies his attention. The rear of the jeep shows scarring and burn marks, from the explosion on the dual carriageway. On the windows and metalwork, the effects of numerous bullet-strikes are unmistakable. At the front, the wings need major restoration work. I have a day's growth of stubble. After the descent from the Chevin, my clothes have a layer of mud. On my forehead, a deep cut has started to scab. I saw, when I looked in the rear-view mirror, both right-temple and right-eye have turned various shades of purple and black.

I can understand the chap's concern. If it were the other way round, meeting such a disreputable looking character on a bleak moor, I would be happier with a shotgun in my hand.

"What's goin' off?" the farmer asks, stepping further away. "It's clear thar's in trouble. Power's off at home and 't phones are down. Before 'tricity went off, radio started picking-up foreign stations, summat it's not done for years, but nowt local. I found one as speaks English. They say there's trouble all owa't place. Las' night, all we could hear wus loud bangs cummin owa't moors. So, tell us, what's 'appening?"

It is plain the man is both suspicious and worried. I take a deep breath. It is time to start talking. I explain, as best I can, about my predicament and what I understand has taken place around the country. It takes some time. By the end, my throat is dry. Standing in the dank morning air, I am colder than ever. A chill breeze blows and the clouds darken.

"So, yuv lost yer wife 'n kids, ya say?"

I nod. His attitude has softened towards me. He reaches a decision. With his gun lowered, he returns it to the cab of his vehicle. The slam of the land rover door unsettles the sheep in the trailer. They treat us to a chorus of bleats.

"George Smithson," he says, on his return.

"Nathan Andrews," I respond.

## CHAPTER 37

A huge, calloused hand takes mine in a grip that makes my eyes water. It is fortunate that my vehicle is a military model. The spare wheel rests inside the boot, instead of on a carrier attached to the rear-door. From the condition of that, I doubt that any appendage would have survived the RPG attack.

Without George's help, I would be stuck on the moors. After a couple of feeble attempts, I realise there is no way that, on my own, I can undo the wheel nuts - they must have been tightened by a gorilla. George, after a lifetime working the land, turns the brace with few signs of effort. The offending tyre has a large shard of shrapnel embedded in the tread. Twenty minutes later, I park a little further along the lane, while George deposits his load of livestock.

Like many, who live outside the mainstream of national life, he has definite opinions about the way the country has degenerated, since JJ took power. Farm quotas have increased at an inverse ratio to the prices received for meat and dairy products. His sympathies lie with the rebels, but this fails to explain his fervent hatred of the authorities - something he displays when he realises he has an understanding ear. He has said something else, which, at this moment, is of greater importance. I am invited back to his farmhouse for breakfast.

Soon after nine, we are sitting round a table in a stone-flagged farmhouse kitchen. The oak beamed ceilinged room shows its age. Its ancient pine-cupboards and furniture have darkened with the passage of time. Outside, the clouds are grey and threatening. Narrow stone-framed windows, overlooking a mud, straw and cow-pat covered yard, provide little light. Rain pours down the glass. The glow from a couple of ancient hurricane lamps provides more comfort than brilliance.

Ethel, who George introduced on arrival as 'the wife', is a kind woman with a tendency to mothering. Grey-haired, and wrinkled faced, her apron appears to be a permanent fixture round her ample waist. She has cooked one of the largest breakfasts I have eaten. Lack of power is no problem when you have a wood-burning cooker. Heat from the stove and the high calorific content of the food has warmed me at last.

Ethel fusses over me, tut tutting as if at a small child. She bathes my forehead before she sticks an enormous plaster over the cut. Satisfied with her handiwork, she sits down. She repeats the same questions George asked on the moors. This time, with the aid of a large mug of strong tea to ease my throat, I repeat what I had said earlier.

"Oh! You poor man, what are you going to do to find your family?" Ethel asks at the end of the question and answer session.

"There are people I must contact, but I need a 'phone to do so."

"All 'phones are down, even me mobile," George says.

"There are special, military ones that work on a separate network," I explain. "If I can acquire one of those, I might be able to make contact. Fia, my wife, has one. If that fails, the person, who arranged for us to be taken to safety, must know where they are."

George leaves the room, to return within minutes. In his hand, he carries a satellite 'phone. It appears to be an old model, but one of military provenance.

"Will this do?" he asks.

"Where'd you find that?" I ask in amazement.

"It was our son's," Ethel says, a tear in her eye.

"Aye, 'e wus in t' army," George says, a look of fierce anger on his face. "Them murdering bastards in t' NSF killed him. All 'e did wus try 'elp a friend they arrested by mistek. They raided a nightclub they wus at. When our Fred went to remonstrate wi' 'em, they shot 'im in cold blood. This wus among 'is belonging they returned to us. A supposed a should 'ave sent it back, but a couldn't be bothered."

This would explain George's anger at the authorities. Wrapped around the 'phone is a wire, from which dangles a charger. The unit is newer than at first I feared. If it works, I may be able to contact John or Harry. What we need is a restoration of the electricity supply.

"'ang on," George says. "I'll go power-up t' generator. We 'ave one 'cos we sometimes gets cut-off fa days i' winter. 'Cos fuel's expensive these days, wi don't use it much, 'less we're off a long time. You ought to be able to charge 'phone then."

## CHAPTER 37

After George's third attempt, and a loud bang from a barn on the opposite side of the farmyard, the lights flicker. They stay on. A cloud of blue smoke wafts across the yard. On a shelf near the window, a radio springs into life. George returns, red in the face. Starting the generator must be harder work than replacing a wheel. Music over the airways stops and a voice speaks in French.

"Must be 't channel I 'ad on las' night. They wus speaking English then," George says.

He presses a button. The ten o'clock pips sound. This time a voice speaks in English.

"BBC," George states, "they mus' be back on air."

The newsreader reads out his bulletin. We listen in silence. It takes some time. The gist is that JJ, along with many of the leadership, is under house arrest. Intermittent fighting with hardcore members of the NSF, who refuse to surrender, goes on throughout the country. These will be the ones with the most to fear if brought to account for their actions.

An estimated fifty-percent of NSF personnel have mutinied. They have backed their colleagues who, with the support of many key-units of the armed forces, instigated the insurgency. An overnight change of leadership, at the top of the military high-command, has led those members of the army, whose units, yesterday, refused to leave their barracks, to join the rebellion. Members of the public should stay in their homes and avoid travelling, unless in an emergency. That last comment brings a smile to my face. It could be a snow warning.

In silence, we look at each other. George turns-off the radio. From another room, comes the murmur of voices. A television, left on since yesterday, has come back to life. As one, we leave to enter another world. The lounge is bright, airy and cheerful, a little old fashioned in decor, but a century ahead of the kitchen.

A large television stands in one corner. George and Ethel sit in their own armchairs. I take the sofa. Images flash across the screen, damaged buildings and infrastructure from around the country predominate.

Flak-jacketed reporters are on the front lines with members of the military. NSF officers, complete with green armbands are fighting their former colleagues. In parts of the south of the country, in particular, the battle for control seems fierce.

Other camera shots show members of the NSF dangling from lampposts and bridges. Local communities have been swift to take their revenge. Again, announcers come on, pleading for calm. Leave it to the professionals to end the conflict. Several member states of the Commonwealth - Canada, Australia and New Zealand are among the first nations to offer support for a new interim-government. Mesmerised, we sit and watch until a brightening sky, and a shaft of sunlight through the window, distract our attention.

I had forgotten about the satellite-phone. The landlines and mobile-networks remain down, but I have a clear dial-tone on the one given to me by George. With it plugged-in and charging, I try, first the number of John's old 'phone, the one Fia had put into her pocket. The call goes to ansaphone. Disappointed, I leave a message. I attempt to contact John on his new number. His 'phone rings, several times. It goes to ansaphone. I leave another message. Damn it, where is everyone? As a last resort, I try Harry. An electronic voice tells me he has switched-off his phone. Frustrated, I glare at the device, but resist the urge to smash it against the wall.

Noon passes. For lunch, Ethel makes a 'snack', as she calls it. Huge wedges of bread, filled with home-cured Yorkshire ham, come piled high on a plate. At first, I think it is for us to share, but no. I realise this is my portion when she returns with a larger pile for George and herself. If I stay here much longer, I shall have to move the car seat back a couple of notches to fit behind the steering wheel again.

The sound of a phone ringing penetrates the noise of the television. In haste, I put down my sandwiches on my way to the kitchen.

"Hello," I say, as I grab the phone from the edge of the work surface.

"Nathan, is that you?" John's voice comes loud and clear.

"Yes, are you okay to speak?" I ask, mindful of how busy he might be.

## CHAPTER 37

"For the moment, yes," he says. "Most areas here in Leeds are under our control. There are a few pockets of resistance left, which the army boys have in hand. How are Fia and the children? The driver left a message to say he had dropped off everyone somewhere near Skipton. Did everything go all right?"

"I don't know. We became separated," I say.

I explain what happened when Bradley came to collect us.

"Blast, I'll try to contact them," John says. "Where are you now? I've a chopper going to Skipton Castle; I'll divert it your way."

"Hang on," I say, going outside, "I'll give you the co-ordinates from the sat nav."

Half an hour later, in the field at the side of the farmhouse, I bid my farewells to George and Ethel. They have been true Samaritans to me in a time of need. I cannot thank them enough. I leave with a bag of ham sandwiches, large enough to feed me for several days. Soon afterwards, the way the pilot and co-pilot of the chopper help themselves to them, I realise I could be wrong about that.

Within minutes of take-off, we are over Wharfedale, heading towards Skipton. We change direction.

"Sorry," the pilot shouts over the noise of the engine. "New instructions, we've to head to Ilkley first."

Before long, the chopper lands in the car park of a large supermarket. Military vehicles take up a part of the huge space, along with a mixture of army or civilian ambulances. As the rotors come to rest, a lance-corporal from the medical corps reaches up to open the door.

"Mr Andrews?" he asks.

"Follow me, please," he says when I nod, then step down.

The supermarket, I find, has become an emergency-treatment centre. Why am I here? Has something happened to Fia and the children?

The lance-corporal races on ahead. I have to run to keep up with him. He stops at the side of a medic in military-fatigues. The NCO whispers something to her. She leaves a nurse to finish bandaging her patient then turns towards me.

"I'm Captain Keith, army medical corps," she volunteers.

Her voice sounds weary. She looks exhausted. I'm pleased she doesn't offer me her hand. It has a covering of blood.

"I believe you're looking for a woman and two children?" she asks.

"Yes," I say. "Are they here, are they wounded?"

"I have a woman, a boy and a girl of about the right ages to the ones you seek," Cap. Keith says. "A patrol brought them in earlier."

I have gone cold inside. The woman's tone is too clinical. It is one of someone with bad news to impart.

"I'm sorry, but there was nothing we could do for them," she says.

"Can I see them?" I ask, my mind freezing with panic. "I must know."

"Of course, follow me," she says, walking to the rear of the store.

I trail behind, my mind unable to focus. "It cannot be them, it cannot," I say to myself, over and over again. We pass through a pair of rubber swing-doors, on the way towards a giant walk-in freezer - an ideal place to store the dead among the frozen peas. Inside the temperature is sub-zero, I am hot and sweating. On a table, at the centre of the space, surrounded by body bags, lie three others. The captain nods at a young medic who has joined us. One-by-one, he unzips the top of each bag. Taking my arm, Keith guides my faltering footsteps to the top of the table. My knees buckle. I force my gaze towards the three lifeless faces below.

# 38

Captain Keith is stronger than she looks. She keeps a firm hold on my arm, as I sway. My whole body shakes.

"Is this your wife, and children?" She asks, as I try to stem the tremors.

I shake my head. For a moment, I am unable to speak. My relief is tangible. On the table, the remains are those of three strangers. The horrors of the past few minutes wash-away on a wave of emotion. Keith leads me away from the makeshift mortuary. I may dare to hope again, but I am no further in my quest. Where is my family? What has happened to Fia, Ian and Caroline?

"You are certain?" Keith asks, her tone less so.

The hoped for positive identification, of three of her case-load of unknown victims, has receded.

"Oh! Yes," I answer, taking a recent family photograph of them from my wallet.

All of us are happy and smiling, standing windswept on the ramparts of Bolton Castle in Wensleydale, a late-summer outing. Keith studies the image, taken with my camera by a fellow visitor. She shakes her head.

"I've not treated them. May I?" she asks as she walks off with the photo.

For several minutes, Keith wanders round, showing it to each nurse, doctor or ambulance-crew member she can find. I follow, relieved to find no-one recalls seeing the three among the dead or wounded brought here. My pilot comes in search of me. I have to go now, otherwise he will leave without me. Keith hands back my photo. I run to the helicopter.

Within minutes, we land on the lawn at the side of Skipton Castle. Military personnel and armoured vehicles guard the entrance by the gatehouse. Before I leave the machine, the pilot hands me a new 'phone, courtesy of John. He had forgotten to give it to me. No sooner do I clear the rotors than they pick up speed. With a final wave from the pilot, the chopper disappears over the castle. The 'phone rings. I notice a couple of missed calls.

"Nathan, it's John. What happened at Ilkley? Were the people there Fia and the kids?"

"No," I say. "Some other poor souls."

"Thank heavens. Are you in Skipton?"

"Yes, landed a few seconds ago."

"Good. Listen. All I know is, Bradley took Fia to a police safe-house, on the outskirts of Skipton, but no-one's been able to contact them there. The local police-chief has details of the house's location. There'll be a police driver with you within the next half hour, someone who's familiar with the area. Should you run into trouble, the man's trained in the use of firearms. The army will provide a vehicle for you. Sorry I can't do any more for now. Good luck. I have to go."

A disconnection tone follows a faint click.

"Mr Andrews?" a young soldier has approached, unnoticed, while I was talking.

"Yes."

"If you could come with me, sir, while we sort-out a vehicle for you. I understand it won't be long before your driver arrives. Time enough for a drink."

Still shaken by my stop at Ilkley, I accept the offer with gratitude. Inside a tiny room within the gatehouse, a corporal thrusts into my hands a metal mug, brimming with tea the colour of tar. Still bloated from lunchtime's sandwiches, I decline an offer of bacon and eggs. The drink is scalding. Before I have time to finish it, a police patrol car pulls-up outside the gate. It deposits a tough-looking man, dressed in a dark-blue uniform. His step is confident as he walks up to the

## CHAPTER 38

gate. After a brief conversation and a check of his ID, one of the guards shows the newcomer into the cramped room.

"Sergeant Braithwaite for Nathan Andrews," he says.

"I'm Nathan," I say.

A hand, with a grip similar to that of farmer George, takes hold of mine. Unlike him, Sergeant Braithwaite seems to be aware of his strength. He releases the pressure before I suffer any real pain.

"Pleased to meet you," he says. "I'm told I'm on protection-duties, until you no longer need me, or I'm re-called."

"Thanks, sergeant," I say, much relieved by his words. "We should have a vehicle at our disposal soon. Please call me Nathan. Do you have a first name?" I ask.

Sergeant Braithwaite is a bit much to keep repeating.

"Yes. I answer to Tony, unless it's my mother," he grimaces, "then it's Anthony."

He accepts a mug of tea. I have the chance to study him. In his mid thirties, I estimate; ex-army at a guess, his hair dark and cut tight against his head. Doubtless, he shaves daily, but a dark shadow traces the lines of his facial hair. His eyes are grey, his gaze steady and penetrating when he looks at me; his face is lean. He looks fit, without an ounce of fat on his body. In a holster attached to his waistband, the grip of an automatic shows below a safety strap.

"Are you armed, Nathan?" he asks.

"Yes," I answer. "I have a gun I found yesterday."

"Are you prepared to use it?"

"If necessary. I have used one, but have little experience."

"That will have to do. Don't draw it unless you have to. I should be able to handle most situations on my own. If something happens where I can't, I'll expect you to have my back."

"Understood."

Minutes later, a black Range Rover pulls-up outside the gatehouse. We take possession of it. Tony inspects the vehicle. Inside the back is a gun-safe, a key in its lock. He whistles at what he finds inside.

"These should come in handy if we run into trouble," he says, showing me a high-powered rifle and a couple of carbines.

He leaves the rifle where it is, but pulls out the carbines to examine them. With practised ease, he inserts their magazines.

"We'll keep these with us," Tony says. "In an emergency it may be impossible to retrieve them from here in time."

We sign for everything in triplicate. Ten minutes later, we pull away. Despite it being late Saturday afternoon, the market-area, through which we drive, shows no signs of any traders. I would have been surprised had anyone risked coming into town. A marked military presence is on the streets. We have to wait at the junction at the bottom of high street, while a long convoy of trucks and armoured vehicles rumble by, going in the direction of the Addingham road.

Our destination is near the village of Carleton, on the outskirts of Skipton. Tony is pessimistic of a speedy result to our visit. No-one has been able to make contact with the people who run the establishment, which is a cause for concern. There should be someone on the premises at all times. Its cover is that of a guest house. Its only occasional guests are those whose identities the authorities wish to conceal.

At a bend in the road, Tony turns left onto a side-road. A hundred metres further on, he takes another sharp left, onto a long driveway. *Primrose Guest House* is the name on the sign affixed to the wall beside the entrance. Beneath is attached, 'NoVacancies'. A large stone-built converted farmhouse nestles behind high hedges and a row of trees, at the end of the drive. On the other side of a cattle grid, a metal gate stands open.

"Something's wrong," Tony's voice is troubled. He brings the car to a halt. "That gate should be closed and locked," he indicates a keypad set into stonework at the side of the way.

He draws his gun and places it on his knees. At a crawl, we bump over the metal bars of the grid. Once past the main entrance, a gravel-drive curves round into a space, large enough to hold half-a-dozen cars. Parked sideways across two bays is a single vehicle. My heart lifts.

## CHAPTER 38

Someone must be here. Tony ignores my optimism. I am to remain with the car. He opens his door, then steps outside.

"Police," he shouts as he zigzags away.

With the vehicle locked, as instructed, I watch as Tony scrunches over the gravel surface. It is late in the day. The overcast sky is dark and gloomy. Through the mullioned windows of the substantial building, no lights are visible. Gun in hand, Tony approaches the ivy-clad walls and stout oak door. He presses the doorbell. After several attempts, he tries the handle. The door swings open. Tony steps inside, out of my line of vision. I await his return, my nerves on edge. With a gun in my hand, I am ready, I hope, for anything.

After what seems an eternity, Tony re-appears in the doorway. He beckons me. While he has been inside, various lights have come on. With some haste, I join him.

"Are they here?" I ask, anxious for a positive response.

"No. The place is deserted. Clothes belonging to the couple who run the operation are missing. Their wardrobes and drawers are half-empty and left open. This was on the floor in the lounge," Tony adds, showing me what is in his hand.

"That's Caroline's teddy bear. She takes it with her everywhere. This confirms they reached here, but then what?"

"I don't know. There's no sign of trouble, nor disturbance. The people here have packed their bags, and gone. The authorities pay the couple to look after the place, and its 'guests'. Both are trained in self-defence, the use of firearms and have access to weapons. I've rung their emergency-line to the local police headquarters. They've heard nothing. I found this," he says, leading me into the kitchen.

On a worktop, lying beside a hammer, are the remains of a satellite 'phone. I take a moment to study it.

"That's John's old 'phone, the one Fia had," I say. "No wonder it went straight to ansaphone."

We search the house from top to bottom, but find nothing else that might help us. In frustration, I sit in an easy-chair in the main lounge.

In my hand, I hold Caroline's pink teddy bear. It still wears a little jacket, which my mother made for it. Something has lodged between the tiny garment and the bear's fur. Curious, I take a closer look. I fiddle around for a moment, to find a folded piece of paper. On unravelling it, I discover a page torn from a pocket diary. Despite a collection of electronic calendar-aids, Fia prefers to carry an old-fashioned paper diary. Scribbled in a hurry and close to illegible, the writing, is hers. I hold it closer to a light.

*N, hope you find this. Bradley is not who she seems. The couple who live here are well-known to her. Don't know why, but they appear to have a long-standing grudge against you. We're safe for now, but they're all acting strangely. Don't know where, but we're to be taken somewhere else. They're standing guard outside the door. F*

Poor Caroline, she is without her favourite toy, but the bear is something Fia knows I will recognise and be certain to pick up.

"Here, Tony," I call as I go in search of him, "I've found something."

I come across him in an office, rifling through the drawers of a desk. He reads the note, after a struggle with the writing.

"Bradley," he says "Isn't she the PC who's supposed to be protecting them? What's her problem with you?"

"I don't know. Apart from Friday, I've seen her only once. She and an inspector visited us earlier in the year, to break the news about the death of Fia's uncle," I explain.

"Before that?"

"No."

I can think of nothing about PC Bradley that is familiar. Prior to this year, I have no memory of meeting her, nor coming across her name. She seemed pleasant, attractive in a no-nonsense way, and professional in her attitude to work. Between five foot seven and eight in height, blue eyes, slim face and body, her hair was blond and tied back. I have a vague memory of darker roots. At our first meeting, she had studied me, but I had thought that a habit formed by the nature of her work. I assumed she did that to everyone she met in the course of her duty.

## CHAPTER 38

Tony shakes his head at my description. It could describe a number of other officers. He returns to his search of the desk.

"Hang on," he says, "is this her?"

He hands me a photo-frame uncovered from beneath a pile of old invoices and papers, now returned to the drawers.

"When I came in, I didn't take any notice if it," he adds.

The picture is of three people, standing in front of an expanse of water, Wastwater from the scree-slopes on the opposite bank. The trio appear happy, relaxed and smiling. Two are strangers, a man with his arm around a woman. Bradley has knelt down in front of the pair. She holds a pair of trekking poles.

"Yes, that's Bradley, at the front," I say. "The other woman, with the dark hair, she has a similar look to Bradley. I wonder if she's an older sister, or cousin?"

"Those two are Stephen and Joanne Smedley, employed to look after this house. Damn it," Tony says as he picks up the 'phone on the desk.

He presses one of the preset numbers on the key-pad. Within seconds, it connects to the local police control-centre. Other landlines may be out of action, but this one runs independently.

"Sergeant Braithwaite, put me through to Chief Superintendent Smithers."

As this is an emergency line, the murmur of a voice at the other end is swift. Salient and to the point, Tony explains the situation. After a few, 'yes sir', 'no sir' and, a couple of times, 'immediately', Tony drops the 'phone into its rest.

"Right, we've to head back to Skipton. The chief super's having copies of Bradley's police-file, and those of the other two, faxed to the station there. Email is still down, but they have a 'phone-link established to central records, and an ancient fax-machine for emergencies. They should be ready for us when we reach town. It's usual for the station to close on a weekend, but with everything that's happening, the local police are back on duty. I'm hoping there might be something among the paperwork to explain what's going on.

On the way out of the house, we find the rucksack I had packed with my clothes at home. The other three, Fia's and the children's, have gone. I fetch it away with us; I am overdue a change of clothes – but first a shower and a shave.

Outside, we inspect the car left behind in the car park. Tony has found the keys for it in the kitchen. Inside the vehicle, there is nothing of significance. No helpful maps with an X marking the spot where the owners might have gone. Tony presses the boot release. I look inside. It too is empty.

"I've asked HQ to find out what other vehicles are registered here. We have classed Bradley and the Smedleys as kidnappers. Don't worry," he says, seeing my expression, "we'll find them."

I hope so, but because of the upheaval going on countrywide, that will be anything but easy. They could be anywhere.

# 39

In the middle of a downpour, we pull up outside the police station in Skipton. An officer shows us into a back office, where sheets of paper crawl out of a fax machine. Used to digital copy, and the clarity of its content, I had forgotten how appalling faxes can be. Twenty minutes later, a young PC, who had left minutes after our arrival, returns. In his arms, he carries a large plastic bag filled with paper-wrapped packages. One of the local fish shop owners, who has braved the chaos, is set to make a fortune from the troops who pass through the town.

The smell of fish and chips drives away any memory of Ethel's food at the farm. Despite a heavy coating of salt and vinegar, we tuck into this unexpected feast with relish. A new shift comes on duty. Tony and I collect the faxes, which have stopped dribbling from the machine. Between us, we sort them into order.

"Ah!" says Tony, after studying one of the sheets. *"Joanne Smedley*, née, *Bradley*. Parents, *Duncan* and *Samantha Bradley*, both ticked as deceased, one sister, *Dianne Bradley*, living. Place of birth, *Sheffield*."

"*Dianne Bradley, PC*, stationed at *Weetwood Police Station, Leeds*. Parents, *Duncan* and *Samantha*, again, both ticked as deceased, one sister, *Joanne Smedley*, née *Bradley*, living," I say, extracting information from her records. "Place of birth, *Sheffield*."

The image on the fax I hold is dark; the outlines blurred. Despite its quality, I cannot mistake the face. This is the woman who has stolen my family.

"So, the girls are sisters," Tony says. "That explains their connection. Any thoughts, yet, about why they might bear you, or members of your family, a grudge?"

"Nothing comes to mind, apart from the three of us being born in Sheffield. I spent my childhood there, in a terraced house. Once I'd climbed the local party-ladder, I move to a detached house in the suburbs. It was later I fell from grace. Within months, I found myself living in a back-to-back terrace in Leeds, working as a junior-clerk. It's a long story," I say, at Tony's raised eyebrow. "Over the years, I don't re-call anyone called Bradley."

"It says here, the father was a member of an illegal organisation, a trades union. Several years ago, he died during a riot at a Sheffield factory, when the security-forces opened fire. His wife died two years later."

"What's the name of the factory?" I ask.

I have a sinking feeling in my heart.

"Dawson's Springs and Metal Forgings," Tony replies.

People say, "What goes around comes round." It looks to me as if it is my turn to be on the receiving end. Dawson's was the company for whom I worked. That was the place where, in my naivety, as party-rep I wielded huge power. The same one where, in a moment of stress, a misinterpreted nod of my head caused the deaths of all those workers.

Blood drains from my face. I know what Diane Bradley and her sister want. She must have recognised me, or my name, when she visited us in April. Since then, no doubt, she and her sister have plotted their revenge. By chance, the coup has provided them with an ideal opportunity to take action. It is clear the pair wants me to suffer for the death of their father. Can I blame them? Were it the other way round, I would be the one to seek justice.

"Is everything okay?" Tony asks, seeing my expression.

"Yes and no," I answer. "I believe I know what the Bradley's have against me. What I don't know is how far they're prepared to go to seek their revenge."

We are on our own, in the back office with the fax machine. Tony brings some tea and closes the door behind him. I unburden myself of the guilt over that incident, and many others during my inglorious career working for the party. I expect a look of revulsion to appear on Tony's face, but, instead, a sympathetic one materialises.

"We've all done something, which, on reflection, was neither sensible nor morally defensible," he says with a wry smile. "Hindsight is divine punishment for stupidity. That's why I quit my job with the NSF, to move over to the police."

"Why, what happened?"

"I was in London, working undercover. One night, my supervisor called me in for an urgent meeting. He informed me about a gangland drugs dealer, a killer whose disposal was a matter of urgency. I said I was not an executioner. My boss told me the target was the dealer who, a few years before, had supplied the tainted drugs that killed my younger sister at a party. The following night, I waited outside the man's house. When he drove off, I tailed him into a supermarket car park. It was the middle of winter, dark and pouring with rain. Under a flight path to Heathrow, it was noisy. From behind, I walked up to his vehicle. Before he knew I was there, I'd put two bullets through his head. Nobody noticed. Within minutes, I was a couple of miles away. Job done!

"A few days later, I discovered the man was none of the things I'd been told. He was a junior party member. His 'crime' was to have a wife who, unbeknown to him, had become the mistress to one of the party hierarchy, a man who had grown weary of his current wife. I had been the instrument of his private intrigues. Six months later, I transferred to the regular police, with dire warnings as to what would happen if I divulged details of what happened."

"From what I know about some of those at the top, I'm surprised they allowed you to live," I say.

"I made it known, if anything happened to me, a full report, names, details and evidence of the operation, would be handed to the man's enemies, with a copy to JJ. He might be a tyrant, but he has strict ideas on the example his fellow leaders should set. Whereas having a mistress is acceptable, arranging the murder of her husband is not.

"Until this weekend, the man who ordered the hit was a senior government minister. Last night, I hear, when rebel forces came to arrest him, he grabbed his mistress and fled. His driver took a wrong turn. They fell into the hands of a large mob in Basildon. What little the crowd left of them could have been taken away in a bucket, by the undertaker."

"What happened to the man's wife?"

"Two weeks after the original killing she disappeared. This allowed his mistress to move in with him."

"He had his wife killed, too?"

"I don't think so. The rumour is, she contacted an underground escape group, emptied his bank account then fled abroad."

A knock on the door interrupts us. A constable enters.

"The vehicle allocated for the use of Stephen Smedley," the constable says. "It's a government registered nine-seater kombi-van, black with tinted windows. We've checked its tracker, it's disabled."

"There's nothing better for transporting people, or goods, you don't want others to see," Tony says in disgust.

"We've issued an APW (all points warning)," the constable explains for my benefit, "and descriptions. We've advised that three of the vehicle's occupants are armed and dangerous, and that three others, a woman and two children, are hostages."

"Thank you," Tony says. "There's nothing else we can do until we hear something. Is it possible to find somewhere for us to stay the night, constable?"

She nods. Ten minutes later, she returns.

"I've found you a couple of rooms at the Lodge, near the roundabout," she says.

I realise how weary I am. Apart from a few, uncomfortable hours sleep, in the front of the borrowed jeep last night, I have been on the go since Friday morning. I look at the clock on the wall. It is approaching one o'clock, Sunday morning. A shower and a good night's sleep are what I want. After leaving our mobile numbers with the officer on

## CHAPTER 39

duty, we set off to the hotel. As Tony said, all we can do is wait, and pray the Bradley sisters do no harm to Fia and the children before we find them.

I am sure the couple intend to vent their anger against my family. Because I destroyed theirs, they wish to do the same to mine. Would it make any difference to them if they knew how much I regretted the results of my actions that day, or would they care? Their grievance has festered too long. What I believed would be a baton charge turned into cold-blooded murder. I doubt they will listen to explanations. Without hesitation, I would offer myself in exchange, but I have little hope that would satisfy them. I suspect they want me to live long, to suffer for my past actions. They haunt me enough as it is.

After a shower, I feel human again. I sink into the comfort of my bed, to find my mind too active for sleep. An underlying sense of panic keeps me tense, my stomach knotted. After a restless hour, I give-in to the inevitable. With the lights on, I wrap the hotel dressing-gown round my shoulders. The mini-bar tempts me, but I want a clear head. Instead, I make a hot drink. With the fax copies spread out around me, I sit cross-legged on the bed, while I read and re-read them. Somewhere, I am confident there is a clue to where the Bradley sisters have decamped. An hour later, with my eyes drooping, I slide between the sheets. This time, I sleep.

I awake. It is seven-thirty. The clock-radio has switched-on by itself. Some previous guest must have set the alarm. The rest has been good for me, although I am a little thick-headed. A cold shower, clears my mind. Something niggles at the back of my consciousness. Dressed, I return to the sheets of paper, spread in a haphazard fashion over the bed and the floor. Back in order, I leaf through them until I find the page I had been looking at before falling asleep.

Half way down, I find the entry for which I seek. Stephen and Joanne Smedley own a caravan, on the coast, off the road to Sandsend from Whitby. It might be false hope, but it is worth following-up. In the safe house, we had failed to uncover any documents related to this. The couple's service-record has the caravan registered as somewhere to contact them, in an emergency, when away from home.

Later, at a table in the dining-room, I stare with impatience at the clock as I wait for Tony to appear. It is unfair of me, I know; it was a late night. I nibble at a second slice of toast. A few minutes before nine, Tony arrives. He looks cheerful and rested. After a quick 'Good morning', he scans the menu. He orders the full English, which I declined. I am too much on edge to digest anything that substantial.

Coffees arrive. As we drink the strong, bitter liquid, I inform Tony about my discovery. He is wary about raising too many hopes, but agrees it is a good place to start. He 'phones through to Police HQ. They have nothing new to tell us. There are no sightings of the vehicle, nor its occupants. With fighting still going on, my problem is low on their list of priorities. Tony gives them the location of the caravan. He requests they ask the locals to send an unmarked car to inspect the site. Under no circumstances should they approach the caravan, nor do anything to alert any occupants.

Half an hour later, Tony scrapes the final crumbs from his plate. His mobile rings.

"Yes," he answers the call. He listens carefully. "The kombi-van is behind the caravan," he says to me, before turning his attention back to the 'phone. "Is there any sign of anyone?...No! That's good. How many of the other caravans appear occupied?...Yes, I appreciate it's the end of September, freezing-cold at the coast, wet, windy and there's an uprising taking place. I take it that means few others are resident on site...Excellent. Don't do anything, unless anyone attempts to leave. Keep the area under surveillance, and your people out of sight. We can be there in a two or three hours." Turning to me, as he disconnects, he says, "That was the Whitby police. Did you follow most of that?"

I nod.

"Good, let's collect our gear."

Within twenty minutes, we are away. An hour later, in the Vale of York, with the North York Moors rising to the east, tension rises with

## CHAPTER 39

each mile we drive. On the motorway near Northallerton, a major checkpoint delays us for a while. Tony loses patience. He switches-on the siren. With that blaring, we are fast-tracked through the stream of vehicles. In the distance, a cloud of smoke rises from the direction of the town. We wind-down the window, to speak to a soldier. The sound of small arms, with the occasional blast of something heavier, carries on the breeze.

"There's a pocket of NSF resistance near the centre," the soldier says. "It's nasty, hand-to-hand street fighting, but they're surrounded. We'll have 'em by tonight."

We drive on, to skirt round the edge of the moors. Near Guisborough, we turn east and head over the bleak moorland towards Whitby. We are about five miles from the seaside town when, up ahead, near to a signpost pointing towards Grosmont, halfway through a hedge a van lies on its side. From the side-road, the driver appears to have taken the corner too fast. The vehicle has flipped over, then slid across the main road. As we draw closer, flashes of light appear at the rear of the van, followed by the sound of bullets slamming into the front of our vehicle. It has sufficient protection to keep us safe from small arms fire. Tony slams-on the brakes. We skid to a halt, sideways-on, front-end off the road, close to adjacent woodland on our right.

He grabs a carbine. Protected from the snipers by the range rover's bodywork, he slips out of the vehicle.

"Stay here," he says, as he closes his door.

At a run, he disappears from sight, into the copse. I keep a low-profile while I watch the area from which our attackers opened fire. A man with a rifle appears from behind the wrecked van. I remain motionless. He approaches, his weapon aimed in my direction. He wears an NSF uniform. Another, uniformed figure steps out from behind the overturned vehicle. He, too, carries a rifle. The man moves towards me. They must have missed Tony's swift exit and believe us injured and trapped.

"Get out of the car, now," the first man shouts.

I ignore him.

In quick succession, two shots ring-out. With blood spurting from his throat, the man closer to the van collapses. The one nearer to me spins round. He falls victim to more bullets fired from the copse. He staggers across the road, to collapse onto the nearby grass-verge. Several more shots come, this time from behind the van. From the edge of the wooded area, where it adjoins the side road, Tony's carbine barks three times. Silence. Tony comes into view, weapon at the ready. He reaches the van then disappears behind it. After a few seconds, he reappears. Before he returns to the car, he confirms the men in the road are dead. As he re-joins me, I notice a speck of blood on his cheek.

"Splinter," he says. "A bullet struck a tree at the side of me. The man behind the van was a bloody fool. If he'd waited a little longer, he could have shot me when I stepped onto the road. I hadn't seen him, but he was too eager. Let's go, we're almost there."

He starts the engine. Seconds later, he switches it off.

"Damn," he says, "we have company."

I look through the side window. Coming our way, from the direction of Whitby, is a convoy of military vehicles.

"These are on our side," I observe. "These are regular army."

The column comes to a halt. Several soldiers, under the command of a captain, leap down, their weapons trained on us. Tony steps out of our car, police ID in his right hand. His weapons, he leaves behind. With hands out wide and his papers in clear view, he walks towards the captain. Most of the troops keep their weapons trained on him. Two move to the side of our vehicle. After a couple of minutes, and a command from the captain, they indicate I should step outside and join them. I comply. Faced with overwhelming odds, it seems the sensible thing to do. The captain has his mobile to his ear.

With slow movements, I take out my ID and join Tony.

"That's all right sir," the captain says, putting away his mobile. "Sergeant Braithwaite has apprised me of your situation and North Yorks Police HQ has confirmed his story. We're here to patrol the road between Guisborough and Whitby. Over the past twenty-four hours, we've had reports of several shootings along here, and a number of fatalities. It's lucky you were in a lightly-armoured military vehicle, and with Sergeant Braithwaite, here, who's a specialist protection officer. He's saved my men a job by removing these," he points in the direction of the bodies of our attackers, who now lie together at the side of the road.

So, Tony is a specialist protection officer, of that I was unaware. It explains a great deal about his actions.

"I'll leave a vehicle to escort you into Whitby," the captain says.

Within minutes, the convoy moves off. Tony reverses onto the carriageway. In the opposite direction, we fall-in behind the remaining jeep. For the last hour, the skies have darkened and the wind has picked up speed. The nearer to the coast we approach, the lower the temperature drops.

# 40

Out over the North Sea, the dark line of a sea-squall heads towards us. Moving at speed, ragged dark grey clouds stream low overhead. White horses race into shore on the incoming tide. The air is damp with spray, whipped up by bitter winds that howl over the cliff tops. I lie flat, on wet grass, thankful for the waterproof clothes I decided this morning to wear again. At the side of a static caravan, three rows away from that owned by the Smedleys, I have strict instructions to remain where I am. Tony is several metres ahead of me, crawling towards our target. A dozen soldiers, who have taken up positions a similar distance away from the caravan and kombi, have them surrounded. They too close in, using the rows of holiday homes as cover.

The squall hits land. Within seconds, driving rain obscures much of my view. I crawl beneath the home beside which I have been lying. It helps little. The gusts whip the torrent sideways. The door to Smedleys's caravan blows open in the wind. Its banging against the outer van-wall becomes a steady beat.

Tony, bent double, zigzags towards the doorway. I cross my fingers and pray, although, from the swinging door, it would appear no-one is inside. He gauges his move with precision. As the door swings wide-open, Tony, gun in hand, dives through the gap to roll out of sight. The soldiers have moved closer and taken up positions a few metres from their target. Two of them check the kombi, but, from the shakes of their heads it is clear they have found nothing.

After a few moments, Tony appears in the doorway. He shouts for a medic. In response to his beckoning, propelled by wind and rain, I race across the intervening space. I hurtle inside the caravan. Of Fia

## CHAPTER 40

and the Bradley sisters, there is no sign. At one end of the interior, slumped on the floor between two long seats, is Stephen Smedley. He is unconscious or dead, his head down and back against the wall, his shirt and trousers soaked in blood. A pistol is on the floor nearby. My heart misses a beat. Lying on top of the seats, one on either side, are Caroline and Ian. For a second, I fear them dead. I see movement. Both of them struggle against their bindings.

Tony cuts Ian free. I do the same to Caroline. Both are stiff and cold, but, at first glance, neither seems harmed. I gather them into my arms and hold them tight.

"Please, help the man, daddy" Ian pleads. "He saved us from that horrible woman. She wanted to kill us, but he wouldn't let her. After she'd gone, he tried to untie us, but he was hurt. He groaned, then went to sleep."

"She took new mum," Caroline says.

For once, Ian fails to correct her. It is usual for him to be pedantic about calling Fia by her name. Caroline has formed a deeper bond with Fia and has taken to calling her 'new mum'.

"Early this morning, that nasty Joanne woman made the nicer one untie Fia's feet, then they dragged her away from us," Ian says. "They put her in a car that was here when we arrived. That Joanne woman came back. She told Stephen to kill us and to hurry up. He said, 'No, I'm not killing anybody'. She said, 'Fine, I'll do it'. She took out a gun, but he already had his in his hand. He fired above her head. She ran away. When he reached the doorway, I heard her gun go-off. Stephen fell backwards. There was blood all down his shirt. You won't let them hurt Fia, will you dad?"

"We're all doing our best to find her," I comfort them, my relief at finding my children diminished by concern over Fia's safety.

Several vehicles pull-up. Flashing blue lights are a blur through the water cascading down the caravan windows. Tony leads us out to a waiting police car. A paramedic hurries inside to treat the wounded man. I wish the medic luck with that. Stephen's chances for survival look slight. The man would seem to be complicit in the abduction of my family, but he did save my children's lives. For that, I hope he lives. To be honest, if he dies my tears will be few.

The squall passes. A helicopter approaches. It hovers nearby, the sound of its rotors deafening. It is too risky to attempt a landing in these winds. I hear the medics are to winch up Stephen Smedley for a flight to James Cook Hospital in Middlesbrough, a few minutes flying-time away. There is still no sign of Fia, nor any indication of where the Bradley sisters might have taken her. Stephen may be the one person we have with a clue to her whereabouts. I realise I need him to live, at least long enough to talk.

A constable jumps into the police car.

"I've to take you to a local hotel," he says. "Sergeant Braithwaite will stay here while we search the caravan. He'll join you later."

Both Ian and Caroline are shivering from the cold. No heating was on in the caravan. In what seems no time at all, we have booked into a large hotel on the edge of Whitby, overlooking the bay. The lounge where we sit has, on a fine day I imagine, a splendid panoramic view of the sea. Now it is lost behind another squall. With heavy blankets wrapped round them, hot drinks in their hands, the children look and sound much better. Their resilience amazes me. A member of staff approaches, carrying a large Pizza. We are all hungry. The food soon disappears, as do the cakes that follow.

Over time, I piece together what has happened to Ian and Caroline since their disappearance on Friday night. With ease, their police-driver had lost the pursuing NSF vehicles. Afterwards, he had taken his passengers to the safe-house. Until the driver left, everything had gone without any hint of trouble. He had stayed long enough to have a drink with Dianne, her sister and brother-in-law. The Smedleys had been hospitable. Once the police car's tail lights had disappeared down the driveway, everything changed. At gunpoint, Joanne Smedley had locked Fia and the children in an old coal cellar. Apart from the steps leading to the door by which they had entered, the only other way out was through a disused coal chute leading to a small hatch, padlocked from outside.

Soon after midnight on Saturday morning, at gunpoint, the captors released their victims from their prison. With a bottle of water to share, Smedley left the three in the lounge for a while. That allowed Fia the opportunity to write her message to me. Before dawn, the captives were inside the kombi, hidden under blankets on its back seats. A number of times, while travelling, they heard gunfire. Twice bullets hit the vehicle, but all escaped injury. Whatever the abductors travel papers had said, on the occasions the vehicle halted at checkpoints, the party passed through without a search. Later that morning, the travellers arrived at the caravan. Here they had remained, with the occasional sip of water and a biscuit for sustenance.

Whatever the sisters' intentions were, the children never found out. Whenever their captors wanted to discuss anything, they went outside to talk. Their prisoners remained inside, bound and gagged. Neither Stephen nor Dianne seemed happy at the situation in which they found themselves. Neither appeared to know the reason why, but finding Fia in the advanced stages of pregnancy had infuriated Joanne. Because of that, it appeared she had changed her plans. This last minute alteration had upset Stephen and Dianne even more, but Joanne was the person in charge.

Up in the children's room, by eight they are in bed. Caroline, relieved at the return of her teddy bear, hugs it to her chest. Neither Ian nor she has slept much over the last two days. A PC brought their bags earlier. Despite a promise to leave the adjoining door between our rooms open, both children become agitated when I leave them on their own. To settle them, I promise to stay the night, in an easy chair placed between their beds. Exhausted, both are asleep within minutes.

For a while, with the television volume turned down low, I catch up on the news. My own problems have occupied my mind too much to worry about what has been happening elsewhere. Apart from those members of the former government who supported the uprising, most of the others are under arrest. A few minor figures have escaped abroad. The army is in control of most of the country.

As with Northallerton, isolated pockets of resistance hold out. There have been numerous reports of violence, as various groups try to evade capture. Outnumbered and outgunned, their eventual surrender is inevitable. After Friday night and Saturday's disturbances by those seeking revenge, huge rallies have taken place today in support of the uprising. Sheer weight of people-power does more to influence the undecided members of the NSF than does anything else. Outside Britain, most leading countries, apart from Russia and China, have recognised the interim government.

A soft knock on the external door to my room interrupts my viewing. Tony has arrived at last. When I let him in, he looks weary and cold. Through the open doorway, he takes in the sleeping figures in their beds and smiles. He takes a seat in a corner of their room while I 'phone room-service for hot drinks. Tony has already eaten. I pull-up another chair, nearby. We watch the news until the drinks arrive. Afterwards, to avoid disturbing the children, we talk in undertones.

"We took the caravan and the kombi to pieces," Tony says, adding a splash of whisky from the mini-bar into his coffee. "SOCOs stripped everything back to the frame and chassis on both, but we found nothing to help us. Same as at the guest house, Joanne Bradley has covered her tracks."

"What's happened to Stephen Smedley? Is he still alive?" I ask.

"I contacted the hospital earlier. Smedley's alive, but he's in a poor way. I spoke to the surgeon. All he would say was, the next twenty-four hours are critical. The operation to remove the bullet was lengthy and delicate. It had lodged next to the spine. They've patched-up Smedley, but he lost a great deal of blood. The doctors insist on keeping him sedated. They say it's doubtful we'll be able to talk to him before Tuesday. He's in a private room, under armed guard."

"So, we wait," I say, my anger and frustration directed at the delay, rather than Tony.

## CHAPTER 40

The longer the hold-up, the further-away Fia could be from me, the greater the time for her captors to cover their tracks.

"There's nothing else we can do," Tony says. "I've spoken to your friend, John. He says to tell you Harry has people digging into both the Smedley's and Bradley's backgrounds, to see if they can find anything useful." He stands, stretches and yawns. "Try to sleep, you look exhausted. That's what I'm going to do. We'll speak over breakfast."

Alone again, with Ian and Caroline, I collect a blanket from my room. Stretched out on the easy-chair between the twin-beds, I take Tony's advice. I might look exhausted, but I feel far worse. Where the hell have they taken you, Fia?

# 41

The background sound of a children's TV programme disturbs me. Ian and Caroline have found the remote control. To my surprise, I have slept through the night. Worn out from their adventure, the children have wakened much later than is usual. We are late for breakfast. Downstairs, of Tony, there is no sign. I ask after him at reception. A young woman hands me a note. A call, by him, first thing to the hospital has provided some news. Stephen Smedley, contrary to expectations, has spent a comfortable night. He shows signs of improvement. Later in the day, his doctors have suggested, it might be possible for someone to have a brief talk with their patient. Tony has driven to Middlesbrough, to await his chance to see Smedley.

Refreshed and wide-awake, Ian and Caroline are full of energy, and incessant questions. The horrors of the weekend have receded and both, unlike me, have a healthy appetite. Yesterday's storm has passed-over, which means a morning of bright sunshine and clear blue skies. Filled with concern about Fia, I fail to appreciate the fine view from the dining room windows. My 'phone rings. It brings me several disapproving looks from a party of elderly ladies, stranded here by the weekend's events. I mutter apologies as I move to the doorway, away from theirs, and the children's, hearing.

"Nathan? It's Harry. How are you bearing up? Are the kids all right?"

"We're coping," I say. "Have *you* any news?"

"Nothing concrete," he admits. "We're looking deeper into the Smedleys' background. Unlike Bradley, they have amassed considerable sums of money, spread over several bank accounts. A couple, they emptied on Friday. We've frozen the others, but we can't rule anything out. Under assumed names, they may have access to further funds. They seem to have led a double-life. As to where the sisters are holding Fia, we've drawn a blank. Is Tony with you, I'd like a word with him?"

"No, he's at the hospital. The doctors think Stephen Smedley may be fit enough to answer a few questions later today. He's our only lead. How are matters elsewhere?" I ask. "What happened at Orford?"

"The initial air strikes destroyed much of the stockpiled vaccination doses and syringes awaiting shipment. Once our troops landed, after a couple of hours of heavy fighting, the garrison surrendered. Our men laid charges. They destroyed everything left standing. The research labs, data and storage units have gone. Raids have taken place at all major manufacturers of components, including Aitkins, and the labs that created the chips. We've taken and destroyed their related files, prototypes and samples. We have a few places left to visit, including the centres that hold the scheme's current back-up data. We've locked down those for now. By the end of the week, the threat from them will be over."

"So that's the end of it," I say.

"We can only hope. Both the Americans and the Russians have heard rumours. They are curious. We've denied everything. The scientists, who invented the wretched program, and designed the chips, were among the casualties at Orford. Those at lower-levels are in custody, but have no knowledge of the technical-processes involved in the chip creation. What we cannot discount is that someone, somewhere, may have sufficient documentation, that could allow them to re-create the whole damn mess.

"Our people remain on alert. We've taken action now because, politicians being politicians, once they're back in power, they might be tempted to re-instate the research. Better to eradicate everything, before they have a chance.

"Elsewhere, matters are much calmer. There's been a couple of rallies today, but nothing on the scale of yesterday. Most people have followed our advice, to stay at home or return to work. Over the coming days, we are to commence processing prisoners at correctional facilities and forced-labour camps, prior to their release. Released from prison over the weekend, leaders of the opposition have arranged meetings with the interim government. Many others, who, over the years escaped abroad, are to return to join in the talks. Over the coming days, they expect to agree a provisional timetable to stage elections, to bring about a full transfer of power to civilian rule."

"What's happening about the NSF?"

"Good question. For now, we have confined most of them to barracks. We shall integrate those units that changed allegiance at the start of the uprising, or were already working for us, into the regular army or police. Units that fought against us, we intend to disband. To the isolated few who continue to resist, the provisional government has issued an ultimatum. Surrender, by two o'clock this afternoon, or face an all-out assault. We'll arrest, and charge with treason, those who survive."

"What's going to happen to the people who were on the periphery of NSF or PNU operations?" I ask. "There must be hundreds of thousands who have reported friends or neighbours to the authorities. Because of their actions, many have gone to prison, suffered injury or died."

This is of some importance. Victims, relatives and friends, such as the Bradley sisters, will demand justice. What I did was wrong, that I cannot deny, but in many ways, it was minor in comparison to the deeds of others.

"That will have to be decided," Harry says. "I'm in a similar position to you in regard to my past. I know a Mandela-type solution is on the table, where everyone admits to what they have done and, as a nation, we move forward. I believe the alternative is that the country will wallow in show-trials and navel-gazing for decades to come. From spying and betrayal of neighbours, right to the top of the leadership, it would be difficult to know where to draw a line.

"Half the population is of potential interest. It would be impossible to investigate everyone. The numbers are too vast to contemplate. I think

## CHAPTER 41

there'll be a cut-off point, and amnesty, for most people, otherwise, we'll be little better off than before the uprising. There are a few exceptions. Those at the top, who gave the orders, members of kill-squads and those involved with torture, will be major targets. The instigators of schemes, such as the one that claimed the life of Fia's brother, will face justice, too. It won't prevent individuals seeking to take matters into their own hands, but those will be a tiny minority."

In the background, someone calls to Harry. Closer to me is the sound of a squabble. In the dining room, between Caroline and Ian, a disagreement has broken out over possession of the last slice of toast. The elderly ladies glare in my direction. I explain about the altercation to Harry.

"I have to go, anyway," he says chuckling, "and I think I have problems!"

He disconnects. Peacemaker dad returns to the battlefield of the dining room. I solve the problem by ordering extra toast. I am sure the oldies believe I should have boxed the children's ears.

The day is ours to spend, as we wish. First, although the morning is bright, it is cold. The children's clothes are no defence against the strength of the winds blowing in off the North Sea. We have run out of other garments. A taxi into town and a slight emptying of the bank account sees them kitted-out for the weather.

After a walk on the beach, we have fish and chips for lunch. I eat little. Worry has destroyed my appetite. After lunch, we climb the hundred and ninety-nine steps to St Mary's Church and the Abbey. The ruins fascinate the children, more so when I tell them about its links to Dracula. We return to the beaches that provided inspiration for Lewis Caroll's poem The Walrus and the Carpenter. The absence of Fia is noticeable. On our previous trip to Whitby, she made everything such fun for the children. From their comments, I can tell they miss her too. Each time I check my mobile there are no missed calls. I curb my impatience. I am sure Tony will make contact when he has something to tell me, or he is able.

After dinner, we take possession of the lounge before the elderly ladies arrive. I flick through the channels on the large-screen television, to find the BBC has unlocked the doors to its archives. Added to the evening's schedule are several programs I remember from childhood. In a civilised manner, we negotiate a compromise with the old ladies when they put in an appearance. We shall monopolise the viewing until seven thirty, after that, they can indulge in whatever programmes they want. We shall have gone to our rooms. Despite a constant mutter of discontent from a minority, most of our fellow guests are happy with our choice of entertainment.

Tonight, the children are more secure. With a wall-light left on for Caroline, I leave them sleeping. In my room, with the connecting door left ajar, I sit back in an easy chair. As I change channels, on the much smaller room television, I find an occasional English-language broadcast from abroad. I observe their take on the British Revolution, as they call it.

Sometime after nine, I hear a faint knock on the corridor door. Within seconds, Tony joins me in my room. Again, he looks tired. I ring room-service, order coffee and a round of sandwiches for him. Grateful, he sinks into the armchair. I sit on the edge of my bed.

"What a tedious day," Tony complains. "I've spent most of it in a stifling waiting-room. It was half-past-seven before I left the hospital."

"How's Smedley?"

"He remains in intensive-care, but mid-morning regained consciousness. The wretched doctors insisted I wait until this evening before I could see him."

"Did he have anything useful to say?" I ask, daring to hope.

If the answer is no, we will struggle to move forward.

"A little," Tony answers. "My time with him was brief. He has difficulty talking, but does want to help. The first thing he said was, 'are the children safe?'"

A knock at the door interrupts him. Our coffee and Tony's sandwiches have arrived. I curb my impatience. By the way he tucks into

## CHAPTER 41

the food, it looks as though it is a while since he last ate. After a few minutes, he notices my anxious face.

"Sorry," he says, "I've had nothing but a bowl of soup since breakfast. Okay, back to my visit with Smedley. I doubt what he said will make you feel any better."

I brace myself.

"To put your mind at rest, the good news is he thinks Fia is still alive," he says. "Let's start from the beginning. Joanne Smedley, nee Bradley, is the driving force behind everything. Her husband seems somewhat afraid of her. It's apparent she dominates most aspects of his life.

"After Dianne Bradley saw you at your home, she mentioned the meeting to her sister. Your name, of course, was familiar, but neither had seen you before then. Joanne was desperate to know whether you were the same Nathan Andrews, whose involvement led to the death of their father. Despite pressure from her sister, Dianne refused to jeopardise everything she'd worked for in her career. She knew any attempt to access your information, the NSF would trace back to her.

"Much younger than Joanne and, unlike her, Dianne was never close to her father. By the time she was born, he was involved in illegal Union-work so was absent for much of the time. For most of her life before his death, Dianne was brought up by her grandparents.

"According to Stephen, Joanne has a tendency to fixate on matters. Within weeks, via her own sources, she confirmed your identity. With little to do at the guest house, she spent her days obsessing about making you suffer. It's probable it would have remained a fantasy, had not chance brought Dianne back into your life, on Friday night.

"When the call came through from Harry's unit about people who were in need of protection, Dianne was chosen at random to shepherd your family. She grabbed the first driver and vehicle that returned to base, then set off. They knew the city was insecure. It would be a struggle to find a place of safety there. When they reached your house, they had to flee with Fia and the children. By the time they lost their NSF pursuers, the party was heading north.

"Away from her home ground, Dianne knew of only one other official safe-house within easy reach. She directed her driver there. Joanne had kept secret her findings about Nathan from all but her husband. Somehow, she had obtained a photograph of Nathan and Fia. As soon as Dianne introduced her companions, Joanne realised who the people were who had walked into her lair. It wasn't until after Smedley produced a gun, and took Fia and the children prisoner, did Dianne find out that you were *the* Nathan Andrews responsible for her father's death. Joanne's dominant personality overwhelms those close to her. Unable to stand up to her in person, with some reluctance, both Stephen and Dianne fell in with her spur-of-the-moment scheme."

"What is her plan?" I ask. "I know, from the children, it changed after they reached the coast and that Stephen and Dianne were even less happy with that than Joanne's earlier one. For some reason, Fia, being pregnant, angered the older sister."

"Joanne's initial thoughts were to kidnap Fia and the children, then hold them for ransom. She had the idea she could bankrupt you. It was later, when they were on the way to the caravan, that Joanne's thoughts became darker. She decided that money was not enough. She wants to break you," Tony warns, as he moves over to the mini-bar.

He pours out a stiff-whisky. To my surprise, he hands it to me. With some trepidation, I take it. This is an ominous development.

"Carry on," I say, taking a sip.

"When they arrived at the coast, Joanne told her companions she'd decided to kill the captives. Later, she changed her mind again. This time, only the children were to die. When the others objected, she threatened them. Then, when Joanne went outside for a cigarette, Stephen retrieved a back-up gun from their bags. Between Dianne and him, they decided that he would protect the children from Joanne and, if possible, she would stay with Fia and try to save her. This is what they did, and how he received his wound."

"Why did Joanne decide to spare Fia?" I ask. "Given what you've said, it seems strange. Does Stephen know where Joanne has taken her?"

## CHAPTER 41

"He knows the first stage of her route. He and Joanne are part of a smuggling and trafficking operation, about which Dianne knew nothing. As a result of their operations, the Smedley's have acquired a large amount of wealth. They bring goods into the country, and ship people out. They have contacts here, in Whitby, hence the location of the caravan.

"Seeing Fia's condition did more than anger Joanne, in time it gave her a brainwave. She contacted her coastal friends to arrange passage abroad. Unable to have children herself, her idea is to keep Fia a prisoner until the baby is born. Then, after disposing of Fia, Joanne intends rearing the child as her own. She believes losing everything is a fitting punishment for you."

"As Stephen's told you the first stage, can we not catch them before they move on?"

"When they left the caravan, they headed for a fishing boat, the Greydon Skua, moored in the harbour. Her intention was to rendezvous with another vessel, out in the North Sea. I've spoken to Harry, but, until first light, there's nothing we can do. Smedley expects the group to have transferred between boats, sometime yesterday-afternoon. Although, it's possible the three are still on board that one, Smedley thinks it probable the smugglers will have landed them somewhere on a quiet stretch of coast, in either Holland or Belgium. Joanne has contacts in both countries.

"At first light, the coastguard and a helicopter will be out looking for the Greydon Skua. I'm afraid tracking Joanne Smedley will be much more difficult. By morning, she'll be two days ahead of us. She could be heading anywhere. The smuggling operation has links worldwide. It's possible, too, she's yet to decide on her final destination."

None of this is what I want to hear. Joanne Smedley's plans for revenge have shaken me. The woman has to have gone over the edge. Her intentions for Fia are diabolical. We have to find the three of them. Dianne Bradley's inclusion in the party is the one positive thing I can take out of the whole affair. It is apparent she is less than a willing participant in the kidnapping and, like her brother-in-law, may try to counter her sister's madness. In doing so, Dianne will be putting her own life at risk. Joanne had no qualms about shooting her husband. I fear, if challenged, Joanne will kill her sister.

# 42

With no news about Fia's whereabouts, I decide to stay an extra day in Whitby. Late in the morning, Tony rings to tell me the Greydon Skua slipped into port at first light. Any contraband it might have carried, the crew must have put ashore in one of the isolated bays along the coast. The boat's unsuspecting captain, unaware that a search for them was about to start, had queued in line for the swing-bridge to open. The port authorities delayed the bridge's operation, to prevent the boat's passage into the upper harbour, until an armed police response unit was in position on the quayside. When the boat docked, the officers stepped aboard. The crew had no alternative but to surrender.

On edge, I wait until late afternoon before Tony 'phones me with the preliminary results of the interrogation. As accessories to kidnapping and smuggling, the crew face lengthy terms of imprisonment, as well as confiscation of their vessel, property and bank accounts. It has taken some time to convince the captain that Joanne Smedley's threat to kill Fia is real. If she does, he becomes an accessory to murder. The death penalty, re-introduced several years ago by JJ's government, will take an act of parliament to repeal. It is doubtful it will be a top-priority before he comes to trial. The captain, anxious to save his neck, talked.

"Nay the 'ell, am not gonna swing for that crazy bitch," he had said.

It is unfortunate his knowledge of Joanne Smedley's personality is greater than that of her intended movements. He offers the name of the Dutch trawler with which he exchanged cargoes. The vessel, the Adriana van Hoek, he says, sails out of the port of IJmuiden, north of Haalem in Holland. Before its return to port, the captain believes the Adriana will make a pass close to the coast, to allow an inshore-boat to collect its passengers. That, he anticipates, will have taken place already. Joanne Smedley and her captives will be in Holland now, some distance away from the coast.

Before ringing me, Tony has passed the information onto Harry. He will contact the Dutch police on our behalf. Under JJ's leadership, the UK had an abysmal record of co-operation with our neighbouring countries. Harry is unsure how this recent history will affect our case and the speed of the Dutch response.

This evening we have the lounge to ourselves. With travel reported to be much safer on the roads, the elderly ladies have departed on their coach, back from whence they came. We, or should I say, Ian and Caroline, are free to watch whatever they want. A day spent in the fresh air has left me short of energy. My mind is in too much of a whirl with thoughts of Fia. Tony wanders in to advise the Dutch police have acted on our information and, within the last half-hour, rung back.

The Adriana is due in port in the morning. Their coastguards are shadowing the vessel by radar. Unless it diverts towards the coast, they will keep their distance. The authorities in Holland take smuggling seriously. Once the Adriana docks, customs officials will search it then question the crew. Dutch police have commenced enquiries along the coast, too, to see if there are any reports of unauthorised landings. They hold out little hope. There are numerous places, they say, where such events could, and do, take place in secret.

The following morning, after breakfast, we check-out. In the lobby, we wait for Tony. He is to drive us back to Leeds. There is no further news from Holland. I assume, by now, the Adriana has docked, and search and interviews are under way. The weather has reverted to grey skies. A light shower splatters against the glass doors. Again, at breakfast, I struggle to eat more than a slice of toast. I am grateful for Ian and Caroline. They keep my mind occupied, a distraction from the dark thoughts that fill it whenever I allow them an opportunity. I want to be doing something, anything, to find Fia. The frustration of waiting eats away at me.

## CHAPTER 42

The journey home is uneventful. We cross the North York Moors towards Guisborough in a convoy escorted by two armoured vehicles. According to the sergeant in charge of the escort, this is the last day they are to mount this operation. Over the last forty-eight hours, there has been no trouble. Along the motorway, checkpoints remain manned, but we see no vehicles flagged down.

Over much of our journey, signs of battle are evident, from bullet-riddled vehicles at the roadside, to burnt out buildings and abandoned military hardware. In some places, bodies litter nearby fields. In others, men in protective clothing load body-bags into trucks as we drive by. We pull-up outside my driveway. The one o'clock pips sound on the car radio. A ragged line of bullet marks scars the wall above the lounge window. Windows are boarded-up on the house opposite.

We say a warm goodbye to Tony. Over the last few days, he has been a good friend and guard to us. His skills are in demand elsewhere. Our risk-level has lowered. Inside, I hear the ansaphone beeping. Hoping for news of Fia, I press the recall button. There are two messages, one from each of the children's schools, to say they are to re-open on Thursday. I have lost track of the days. I discover that is tomorrow.

I leave the children to play games on their tablets, while I go upstairs to unpack. As soon as I step into the bedroom, the sight of Fia's nightdress on the bed stops me mid-stride. I close my eyes and picture her lying there. I curl up on the bed hugging her pillow, the delicate scent of her perfume still fresh on the fabric. Willpower might have kept me going for the past few days, but now, in the room where I have spent some of the happiest moments of my life, I break down and sob like a child.

John 'phones during the evening. Harry has put him in charge of co-ordinating the effort to find Fia. The Dutch police, apart from a short response to say their enquiries continue, remain silent. Further questioning of the Whitby trawler crew has thrown up some leads, the details of which, to my frustration, John cannot discuss, apart from to say a couple seem significant.

Morning comes. The alarm wakens me. Half asleep, I stretch out, but the other half of the bed remains empty. My dreams fade and I am back to reality. With Ian and Caroline up, washed, dressed and fed, I drop them off at their respective schools. It is time to head to Aitkins. Signs of heavy fighting are everywhere. Wrecked cars and rubble from burnt-out buildings litter the way. Numerous craters in the main roads cause me to divert my regular route.

On arrival, I find the factory quieter than usual. The office, where Harry and, later, the new party-rep worked, is an empty shell. James and Rachel greet me with delighted surprise. They had heard about the shooting, outside my home, and my family's disappearance. My subsequent no-show at work, and lack of contact, has led them to believe we might all be dead. I give them a rough outline of what has taken place since last I saw them.

Over tea and biscuits, horrified, they express their sympathy. Our conversation turns to their experiences over the past few days, before we address our workload. We have little to do. Men in suits and dark glasses, accompanied by a unit of soldiers, visited the factory on Monday. Their main priority was experimental. They removed several truckloads of papers, prototypes and computer equipment. My laptop was at home. It has the software to link me to the server in Experimental, but holds none of their data. With the removal of their server, access is no longer a requirement.

All military contracts are on hold until further notice, according to instructions received from the ministry of defence. Much of our other work is on hold, too, while Sales attempt to contact customers to ascertain their needs. We fear some businesses may have suffered much over the past week. James and Rachel know of several of our customers and suppliers, whose premises suffered severe damage during the upheaval.

Later that morning, the CEO and HR director call me into a meeting. With the change of government, there is talk of huge foreign investment and a rapid increase in international trade, but these improvements

## CHAPTER 42

could be a long way in the future. In the short-term, the outlook is bleak. The company has to make many cutbacks, which includes staff downsizing. Of those who remain, many will go onto reduced hours.

After this twenty-minute preamble, it comes as little surprise to find they have someone from my department in mind for redundancy. One of my two juniors must go. Which one? I have until Monday to decide. As if I did not have enough on my mind. Weary, I trudge back towards my office. Before I can face my colleagues, I decide on a strong black coffee. Each of my staff is good at their work, their strengths and weaknesses cancel out each other. Alone in the canteen, two coffees later, the caffeine boost triggers an idea. There might be a solution. It is something Fia and I have discussed over the past month or two.

I ring Andrew Faulds to arrange a meeting. In the hope of Fia's speedy return, I have put-off telling him about what has happened. Both she and I have signed powers of attorney. They anticipate a situation, such as this, where one of us is unable to participate in company affairs. The documents give temporary control of our individual shares in the business to the other. In effect, until Fia returns, I, have the say in all matters Sandiman.

Saturday morning, with Ian and Caroline beside me, armed with books and their faithful tablets, we enter Sandiman's offices. Andrew is already at his desk. We leave the children, armed with the office Wi-Fi key, content to play on their machines while we retreat to Fia's office. As with James and Rachel, I give Andrew an abbreviated explanation of what has taken place. The news appears to affect him much more than did that of Joe's death.

"I can't believe it," he says, shaking his head. "This is too horrible to contemplate. Have the police any leads, yet?"

"They had nothing new as of first thing this morning. I believe the Dutch police have contacted Interpol. This smuggling-ring is new to them. Since the middle of the week, the Dutch have made dozens of arrests and closed down their end of the trafficking pipeline. They expect further raids and arrests to take place across Europe. Inquiries have spread to North Africa, but of Fia and her captors, there is no sign."

Andrew is aware of the power of attorney documents, but I show him my copy as proof. Fia, it seems, has discussed our ideas with Andrew. He has no objections about my decision to implement them. With Ian and Caroline to look after, and a baby on the way, she had decided to take a sabbatical from the main work of the business. Her intention was to keep a couple of key clients, but, for the foreseeable future, work part-time.

Now the living-cell program is no more, and the government overthrown, the relevance of my position at Aitkins is over. A number of times Sandiman's has used my knowledge of industry, on a consultancy basis. With Andrew taking on much of the commercial-side of the work, Fia and I thought it would be better if I join the company full-time, to run the industrial arm. With Fia missing, for a while, wherever I am, I shall have to work part-time at the office and the rest from home.

At Aitkins, I know James can ill-afford redundancy, nor a vast reduction in his hours. With Leila, he is in the process of buying a house. Rachel is a single mother and, likewise, needs the income. If I leave, the reduction in departmental wages will be far greater. To achieve the required savings, the other two would have to reduce their hours by a much smaller amount. It sounds noble of me, but the truth is I am ready for a change, and a new challenge.

Two members of staff have come in, to catch-up on work. In between their tasks, they keep Ian and Caroline occupied. By lunchtime, Andrew and I have a clear outline of what we want to achieve and how to take our working partnership forward. At Aitkins, I will tender my resignation on Monday. I doubt they will complain about a week's notice. They want to reduce their overheads as soon as possible. In nine days time, I shall start work at Sandiman's. Over the weeks to come, I shall learn the business from top to bottom. Andrew will retain overall control of the day-to-day running of the operation, but,

## CHAPTER 42

where necessary, I will be the stop where the buck goes no further. Over these past few months, Andrew has grown into his role, but he is happier when someone-else is there to take ultimate responsibility for the big decisions. I shall operate from Fia's office. This will send a clear message to staff, and visitors alike, as to my position.

First thing Monday, at Aitkins, I meet with the directors. James and Rachel watch me go, worried expressions on their faces. Over the last few days, they have heard rumours, and seen other members of the workforce issued with redundancy notices. Both know the current workload for our department means we have a surfeit of staff. I cannot say anything to re-assure them, until after my meeting.

The board express surprise at my decision to leave, but see the advantages of keeping both of my team with only a slight reduction in their hours. We agree a redundancy package. I go at the end of the week. I foresee few problems; the pair has covered for me in the past. James and Rachel are relieved that I have chosen to leave. James steps up to take over my position. After me, he is the longest-standing member of the team. There is no increase in salary involved; a title has to suffice. Rachel accepts the change without a quibble.

On Friday night, Ian and Caroline stay over with friends, while James, Rachel and I celebrate my leaving. Next day, the few drinks I have leave me with a migraine, a situation that the boisterous return of the children on Saturday afternoon does little to help. Sunday morning, two police officers arrive at the door. Under caution, they take me, and the children, to the local Police Station. Here, a pleasant young woman in uniform looks after Ian and Caroline. An interview room awaits me.

For twenty minutes, I sit, with no explanation as to why I am here, although I have my suspicions. In the white-painted room, a microphone and digital recorder rest on the imitation-wood topped table in front of me. My seat is an uncomfortable plastic chair, with two similar, but empty, ones on the other side of the table. Harsh LED lights shine down from vandal-proof security fittings, to cast sharp shadows wherever their beams touch. Near the door, a constable stands at ease, his gaze fixed on a point somewhere on the wall, above and behind my head. His conversational skills he declines to practise. We remain in silence.

The door opens. Two men in plain clothes enter. They introduce themselves as DS Fletcher and DC Iverson. The pair greets me in a neutral manner. They switch on the recording equipment, announce start times and name the people involved in the interview. They have a file in front of them, which they open. As I suspected, this meeting is about my past association and deeds with the PNU.

Without pre-amble, the pair launch into an intense grilling. The police have taken possession of huge numbers of meticulous files, amassed by the NSF over the years, mine among them. Their record of my past deeds appears comprehensive. I admit to everything.

There is one startling revelation. The mass shooting, that for years I have blamed myself, and for which Fia suffers the consequences now, was a set-up. The party hierarchy had decided to make an example of the workers. The captain's orders had come from the top. It had been no misunderstanding between him and me in the heat of the moment. His instructions were to fire on the crowd, no matter what I said or did. I was there to take the blame.

I cannot describe the sense of relief I feel at this moment. Not that it will help return Fia to me. I doubt Joanne Smedley would believe the truth, even if I was in a position to tell her. Her hatred has festered too long. I was there and, to all intents, in charge, ergo it is my fault. My interrogation, or interview, as DS Fletcher calls it, lasts over two hours, with a brief halt for coffee and a sandwich. At last, he terminates the interview at thirteen fifteen hours, as he announces to the microphone. A car will take the children and me back home.

"What happens now?" I ask, unsure what the future holds.

"Unless we receive further information," Fletcher replies, "or we require clarification on anything, which I doubt, your file will go to the CPS sometime in the next few weeks. Your answers have been frank.

## CHAPTER 42

Apart from a few amendments, the information you have supplied matches that which we have.

"There's a recent testimonial, attached to your file, signed by one of the leaders of the recent uprising, Colonel Harry Wardman. It praises you, and the work you did, which contributed towards the success of the revolution. My personal opinion is, in a few months, you'll receive a letter stating no charges are to be levied against you. That will be the recommendation I shall put with your file. Compared to some cases I've studied, yours ranks low in matters of interest, but we have orders to interview everyone with whom the NSF had a file. If I were you, I would not be unduly worried. Go home and take care of your children," he says, which is what I do.

# 43

Since the overthrow of JJ's government, the change of attitude in the local community is remarkable. People have moved out of the shadows. They talk without fear. No longer do they look over their shoulders to see who might be in earshot. Smiles and laughter have returned to the streets. Albeit in small quantities, luxury goods, once the preserve of party members, have re-appeared in general-stores. Grocery shops stock a greater variety, quantity and quality of produce. Week by week, as the country stabilises, business fears ease, although confidence remains low. A few companies start hiring again. The first sales teams head into Europe or further afield. Violence against the individual is dropping. The provisional government is working hard, healing divisions and promoting reconciliation.

The third week in October brings with it the joys of the school half-term. On two of the days, while Ian and Caroline visit friends, I sneak into work for a rest. Of the other days, half are cold and wet, where I become chief entertainer for return visits by the children's friends. I suppose it is fair I take my turn. On the few days when the weather is kinder, we explore the area's attractions or walk in the country.

Of Fia, there is no news. My mood swings from moments of high-hope and expectation to longer periods of abject despair. Caroline, in particular, wants to know, when will her new mum come home? When the children are around, I put on a show of confidence, and pretend that everything will be all right. On my own, in bed on a night, my fears threaten to overwhelm me.

Uncle John and aunty Linda, as the children call them, drop-in several times to visit. They bring treats and play games with the young ones.

## CHAPTER 43

John professes optimism, but he is unable to provide any answers as to where Fia might be. For several years he has looked out for her and done much to keep her safe. Her disappearance has hit him almost as hard as me. He considers Fia more an honorary younger sister than anything else. As do I, he knows time grows short. In a few weeks the baby is due. After a series of arrests on the continent, John has pieced together Fia's arrival in Europe and some of her journey onwards, but, for the moment, her trail grows colder by the day.

We now know the Adriana Van Hoek, with its human cargo aboard, had approached the Dutch coast a few hours after the Greydon Skua arrived back at Whitby. Half a mile off shore, a powerboat collected the passengers. Within minutes it landed the trio on a beach, to the north of the South Holland resort of Katwijk. Two men had awaited their arrival. From there, it was a matter of minutes, on foot, before they reached the Noordduinseweg car park, where, earlier, the men had left a mini-bus. Using available CCTV footage, the Dutch police had traced the vehicle's journey through Holland, until it disappeared, close to the German border.

On a side road, off the A34 motorway, several kilometres short of the border-crossing, a police patrol discovered the burnt-out skeleton of the mini-bus. To my relief, no human remains were among the ashes. On the following afternoon, outside a café in the German town of Dortmund, CCTV recorded Diane Bradley, accompanied by the two men. The German Federal State Police, the Bundeskriminalamt (BKA), joined the hunt. They co-ordinated inquiries there, and liaised with John's department here in England, as well as with the Dutch police. The German authority's identification of the two men, as the Baumann brothers of Nuremburg, was rapid. That night, police raided their homes and arrested the pair.

With overwhelming evidence against them, the brothers soon confessed. In the back of a delivery truck, inside empty crates, they had smuggled their passengers over the border. It was later, when the brothers stopped to buy food in Dortmund, that the CCTV recorded them. The last time the pair had seen the women was when they parted company in Erlangen, a town a few kilometres from Nuremburg.

There, Joanne Smedley had arranged to meet a forger who could provide them with counterfeit passports and identity papers. Whoever this person might be, the brothers have no knowledge. Little more than hired-hands, at the bottom of the network's chain of command, such important information is above their level of trust. So far, the German police have failed to identify the forger.

Once Joanne Smedley obtained her passports, John believes the group's departure from Germany would have been swift, via Italy or Switzerland. With new hair-colours, styles and clothing, the three would be almost unrecognisable. Stephen Smedley had confessed that the couple, under assumed names, had possessed two bank accounts in Germany. On inspection, both were empty. Somewhere in the world, Joanne Smedley, or whatever she now calls herself, is in control of a several million-Euro fortune. Despite the number of people working to trace the money, she has proved as adept at hiding her financial trail, as she has her physical.

The first of November arrives. I turn over the calendar to the new month. In bright blue felt pen, Fia has ringed the eleventh. This is the date our baby is due. The birth is her first. It could be late, yet, I fear, with the stress of her captivity, it may arrive early. Once our child is born, Fia's usefulness to Joanne Smedley is over, as is her life. Smedley will take her revenge. Will I ever learn what happens to her or my newborn son or daughter? Of one thing I can be sure - his or her upbringing will be in an atmosphere of hate.

On Friday evening, after our regular trip to the supermarket, Ian, Caroline and I sit in front of the fire. Our attempts to play junior scrabble are fraught. I struggle to persuade the children their interpretation of English spelling is neither standard, nor acceptable. As usual, my thoughts wander to Fia and my attention lapses. Ian, I suspect, uses these moments of distraction to manipulate the results. Whether this is true, he does win an unusual number of games.

## CHAPTER 43

Soon after the pair is in bed, the sound of the doorbell disturbs me. The ten o'clock news is half-way through. I switch off the TV. With some apprehension, I step into the hallway. Closer to the door, with the hallway light shining through the glass panes, I recognise Harry and John's faces. Each wears a sombre expression. The knot that has resided inside my stomach for weeks tightens further. Fumbling, I drop the key. It takes me several attempts before I find the key-hole then turn it in the lock. I open the door. My two friends step inside.

"Hi, Nathan, how are you?" Harry asks.

He gives me a quick man-hug. It is a while since we last met.

"Surviving," I say, wary as to why they are here. "Come in, have a drink."

"Whisky for me," Harry says.

"I'll have coffee, please," John says, "Harry's making me drive."

I hang up their coats. It is soon apparent, without a drink in their hands, they have no intention of discussing the reason behind their visit. Harry helps himself to the Jameson's. I make coffee for John and me. Five minutes later, I am back in the lounge, bearing steaming mugs. Harry and John are deep in whispered conversation.

Fearful of hearing the news I expect, but dread the most, I collapse into the armchair opposite the pair. John takes a dripping mug of coffee from me. I raise mine and take a large drink, before I top up the mug with whisky. Harry clears his throat. He starts to talk. I sit on the edge of my seat, unable to comprehend his words. By the time he finishes, my mind is in a spin. My cup slips from my hand. The carpet appears to be coming up to meet me. Hands grab at my arms. For a moment, I think I am going to faint.

# 44

Calm and relaxed, the captain's voice booms over the cabin speakers.

"Ladies and gentlemen, we are about to start our descent. Please ensure your seat backs and tray tables are positioned fully upright…"

I feel my muscles tense. This is my second time in an airliner, my first, a domestic one, being late yesterday-afternoon. I discount my helicopter trips. During those there was too much on my mind for me to worry about crashing. Another announcement informs we have clearance to land. The butterflies in my stomach go into overdrive. It is Sunday. At five-fifteen this evening, we left Heathrow. Nine and a half hours later, as it approaches 7pm local time, we land at Vancouver International Airport.

On either side of me, sleeping, are Ian and Caroline, their seatbelts fastened by helpful flight attendants. The first *'are we nearly there yet?'* came twenty minutes into the flight, and again at similar intervals until they fell asleep. Despite current local time, the reality is that it is long-past their usual bed times. Because of the uncertainty over how long I will be abroad, the children have accompanied me. I know other parents well enough to ask them to look after the pair for an occasional night, but not for what could turn into an extended period. Also, after years of enforced separation, I cannot bear to be away from them.

Seated in the row in front is Tony Braithwaite, borrowed for this trip from his current protection duties in London. He appears delighted at the chance to travel overseas. An all-expenses paid trip to Canada, even in November, must make a welcome change from his dreary London routine. As for me, I am glad someone as capable as Tony, with knowledge of the country, is with us.

## CHAPTER 44

I find it hard to believe everything that has happened since Friday evening's visit by Harry and John. Convinced they had come to tell me they had found Fia's body, the relief, when I realised they had good news to impart, had overwhelmed me. After they had given me a stiff drink, they had to explain everything again.

"So, you say you know where Fia is?" I had asked.

"No, not her exact location, but we do know when, where and how she and the Bradley sisters left Germany," Harry said, "their initial destination and the general area where they are now."

"Where's that?" I had tried to interrupt.

Harry ignored me. He had a story to tell and he wanted to tell it his way.

"Since Fia and her kidnappers disappeared, across Europe there have been dozens of arrests. Furious over the trouble Smedley has caused them, several captured network-members have provided information about her movements. Once Joanne's party obtained their forged papers in Erlangen, they travelled to Munich Airport, where they boarded a private Learjet.

"Fia was given something to make her drowsy. They took her through check-in, under the guise of an invalid, in a wheelchair. Because the pilot filed a domestic flight-plan, passenger checks were less rigorous than for an international flight. The gang's contact in Hanover, where they landed, had slipped three women, airside, into the airport. They took-on the guise of the passengers, so cleared arrivals without raising suspicion. On submission of a new flight-plan, refuelled and with the sisters and Fia still hidden on-board, the jet flew on to North Africa. After the women left the plane, at a private airstrip belonging to an oil facility in Libya, the aircraft collected a legitimate group of oil executives then returned to Germany.

"Using a series of private-jets and airfields operated by the trafficking-trade, the three moved around the world. In doing so, they changed passports and identities again, before their final landing in southern Texas. Here Smedley, under the 'original' alias of Smith, hired a car.

We have CCTV confirmation of this. They crossed into Canada, using passports in the names of three fictitious Smith sisters.

"They left the car at the rental company's lot in Vancouver. After that, they went off the grid. It's probable, Smedley used an associate to purchase another vehicle for cash. There's no evidence they have left the region. The authorities have examined CCTV footage from around the area, but have to identify yet anyone who matches the descriptions of any of the women. The man, who left the vehicle at the rental-offices in Vancouver, wore a thick padded jacket, sunglasses and a baseball-cap. He paid in cash, but kept his face away from the security cameras. Our description of him is basic."

"We can assume they have changed aliases again," John said. "The Canadians are certain Joanne Smedley, somewhere on her journey north, hired a pair of bodyguards in the states. Ever since Joanne split from the Baumann brothers, she has had help along the way, to keep her prisoners under control. I say 'prisoners' because we believe her sister, Dianne, is as much a captive as is Fia. Please understand, this work has taken some piecing together. The trafficking-operation has links worldwide; drugs, people, prostitution, stolen high-end cars, antiquities and a host of other illegalities."

"We learned yesterday, the RCMP has received reliable intelligence the people at the top of the US-arm of the illegal operations have traced Smedley's whereabouts. News of mass arrests in Europe reached the US at about the same time as did she. On her arrival in Texas, their people sent two men to take her to Dallas, where it is probable she would have 'disappeared'. Somehow, Smedley avoided them and escaped. Because of the disruption and financial losses she's caused, it seems now there's a contract out on her."

This last piece of news came as a shock. Killers for hire have a tendency to leave no witnesses. Fia is in as great a danger from this new development as is she is from Smedley.

"There's no need to worry," John said. "The Canadians know the identities of the killers, if not the location of their target. Only the team

## CHAPTER 44

and their bosses know that. We have narrowed it down to somewhere on, or close to, the west coast of Canada, which could include any one of the numerous offshore islands. It's a vast area. It covers thousands of square miles, much of which is mountainous."

"If the Canadian police know who the killers are, why don't they arrest them and make them talk?" I demanded.

"Such men and women don't talk," Harry answered. "If they did, they know their paymasters would have them killed in prison. Arresting them now would mean someone-else taking their place, people unknown to the authorities. We have to make use of what we have. Besides, at present, the contractors are in Central America. We know they are to travel on a private flight, due into Vancouver on Tuesday lunchtime. A vehicle awaits them, weapons, too, and a place to hide out. Once the hit-team is on the ground, the RCMP will keep them under surveillance. Vancouver has an ERT - Emergency Response Team - similar to the US SWAT teams. They are on high alert."

"So, what can we do, besides sit here and wait?" I asked, frustrated.

"We wait, you go," Harry said. "You're booked on a flight to Vancouver. It leaves tomorrow-night from Heathrow. Tony Braithwaite will accompany you. He has worked in Canada. Tony has contacts within the CSIS, the Canadian Security Intelligence Services, as well as the RCMP. Tony has official accreditation as an observer, whereas you are there as a private citizen, to assist with identification as and when required. All the documentation you need, passports etc will be ready for you to collect when you arrive at Heathrow."

Harry was unhappy about my insistence the children accompany me, but, in the end, he backed down. The result of which is why they are beside me now, snoring gently. Arrangements are in place for us to stay at a safe-house, with someone to guide and guard us while Tony liaises. Our protector will look after Ian and Caroline when I have to leave them. As the sole adult, on this side of the world, able to identify, physically, both Fia and Dianne Bradley, that will happen sometime. In Fia's case, alive, I pray.

Treated as VIPs, our passage through customs is swift. With our baggage, we make our way through the international reception-lounge towards the glass exit doors. Once through, into the public greeting area, I notice, to one side, a youngish woman. She appears to study everyone who passes through the entrance. Her blue eyes squint in concentration, as she peers from under the fringe of her shoulder-length blond hair. She steps out from behind an advertising board, to reveal an outfit of dark slacks, tucked into knee-length boots, and a thick, dark-grey sweater. Its snug fit emphasises her figure. A large bulge spoils the line of the fabric on her right hip. A heavy overcoat drapes over her left arm. In her right hand, she holds out a piece of card with 'Braithwaite' handwritten in large letters.

Tony steps out from behind me and looks around. The blonde-haired woman breaks into a broad smile as she catches sight of him.

"Tony, hi," she calls.

She runs towards him. To my surprise, he drops his luggage to throw his arms round her. He lifts her high into the air. A long embrace and a lingering kiss, which goes far beyond that of two old acquaintances meeting after a long absence, encourages me to move a little away, to give them space. Caroline looks on, wide eyed in amazement. Ian pulls a face and says 'Yuk!' under his breath.

"Nathan, Ian, Caroline, meet Stella, Stella meet Nathan, Ian and Caroline." When they disentangle themselves, Tony makes the introductions.

"Hi," Stella says.

She shakes hands with everyone.

"Stella's, er, an old friend," Tony says. "We worked together in Ottawa a while back. She's our RCMP liaison-officer. Stella's staying with us during our visit, to keep an eye on everything."

I have a good idea theirs was much more than a working relationship, during Tony's previous stint in Canada.

"Less of the old," Stella says, smiling. "God, Tony, after your people re-called you to England, I thought I'd never see you again. When

## CHAPTER 44

trouble started over there, I was worried to hell. Boy, was I happy after I'd gotten your message. For how long are you over?"

There is an anxious undertone to the question, which goes beyond simple courtesy or curiosity.

"For as long as it takes to find Nathan's wife, Fia, and return her to him. After that, I am due a few weeks leave. I intend to spend them over here. We'll have to see what happens then."

Stella flings her arms around Tony and gives him a huge hug, before regaining her composure. In an instant, she is professional. Her on-duty persona takes over.

"Right, follow me," she says, picking up some of the children's bags. "Don't you worry," she says to them, "we'll soon have your Mom home safe."

We follow her outside into the darkness. The evening air is raw and chilly. We cross a couple of roadways to the passenger pick-up point, where a black Chevrolet SUV awaits us. Its driver, alerted by a quick 'phone call from Stella, stands beside the vehicle. Within minutes, our luggage is inside, we are on board and the Terminal is behind us. Back in England, it is early morning. Our body clocks are still at Greenwich meantime. I am ready for bed, while Ian and Caroline keep falling asleep. Tony and Stella are deep in whispered conversation.

In New Westminster, after a half-hour drive, we pull into a driveway, on the opposite side of the road to what appears to be leafy parkland. As with many houses in the area, this two-story one is a craftsman built, timber-framed structure, brick-sided, with a shingle roof. Inside, the dimensions are impressive compared to the home we left behind. Open plan, with hardwood floors and a kitchen the size of my complete downstairs floor-plan, the house is unlike anything I have seen. Before we went inside, I noticed, unlike many of its neighbours, a high, solid stone-wall, complete with an electrically operated gate onto the roadway, surrounds this building.

Ian and Caroline are sleepy. Stella shows us to their rooms. Again, they are enormous, en-suite, complete with double beds and easy chairs.

I swear, if we shouted we would have to wait for the echo to bounce back. I settle the children. Downstairs, Stella and Tony have made coffee and sandwiches. Stella is still on duty. Despite her professional manner, there is a familiarity about hers and Tony's interaction, which is indicative of much time spent in each other's company.

An intercom speaker buzzes. Stella answers the call. The night-watch has arrived to patrol the grounds. Armed with flasks of coffee, and several rounds of sandwiches to sustain the new arrivals through the dark hours, she goes outside to meet them. On Stella's return, she locks the door. For the first time since we met, she unclips the holster from her side. Despite its removal, it stays within easy reach, even when she comes to sit on the couch beside Tony.

It is a four-bedroom house. Seeing the way they keep looking at each other, I doubt either of them will be sleeping on the couch. Stella is off-duty. They have much catching up to do. I make my excuses and go to my room.

Worn out, I sleep through. I waken at first light. After a quick peek at the children, still asleep, I shower then dress. I head downstairs in search of a cup of tea. Stella and Tony look-up from the kitchen table, a large plateful of pancakes between them and a jar of maple syrup to one side. Stella is tousle-haired and has the look of a feline that has been in a catnip patch. From the expression on Tony's face, too, I assume their reunion went well. Resting against Stella's hip is her gun. She is back on duty. Within minutes, a car arrives for Tony, to take him to the control-centre set up to co-ordinate the search for Fia.

"Help yourself to pancakes," Stella says. "I'll make extra when the children waken. Oh! I'll do them now," she adds as, in their pyjamas, two hungry waifs wander into the dining area.

"Hi Stella, hi Dad," says Ian. "Have you seen our rooms?" he asks, his eyes wide.

"We've our own bathrooms," Caroline says.

"They're the biggest rooms ever," Ian boasts.

"Mines bigger than yours." Caroline resorts to one-upmanship.

## CHAPTER 44

"No it's not," Ian counters.

After a moment or two of outlandish embellishments, Stella steps between them, holding a plate filled with fresh pancakes. Caroline loves them. Ian tries one, but pulls a face. He settles for cereal and toast instead.

By mid-morning, a pale sun is visible through the thinning cloud. To occupy Ian and Caroline's time, Stella takes us to Greater Vancouver Zoo. No longer high season, some events are unavailable, but we hire a quadra-cycle, ride the miniature-train and photograph many of the animals. The outing is great fun, as much for our guide and protector, who joins in with everything, as the children.

Over lunch, I succeed in extracting from Stella, some of her history with Tony. He first arrived in Canada as a protection officer with the Royal Family, when they went into exile. Stella's assignment as a liaison-officer brought her into regular contact with him. Friendship turned into a close relationship.

With some reluctance, when his tour of duty ended, Tony returned to England. Stella was aware of his thoughts about the government of the day. He had tried to stay, but his visa had expired. Soon afterwards, the British government cut external communications. This left her with no way of knowing what had happened to him. Tony, it seems, had sent several messages by underground routes, but a change of duties had taken her to the west coast. None of his letters had reached her.

Several weeks ago, with many freedoms restored in Britain, Tony, with the help of a former colleague in Ottawa, had tracked her down. They re-established contact. He is the love of her life. I suspect that if Tony leaves Canada, it will be with Stella at his side. Somehow, I doubt that will prove any hardship to him. They had planned to meet in Toronto, over Christmas, but this mission had proved opportune. Stella had called-in a few favours from friends in high-places. They had pulled strings, with the result of a rapid deployment to the case.

We meet Tony at a diner for an evening-meal before we return to our temporary home. Stella uncovers a stash of games. We spend a pleasant time in friendly competition. Tony waits until Ian and Caroline are in bed before he updates us on his day.

The airport has confirmed a twin-engine Cessna, hired for the killers, is due to touch down at one-fifteen tomorrow afternoon. The airport police have identified a vehicle, hired for the hit-team, parked in the long stay car park. Technicians have added a tracking-device, its operation will be independent of the one fitted as standard by the hire company. By the time the new arrivals have cleared customs, the surveillance-team will be in place.

As with today, Stella has plans to entertain the children and me tomorrow. Tony will join the surveillance-team. We have to wait, and pray for a successful conclusion. Thoughts of failure I cannot countenance. I need Fia rescued, without harm to her, nor our unborn child. It is late. I leave Tony and Stella on the couch. The television is on in the background, but neither of them pays it any attention.

I anticipate, tomorrow will be a long day.

## 45

The first grey light of Tuesday's dawn brings detail to the views across Queens Park. In stockinged feet, I creep down the wooden staircase, in an attempt not to waken Ian and Caroline. When I reach the kitchen, I find them halfway through their breakfast, chatting to Stella. I am the lazy-one today. Tony has left to spend the morning with the surveillance team, while they finalise their plans for the operation. Before noon, he expects to join the field-operatives at the airport, to await the touchdown of the hit-team's aircraft. At this stage, my presence would be an encumbrance.

To fill our day, Stella takes us to the aquarium in Stanley Park. By noon, after yesterday's visit to the zoo, Ian and Caroline's concentration on anything animal or aquatic has waned. Despite the park being a favourite summer tourist-attraction, on a damp, cold November day, its attractions are something we are prepared to miss. Instead, we indulge in a late lunch at a pizza restaurant. Afterwards, we go to a large toy-store on Granville Island. An hour or so later, we almost have to drag away Ian and Caroline, before we drive back to our temporary home, laden with a variety of new playthings. Content with their new acquisitions, Ian and Caroline lose themselves in a world of make-believe. My concentration is poor. I can find nothing to interest me on the television. There is too much advertising for my taste.

Of Tony, we have neither sight nor message. After a late meal, Ian and Caroline are soon asleep. Stella 'phones the command centre. All they can say is, Tony's situation is fluid and ongoing. They confirm the surveillance-team has its targets under observation. They are on the move, somewhere north of Vancouver.

"Go to bed, Nathan," Stella advises. "Once the night shift comes on duty, I'm going to do the same. We'll not hear anything before morning. I doubt Fia is in any greater danger tonight than she has been. The gunmen are pro's. They won't want to be here a moment longer than necessary, but neither will they want to rush. That's when mistakes happen. They'll want to study the target area before they strike."

"I suppose you're right," I say. "This waiting is hell. One moment I think no news is good, the next, because we've heard nothing, I fear something dreadful might have happened."

"It would be patronising to say I understand what you've gone through, and still are going," Stella says. "After Tony left for England, my life was hell. That was bad enough. This must be torture for you right now. If it helps, we have the best people on the job.

"With a rifle, Tony's a dead shot, and exceptional with a handgun. His hand-to-hand combat skills he learned with the Special Forces. He's lethal with a knife. On his own, I would favour his chances on going against either the killers or the kidnappers. The team he's with is no less professional. You *must* believe, Nathan. We *shall* find Fia and we *shall* bring her back alive. Don't ever doubt it."

Stella leans over and gives me a motherly hug in support. I leave her to sort out the night shift whose arrival the intercom has announced. She is right; I must not give up hope. Apart from that, I have nothing onto which I can cling. Ian and Caroline are asleep when I look in on them. Later, alone in my cavernous room, a diminutive figure stretched out in my super king-sized bed, Stella's reassurance dissipates. My fears magnify. They fill my mind. What shall I do if anything happens to Fia? I face a black void, a total emptiness in my life. With the lights back on again, I sit up in bed and face my demons on my own. Sometime later, the door clicks open and in walks Caroline.

"I had a bad dream, daddy," she says, tears in her eyes.

I put out my arms and she clambers up, teddy in hand. I dry her eyes and hug her. We talk of pleasanter things. She curls up beside me and goes back to sleep. I doubt whether she was fully awake to start

## CHAPTER 45

with. With a protective arm around her, I contemplate my future. No matter what happens over the following hours and days. I still have my children to consider. I drift off to sleep, Caroline's head resting against me as she snores in the background.

I waken early. Caroline lies sprawled across the bed. Careful not to wake her, I carry her back to her room. Tucked up in her own bed, when she awakens, I doubt she will remember anything of her nightmare.

Soon afterwards, showered, shaved and dressed, I am downstairs eating breakfast opposite Stella. I wonder what time she rises. When I arrived, she was already in the kitchen. Although she hides it well, she must be concerned about the lack of contact from Tony. Earlier, she rang the office, but they have nothing new to communicate. Operations remain ongoing. An hour later, Ian joins us, followed by Caroline. As I thought, she has no recollection of waking during the night.

Nine o'clock comes and goes. The children play their computer-games. Noon passes without a 'phone-call. The minute-hand creeps round to 2pm. The sound of a car, pulling up outside, reaches us. Both Stella and I jump at the noise. The key turns in the front door and Tony enters. He looks exhausted. Black rings are around his eyes and his clothes are rumpled. The faint smell of stale sweat wafts across the room. In his hand, he carries a large envelope. Stella runs to welcome him with a hug and a kiss. Fatigue makes him sway, but his face lights-up at her touch.

"I've some images for you to look at, Nathan," he says.

Still smiling, he walks over, his arm round Stella's waist. We go through to the kitchen area, away from the children. Seated round the table, I pour Tony a drink. He pulls-out some prints from the envelope.

"Are these Fia and Dianne Bradley?" he asks, as he places the copies on the tabletop. "We received them by email an hour ago."

I look at the images. The photographer has found a vantage point, high above a clearing in an area of dense forest. Blown up, the photographs are of low quality, at a guess taken from a distance with a

357

camera phone. The first few are general images of the area. One of the people in the shots could be Fia. She is outside a large, modern-chalet style log-cabin. By the look of its steep, pointed roof, I assume this must be in an area subject to heavy seasonal snow. The woman's hair is unkempt, feet shackled. She is in an advanced stage of pregnancy. The baby cannot be far from full term. Nearby, is a blond-haired woman, Dianne Bradley? Both women look away from the lens. The second woman, too, appears to be wearing shackles.

On the porch of the cabin, a stocky-looking man sits in a wooden rocking-chair. With a rifle in his hands, it is apparent he keeps watch over the women. Nearer to the photographer, opposite the group on the other side of the clearing, near a woodpile, another man wields an axe. Propped against a white picket-fence, close by, is what appears to be another rifle. To one side of the building, at the end of a gravel driveway that leads into the woods, stand a small van and a four x four. On several of the later shots, the camera has zoomed-in on people. Although blurred, Fia and Dianne's faces are recognisable, but the men are unknown.

Near the end of the set, a couple of images, show Joanne Smedley coming out of the house, carrying a drink for the guard on the porch. The other man has disappeared. Unlike Fia and Dianne, whose clothes are almost rags, with blankets wrapped around for warmth, Smedley wears heavy jeans, western-style boots, and a checkered shirt beneath an open sheepskin coat.

The final shots shows Fia and Dianne herded into, what Stella believes to be, a basement-storage, utility room. A metal bar, with a large padlock, seals their prison door. Smedley does allow them some fresh air during the day. I suspect she wants Fia fit and healthy until the baby is born. It occurs to me that Smedley could be keeping her sister alive as a companion and carer for Fia.

"Yes that's Fia, and Dianne Bradley," I say handing back to Tony the best of the images. "Joanne Bradley is the one in the sheepskin. So, what can you tell us about what happened yesterday and today?"

## CHAPTER 45

Stella is busy at the stove. The smell and crackle of bacon and eggs fills the kitchen. Apart from a couple of chocolate bars, Tony has had nothing to eat since yesterday lunchtime.

"We were in position, in plenty of time, before the gunmen's plane landed," Tony says. "After they cleared customs, they collected their hire-car. They drove it to a house, in a quiet area of West Vancouver, off Marine Drive. It's a short-term rental. Whoever rented it for them, they'd used a letter of credit to pay for it until the end of the month. We traced the rental company, then looked into the details provided by the payee. That trail ends at an empty back street office in Vegas. It opened a few days before the transaction. A day after the money went through - it closed. Occupiers unknown; office rental paid in cash."

A stacked plate lands in front of Tony. I allow him to eat in peace. I use the time to compose myself. To see photos of Fia, and to know she is alive and unharmed, has lifted my spirits. Tony soon devours his meal. A large apple-pie appears on the table, of which I take a slice. Replenished, Tony sits back. He looks less stressed. Ian and Caroline are like gannets, the smell of food has attracted them. Stella hands them each a Hershey Bar to eat. Satisfied, they return to their games. Tony picks up his mobile.

"Hi, Francine," he says. "Can you connect me to the boss, thanks? Oh! Hi Sam, it's Tony. Nathan has confirmed the two in shackles are Fia Andrews and Dianne Bradley. The woman in jeans and sheepskin is Joanne Smedley. The men are unknown. You can take-out the hit-team whenever you want. Do you need me? No! Good, I'll leave it to ERT. You'll let me know what happens? Great. What time in the morning? Six. Okay, I'll bring Nathan along," he disconnects. "Did you follow that?" he asks me. I nod and he continues. "We leave at six in the morning. A helicopter will fly us up-country to the heliport at Whistler."

"What happened after the gunmen reached West Vancouver?" I ask.

"No sooner had the trio arrived at their base," Tony begins, "when one of them, Franco Delvira, visited a lock-up a mile away. He collected a large package, which we assume contains the team's weapons. Once he returned to the house, the other two, Johnny Wiston and Reg Stones, took the car. They drove towards the Sea-to-Sky Highway, where they headed north towards Whistler.

"A little over two hours later, on the other side of the town, half way between there and Pemberton, they turned off the highway onto a dirt track. Our local guide told us it led to a campsite, which, at this time, would be empty. We parked our vehicles in the woods, on a service-track a little further on. From there, we went on foot."

"Wouldn't they spot or hear you coming?" I ask.

"A couple of ERT trackers were sent on ahead. They move through the woods like ghosts. They kept in touch by radio. The killers, as we thought, had parked at the campsite. Our men tracked them through the woods, over a low ridge to a spot overlooking the house where Fia is a prisoner. Apart from automatics, Wiston and Stones carried with them nothing more lethal than binoculars and a camera. While the trackers kept an eye on them, we stayed out of sight, but within easy reach of their location.

"Soon afterwards, it dropped dark. By dawn it was bloody freezing. I could have murdered a round of bacon and eggs. I cannot remember ever being that cold. In case we made any noise, it was impossible to move around to keep warm. Up there, on a still night, the sound of someone stepping on a branch would travel a long way."

"What happened in the morning? What did Wiston and Stones do?" I ask.

"They had returned to their car overnight, where they had blankets to keep them warm. At first light, they went back over the ridge to keep watch. From time to time, they changed their position, to study the terrain from various angles. They took dozens of photographs while waiting for Joanne Smedley to come out of the cabin. When she did, her bodyguards were with her. She opened the basement door to allow Fia and Dianne out for some exercise. Wiston and Stones took several photos of Smedley. They compared these against one they had

## CHAPTER 45

with them. Soon afterwards, they left. The trackers remained behind to keep watch on the house.

"We'd left two people with our vehicles. Once Wiston and Stones reached the highway, our officers tailed them back to their hideaway in Vancouver. We followed on afterwards. After we'd gone, the men we left behind took the photos I showed you. They forwarded them to HQ from their mobiles. We've sent back-up and a mobile-communications truck to support them. Between them, they'll keep watch until we move-in tomorrow. They have instructions not to intervene, unless the captives appear to be in imminent danger."

"What's happening with the gunmen?"

"Sam and his team will raid the house in West Vancouver later tonight. He has the place surrounded. We fly to Whistler in the morning. The ERT will move in, once Fia and Dianne are out of the house, and we can confirm the whereabouts of everyone else. According to the architect's plans, there's direct access to the basement from the living quarters. Any delay in gaining access to that could allow Smedley time reach the prisoners if they were inside.

"The cabin's new. It's well constructed. The owners built it as a holiday rental. This summer was their first season in business. They were happy to find someone who wanted to lease the place for the whole fall-winter period. Smedley paid cash, six months in advance. She was personable, said she was a travel writer, working on a guide to BC for a British travel company. The rental agency saw Smedley but no-one else. She said she had an invalid sister, a nurse and some staff staying with her."

Tony can tell us little else. Exhausted, he goes to bed. Stella accompanies him, but returns a few minutes later smiling.

"He's asleep," she says.

A little before eleven, from Tony's coat, comes the sound of a mobile. Stella retrieves it. She answers the call. After a few minutes, she disconnects.

"Good news?" I ask, my heart racing.

"Sam's team have raided the gunman's base. They took two of the men by surprise. They arrested them without a fight. The third one is in a critical condition. Stones was in a back-room and had time to reach his weapons. As he attempted to escape through a window, he opened fire and wounded two officers. A marksman outside shot him before he could jump."

That is one worry out of the way. It is time to rest. I have an early start in the morning. In the darkness, thoughts of Fia threaten to overwhelm me. One moment I am high on euphoria at the thought of finding her, seconds later in the depths at what could go wrong in the rescue attempt. It seems an age before I fall sleep. Moments later, or so it seems, a hand shakes me awake.

"Come on, Nathan," Tony is saying, "it's four-thirty, time for us to be moving."

# 46

The sky is dark when we arrive at the heliport in Burnaby, a quarter of an hour's drive from where we lodge. A blue Bell 407 helicopter sits on a circle of tarmac. The ERT team is already in place in the mountains. With impatience, we wait for two medics, who are to accompany us with their equipment. By six-thirty, we are on-board. As we lift off, I clench onto my seat. We fly over Vancouver and the estuary, soon the lights are behind us as we head north. The land rises. Thirty minutes later, the sky lightens. Dawn breaks over a spectacular landscape of white-topped mountains and dark valleys. We land at Whistler Heliport. Yesterday's clouds have gone. The rays of the sun sparkle and flare as it rises over the tips of the Canadian Rockies.

As the rotors stop, a dark SUV moves towards us. The driver nods a greeting to Tony. The medic's put their gear into the back. We take our seats. Soon afterwards, we are on a gravel road, approaching the campsite. The area is no longer deserted. A communications truck, several SUVs, and a number of men in dark uniforms, fill the space. With 'POLICE' highlighted on the breasts of their protective vests, a group, wearing ski masks and protective helmets, stands apart. These people are members of the ERT squad. I count a dozen.

I stand to one side; Tony talks with their leader. They provide him with a vest and helmet. What amazes me most, despite the number of people and vehicles, is the lack of noise. The air is bitter; the ground crackles under foot. The nearby woods shine with hoarfrost.

"Here, put these on," Tony says. He hands another vest and helmet to me. "We go with the team leader. When we're in position, he wants you to confirm identities."

Without delay, I put on the protective garments.

"Hi, I'm Tom Lederson," the sergeant in charge of the ERT team introduces himself. His handshake is firm. "I want you to follow me. Step where I step, freeze when I say freeze. If I say 'Drop', do it. Don't think; do everything I tell you, when I tell you. I don't have time to nursemaid you."

"Understood," I respond.

"Good, let's move out."

In pairs, his men spread out to enter the woods. They disappear. They have their orders. Everyone has to be in position, before Smedley and Co venture outside the cabin. After that, the least movement on our part, the better it will be. Thankful for my regular walks in the Dales, I keep up with the long-striding sergeant and Tony. In the icy air, I gasp for breath, long before we each the ridge top. We descend the other side. Here, the sergeant's footsteps are like those of a woodland creature. He has an uncanny instinct for where to place his feet. I follow his steps precisely. Stealth, rather than speed, is what we need now. For most of the descent, the dense forestation hides our movements. On several occasions, we have to crawl, to remain hidden from the cabin windows.

As we approach to within a hundred metres of the clearing, on the opposite side, smoke rises from the cabin's chimney. The occupants are awake. A door bangs open. We drop to the ground. One of the guards walks in our direction. The sergeant has his carbine, suppressor fitted to its barrel, aimed at the man, but he stops at the woodpile. With arms laden with logs, he returns to the cabin. He makes several trips.

My companions remain on high alert, until the door closes for the final time. We move closer to the clearing's edge. A series of voices sounds through earpieces built into our helmets. Each team of two has reached its designated position. We are set. Now, we have to wait for the best moment to move in.

The sun rises higher. Distant peaks glow in the brightening light. Soon after nine-thirty, accompanied by one of her bodyguards, Joanne

## CHAPTER 46

Smedley strides onto the porch. The pair steps onto a gravel pathway. Down the slope they stroll, to the padlocked basement-door, which she unlocks. The guard lifts a heavy metal-bar. He places it on the ground. The door screeches as he pulls it open. Blinking and shading their eyes in the bright sunlight, Fia and Dianne Bradley emerge from their burrow.

"It won't be long now, bitch," Smedley says, laughing as she pats the bulge around Fia's waist. "A few days now and I shall have me own family."

"For God's sake, stop tormenting her," Dianne speaks out, hobbling her way between them.

Smedley backhands her across the face. The blow knocks Dianne to the ground.

"You ought to be careful what you say, little sister, I've still to decide what to do with you," Smedley snarls and stomps off to the house, unaware of the guns trained on her and her companion.

The watchers have several clear shots at each of them, but Lederson holds back. Alerted, the man inside could target the prisoners through the window with ease. Before we can strike, we need to know the exact positions of each one of our three targets.

I take a careful look at Fia as she helps Dianne back to her feet. There is defiance in her manner, rather than defeat. To whatever Joanne has subjected her prisoners, the woman has failed to break their spirit. From this distance, I can see that Fia shivers in the cold air. Her clothing consists of a loose-fitting grey dress, a blanket and ankle boots with holes in them. Dianne removes her blanket and wraps it around Fia. The guard has moved away. He sits on the porch, in the rocking chair, wrapped in a thick fleece-jacket, a blanket over his legs. A rifle rests on his knees.

"Please, throw us another blanket," Dianne pleads.

"Go to hell," is the guard's response.

"Bastard," I hear Tony mutter under his breath, which echoes my thoughts exactly.

Fia and Dianne appear to have a routine. With shackles, they walk, as best they can in a circular route on a path they have worn through the grass in the clearing. For Fia, it is difficult to waddle. Her back appears to be paining her. Dianne supports Fia with a steadying arm. To keep on the move is the only way they can stay warm.

They come within twenty metres of our position, but, the further away from the guard they wander, the greater his attention. It is a temptation for Lederson to have the guard 'taken out', while we attempt to snatch the women, but there are frequent shadows at the cabin windows. While, at this distance, the guard is an easy target for the sergeant's men, Fia and Dianne are the same from inside the building.

Shadows shorten, the morning advances. If today is similar to yesterday, it is time for Fia and Dianne's captors to re-incarcerate them inside the basement. The cabin door opens. For a moment, Joanne Smedley is visible in the gap. She stops, half in, half out. At the edge of the clearing to our right, something has attracted her attention. Without warning, she steps back inside. The door closes behind her.

"What was that about?" I whisper.

"Standby," Lederson talks into the microphone at the side of his mouth. "She's spotted us."

No sooner does he speak than the sound of a high-powered rifle comes from the direction of the cabin, accompanied by the sound of breaking glass. A window near to the door fragments outwards. From the edge of the clearing forty metres away from us, there is a yelp of pain. One of Lederson's men rolls into view, clutching his arm. The rifle barks again. Soil and grass splatter in front of the victim's face. Lederson gives the order. A hail of bullets, fired from around the clearing, smashes into the walls and windows. Under their covering-fire, the wounded man's companion drags him to safety.

At the sound of the first rifle-shot, the gunman on the porch disappeared. The rocker lies on its side. At the lip of the hollow, at the front of the basement door, I see the barrel of his rifle as he brings it to bear. On my feet, I yell at Fia and Dianne to drop to the

## CHAPTER 46

floor. Tony has seen the danger, too. He brings his carbine up and fires towards the gunman. Splinters, from bullet-strikes, fly from the cabin walls behind him. The man dodges from sight. Tony runs forward. I am at his side. We head towards Fia and Dianne. Fia has caught sight of me. Oblivious of our shouted words, both she and Dianne hobble our way.

From inside the cabin comes the sound of explosions as stun-grenades smash through the windows. Through the corner of my eye, I see four shapes, guns at the ready, smash through the cabin doorway. Smoke pours from the windows. From inside comes the sound of rapid gunfire.

I am almost in reach of Fia. Dianne has moved behind her, to allow Tony sight of his target. The gunman has taken cover behind a rock. He opens fire, again. Dianne screams as a bullet rips through her side. She falls to the ground. Tony fires as he runs. His bullets ricochet off the stone and earth around the gunman's position. Other weapons fire in the same direction. The man seems oblivious to the incoming fusillade. Flame comes from the end of his barrel.

As I touch Fia's hand, she stumbles, screams, then collapses onto me. Arterial spray spurts from her shattered leg. I ease her onto the ground. Her face has turned white. For an instant, she looks at me with wonder, before her eyes close. From her dress, I rip a large piece of fabric. With it, I try to stem the bleeding.

"Fia, Fia," I cry, "Stay with me," but she is already unconscious.

A pool of water forms beneath her. Her waters have broken. Strong arms pull me away as medics take over.

Tony zigzags towards the cabin, carbine discarded, automatic in hand. He drops to one knee then, gun held two-handed, he empties his magazine into the gunman. The man slams against the cabin wall, his body jerking with each strike, but he refuses to die. He raises his rifle and fires. The bullet's impact flings Tony backwards, his life saved by his vest. Other weapons open up. The gunman, body riddled with bullets, slides to the ground in a smeary mess.

Now, proceedings become a blur. I am at Fia's side, gripping her hand. Everything appears to happen in slow-motion. A dark shape looms above my head. A loud-beating sound drowns out everything. A shadow descends onto the clearing. People run towards us. Again, arms tear me from Fia. Stretcher-bearers carry her away, medics still working on her.

Dianne Bradley, about whom I had forgotten, is already inside the waiting helicopter, alongside wounded members of the ERT team. Lederson's men have to restrain me from trying to reach the aircraft. There is no room for passengers. Helpless and dazzled by its landing lights, I stand and stare as it lifts-off. After months of deprivation, for this to happen to Fia at the moment of her rescue - has she not suffered enough?

My legs give way. I sink to the ground. In shock, I stare at my hands. Fia's blood covers them, as it does my clothes. Tony, his vest removed, staggers towards me. He sits down beside me.

"I think the bugger's cracked a rib," he says, wincing. "Look, mate," he adds, looking at my expression and bloody state "Here in Canada, they have some of the best doctors in the world. They'll take care of her."

In silence, we sit. Around us is hustle and bustle. An ambulance, lights flashing, siren whining, speeds up the driveway. We watch, as attendants doctor some minor injuries. Smedley, and the gunman inside, we learn, did not survive. A fire-engine arrives next. The stun-grenades have set alight furnishings. The cabin is in flames.

Officious newcomers move us back. More vehicles pull-up. They park at the edge of the clearing. People insist on asking damn-fool questions. I ignore them. All I can see is Fia's white face, the look in her eyes at seeing me again, followed by the awful blankness that replaced it. Like a film-clip, the moment replays over and over again.

A driver approaches. She escorts us to a waiting patrol-car. With siren blaring and lights flashing, we hit the highway. At speeds that, under normal circumstances, would have set my heart racing, we hurtle

## CHAPTER 46

back towards Vancouver. Images still loop through my mind. With an escort of highway patrol vehicles, our driver accomplishes the usual two-hour-plus journey to Vancouver General Hospital, in little over half the time.

We reach the hospital gates. By now, I have recouped some of my faculties. If I concentrate, I can switch-off the recurring images. Our driver does her damnedest to sound encouraging and positive. The hospital, she says, is a level-one trauma centre, one of a kind in British Columbia. Fia's helicopter would have landed on the roof and she would have had a team of doctors standing by, to work on her. I nod, too numb to take in her words.

Tony is a true friend. Despite the pains in his chest from his suspected cracked rib, he guides me through the hospital, to the special-care trauma unit. There is no sign of Fia. She remains in surgery. Tony fetches me endless coffees from the vending machine. He helps me clean the blood from my hands and face. We wait for news. An hour passes. Each time a nurse comes in, we stand but their visits are for others in the waiting room. When we ask, the nurses say Fia is in surgery, in good hands.

Two hours later, awash with coffee, I leave the room for a moment. On my return, a grey-faced surgeon is with Tony. They lead me out, into a side-room where they sit me down on a black plastic chair. The surgeon begins to talk, a serious expression on his face. In a daze, I brace myself for the worst. I know what is to come. I shudder. His voice comes, as if from the distant end of a long, dark tunnel.

## 47

The sun is hot this late August day. We walk the well-worn path overlooking Langstrothdale. Ian and Caroline race round me, playing tag. On a rock beside the path, halfway between Scar House and Yockenthwaite, the three of us sit and eat our lunch. For a moment, I look back along the trail. I close my eyes and allow my mind to wander back in time.

*Through a gap in the dry stone-wall, steps a woman. Dark haired and attractive, she has a figure that makes me take a longer look as she approaches along the dusty path. Late twenties, early thirties, I guess. Her hips swing with an easy stride. On the path, near to me, she pauses. She takes a deep swallow from a water-bottle. Between her pert breasts, perspiration darkens her bright green tee shirt. The woman turns to me, a beaming smile on her outdoor tanned face, the upper part of which lies shaded by her floppy sun hat.*

*"Beautiful day for a walk," she says cheerfully.*

"Daddy, Ian won't let me have another biscuit. Can I please, pretty please?"

The vision fades, I am back in the present.

"Of course you can, Sweetie," I say, raising an eyebrow at Ian and trying to look stern.

He grins wickedly. His protectiveness, towards his sister, only manifests itself whenever someone tries to bully or make fun of her. To him, she is fair game; he knows how to press her buttons.

"I do wish new mum was here," Caroline says.

I give her a hug, before I smear both of them with an additional layer of sun-block. A couple of hours later, we are at the Rake Tearooms in

## CHAPTER 47

Buckden. By chance, each table is full, except the one I sat at, those few short years ago, when first I met Fia. I picture her there now. Her treacherous uncle Joe's face has faded from my memory. Apart from John, I cannot recall any of the others who sat round the garden tables that day. Ian and Caroline chatter merrily. It is time to return home.

As I empty rucksacks and boots from the car, Ian unlocks the door. He helps me carry them into the hallway. Both he and Caroline raid the fridge for drinks and biscuits. I wander through the back door into the garden. Under the shade of an apple tree, sheltered beneath a parasol, baby Alicia is asleep in her pram.

Looking down at her, takes me back to that dreadful day, last autumn in Canada. The helicopter had landed on the roof of the hospital, where a crash team awaited its arrival. They rushed Fia straight to surgery. Doctors performed an emergency caesarean. It had been touch and go for a couple of days, but baby Alicia was a fighter - she pulled through. After they had taken her from the operating theatre, into intensive care, the surgeons had worked for hours on Fia. The bullet that hit her had shattered her leg and severed an artery. On the way to the hospital, the medics had performed miracles by stopping most of the bleeding, but she had lost a great deal of blood.

Fia died that morning, once in the helicopter and twice on the operating table. Each time, they had revived her. She had received countless pints of blood in transfusions. The team of surgeons pieced together what they could with the bones in her leg. She was in intensive care for several days. I split my days and nights between her and Alicia. Stella brought in Ian and Caroline each day. As Fia's condition improved, her doctors reduced her medication. The moment she opened her eyes, recognised me, and squeezed my hand is one that will stay in my memory forever - as when I introduced her to Alicia for the first time. Despite warnings of possible brain damage, Fia has shown no lasting effects.

Dianne Bradley survived her wounds, too. Fia later testified, on Dianne's behalf – as to how the younger sister's participation in the kidnapping was under duress, and that she had been a prisoner herself for most of the time. Fia is certain she owes her sanity to Dianne's support. The authorities decided not to prosecute.

I bring my thoughts back to the present. On silent feet, I step past Alicia, towards the nearby swing seat. I lean down and kiss the sleeping figure on the lips. Fia opens her eyes then stretches languidly. She puts her arms round me and pulls me down onto the seat beside her.

"Good walk?" she asks, as we break apart, a wistful tone to her voice.

"Great," I reply. "You'll be coming with us again before too long. The doctors say, providing you don't overdo it, you should be much better by spring. The work the surgeons did in Vancouver was incredible."

"I know, I'm too impatient," she says, smiling.

A whimpering cry comes from the pram.

"You look after Alicia, while I check on dinner," Fia says, as I help her to her feet. "She'll need a nappy change."

"Oh! Thanks a lot," I say at that parting shot.

Laughing, Fia picks up her walking stick. She limps towards the kitchen. On sight of me, Alicia's tears dry-up. She smiles and chortles. Her arms stretch-out. I undo the straps that hold her in, then lift her out of the pram. She bounces up and down in my arms, her tiny fingers grabbing at my hair. I wrinkle my nose at the aroma. I have drawn the short straw. I watch Fia, as she eases into the house. Ian and Caroline meet her, to regale her with their day's adventures.

Everything could have been much different. The injury to Fia's leg was severe. Weeks on traction, twice-weekly physiotherapy sessions and daily exercises have improved her walking beyond measure. Her doctors removed the special support-splint from her leg a few weeks ago. Whether Fia will ever be able to reach the high places she loves again is uncertain. The doctors say the mobility in her leg will improve, but we cannot expect her to be a hundred-percent again. Fia knows the odds as well as I do, but I know of no-one more determined. Whernside, Ingleborough and Pen-y-Ghent, I am certain their summits will know, once more, the tread of Fia's footsteps.

Printed in Great Britain
by Amazon